HIDDEN STRENGTH

HIDDEN SERIES OF ELARIA: BOOK 4

BY TIFFANY SHEARN

Hidden Strength by Tiffany Shearn

Published by Tiffany Shearn

Auburn, Washington, U.S.A.

www.tiffanyshearn.com

Copyright © 2024 Tiffany Shearn

All rights reserved. No portion of this book may be reproduced in any form without permission from the publisher, except as permitted by U.S. copyright law. For permissions contact: author@sharisi.com

This is a work of fiction. All names, characters, and events are the product of the author's imagination. Places are either the work of the author's imagination or are used fictitiously. Any resemblance to actual people, living or dead, or historic events is coincidental.

Cover design by Miguel Lobo.

Edited by Maxine Meyer

ISBN: 978-1-7377111-7-9 (Paperback)

I would not have made it to the series finale without the support of my wonderful fans and team. This one is dedicated to Beba and Maxine, who have been with me from the start of this publication journey.

PROLOGUE

Kalachi Desert – Decades Past

Chesik trudged through the desert sand and toward the massive, flat rocks that grew closer with every step. The harsh sun setting at his back highlighted the red and yellow vertical striations in the stone, making it appear as though they swayed to the rhythm of the heat rising off the hot sand. Another month, maybe two, and he would be home. He would likely wait out the winter and spring before heading out again. If he left in the summer, perhaps he would reach the beautifully warm, sandy beaches far to the south.

The trip would require traveling d"nger'usly close to windani territory, but exploration was in his blood. That latest trip took him into the west, all the way across the Kalachi Desert. Rumors of an active volcano had reached his ears from the desert nomads, and Chesik found himself filled with longing to witness the fiery mountain himself. He'd trained in desert travel for a year before departing while winter still held reign. By summertime, he had left the most barren lands behind and plumes of ash floated up in the distant sky.

For nearly another year, he studied the land around the

volcano, but he dared not venture too close. Even at the distance he maintained, when the wind turned, the noxious fumes clogged his lungs and made him cough. It was worth the risks, though. Few others ever made the desert crossing and saw those lands, which was a shame, to his thinking. The elves held no claim there, so perhaps the humans could make use of the fertile soil to find a place for themselves.

He shrugged and tugged on the lead in his hands. "Come along, Shrub," he said to the camel following behind him. "There should be water at the northwest side of these rocks."

Shrub had been his constant companion since the time of his desert training. The camel embodied indifference. He would lead you to water when he smelled it, but with none of the enthusiasm Chesik had seen other camels exhibit. When encountering snakes or other desert threats, he casually lifted a leg or sidestepped and continued on his way. Chesik found himself offering the animal a variety of fodder in batches, just to test if he might generate some reaction. His attempts never worked.

As they neared the large, flat-topped rocks, Chesik made out the crevasses winding between them. Some were mere cracks in the stone, while others were about shoulder wide. The nomads warned him against entering due to the deadly vipers nesting within. Fortunately, disturbing them was not necessary since the water source sat on the outer perimeter.

Long ago, there had been a wellspring, but in the last century, it had dwindled to only a covered well for travelers to use. Chesik and Shrub would bed down near the well for the night, fill their water bags, and resume their journey early in the morning. Each day was the same: rise early, rest in the heat of the day, travel well into the evening, then rest again.

Reaching the rocks, Chesik was about to turn north when movement to the south caught his attention. Five travelers with two camels came around the southern edge. They dressed as he did, in layers of diaphanous robes, light enough to breathe while keeping the blistering sun off one's skin. As they flagged him down, Chesik wondered if some ill fate had befallen them. A couple of camels were not enough to carry supplies for five travelers on more than a day trip. Loading up with well water, though, would be enough for them to reach the nearest desert city and resupply. He would show them where to find the well, if they were not already also heading in that direction.

"Well met," he said to the men as they caught up to him. He saw they were all human and all male. "Are you seeking the nearby well?"

None of them replied. The hair rose on the back of Chesik's neck as one made a gesture. Three others moved to surround Chesik, while one stayed with their beasts. He didn't bother to state that he meant them no harm, and instead fingered the hilt of his dagger beneath his robes.

"You have something of ours," the one who had gestured said through cracked lips.

Chesik shook his head once. "I have nothing."

"That there is our camel with our supplies," he said, gesturing at Shrub. "Wouldn't you say so, fellows?"

Grunts of assent sounded around him as Chesik's other hand tightened on the lead line he held. Taking all his supplies so far into the desert was as good as killing him, if only an indirect way to go about it.

Swallowing his rising fear, Chesik said, "I would be happy to share. We can travel to the city together, and then Shrub will go with you from there."

As he conversed with the leader, another of the men approached quietly from behind. Their answer to his offer was a blow to the back of his head. Chesik crumpled to the ground, dazed, as the group converged on him. They kicked and punched, over and over, as Chesik curled up on the heated sand against the beating. His hand brushed the dagger again, and he pulled it from its hidden sheath, slashing out blindly at his attackers. Blood sprayed, and one of the men staggered back, grasping his throat as blood continued seeping through his fingers.

The leader glanced from his dying companion to the blade in Chesik's hand and finally scrutinized his face. Disdain filled his eyes as he grabbed Chesik's wrist. In one smooth motion, the man broke his arm, took the dagger, and plunged the blade into his stomach. He pushed Chesik back as he pulled the dagger free.

"Grab the camel," the man said over his shoulder as he took a menacing step forward.

Chesik didn't hesitate. Holding his bleeding gut, he turned and ran. Into the nearest crevice he fled, turning his shoulders and shuffling sideways where the walls closed in on him. Two vipers lashed out at him, but he was past before the strikes landed. On and on he ran, winding through the twists and turns and trailing a stream of blood along his path until he could run no further. He dropped to his knees, then fell forward, bleeding out on the hard ground.

Come to me, a voice called.

Sand scraped his face, sticking to the congealing blood, as he turned his head in search of the voice. It called to him, beckoning him forward and offering succor. Chesik struggled to his hands and knees and crawled forward, leaving a blood-smeared train in his wake. Every time his strength failed, the voice called again, offering salvation, offering aid. It lit a strange fire in him, offering justice, offering vengeance.

He pushed himself up against a stone wall, and beneath his bloody handprint, the slab melted away. The hole opened to a cavern breathing a gust of refreshing, chilled air out against his fevered skin. Into the darkness he went, stumbling down, and eventually crawling once more. Down and down he went with the last of his failing strength. At the edge of a pool of liquid, he drew his head up to look upon the symbol of his salvation carved into a small object atop a pedestal in the center of the liquid.

I can offer you retribution, it promised him. The symbol? The object? He didn't know, but it sang a beautiful song in his dying mind. *We will make them pay for their crimes. You have the power within, and I can guide you. Together, we can prevent this from happening to others. We can protect them, but sacrifices will be necessary. Will you join me?*

Chesik was weak and broken. He protected no one, not even himself. He wept for his death while the voice whispered promises to him. The thick water lapped at his wound, offering comfort as he was told how the world could be different.

What had happened to him was wrong. The innocent should not suffer as he had, but the innocent could not prevent suffering, either. He'd killed that man as surely as they'd killed him. Hours passed, maybe days, in a fever dream through which he was remade.

You are Chesik no longer, the voice told him, satisfied, as though reading his thoughts. *You are the innocent murderer. You are the wrathful defender. You are Kahnlair. Come to me, and I will show you how.*

Yes, he thought, relinquishing himself to his new role. He dragged himself forward, further into the pool, releasing Chesik to die upon the ripples floating away from him and embracing Kahnlair. He would cleanse the realm, starting with the greatest threat. It was tragic, but necessary. The humans were too volatile for the realm.

CHAPTER ONE

Scorcella – Magai Capital City

Marto's heart pounded harder in his chest with every mile they flew. The speed and altitude were not the cause though, no matter how thrilling he found the wind rushing through his hair as the ground sped by below. Each second, they flew closer and closer to the main stronghold of the magai. He'd never been there, having grown up closer to the former mage academy to the southwest. From his early studies, he knew the capital city stood well protected by physical fortifications that were magically constructed and maintained.

They arrived within sight of the walled city around midday. It was so enormous they had no trouble discerning the structures in the distance, and their numbers were so few that they were unlikely to have been spotted by anyone within the walls.

"Your estimate of the distance was a bit long," Karl said from behind to Marto, where he hung in the flying harness. "I suspect the difference is due to the hilled area we flew over earlier. Your map makers likely overestimate the distance involved."

Along with Karl, Marto had been assigned two other medic fairy for his negotiation entourage. Charie and Kade had apparently treated Marto's friends when they first arrived at the fairy sanctuary. While Charie spoke Market, the common language of the realm, Kade did not. Despite the language barriers, their small party had found a companionable routine for their days of travel. If all went well with the magai, and they agreed to help heal the injured from the battle soon to begin to the north, then Karl and Charie would speed the message to Darrin and help with the treating efforts, while Kade remained to assist Marto. With his papilio wings, Kade wouldn't be able to match the speed of the two raptor fairy.

"We should fly lower from here," Marto said to Karl. "And we'll need to walk the final mile."

Though Marto couldn't see his face, he knew Karl's lips twisted in displeasure at his charge crutching along for such a distance while not completely healed. He had never liked Marto's plan, but conceded to the mage's greater knowledge of his own people and their likely reactions to a group approaching the city from the sky, even if there were only four. From the way the magai on both sides of the war blasted opponents out of the air, Marto didn't want to take any risks with his companions' lives.

Karl took their flight nearer the ground and covered about three-quarters of the remaining distance skimming the treetops. By the time they could make out people on the wall, it rose like an impenetrable barrier before them.

"If I hadn't seen this from the sky first, I might have thought it too high to even fly over," Charie said in wonder.

The people in the tiny huts on top were nothing more than gnats scurrying about.

"How does it stay up?" Karl translated the question from Kade. "Bracers on the inside?"

Marto gave a dismissive shrug. "Years of architect

magai adding to the internal stability."

He didn't know if the casual gesture concealed his own awe at the magnitude of the wall surrounding the magai city. The wall around the academy had been human constructed with magai magical support, but it had been nowhere near that tall. The stone monolith rose high into the sky, concealing the structures within. Marto thought there were at least a few buildings as tall as the wall, recalling the sun glinting off something stretching high within the city before they dropped down for their final approach.

"Hold here," Marto said, calling a halt to the group. Despite the three fairy having taken turns carrying him until their shift to walking, sweat beaded on his brow from the exertion of swinging himself forward for the few extended periods when he moved on his own.

Karl gave him an assessing scan. "Will you consent to be carried again?"

Marto restrained himself from rolling his eyes. "Not yet," he said. "We should wait here though. They'll have noticed us by now, and an artist will probably send instructions soon. If I recall the protocol for visitors correctly, anyway."

"What do you mean?" Karl asked, looking at Marto briefly, only to startle when his glance returned to the wall.

In that instant he turned away, a woman appeared out of nowhere, standing ahead of them where no one had been a moment before. She wore a long, white dress with long dark hair flowing down her back as she waited patiently for their group to approach. Her hands were clasped delicately in front of her, and she had a warm smile on her face while she stared off at a point in front of her.

"Welcome," she said, still staring.

Karl waited for Marto to respond, but when he remained silent, the fairy gave a small bow and spoke before Marto could correct him. "Thank you, we—"

"You are approaching the magai capitol of Scorcella," the woman said, gesturing. "Home of the magai council and secondary mage academy."

"She's not real," said Marto as the image continued, sounding more scripted with each word.

"The war requires that we take additional precautions with our safety, including taking added care for who we allow within our fortifications. We regret if any of these added precautions cause discomfort. If you have friendly intentions for coming here, please do the following: have your party wait here, send no more than two representatives to the city gates, speak your cause and intentions for visiting at the gates. If all is in order, we will send word for your companions to join you within our walls. If, however, you intend us harm, then you should leave now or face the full might of our anger." The illusory woman stared for a moment longer before disappearing as silently as she'd arrived.

"You two should go," Charie said. "We'll await orders here."

Karl nodded and raised his eyebrows at Marto. "Can we at least fly to the gates?"

Marto thought about it as he considered the distance remaining. *It's not likely the best decision, but I don't have the strength to walk that far, and Karl cannot carry me on the ground the whole way either. If the magai attack, I can probably shield us long enough to escape.* "Yes," he said. "Let's fly, but remain close to the ground."

Without bothering with the harness, Karl gathered Marto into his arms and took off, skimming over the open ground between them and the wall, with Marto pointing out what appeared to be a small, arched hole at the base. Marto kept an eye on the people above and across as much of the stony expanse as possible, on alert for any attack.

None came, and they arrived safely. At the gates, he

took another look at the wall, tilting his head all the way back to make out the top edge against the sky. It didn't even appear curved from this close, but rather like an unsurpassable barrier.

The hole ended in a wall. Ten paces wide and ten deep, it was only an alcove until that back wall melted away, revealing five magai. Two stood with their hands upon the walls of the tunnel, looks of concentration on their faces. The other three stood together, facing their visitors with a shield between them. Shock and suspicion warred on their faces as they took in Karl's feathered wings folded gracefully at his back. None of them spared a second glance for Marto's crutches and missing leg, even though he represented the greater threat if it came to a fight.

These magai are too sheltered if this is how the combat magai of the city behave, Marto thought to himself. "Greetings," he said. "I am Mage Marto from the Northern Council in the Palonian Woodland. The magai council should have been informed of my recent mission. I'm here to report its success, along with a request for immediate aid. My companion is Karl of the fairy people, and we ask that our two companions be allowed to join us in entering the city."

By the end of his brief introduction, the two architects had joined in staring at Karl.

"F-Fairy?" the central mage asked once before collecting himself with a brief shake of his head. "An illusion mage could produce the image before us. What proof do you offer?"

Fortunately, their group had discussed such a situation, and Karl took one small step forward, bowing his head briefly before speaking. "I can offer proof, if you will allow me to approach one of you."

The mage considered them before looking to and nodding at the woman on his left. "Very well. Bellanna will meet you in the middle."

They walked forward cautiously, stopping with an arm's length distance remaining between them. Karl slowly brought one wing out to curl around in front of him and reached across to stroke his own feathers, appearing to search for something. Finally, he stopped and spoke. "This one is loose," he said to the woman. "If you pull on it gently, the feather will come free and provide the proof you request."

She slowly reached out until her fingers stroked the soft vanes. When her hand pulled back, she held a giant, blue-black feather larger than any crow's. Her eyes held amazement as she turned back to the other magai. "It's real," she whispered.

Their leader turned to his companions, sending one of the architects and the other combat mage off on errands. "Your companions will be invited to join us momentarily, and the council is being notified of your arrival," he said to Marto and Karl. "Please, follow me. We can await them in the courtyard."

They followed him through a short tunnel opening into a walled area open to the sky. The mage leader was a shorter man, rising to about the height of Marto's shoulders, with thin, bristly, straw-colored hair and beard. He was older than Marto, but age became nearly impossible to discern in magai for most of their lives. As they waited for Charie and Kade to make the flight in, a young woman hustled into the area from the opposite side. By her robes and age, Marto guessed her to be a student healer a couple of years younger than him.

"Mage Marto, honored guest," the mage leader said as the woman approached them. "My name is Alastair, and this is Patience," he said, gesturing at the young woman. "She is our student healer on duty at the watch post right now, and I wondered if I might offer her services."

Marto's heart thumped against his ribs as Alastair gestured, open-handed, from her to his missing leg. His breathing became shallow, and he grew light-headed as he swallowed against the sudden lump in his throat. He found it impossible to form words with his suddenly dry mouth.

Karl placed a hand on Marto's back, bringing it up to his shoulder and giving a comforting squeeze in one smoothly familiar motion. "I have heard wondrous tales of magai healing powers," he said to the magai, then met Marto's panicked eyes. "Would you allow me to observe your healing, my friend?"

Swallowing once more, Marto found his voice while staring at Karl. "Of course. That would be fine."

The three of them maneuvered to a nearby bench, while Alastair graciously allowed them space and privacy.

"May I ask what happened to cause such an injury?" she asked Marto as he sat on the bench and reached to undo the knot holding his pants leg close.

Her brown eyes were warm with curiosity and care as they stared into his, waiting for an answer, but Marto shook his head and glanced to Karl for help.

"I may be able to offer more insight into the situation than Marto," he told her. "I'm a nurse, a medic among my people, and I assisted with his surgery when he arrived at our homeland. According to the information passed on to us of his condition, he endured a savage attack from a windani over a week earlier. He suffered from blood loss, malnutrition, and dehydration because of the situation he and his companions found themselves in, and the wound had necrotic tissue by the time he came to be in our care. I'm afraid we were unable to avoid amputation."

Karl spoke so simply about his injuries that it loosened something in him.

"You are fortunate to have survived," she said, receiving a concurring nod from Karl. "How long ago did this happen?"

"The amputation was approximately five weeks past," Karl said. "We've been working through rehabilitation exercises recently."

Marto snorted. "Torture," he muttered reflexively at the thought of Karl's *rehabilitation exercises*.

Patience giggled before schooling her expression once more. "Well, let's see if there's anything I can do to speed the recovery process."

He winced as she examined his grotesquely scarred stub, but held still beneath her scrutiny before she placed her hands on his leg and chest. Her eyes gained the distant look of a mage working, and Marto watched as the scars smoothed out, the red faded a little, and the constant ache subsided. Not even a magai like Gregry could regrow what Marto had lost, but perhaps he would not tire as quickly.

"Amazing!" came Karl's whispered exclamation.

She looked at the fairy with a small smile. "The amputation was well done. I have no doubt you saved his life, and for that, we are grateful." She turned back to Marto as he reached for the pants leg to re-tie it. "I'm sorry we can't do more for you."

"Our mission was worth the price," he told her, reminding himself as well.

The walled courtyard in which they sat carved out a small garden space against the massive perimeter wall with another, normal-sized privacy wall curving in an arch opposite. Raised flower beds dotted the walls, while a shrubby tree stood at the south end. Marto suspected the area didn't see much sunlight, which would limit what could grow there. Four benches made up two rows back-to-back in the center of the open space. In addition to the large tunnel through which they'd entered, Marto saw one other door beside it. The room beyond most likely wound up through the wall to the top, acting as an access point and break room for those on shift watching outside.

While there were no other visible exits, that meant little for a city of magai, many of whom could create and conceal access points at will. From Marto's lessons, he knew it was more challenging to alter a structure that had been magically reinforced. If Kahnlair wanted to conquer the city, he would need to either limit his forces by following the predefined paths within the stone, or exert more effort through his magai followers than ever before. As his forces had traveled to the dwarves instead, he seemed content to wait out the magai.

Patience raised her head from its bowed position healing Marto. "Your companions have arrived," she said.

He glanced up from retying his pants leg, then quickly finished as Charie and Kade were guided over to them by Alastair. Marto and Karl stood to greet them. Karl held himself prepared to support Marto, but the healing had done more than age his scars. The aches and pains from exercising faded to the background, and he knew any internal damage from his deprivation had also been repaired. The sore muscles would return as he continued to rebuild their strength and endurance, but he was steadier then than he had been since the battle with the windani.

An archway opened in the interior wall to the north, close to where it touched the perimeter, and a young man walked through. He had brown skin, dark hair clipped close, and his robes were so pressed you could see the sharp creases with every step.

"Greetings," he said, bowing formally to the three fairy while ignoring the other magai, including Marto. That meant he was representing someone high-ranking. "My name is Beldar, and I am an assistant to our magai council." *There it is,* he thought. "They would prefer to meet with you themselves before word of your arrival spreads. So, with your permission, I will guide you to the council chambers immediately."

Karl glanced between his three companions, receiving nods or shrugs from each. "If you're not already including my friend, Mage Marto, in the invitation, then I would request that addition. Otherwise, we are agreeable."

Beldar did not miss a beat. "Of course! If the four of you will please follow me?"

They were led around the perimeter of the city, always keeping the massive wall to their right. Periodically, they passed a section of another wall, and a couple of architects trailing behind would close the archway through which they had walked.

Tall spires rose to the east. The glimmering tops of those buildings could be seen above the internal walls. The city probably would have been miraculous to behold if they were allowed to view it, but they were guided around in secrecy to a moderate-sized, unimposing building. At least, the outside was unimposing and unimpressively constructed of blocks of sturdy gray stone. They walked inside and were guided to the center of the room before the magai council.

A broad dais took up most of the far side, holding five chairs situated before colorful banners. Benches faced the dais in four sections, with three aisleways between. Another three smaller platforms stood between the rows of benches and the dais, each containing another bench and table facing forward. Beldar guided them to the central platform, bowed once more, and took his leave. Marto frowned at the bench for only a moment before moving to stand behind it and lean against the backrest instead of sitting.

Marto couldn't deny that magai had a flare for the dramatic when it came to demonstrations of power. The audience room was not threatening, but it wasn't designed to put visitors at ease either. The immense room, likely built and maintained by architect magai, placed the council members physically above people on any of the benches. They were as open with political power as they were with magical abilities, and Marto missed the simplicity of the Palonian Woodland.

"How?" A middle-aged man with salted brown hair and beard spoke down at them from a dais with wonder in his voice.

Appearances were deceiving in his case, because the man was most likely centuries-old to have any white in his hair at all.

"What does it matter how, Goran? These are fairy!" That was said by a mage much older than the first. His gray hair was well on its way to white. A large belly pushed against the buttons of his shirt, and his clean-shaven face made his additional chin clearly visible. For all his girth and age, the old mage moved with surprising speed as he rose from his seat and descended to the floor.

"Well," he said and circled their platform with a critical eye, "no elf-like ears. You are taller than we thought, and less sparkly than we imagined, but…oh, the wings!" He clapped his hands together.

"I'm afraid we must ask your forgiveness for Councilor Trennor's behavior," said the only woman among the five. Her voice was airy, despite her attempts to put more volume into it. "The artists have long created images of fairy from legend and imagination, so seeing you now is an opportunity to refine and correct their works."

Her age, as well as that of the remaining two magai, was somewhere between Goran's and Trennor's. She had a strong, broad face with sharp lines beneath yellow-brown skin. Her black hair fell straight down except for the two small braids framing her face.

"An understandable reaction, I assure you." Karl gave a short bow of his head. "My name is Karl. I was asked to come here with Mage Marto by my king to request your aid now that we have joined in this war as allies."

"Please do not take this as an accusation, sir," Councilor Goran said, "but why would you wait until we have all but lost?"

"We, as a rule, do not leave our sanctuaries. Your war was unknown to us until recently."

"I would say the war was impossible to miss," came

Councilor Goran's reply as he leaned back and folded his arms, "but you have hidden from the world for so long that we cannot deny the possibility."

There was an audible sigh of frustration from one of the men yet to speak. "I feel we must ask your forgiveness again for our poor manners," he said. "It seems the war has taken even those from us. Please, allow me to introduce myself and my colleagues. I am Mage Kaft, elected councilor of the healing magai. Mage Goran is before the red, and represents the combat magai, Mage Setioral before the green represents the architect magai, Mage Katira before the yellow represents the chemical magai, and Mage Trennor represents the artist magai. Welcome to our capital, Karl of the fairy, as well as to your companions and Mage Marto. We are honored to have you."

Mage Kaft was utterly nondescript in appearance, with light brown hair and features neither off-putting nor stunning. In a crowd, your eyes would slide over him without notice. The opposite was true for Mage Setioral. His skin was a rich red-brown, his hair a sleek black in a short, tousled style, and his striking brown eyes captured your attention.

Marto jumped on the opening the inclusion of his name provided. "Honored council members," he said. "I hope you will forgive me for interrupting, but would it be possible to take our discussion to a more comfortable location? Perhaps we could offer seating accommodations suitable for my companions?"

The five magai exchanged glances before Mage Goran answered. "Thank you for calling this to our attention, Mage Marto. I suspect this will be more than a quick reception, so the conference hall is more appropriate. If you'd care to follow us, when we arrive, we'll do what we can for appropriate seating."

As the other four descended with more grace and restraint, Councilor Trennor spoke to Karl. "May I…? It's just…" His eyes were fixed on Karl's wings, and his hands twitched unconsciously. "Texture is such an integral part of visual re-creations."

"You want to touch my wings?" he asked.

"Not if it is something your culture would frown upon," Councilor Trennor said. "I would never want to give insult."

Karl and Charie laughed at his genuine, child-like curiosity. He was not only an artist by trade, it seemed, but by heart as well.

"Nothing of the sort." Karl stretched his closer wing slightly. "Go ahead. For everything other than wind currents, our wings are less sensitive than most other parts of the body."

After Mage Trennor gave a few giddy strokes, Mage Goran led them deeper into the building, down hallways lit with slowly burning torches until they finally left the winding hallways and entered another room. A fire burned in the hearth, adding to the light from the various oil lamps along the walls. Marto suspected the dining room was rarely used except to host large delegations. The size fit, and the décor was general enough to not offend. It was perfect to host a group of visitors and five magai councilors. There was only one problem.

"Mage Setioral," Marto said. "Would it be possible for you to modify two chairs so the seatbacks are much lower?"

The leader of the architects scrutinized the chairs and the fairys' wings before giving a knowing smile and nod of understanding. Without further delay, the mage pushed his magic into two chairs at once, until the backs were little more than cups to support the lower back. When his striking eyes returned to the fairy, Karl grinned at him in awe and gratitude.

"Please, be seated," said Mage Kaft. "We will have something to eat brought in shortly."

When everyone situated themselves, Mage Goran spoke again. "Now, please, tell us what aid you are seeking and how you came to join the war."

CHAPTER TWO

Trazine Range

Darrin gave Braymis command of the recovery efforts after the surviving gilar and vampires fled the field. The medics arrived and treatment tents were hastily set up away from the worst of the bloodshed. Dwarves set to work clearing space and transporting stable patients within their stronghold to receive food, rest, and other care. Fairy flew patrols over the battlefield searching for survivors.

Despite protests against him flying out again, Darrin left his colonel to organize everyone and joined the sweeps moving slow and low to the ground searching for sound or movement. More than enough able bodies remained behind to help on the ground, while the search field was enormous. He still ended up with a full guard complement ranged around him to ease everyone's minds. They were an hour into their post-battle activities when a small group of gilar rose from the mass of bodies to attack a low-flying fairy patrol.

Shouts rang out in the deepening night, and Darrin's guards converged on him, driving him up and away from the ground. He held back from voicing frustrated protests, knowing he had no valid reason to risk himself. Even as they scanned the skies for vampiric threats and headed back toward the small command tent erected outside the dwarven gates, three other patrols converged on the scene of the attack.

He entered alone without waiting, interrupting Braymis, Mayor Natalia, and a dwarf unknown to Darrin. "There has been an attack on the field," he told them.

Natalia turned to him. A petite woman with a small frame, her wings appeared too large for her as she held them high and at an angle to keep them from brushing the ground. Her wings mirrored her brown skin and black hair, with dark striations at the edges and otherwise primarily brown feathers. She had traded assignments with Chalise and acted as their general commander out of Essence, allowing the papilio mayor to join the forces who had gathered at Earth.

"I'll inform the triage doctors," she said with quick nods to him and the other two before exiting.

"Prince Darrin, this is Clanlord Fwendilg," Braymis said as a quick introduction. "Clanlord, I introduce to you Prince Darrin of the fairy."

Clanlord Fwendilg kept his russet hair and beard cut short, not more than a thumb length, against his dark brown skin. He wore armor dented and dirty from combat, but his greataxe gleamed from recent polishing. He seemed no older than Nurtik to Darrin's untrained eye, and he held himself confidently with one hand on his axe and the other on his hip as he jutted his broad chest forward.

His nod was a brief acknowledgment from one leader to another. "Well met, Prince Darrin."

"To you as well, Clanlord Fwendilg," he said. "I'm certain we'll receive a report shortly. It's unlikely a significant force could hide for so long among the fallen."

"I wish we could've killed them all," Fwendilg said. "Those who escaped will remain a plague upon these lands until they're driven back to their territories."

Though the dwarf leader bore an accent, it was nowhere near as thick as Nurtik's. Darrin felt a moment of surprise, but it made sense for their leadership to speak the common language. If his own people saw the need while safely isolated in their sanctuaries, then the people out in the world would understand the necessity of their Market speech even better and strive for fluency.

Braymis looked at the dwarven leader in surprise. "Do you think they'll linger?" he asked. "We've seemingly won and more than decimated their forces. It would seem the better course for them to return to their lands to regroup."

"Or at least for the vampires to head west to join the main army, as we intend," Darrin said.

Fwendilg shook his head and snorted out a breath. "None of our enemies behave as they should in this war. From all the reports sent to me from the northern council, Kahnlair maintains unchallenged control and orders his troops about however he wishes. The gilar would have never been this far north otherwise. These have always been vampire and windani hunting grounds."

"So where—"

Darrin's question was cut short by the entrance of two additional fairy.

"Sir." The woman in front glanced around, then faced Darrin to report. "One of our patrols was ambushed by a group of gilar hiding within the field of battle. We lost three fairy and another four are severely wounded. They are being treated now."

He clenched his jaw against the pain of the additional loss, but otherwise restrained himself. "Thank you. Do we know how this happened?"

"Based on their positioning," she said. "It appears the gilar were caught too close to the center of the fighting and unable to flee with the back line. They instead waited to ambush anyone looking for survivors."

"How many gilar?" Braymis asked.

"Twelve. Three other patrols responded quickly and eliminated the threat."

"Good work. Order the search patrols to increase their altitude for the remainder of their efforts," he told her before turning to Darrin.

"No need." Darrin held up a hand to forestall Braymis' inevitable instruction following this turn of events. "My patrolling is done for the night. I'll help where I can with the injured."

"And—"

"And have my field stitches seen to again," he said, sounding harassed.

Fwendilg chuckled and prodded his arm to reveal a break in his chainmail armor where a cut still oozed a little. "My men have been harassing me as well," he said with a wry grin. "Come, Prince Darrin. I will show you to the healers and we can both ease the minds of our people."

He returned the grin, and they left the tent together with the sound of Braymis' exasperation following.

A whistle blew in the distance, rousing Darrin from a fitful sleep. He needed to rest, but war was *loud*. In the sanctuaries, fairy were respectfully quiet. At night, you flew silently, not calling out or walking heavily. Out there, however, dwarves stomped around in full armor, watch rotations and scouts came and went with reports at all hours, and notifications whistled through the air constantly. The sheer level of noise would kill him before vampires got a second chance.

Rolling onto his back, he thought through the signal pattern. It wasn't one of the 'all clear' check-ins keeping him half-awake over the past few hours. No, that one had been an alert notification. Nothing to indicate a crisis, but something was happening. If Darrin wanted to know, he would need to rise and ask, though. The full pattern and the message it conveyed remained lost in semi-consciousness.

Darrin groaned as he pushed to his feet. He rubbed his neck and stretched through aches that had settled bone-deep as he rested. His back remained one massive bruise from crashing into the ground, the stitches pulled and itched, and his head and stomach throbbed in time with his heartbeat. The latter two must have been from lack of sleep. After splashing water on his face, and setting his clothes in some semblance of order, Darrin pushed out of his tent and into the pre-dawn light.

The dwarves had offered him a room within their stronghold, but the halls were close enough to feel cramped for raptor fairy. Taller fairy had reported scraping their wings on the ceiling or floor at times, so Darrin elected to remain with the bulk of his forces camped outside.

Perhaps I should reconsider the offer for a nap today, he thought. *The stone walls might dampen some of the noise.*

Despite the hour, the camp remained active, though it had calmed some from the immediate aftermath of the battle. Flights marched by or flew overhead to assigned positions or carry out new orders. The injured were either tucked away to rest or still receiving treatment from overworked doctors, nurses, and medics. A fair portion of their medical personnel had fought in the battle and immediately shifted to treating their fellow soldiers.

"We should find earplugs for the injured and the medics so they can actually sleep," Darrin said as he entered the command tent.

Four fairy stood and turned to greet him. His statement shifted whatever conversation they had been in the middle of, but his tired brain had been caught up in the momentum of his thoughts and spoken them aloud without waiting.

"A good thought, Your Highness." Braymis nodded. The shadows beneath his eyes attested to the fact he had not taken a moment to rest yet.

"Hmm," Darrin grunted. "You already thought of it, didn't you?"

His lead colonel chuckled. "Not I. The medicals took care of it." He paused and narrowed his eyes at Darrin. "We'll have to find you a set."

Darrin waved him off. "What did I interrupt? I heard the signal."

After a nod from Braymis, a young captain spoke. "We spotted a small group approaching from the south. A flight is intercepting with another in reserve."

The news cleared the remaining fog from Darrin's head.

"The magai?" he asked, thinking about the people sent with Mage Marto. Their mission was to both inform the magai of the fairy's involvement in the war and request their assistance with healers there.

"We'll know shortly, sir."

"How many in the group?" Braymis asked.

"Three separate forms."

"Three?" Darrin's question was more to himself than requesting confirmation, but the captain responded in the affirmative, regardless. While they only expected two from the magai capital city, three fairy *had* traveled with Marto.

They were not left to speculate for long. Karl entered, eyes alight with excitement, only minutes later. Darrin was not the only one to breathe out a sigh of relief.

"It's wonderful to see you, Karl!" Braymis grinned at the nurse, who had been a frequent presence at their meetings as he supported Marto in his recovery. "How did your meeting with the magai progress?"

"They sent three healers here with us and a large supply

of their antivenin," the man said enthusiastically, jumping right in. "It took all three of us to bring it here. Charie carried two of them all on her own! There are two masters and an apprentice. The three of them asked to be led directly to the injured, and I saw no reason to hold them back."

Healers and the medicine we so desperately needed? Darrin fought against the flood of emotion at the thought. They had not dared to dream the magai would respond so strongly and swiftly. *How many can they treat? What do they need?*

Karl hesitated at Darrin's stunned lack of a response, possibly wondering if the action had been the wrong decision.

Braymis recovered first and wasted no time in assuring him. "Our medicals will coordinate with them better than us here, and they could use the support right now. Does this mean the magai are joining us?"

Excitement turned to fire as Karl met each of their eyes. "As many as we can carry," he said. "They have been receiving reports from the elves as well. They said that as long as we succeeded in routing the gilar from this area, they would send the bulk of their forces remaining in the city. Marto will coordinate as much as he can while we are away."

Darrin wondered if the young mage knew how much they had come to trust and depend on him in recent weeks. His caretakers would not betray his confidence, but Darrin knew his injury weighed on him still. The tent flap opened again, and another fairy entered, making the small tent feel overcrowded.

"Sirs." The newest entrant drew himself up to report. "Colonel Braymis, Doctor Gorryck has requested your presence."

Braymis chose the smarter path and didn't attempt to keep Darrin from joining him. They crossed to the primary triage tent and entered to find organized chaos. People darted back and forth between beds and across aisles. Orders rang out over the moans and cries of those still injured and suffering.

Karl excused himself and passed Darrin and Braymis to join in the madness as a wiry papilio man, with fair hair and freckles faded from the winter, crossed to where they stood by the entrance. Doctor Gorryck had been placed in charge of the medicals assigned to the northern forces. When they turned west, he would remain there with a small group to continue tending to the injured.

"We can speak outside," he said, gesturing back and following them out before he continued. "The healers…" He drew a hand through his hair and blew out a breath. "I've never seen anything like it."

"They're helping then?" Darrin asked.

"Oh, yes," he said emphatically. "I wish ten times as many were here. That's actually what I asked you here for. After conferring with Healer Mage Prescolnt, we divided the patients into groups. They have left those we are confident we can treat to us and are working primarily on the injured who we are uncertain if they would recover, beginning with those most likely to survive. According to Mage Prescolnt, this will best extend their strength over the greatest number of patients. He informed me they're preparing for an influx of injured in Scorcella, and we should send those who are stable enough to make the multi-day trip now. I'm coordinating medic units, but we'll need at least four flights to help carry them and the necessary supplies."

"They'll be safe approaching the city?" Braymis asked.

Gorryck nodded. "The apprentice will be returning with them. Mage Prescolnt is having the young man exhaust his power—they tell me it will do him no lasting harm—and he'll rest on the return and provide the necessary signal to the magai upon their arrival at the city."

Braymis looked to Darrin, who nodded approval.

"Very well," he told the doctor. "How soon do you expect to need the units ready to depart?"

"Two hours, please, Colonel." He turned at a call of his name from within. "Thank you both. If you'll excuse me."

The doctor was gone in a blink, leaving the two men staring after him. Braymis turned a crooked smile toward Darrin and scratched his head.

"Do you think we dare go back in and pull Karl out for more of a report?" he asked.

Darrin snorted a laugh. "I think we go organize four flights for departure in two hours to the mage city." He grimaced and sighed at another thought. "Though, that means we'll not likely have a full reply to send with them."

"That's simple enough," the colonel said with a suspicious glint in his eye.

"Oh?" Darrin asked as they strode off.

"Yes. You'll go with them, Your Highness."

CHAPTER THREE

Derou Woodland

Annalla sat at the small dining table in the central room of Larron's Derou home, studying a couple of maps spread out on the flat surface. Larron had requested them early that morning for her, and they were delivered only a short time ago. While she inspected the maps, he stood at his stove cooking a stack of flat cakes made with fruit and oats. There were more than the two of them could eat, but Erro slept in Larron's spare bedroom.

After spending half the night shifting between excitedly reviewing reports about the Woodland and horribly retching because he remained ill from Annalla using her essence to cleanse the Derou, Erro had passed out nearly mid-sentence. Annalla had helped Larron carry his nephew down the hall and remove his boots before they tucked him in and left for their own bed. When she asked Larron why he was less affected, he replied that he thought it was because most of his royal connection had been passing to Erro since his birth. As Erro held the stronger connection, the after-effects of her power flowing through that connection would be greater on him.

Annalla felt tired, but her power regenerated quickly enough. The essential exertion set her overall recovery back a day or two, but after the full day of rest when they first arrived, she had enough energy to resume their travels. Based on the initial estimates of the fairy, they would be entering some of their initial battles shortly, if they hadn't already.

"Larron," she called over to him absently and pointed to a spot on the map before her. "What is this word here?"

While Annalla spoke many languages, she only read one, and only knew basic lettering in Market.

He flipped the cake, took a few steps over to the table, and leaned over to look. "Camp," he said in Jularian, the language of the elves. "Kahnlair established a few prisoner and labor camps early on and was setting up more when we lost contact with our allies. The confirmed camps don't have that extra symbol at the end."

She nodded and continued her perusal when there was a knock at the front door. Larron started to wipe his hands off, but Annalla waved a hand in his direction and headed toward the door herself. They hadn't asked for any other deliveries, so it was likely someone searching for Erro. Larron had been close to waking him regardless of their visitor.

"Hello— Wow!" Her word of greeting blended with the soft exclamation when she saw the man at the door.

He was perfection. A work of art carved from the finest gemstones. Skin the color of a polished brown moonstone, hair as dark and shimmery as obsidian in hundreds of tiny braids framing a face sculpted by the divine, and eyes of a piercing tiger's eye with flecks of amber staring into your soul. The man stood slightly taller than Larron. A form-fitting shirt showed off his leanly muscled torso, paired with billowing pants and a long, flowing overshirt.

"May I enter?" he asked, appearing unfazed by her staring.

Annalla heard herself whimper. *By all that is sacred,* she thought, *even his voice is decadent. Just deep enough to melt into your bones.*

"Yeah." Her answer came out as a breathy squeak as she attempted to regain some semblance of composure under the sensory onslaught and stepped back to allow the god-among-mortals to pass.

He brushed past her into the house, and she watched Larron turn, take in the two of them, and give a small smile and snort of laughter before greeting their guest. Annalla's face flamed, and she took her time shutting the door.

"Hello, Sandrala," Larron said. "What can we do for you?"

"Well…" The smooth voice bore hints of nerves.

Annalla's embarrassment became somewhat subdued in the face of renewed curiosity. She returned to the table to clear off the maps and invited Sandrala to sit as Larron turned off the stove and joined them, setting the plate of cakes on the table.

"I came to ask after Thanon," he finally said.

Larron's face went from smiling to blank, and his narrowed eyes spoke of frustration and disappointment to her through their bond. "Oh?" he asked, filling the one syllable with mountains of meaning.

Her mind reeled with trying to puzzle through the sudden tension between the two men over Sandrala asking how Thanon had fared on their journey. She didn't think they were related, though it could be difficult to tell with elves, as they didn't always appear similar to their relations.

Sandrala sighed, seeming resigned to Larron's anger. "We were in a relationship before your journey was announced."

"So you both lied to me." Larron's jaw worked as he clenched his teeth.

Ah, yes, Annalla thought. *The suicide mission.* No

attachments allowed."

"No," came Sandrala's firm reply. "No. We did not lie. Our relationship ended, by mutual agreement, as soon as we found out about your mission."

"Why?" Annalla asked him.

He turned to her, appearing relieved to have a reprieve from Larron's scrutiny. "Thanon is the best. He needed to go."

"That is not how relationships work, Sandrala," Larron said. "You cannot simply turn one off for convenience."

Annalla raised her eyebrows and slowly, deliberately, turned her head in his direction.

Larron pointed at her. "Do not. That is a completely different situation."

"Are you saying," she said, "that two people who care for each other cannot set aside further emotional attachment to focus on the needs of duty and responsibility?"

His lips pursed. He took a deep breath in through his nose, and his eyes closed on the exhale before his face fell into his hands so he could massage his temples.

She felt Sandrala's regard and peeked over at him, receiving a grateful grin. The gesture took his face from stunning to blinding, but the playfulness reminded her of Thanon and she grinned back.

Larron breathed deep once more. "No. That iss not what I am saying." He looked up and met her eyes. "But duty does not stop the pain. Palan's death still lingers on my heart, and I considered him a friend."

"As did I." Sandrala swallowed. "I am sorry to hear of his passing."

"Thanon was well when we last saw him in the Palonian Woodland," Larron quickly said. "We departed in early winter, before the first snowfall."

Sandrala released a relieved breath, fighting back tears as he nodded his thanks. For his part, Larron rose, giving

Sandrala's shoulders a comforting squeeze before bringing over a tray with three more dishes filled with toppings upon it as well as a stack of simple wooden plates.

"Eat," he told them. "Before Erro wakes to consume them all."

Erro emerged from the hall as his name was spoken. "You asked for me?" he said and sniffed the air. "Ooh, oatcakes!"

The three of them laughed as the young elven prince took the final seat at the table, topping a cake with a spread of soft cheese and a drizzle of honey. Annalla's stomach rumbled, and she quickly copied him.

"Good morning, Sandrala," Erro finally said. "What has you away from your workshop so early?"

A beautiful blush stole across his features as he shrugged. "Thanon."

"Ah." Erro grinned and nudged his arm. "I am sure the Palonian are taking good care of him."

Sandrala laughed. "You mean 'tolerating' him well enough."

As they told stories about Thanon, a pang beat in Annalla's chest at missing her friend. She easily imagined the carefree, hopelessly romantic hunter alongside this somewhat shy, and—the more they talked, clearly intelligent—gorgeous man sitting beside her. Eventually, someone came calling for Erro, and he had to depart.

"I should go as well," Sandrala said as they took care of the breakfast dishes.

"Before you do," Larron said to him, "I intended to contact you for assistance on another matter today or tomorrow."

"How can I help?"

"Do we have any remaining stores of the magai's vampire antivenin?"

Annalla knew why he asked. As a fairy, she was particularly susceptible to the venom within vampire claws. Fairy had a fifty percent, at best, survival rate from even a small scratch, and the magai cure would be necessary if the worst happened.

"The magai creation?" Sandrala asked. "No. We exhausted our supply more than a year ago."

Larron paused and grabbed his arm, stopping his movement, staring at him in confusion. "What do you mean more than a year? We treated at least two vampire injuries before I left last spring."

"Yes?" Sandrala studied Larron. "Did Zeris not tell you? I developed my own version of their antivenin. It is nowhere near as effective, but only from the perspective of a longer recovery period."

"How did you create it without magic?" Annalla asked.

"I work with the medicinal properties of many plants and other biologicals."

"He is being modest," Larron said. "Sandrala is as close to a chemical mage as you can be without magic. He alone discovered the majority of the medicinal treatments we use today, including the leaves to treat pain, and the distillation of the trakin anesthetic. How did you replicate this one?" he asked Sandrala.

"We have the two trees the magai use here in the Derou. I had already been dabbling in different methods of reproducing the effect of the magical merge. When the war began, I simply shifted to focus on the effort. We tested it and shifted to using my version on all but the worst vampire wounds to stretch our supply of the magai version. While we are out of theirs *now*, we have plenty of mine, if you are in need."

"I am a medic," Larron said incredulously. "How did I not know about this?"

Sandrala shrugged. "Here, you are a commander. Your

medics were aware, and they did their jobs. I will send you a full medical kit, including several doses."

Larron sighed and shook his head with a smile. "Thank you, Sandrala. I appreciate your efforts."

"Of course." He started toward the door. "And it was a pleasure to meet you, Annalla. Thank you for your stories of Thanon."

They waved goodbye, and Annalla turned back to the room to see Larron placing the maps from earlier back on the table.

"So," he said with a sweep of his hand. "Have you decided where we're headed next?"

Annalla shook her head, amused at his anticipation of her anxiousness to leave. "Not yet. It depends on where we intend to meet with the army."

CHAPTER FOUR

Ceru Lines

Jarin would be late rejoining the army. That day marked the target for his estimated arrival at the main army camp on a final messenger horse held for him. The horse, and the camp at which it rested, remained a day or two away at his current rate of travel; the final muster before the Karasis Mountains sat another two days beyond. The reasons for his tardiness arranged themselves around him for their continuing trek south through the western fields gifted to Ceru by the elves long ago.

No crops had grown in the region in decades. The area remained too dangerous for the human farmers, and any effort expended would be wasted the moment a battle was fought over tender sprouts. They were contested lands a year ago, before Walsh planned and coordinated an inspired forward press against Kahnlair to regain precious farmland to the east. After so long, with only transitional troop movements over them, the grounds appeared almost like the wild, open plains they were long ago.

"Do you think these fields will be replanted this year, Apua'alar?" the man walking at his side asked, struggling over the name Jarin had given him.

Captain Darnes led the group of twenty, flanking them and scouting ahead. He was a balding man of early middling years with a bushy brown beard he split into two crude braids. A big man, he stood burly and muscled in a way no elf would ever achieve, no matter their training and exercise. More than half of his men were as large as he, and all of them wore and carried standard equipment for the Ceru army. Despite the accouterment, Jarin possessed no means of verifying their identities.

If it were only a handful of people, he would simply take them back to the closest camp. The twenty men in that unit presented more of a problem for Jarin, as Captain Darnes handled his men diligently and always had scouts and rearguards far enough away to remain out of Jarin's control.

Walsh counted on an element of surprise for his planned strike into the Karasis Valley, which meant they could not take a chance of some random infiltrator discovering the army's movements and sending word back to Kahnlair. Jarin found himself caught in indecision with no clear, best course of action. Instead, he used the name of an Auradian scout Jarin often dined with and walked with them while they used his horse to carry supplies.

"Our orders are simply to monitor the area, Captain," he replied to the man's question. "I have received no further word on the king's intentions for the land."

Captain Darnes nodded but made no additional comment on the subject.

"How fare things in Ceru?" Jarin asked him.

Upon their meeting that morning, Captain Darnes informed him their unit traveled from the human city. A combination of veterans from the city guard and new recruits conscripted for service by Prince Lukas. Their—alleged— mission was to scout and patrol the reclaimed lands to ensure they remained clear of enemy forces. They held signed orders from their prince and commander and told him their names would be with Walsh and the various camp leaders.

Jarin had no familiarity with Prince Lukas' seal, and since the horrible incursion years ago, the standard protocol would be to verify those names separately at a camp based on their independently received communications. Everything they said made sense to him, but he remained jumpy and nervous about potentially ruining Walsh's plans and inadvertently costing lives. So, instead of turning back, Jarin continued forward at a crawl to the next camp location and hoped clarity would come to him. Of everyone in the army, he bore the least risk of assassination.

"Same as most," came his answer. "People are tired of the war they don't see, tired of the restrictions, and flat tired of losing. Not my words. Most are either too scared or exhausted to say anything at all, but those as have means talk and complain enough for all."

Jarin did not like the sound of that. It made little sense to his elven nature. All of the Woodlands contributed whatever possible without complaint, be it supplies, personnel, or work. The two-decade-long war would not be unique had Kahnlair not made such an effective first strike. It was not unusual for the gilar, vampires, or windani to harry a location for much longer. Since the elves would not push into their territory, the recurring battles often lasted many years until infighting forced the aggressors to contract their holding once more.

"I do not enjoy hearing such news," Jarin said, "but I have heard from others this would not be the first time for such sentiments in the human city."

They continued on in the same manner throughout the day, stopping for lunch around midday. The various scouts rotated in, grabbed their food, inhaled it in a rush, and rotated out again so the next could take their turn. It seemed rather excessive for a group behind their lines, but that only meant Walsh would be well pleased with the discipline instilled by the captain in his men.

Afternoon turned to evening, and Captain Darnes set a watch order as they unloaded the meager supplies from Jarin's mount and set about making a sparse camp. Jarin took care to remove his weapons from the pile one at a time. When the captain gave him what appeared to him an assessing eye, he wondered if he had oversold his struggles.

Perhaps, he thought, *but my weapons are the most distinctive thing about "Jarin," so what else is there for me to do? It is impossible to disguise the fact I have both a greatsword and morningstar in my possession. The best I can do is to pretend I prefer a variety available to me.*

As Jarin lay down in his bedroll, he wished again that he were more of a strategist, like Walsh or Lesyon. Either of them would know better what to do in that situation.

"It's him."

The hissed whisper held enough agitation to rouse Jarin from sleep. His muscles twitched in anticipation of movement, but he otherwise gave no indication of his alert state.

"Quiet," came the softer reply. "We don't want to wake him."

Minutes passed with no further word from the two men, and Jarin started drifting off to sleep once more. They likely waited and watched to ensure he would not rise, as they resumed their conversation at a greater distance after he settled.

"Of course, it's him," the second speaker said in a tone low enough to rouse none but the lightest of sleepers. "You think I wouldn't recognize the greatest weapon the elves bring to bear against Kahnlair?"

Jarin recognized the voice as Captain Darnes then. He

did not wonder long about what had given away his identity to the observant soldier.

"An elf carrying those two massive weapons?" he said. "He must think me a fool to believe a different name would obscure the terrifying presence of 'Jarin of the Elves.'"

While the words appeared innocuous enough on their own, the derision laced through raised the hairs at the back of Jarin's neck. He said 'elf' like the word was a slur or an insult. Jarin didn't need to see his face to know his lips were twisted in a disgusted sneer. Those were not friends and allies. Even if they came from the city of Ceru, their leanings were not in support of the human king and his war efforts opposing Kahnlair.

"We should leave him," said the first again; one of the scouts, Jarin guessed. "We should've parted ways immediately."

"He's part of King Garrett's inner circle," Darnes said as though to a misbehaving child. "Why would we pass up this opportunity to gather information? Why is he so far south of the king's camp? Why is he alone? Where is he going?"

Too much, Jarin thought in fear. *He knows or suspects too much.*

"And what have you learned, Darnes? Huh?" The scout continued when no reply came. "Right. Nothing. You learn nothing and risk our lives. If he doesn't kill us, Kahnlair will."

"No," Darnes said firmly. "No, Kahnlair will not kill us for this. We hold information on Jarin's location at the very least, *and* an opportunity no one would have *ever* thought possible."

"Oh?" came the dismissive reply. "And what 'opportunity' might that be?"

Darnes said nothing, but Jarin listened as his steps moved back to the campsite proper and over to where he lay in feigned slumber. Jarin's blood ran cold as Darnes' movements took him straight to Jarin's equipment, sitting off to his right by his feet. The sound of a long blade being unsheathed split the night.

His heart pounded in his chest. *He cannot be thinking to do what I suspect.*

But he was, and he did. There came a grunt of effort, and Jarin's own blade fell down upon his neck, sliding forward and scraping across his skin until the tip sunk into the ground opposite. His eyes flew open in disbelief, and for a moment, the two of them stared at each other. A slow smile spread across Darnes' face, his eyes alight with malicious glee as he misinterpreted Jarin's shocked, frozen state as the immobility of death.

The scout rushed over. He was the tall skinny one who often ranged far ahead, fast and light on his feet. Darnes raised the sword again, shaking it in jubilation as he stepped over Jarin's supine form. He started to laugh, the sound low and maniacal. The laugh of someone who could not believe a gamble prevailed, giddy with relief and a sense of invincibility.

His glee broke Jarin's shocked state, flaming to life hurt and anger in the pit of his stomach. He had walked and talked with those men all day. They'd shared tales of war and loss. Only the name given by Jarin had been false. The rest had been true and honest, while they lied to him about everything. Those men gloried in the deaths of his people.

Jarin rose with silent, elven grace behind Darnes. His left arm came around the man's throat with bruising force as his right hand reached forward to control his sword. The scout's eyes went wide, and his mouth opened to yell at the sight, but Jarin's blade stabbed into his throat before he uttered a word of warning. Darnes struggled against Jarin's hold, but while he might be larger, Jarin's strength prevailed.

In the end, the fight ended as quickly as it had begun, and two lifeless bodies lay at Jarin's feet. None of the sleeping men had stirred at the brief combat in their midst. A quick count informed him there were only three men on watch. He would not receive another such chance to eliminate the threat. Swallowing his gorge, Jarin braced himself, then strode into the night.

CHAPTER FIVE

North of Earth

Zerdath's death continued to haunt Tyrus, and Patrice remained shaken as well. The young fairy soldier injured when eliminating the vampire scouts had passed away in the night. When breathing became painful for him, the doctor had administered a medicine, rendering him unconscious until the vampire venom had stopped his heart. His end had come almost peacefully, but it had brought home to Tyrus how half the fairy there might end up dead in the first confrontation with the vampires if the army did not have enough antivenin. He hoped the dwarves in the north would have enough for Darrin's forces as well.

In the three days since the first vampire sighting, there had been two others. One happened during full dark, when they'd already set up camp and settled in for the night within the forest below. The army spread beneath the concealing branches and lit no fires to draw attention, and the vampires passed them by with no indication they knew of the forces slumbering below. It was a careful balance of absolute silence and strategic positioning to blend with the foliage.

The other occurrence passed as uneventfully. Just after dawn, as they prepared for departure, the call to hide came in, and the groups halted once concealed and maintained silence until the threat departed once more.

That morning marked the seventh day of travel along the path of the Oasis River upstream toward the north. The river path kept them further from vampire territory surrounding the former magai academy, but they needed to shift their travel to the east soon or risk alerting Kahnlair's forces still surrounding the dwarves in the Trazine Range. Based on Tyrus' recollection of troop deployment and fairy distance estimates, they would reach the southernmost army camps within another two days. From there? It depended on the present disposition of the army. Tyrus had been gone more than a year; there were bound to be changes.

The 'all clear' signal came in, and they departed in a massive flutter of wings, flocking up to hold steady at a comfortable elevation. Tyrus grinned into the wind, closing his eyes, enjoying the cool breeze and dawning sun against his skin. Perhaps a product of constantly wearing armor, he preferred the cooler temperatures and clearer days of spring and fall. After a few hours of flying, they started to shift east, away from the river, and he turned his head toward Ameris.

"Why are we shifting?" he asked.

Ameris gestured, stretching his arm out past Tyrus. "The hills are too rocky here for enough tree cover to grow close to the river," he said. "It's not much better to the east, but enough to serve against distant observation."

Tyrus nodded. If hiding from the vampires was not possible, they would need to bring them in as close as possible before they were discovered. Otherwise, they risked one escaping to alert an entire colony.

"We watch further to the west now, as you suspected vampires in the mountain range that direction as well," Lead

Colonel Zara told him during their brief landing for a break at mid-day. "The clouds coming in will give both sides cover though."

"Is that better for you or for them?" asked Patrice.

"Both," Zara said and shrugged. "It depends on the situation. If a vampire patrol passes by further away, it will make our presence more difficult for them to detect. However, if they spot us, the lower cloud cover complicates our attacks from above. I have papilio patrols ranging wide. If our raptors miss, the patrols will rise to engage."

Tyrus and Patrice shared frowns at the last statement. Engaging meant close combat, which meant a greater likelihood of injuries.

They flew on, and the clear sunny morning turned into a dreadful downpour of an afternoon. Cold wind blew down from the north with torrential rain, slowing their forward progress and significantly reducing visibility. Tyrus shivered against the chill of his wet clothing and felt renewed sympathy for Annalla's early flights into the freezing rain at the start of their journey.

Ameris told him, shouting to be heard over the storm, that they headed a little further east to avoid the strongest southerly winds blowing over the river path. He nodded, but hadn't noticed the change. Between the gusts and jostling of the crosswinds and shielding his face from the rain pelting from the front, Tyrus had no idea in which direction they flew.

After an interminable period, their flight finally began to descend. Ameris soared down, jostled by and fighting against the continuing wind toward a goal Tyrus hoped he saw clearly enough to land safely. The spring rain lashed against them, not stopping even upon the ground. Only once they huddled beneath one of the sparse clusters of trees did they experience some relief.

"Our tents will never withstand these winds!" Yallista

called across the group.

Zara futilely wiped rain from her face. "Use the trees and tarpaulin to create a windbreak! Make sure to allow some airflow to prevent tearing though! That should see us through the storm!"

"How long?" Tyrus asked.

Zara's face took on an absent expression momentarily before she responded. "A couple of hours, maybe! It will pass soon enough! Let's get to work!"

Nods of agreement came from the other fairy as they turned to work. Patrice was miserable and a little ill, but she and Tyrus followed orders and helped where they could to set up some protection from the elements to wait out the storm. The fairy army stretched across the land in huddled clumps around the trees with a cold meal, trying to rest and prepared to set a hasty camp. Tyrus gathered his friend in his cloak so they clustered together. He suspected her shivering was more from the ordeal of the flight than from the cold.

"I don't think I can travel through another storm, Tyrus," Patrice said, her words muffled against his chest.

"The storm slowed us, but we should find an army camp by the day after tomorrow," he said, hoping it was still in the same place. "Hopefully you won't need to."

With neither sun nor stars visible through the clouds, Tyrus had no means of tracking how much time passed before the pounding rain and gusting wind eased off enough for tents to be raised and bedrolls laid. He set a sleeping Patrice inside one of the first erected before helping with the others. When he finally crawled in, he was asleep before he even thought about removing his boots.

It seemed he had just closed his eyes when frantic voices woke him. Tyrus rolled over and crawled out of the tent, stumbling to his feet. Patrice exited on his heels.

Zara saw him while she was in the midst of issuing

orders and strode in his direction as the people around her shot into the air. "You two, stay here."

She ignored their questions and directed her attention behind them to where Jeri stood. "Your unit will remain here to guard them." With no further word, Zara took off to join the others.

Tyrus turned to Jeri. "What's happening?"

Jeri started to shrug, but perked up and waved someone over to join them. Vela, the fairy who usually carried Patrice, trotted up. Her wings were a soft brown with flecks of gold matching the unique tint to her eyes.

"What do you have for us?" Jeri asked her.

"A large force of vampires was spotted coming from the northwest," she said. "Not a patrol. The guess is that it's a full force transitioning between the mountains and the colony to the east."

"How many?" she asked.

"Hundreds." Vela grimaced. "I didn't get the count, but Zara is mustering an overwhelming response to ambush them from all sides. She doesn't want any to escape and bring word of our arrival before we're ready."

The whistles of the fairy and screeches of vampires began as she finished her report.

"Tight to the trunk!" Jeri called out.

Ameris pulled Tyrus with him as the fairy circled in close to the nearest tree and placed their backs to the trunk with their weapons in hand. Tyrus followed suit and pulled his sword, but there was nothing for him to do; he stood there while a slaughter reigned above. Battle cries and screams of pain rang through the night, drifting down faintly through the distance to where they stood.

He stretched his neck forward, scanning the skies, but the faint moonlight showed him nothing. That was worse than battle. In a battle, Tyrus fought; he contributed and made a difference in the conflict. There, he stood blind and impotent against an enemy out of reach while friends and allies acted to protect him.

Something yelled out, and a shadow crashed down to his right, breaking branches and hitting with a sickening *thud* against the ground. Tyrus' heart pounded in his chest. He twitched with a need to *move*, and his eyes strained open, trying to peer into the surrounding darkness. His lips pursed and nostrils flared, trying to silence his heavy breathing to hear anything around him.

More screams came from above, and Ameris threw out an arm, slamming him fully back against the trunk of the tree they surrounded just before a body crashed through the branches to land at his feet. Something scraped down his arm and slivers shot out from the impact to scratch his exposed face and hands. An all too familiar wet warmth hit him with the shards, and he blinked away blood as he dared to peer down at the heap that was recently a person.

"Vampire," Ameris spat out, identifying the body.

Tyrus swallowed back bile. Vampires looked like giant bats or giant flies. Somewhere between black, gray, or brown, with dark bristly fur or hair covering their bodies. Enormous eyes of black or red took up a quarter of their heads, giving them some sort of vision Tyrus could not imagine. Their ears were even larger, curling up and back. Large claws extended from overlong fingers. Though incapable of holding weapons, each claw bore an individual venom sack that leaked out to coat their claw tips.

The body on the ground hardly resembled vampires he had seen. Whatever height it fell from drove the creature down with enough force to break every bone in its body. Some of the flesh had ruptured upon impact, spraying Tyrus with substances he did not want to contemplate, and a reek emanated from the corpse almost immediately. He was going to be sick, or pass out if his lightheadedness was any indication.

Someone grabbed his hand and squeezed it, drawing his attention from the horror before him. Patrice squeezed his hand again and nodded. An unspoken question on her face, asking if he was alright. Tyrus swallowed again, focusing on her comforting gaze, and gave an affirmative tilt of his head. The two of them stood like that, waiting for the fighting to end.

Finally, whistles sounded, and they were able to leave the shelter and torture beneath that tree. Zara returned and captains flew in to report on the situation while Yallista rushed to take notes. Tyrus would have offered to help, but most of them spoke in their own language rather than Market.

In a lull in the reporting, Zara turned to him and Patrice. "We believe all the vampires were eliminated, though there's no way to be certain," she said. "Two fairy were killed, and twenty more injured. It wasn't a bad accounting of ourselves."

"Claw wounds?" Patrice asked.

Zara's head bowed. "Most of the twenty, yes."

Tyrus' heart sank. Losing two to eliminate hundreds represented an enormous victory, but it would be undone emotionally to watch another twenty slowly and painfully succumb to injuries the fairy had no means of treating. For all their medicines, the vampires and their venom were the monsters in the night they feared most. They had driven the fairy into millennia-long hiding.

"No," Tyrus said, though no one had asked a question of him. "We go now. We fly through the night, and tomorrow, and we find the closest Ceru camp."

The faces around him took on miens of sympathy and resignation. Tyrus understood their position, but he knew he was right. They needed to save at least one of the injured.

"I know the chances," he said to Zara, "but we're close enough that we might save some of them. If the southern camp is gone, then secrecy will likely be impossible anyway. But if it's still there, then the antivenin or the healers or both will be able to do something. I think we have to try."

Zara stared at him with eyes shining in the night from unshed tears. "So be it." She tilted her head before addressing the captains. "Pack up and harness the injured. We fly a marathon run."

CHAPTER SIX

Trazine Range to Scorcella

Darrin conceded to Bryamis' logic and traveled with the injured fairy to Scorcella. As the person most familiar with magai—though it was a low threshold for the fairy—Karl returned with him to the mage city. Doctor Gorryck kept all the fully trained doctors with him and placed Karl in charge of the medic units assigned to the group. They brought with them as many of the 'injured, but stable' condition fighters as they could, including fairy and dwarves in their numbers. Karl's task was to keep them stable for the four-day trip.

The first day challenged Darrin. His abbreviated sleep after the battle, combined with his lingering aches and pains from injuries, pushed him toward exhaustion. Karl took one look at him when they landed for the evening and guided him immediately toward the tent in which the unconscious apprentice mage had already been laid. Mage Prescolnt told them he would likely sleep through the day and night after the power he had expended.

"Sleep, before you fall over," Karl said. "You can eat in the morning."

Despite the movement outside setting up camp, the area remained quieter than their location at the dwarven stronghold. As tired as he was, it might not have mattered. Either way, Darrin slept deeply and only woke when morning light brightened the tent's interior. He pulled his wing higher to block out the light, but his stomach took that moment to give a demanding rumble. He heard a yawn and some rustling behind him.

"I'm hungry too," said a young, sleepy voice.

Darrin gave up trying to ignore his stomach for more sleep and turned toward the apprentice mage, where he sat yawning again and rubbing his eyes. Physically, he appeared around the same age as Marto, but the one his people were coming to consider 'their' mage bore years of maturity over that young man. Marto had lost his family, finished his training early, guided a small group in a search for the fairy, and nearly lost his life finding them. Apprentice Brondynn wore innocence around him like a cloak, only recently tattered by the sight of so many injured from the battle with the gilar and vampires.

Brondynn was small and trim, which allowed Charie to carry both him and the petite female healer all the way to the Trazine Range. He had sharp cheekbones and a striking combination of bright hazel eyes against light brown skin and hair. The young man blinked owlishly at him, and Darrin wondered if he would survive what was to come. Their stomachs rumbled in unison, drawing laughter from them both.

"Yes," Darrin said. "I think we've rested long enough and can assist with packing up this morning."

They rose, and Brondynn helped Darrin break down the tent they shared before they sought breakfast in the common area. It was only a quick mash with some rashers fried easily in a pan. Taking their servings, they joined Controller Nurtik where he sat beneath a tree on relatively dry ground. The recently promoted dwarf joined them, on the orders of Clanlord

Fwendilg, to continue to represent the dwarves as Darrin worked to coordinate with the magai.

"Prince Darrin. Mage Brondynn. Good ta see ya both up and about." Nurtik spoke slower than in previous conversations Darrin held with him, but his accent became more subdued as a result.

"You don't need to slow your speech on my account," Darrin said.

His beard twitched in irritation. "I unnerstan jus fine." He paused and slowed again. "Me clanlord told me I need to make a grea'er effert on me pronunciation with me new position."

"Then I applaud your efforts," he said. "I too was forced into language studies. It escapes me how those such as Rolan and his daughter find such delight in their learning. I always much preferred the guard training."

Nurtik pointed at him in a gesture of enthusiastic agreement as he munched on his meal.

Darrin laughed and turned to the mage. "What about you, Mage Brondynn?"

He shrugged and quickly swallowed. "Well, Your Highness, Market is our standard language. We only use our native language for spells," he told them. "And then we are learning spells, so…"

As he trailed off, his facial expression conveyed a sense of 'why would you *not* want to learn spells?' *A fair point,* Darrin thought to himself. He couldn't imagine having the power of magic or essence at his fingertips and not seeking to learn to use it well.

"I suppose—"

Whatever Darrin might have said next was cut off by a shout from near their packed tent. "Mage Brondynn!"

"Here," Brondynn called out in response to the fairy woman's call. His meal was left forgotten where he set it aside, quickly standing and meeting her halfway. A prepared and professional countenance occupied his face as he listened intently, all traces of immaturity wiped clean by his expertise.

"Nurse Karl requests you join him," she said. "One of the dwarves grew worse overnight and they think he has either an infection or bleeding that was missed initially."

From her recitation, Darrin could tell she was not a medic. The cadence indicated memorization rather than understanding, and it seemed Brondynn felt the same. Instead of questioning her further as they walked, he simply asked her to lead the way.

"Are you recovered enough?" Darrin asked, easily keeping up with them.

"I should be," he said. "My orders are to keep everyone stable enough to reach Scorcella and otherwise conserve my strength. I won't heal the dwarf fully, only enough to ensure they will survive the journey. That will help ensure I have the ability to help others should the need arise."

"Good."

Brondynn smiled over at him. "Mage Prescolnt spoke highly of the skill of your medics. I'm sure there will be nothing our combined efforts wouldn't be able to handle."

He continued to the dwarf's side while Darrin and Nurtik stopped at a respectful distance.

"Let's go help pack," Nurtik said, carefully elbowing Darrin.

Doctor Gorryck selected the patients well. Only one other person—a fairy soldier—required Brondynn's attention in the days until they arrived at the mage city. As they approached, a challenge shot up from the surrounding wall. Brondynn went forward with his bearer and the signal to proceed quickly followed, and they set down in a large courtyard milling with magai. Darrin tried to remain out of the way as the apprentice and nurse Karl conferred with the other healers to direct the injured where they needed to go.

"Prince Darrin!" a familiar voice called out as the area began to clear and settle.

He stood taller to peer over the remaining heads and scan the area. Mage Marto crutched toward him, swinging himself with more strength and alacrity than he had previously shown. It was a testament to the healing powers of his people and his own determination and strength.

"Combat Mage Marto," he said, just as formally.

"Just Marto, please. Everyone here is 'apprentice' or 'mage.'" He grimaced. "I see now why my parents preferred living in a human village."

"I will warn you, then," Darrin said with a smile. "Many of my people have taken to calling you 'our mage.'"

The young man blushed, and a wealth of emotion stole across his face. "I can't see that I've done anything to deserve such a distinction."

"What other mage keeps our secrets and calls our protector a friend?"

Marto pursed his lips and dipped his head. He cleared his throat as he met Darrin's eyes once more with a small smile. "The council asked me to meet whoever was leading your group. If you need time to refresh yourself, we can stop by your rooms first. Otherwise, they'd like us to join Councilor Trennor at the city academy."

"I'm well enough," Darrin said, and scanned the area again. "We should find…" He could not stop himself from grinning as the object of his search barreled across the open ground.

"Marto, me boy!"

Nurtik rammed into him, wrapped his arms behind the taller man's rump, lifted, and spun him around. Darrin barely avoided being struck by one of the crutches as Marto cried out and flailed about, trying to stabilize his position. He needn't have bothered; Nurtik remained sturdy on his feet as he spun and shook and squeezed his friend.

"Nurtik! I'm glad you are well," Marto said, laughing and patting the dwarf on his back as best he could.

"I was going to say that we should find Nurtik and ask him to join us, as he is here representing his clanlord," Darrin told them.

"Of course! If you will follow me?" Marto said.

They departed into the late morning sun and onto a wide street. The door from the courtyard opened opposite a building towering above them, standing upon spindly support beams. Darrin knew some of the basics of construction, weight distribution, support, and material strength, but that building defied all logical rules of construction. There were even windows filled with a colorful material beautifully decorating the façade.

"How?" he asked, stopping and staring up.

"I've never lived here," Marto said, "but my father told stories of architects employed to renew the magic strengthening the structures in Scorcella regularly. Actually, one of the reasons we're heading to the academy is to give you an overview of our areas of study to determine if there are any additional applications to aid the fairy in the war."

"And what about the windows?" Darrin asked, still staring up at them as they started walking again.

"Ah." He gave a smug smile. "That's actually a combat mage technique. Two combat magai use shields to mix and spread molten glass and support it as it cools into large panes."

He led them between other buildings stretching toward the sky and shining with sunlight on windowpanes until they reached a more uniform area. The magai might have called the buildings there less grand, but they were amazing in their own way. Square-ish structures reached six, eight, ten stories high, some with glass windows as tall and wide as Darrin with his arms stretched. People peered back from the inside of a few, but there were much fewer than he anticipated. The capital seemed half deserted. All the beautiful buildings, the towering homes and shops, stood quiet and empty for want of families and workers to fill them.

"The dwarven clan was not so empty," Nurtik said, echoing his thoughts.

"The city possesses a few more autonomous defenses," Marto told them. "After the academy was taken, there was a massive outpouring of volunteers leaving to join the army. At this time of day, most people are also occupied with work or study. Between the two, the city appears emptier than it actually is."

Buildings shrank to one or two stories as they followed further into what Marto called their academic district. The windows remained large and filled with glass, but they became fewer and less frequent along the walls. Streets in every direction stayed empty. Only the faint sounds of habitation reaching his ears belied the absence. The distant noise quickly grew louder until it became almost painful to Darrin's ears. No one yelled or screamed, but an excited chatter filled and overflowed what had to be a massive room ahead.

Marto glanced at Darrin as he winced at another squeal and held them up. "Give me a moment, please. I'll quiet them before you join us."

After a minute, it was another's voice Darrin heard call out inside. "Students! Students!" He paused to wait for the talking to cease. "Our guests have arrived. Out of respect, you will speak only when called upon and you will speak softly. Am I understood?"

"Yes, Mage Norstier," came the chorused reply.

Marto exited with an older, heavier mage who

approached Darrin with stars in his eyes as he stared unabashedly at his wings.

"Marvelous!" he said, clapping his hands together. "Like a golden bird of prey!"

"Counselor Trennor," Marto said in a chiding tone. "This is *Prince* Darrin of the fairy." He sighed and met Darrin's eye. "I apologize for Counselor Trennor's lack of discretion, Your Highness."

Before Darrin could respond, Counselor Trennor waved him off. "*Pssh*! I'm too old to offend anyone, and an artist never apologizes."

Marto pinched the bridge of his nose. "Neither of those statements is correct, Counselor."

The older mage turned to inspect Marto. "And would you say the same to Counselor Goran?"

"Why would I not?" Marto asked, confused.

Darrin, however, saw the smile of satisfaction on Counselor Trennor's face and wondered what plans the council was concocting for the young man.

"Quite right, then," he said before addressing Darrin. "My apologies, Your Highness, for any offense given. The wings of the fairy are marvelous to behold and endlessly distracting to one such as myself. I do beg your pardon."

"All is forgiven," Darrin said. "I find myself equally in awe of your magic."

"Well," he said in response, "I hope we can make this an enlightening exercise for you, then! We brought together some of the top students from the various classes." Trennor led the way inside and to the front of the packed room, where a mage older than the students in the room waited to greet them.

"Welcome, esteemed guests." The elder mage bowed to Darrin and Nurtik. "I am Mage Norstier, one of the teaching masters here. Apprentices from each of the magic concentrations are present, with the intent to provide you with an overview of our capabilities and answer any questions you might have. If that's acceptable?"

"Please proceed," Nurtik said with careful dignity.

Mage Norstier smiled, bowed again, and peered around at his students. "Lilah, Mercuric, you are nearing your final testing. Care to provide a brief overview of your concentration?"

Two students to the right of the room came to attention. The way they glanced side-eyed at each other, leaned away while not actually shifting seats, and jutted their chins in unison, Darrin imagined a relationship fraught with healthy competition mixed with hidden romantic longing on both sides. He wondered how accurate his assumption was as the young woman answered first.

"We're learning to be healer magai," she said. "Most of our work relates to mending and manipulating tissue and bones. We can rebuild, re-grow, and strengthen bone structure, or patch and knit flesh injuries back together; though, flesh always needs natural healing time as well."

"We also deal with illnesses, helping the body fight them off, or affecting natural functions like sleeping, but those require the application of more power. Some healers are never able to work them," the boy said.

"Manipulating the body?" said Darrin. "Can you harm as well as heal?"

The two looked at each other again, but it was the man behind them who answered. Once Darrin focused on him, he appeared older than the students, possibly another teacher sitting in on the discussion. "Yes, we can," he said. "Stopping a heart, breaking a neck. However, only an extremely powerful healer mage can do so without touching the person, and even then, the distance is limited. We're not effective in an offensive capacity on the field of battle."

Darrin nodded. "I imagine such an action would also be

emotionally challenging—even damaging—for healers to use their abilities in such a way."

The teacher cocked his head and blinked. "Yes. Though, not many in war acknowledge such a distinction."

"Military service is mandatory for fairy," he told him. "We take care to monitor the impact on all our people."

With a tilt of his head in appreciation, he asked, "Any other questions for my students?"

"Can you heal poisons, toxins, and venom?"

Mercuric, receiving a nod from his teacher, responded. "Not directly. We heal the damage done to the body by the foreign substance, and we can help the body process it. However, it's often more effective to combine our efforts with a chemical mage to treat such a patient."

"How does that work?"

"We heal the damage," Mercuric said, "while the chemical mage deals with the problem substance."

"A chemical mage doesn't need to be present if we have the antidote at hand," Lilah said. "In that case, we would heal as well as facilitate the distribution of the antidote to counteract the poison, as an example."

"If you have no more questions specific to healing," Mage Norstier said, "then we can shift to our chemical magai to help with this topic?"

Darrin thought for a moment. "That would be great, thank you."

"Alright. Amrys, an overview, if you will?"

Another young man, this one with tight, wildly curling hair, sat forward to speak. "The chemical concentration deals with mergers and separations of disparate items and ingredients," he said. "We often work in support roles for the various applications of the other magai. The stained windows in the city are made using a merger of cloth dye and sand.

"We work closely with the healers to do what they

cannot, or what would take too much power for them. If someone were poisoned, as Mercuric described, then we work with a healer to separate the poison from their blood. There are mergers used to put people to sleep or ease their pain. Once a healer and chemical work out a merger combination, we can create it independently.

"We work with architects, often related to impurities in metal ores. They can be filtered out by separating one metal from another, or we can merge metals to find the strongest blend. With artists, we can work to blend new pigments or mediums for them to work with. And we are fantastic cooks." He paused to wink at another student, earning a round of giggles from the group. "Cooking involves less complex or incomplete mergers. Mixing bread without a tool, softening vegetables faster by infusing them at the same time they're cooking. We speed up the process and can work on a larger scale than those limited to mundane means."

"How quickly can you produce the vampire antivenin?" Darrin asked. "I'm uncertain how far we depleted the dwarves' supply."

He smiled sympathetically. "We were told of your need. I'm the only chemical mage here today because the rest are working on creating as much as we can. The greatest limitation is the supply of the ingredients. We grow them in our greenhouses, but growth and harvest take time."

"We are recommending rationing the use," said the healer mage. "Humans and dwarves have proven the most resilient to the venom and most often survive with limited intervention. We'll be reserving most of the antivenin to treat the fairy and elves, who suffer worse symptoms from such injuries."

Nurtik nudged Darrin with his elbow, and the dwarf grinned up at him when he glanced over. "Annalla."

Darrin frowned in confusion for a moment before

understanding dawned. He laughed and gripped Nurtik's shoulder. "Annalla."

Amrys gave them a concerned look. "What are we missing?"

Marto, also smiling, answered for them. "The fairy with essential abilities," he said. "She can accelerate plant growth. If we get you to the front line with a sample of the ingredients, she can grow more."

Amrys smiled with them. "That'll solve one problem. We'll still make as much as we can in advance, though. Anything else we can help with?"

Darrin had remained so focused on the threat of the vampires, he hadn't thought much beyond the one problem.

Marto, though, had no hesitation. "I recommend some of the chemical magai study the medicines used by the fairy," he told the apprentice. "They made advances we may be able to replicate."

Mage Norstier paused for additional insights, then moved them along. "Alright," he said. "Let's go to…Cierless, our only artist apprentice."

That was one of the few people present who looked young enough to be considered a child rather than an adolescent. He spared Counselor Trennor a nervous glance before standing and giving the room a blinding smile.

"I'm only in the first year of my apprenticeship, but I will answer what I can," he said. "Artists create things affecting the senses. Images and sounds like the ones we use to 'greet' visitors are the most basic because they play on weaker distance senses. Trying to impact senses like smell, taste, or touch is impossible from a power perspective. To give the illusion of those senses requires the mage to utilize the real world around their image creatively.

"If you want something to smell real, use a real scent in the area. Is there lavender nearby? Put a sprig in her hair. A fire? Put a bit of soot on her cheek or clothing. As there is nothing to consume, a scent is the only means of impacting taste as well. Touch is difficult because we can't affect anything physically with our creations. Subtlety is key with touch because you can brush past someone as a breeze passes to give the impression of physical movement."

"Useful for spreading false information and misdirection, or for concealing something," Darrin said. "The artist living with the dwarves assisted us in hiding our camp from any vampires flying over."

"Yes." Trennor nodded, unusually subdued. "Unfortunately, Kahnlair finds the tactic just as useful, if not more so."

"Why is that?"

"An artist can often detect the working of another. It depends on if they're looking, their proximity, the power of the mage, the power of the working, duration, and several other factors; but Kahnlair found a way around the limitation. By all reports, we only see through about half of his deceptions, and I think those are the ones he wants us to figure out, to make us believe he doesn't have the ability to fool us at will. He found ways to do things we never thought possible...in all the concentrations." Trennor sighed and held up a hand to stop his line of thought. "We'll have plenty of time to talk about that later. That was a very good overview, Cierless, thank you. Norstier, what's next?"

"Let's go to architects. Riecee, why don't you give us a brief description?"

"Yes, sir," said a tall young woman standing at the back of the room. "Architects work in a way similar to the healers, but we work on inanimate objects, rather than living creatures. They strengthen bones, and we strengthen the materials in structures. They manipulate flesh, we manipulate stone into the shapes we desire. The buildings here are examples of both aspects, with the strength needed for height and the stone molded as neatly as possible.

"We can also become artisans and use our power to create sculptures or pottery of sorts, or—more so of late—create weapons to help with fighting. Our process is safer than working as a blacksmith because we don't have to heat the metals."

Darrin raised a finger at her last statement. He pulled something off his uniform. "Can you create more of these?"

"This is only metal?" Norstier asked, holding out his hand in an unspoken request.

He handed the ammunition over. "Yes."

The small bolt was set down on a nearby table, and Norstier then took off both his belt and the clasp of his cloak, placing them both next to it. His hand hovered over the pieces. Before their eyes, the buckle melted away from the leather and merged with the clasp. Metal swirled along the table and formed into a pointed tube, little bits of metal sliced away to fall unmoving against the table until a near exact replica of Darrin's bolt sat on the table. Only the color was different because of the metal used. Darrin's lips quirked in a small smile and reached for the new bolt.

"We might need to explore the types of metal required," Norstier said, "but it's manageable. What's it for?"

Darrin picked up the bolt and fit it into his wristbow, took aim at the wooden doorframe, and fired. "Our version of arrows," he said, inspecting the impact.

"A little soft. We'd definitely need to look at the material if we want them to penetrate armor or gilar skin. Replenishing our supplies will become more difficult for us over time," he said. "There are smiths in the sanctuaries creating more, but the couriers can only make the runs so quickly."

"My apprentices and I can work with your people to

determine the specifics. That would allow the masters working on arms to take over once we have the details for them."

"I'll make arrangements on my end," Darrin said eagerly. "This could ease another of our greatest concerns. Thank you."

"And with that," Norstier said with an acknowledging nod, "we are on to the combat magai. We have many combat students here, but we'll give the floor to the one about to go through his final testing. Pouldric?"

"I'm sure Mage Marto already shared much of this with you," said the young mage, acknowledging his fellow. "I'll give an overview just in case, though. We have two primary categories of combat magic—defense and attack—though not all applications necessarily have to do with active combat.

"Shielding can prevent penetration in, out, or both, acting as protection or prison depending on the *what* being prevented. Attacks are in the form of fire, energy, or force. Fire works best on things already flammable and takes less power than the others. Energy is like lightning: strong, but difficult to control where it lands. Force is effective and more controlled, but it's not much considered an attack except when used by the strongest magai. Force requires acting on something else to work, whether that's an enemy or an arrow.

"We've used force to try to bring down vampires. A few magai target directly, but the tactic works best for us with elves, who can target higher up, and we add force to their shot to reach the target. In groups, we can also extend the range of the humans' catapults. There are ways to modify the workings and combine them with multiple magai working in concert, but those are the basics."

Darrin grimaced, remembering the fight to the north. "I recently became more familiar with magai in combat. We set some of our teams to search out the enemy magai so our allies could better target them with us."

"I know there weren't many magai with the dwarves," Pouldric said. "It bears considering if, with additional magai fighters, some might join you in the air."

Marto tipped his head toward Counselor Trennor. "It's something we are discussing."

"Speaking of which," the counselor said, rising to his feet. "I must be getting back."

A collective groan rose from the students, quickly cut short by a sharp glare from Mage Norstier.

Darrin bit back a laugh. "I can stay for some questions, as long as I have a guide and am welcome."

"Very welcome," Mage Norstier said.

Counselor Trennor chuckled. "And consider Mage Marto your ambassador, Your Highness." He turned to a surprised Marto. "Mage, I ask you to ensure they are rested for tonight's meeting."

"Yes, sir," he stammered as the elder mage stood and left the room, leaving Darrin prey for eager questioners.

CHAPTER SEVEN

Derou Woodland

Larron lunged forward, his sword tip aimed at Annalla's chest. Her blade sliced in from his left to parry, and she quickly jabbed the pommel back and up at his face. He laughed as he dodged, feeling a carefree exuberance he only experienced when they danced. To let his skill loose when no lives were on the line reminded him of why he loved the forms and movement of sword work. Her answering grin told him she enjoyed the freedom as well.

She closed on him again, driving forward with quick slashes, forcing him to block and back carefully. Her head cocked slightly to the side with the fourth strike. "Someone is looking for you again."

He parried a blow and darted in close, working his blade at an angle to disarm her. "They can find me easily enough," Larron said as he twisted his blade, his eyes flashing in triumph.

Instead of her sword flying off to the side with his motion, it fell straight down when she intentionally released the grip. Her wing slid up between them, blocking any follow-through strike, and the weapon flew back to her hand all on its own. *Essence,* he thought, as Annalla struck out with an upward slash.

He shifted his hands to block and slid his feet back into position, but his right foot snagged on something. Instead of a stable stance, her blow caught him on the unsteady footing and he tumbled backward, landing hard on his rear before he rolled to distribute the fall properly. Laughter and clapping from the door at the back of his house pulled his attention from the new vine waving at him from the ground in the morning breeze.

Tralie, Zeris' lifemate, stood hunched over laughing, her dark honey eyes sparkling. She wore standard guard armor. Hers was dyed a little darker than his to help her black cherrywood skin blend into the shifting shadows of the forest. A pang of regret hit Larron at seeing her shaved head. The lack of hair highlighted her sharp cheekbones and full lips, and Zeris would adore her new appearance. He loved Tralie's smile and often waxed poetically when gazing worshipfully at his bonded's face. Larron had nothing against the style, but it reminded him of *why* she made the change.

When Zeris was captured in a gilar attack the previous spring, Tralie had shaved her hair, left the heartwood to lead the border guards, and vowed to remain there until either the Woodland or her bonded were returned to her. Annalla had restored the Derou to its former vitality, but Zeris was beyond her power and skill. It was the first time he had seen Tralie laughing since well before her lifemate was taken.

"Larron!" she said with another laugh. "I have never seen you bested. Are you injured, brother?"

Larron dusted himself off as he rose and rushed over to squeeze her into a hug. "Tralie. I am glad to see you. I have missed you!" He turned to face Annalla, keeping an arm around Tralie's shoulders. "And you—"

"Cheated?" she asked with a smug grin, finishing his sentence.

"No," Larron said, incredulous. "You should practice more with your power when we spar. That way you will not risk injury the next time you decide to face *thirty gilar* alone."

He shifted to introduce the two women, and Annalla's eyebrows rose in consideration. At Zeris' name, when he mentioned how they were connected, the sorrow and pain returned to Tralie's eyes, and she winced but said nothing as the three of them returned to the house so Larron could begin their morning meal.

"I—" Tralie said, laying a hand upon Annalla's arm. "Our home has not been this vibrant since before the war began. My Zeris cannot be here, so I thank you on his behalf, and on behalf of our people."

Annalla fought embarrassment under Tralie's earnest gaze and words. When her own words failed her, she smiled and dipped her head.

"Erro said most of the gilar were caught in the Woodland when our lands were reclaimed," Larron said to Tralie, saving Annalla from the silence and attention.

"Yes, we counted only a couple thousand beyond the border on the desert side. We suspect they are all that remains of the slaughter sent to overwhelm us. Though, we do not number many more ourselves at this point."

So many of his people were gone from the world forever, but hope remained for the elves. "He also told me we have three more pregnancies to celebrate since I left."

Tralie's eyes lit. "And one of them is Tzarrina again! Those two. So long without children and now two in a matter of twenty years! The boy is not even out of training!" She turned her head to scrutinize Annalla once more. "You know, Anor's parents were Palonian. There is a chance they yet live."

"But my father was Derou," Annalla said.

"Yes, as was his grandfather. Anor's father, however, was born in the Derou, but he never felt he belonged here. He left and found his home Woodland in the Palonian, as well as his lifemate. Anor's path mirrored his."

"Travelers often come from such mixed parentage," Larron said. His own mother had been born in Auradia, leaving and finding her home in the Derou only after she bonded with his father. The olive tones of his skin attested to her heritage in him. Some said those with hints of green in their person were meant to be part of the lost Woodland, and that was the reason they often moved or found it difficult to settle.

"Anor was brash," Tralie said. "He never settled, even here. He was always looking for something different. I am glad he finally found what drew him away from us. And you as well, Larron."

He saw her fond look between himself and Annalla. Smirking, he said, "I am not brash."

She laughed, as he intended. "Perhaps not in the same way."

They reminisced as Larron cooked and tried to pretend that day was another normal morning, despite the hole left with Zeris missing from her side. Annalla mostly left them alone, sitting to the side, cleaning their weapons after the earlier bout. Larron would have liked nothing more than for his brother to be there with them, sharing their lives and their bonds now that he finally understood what it was to have such a partnership.

"So," Tralie said as she sat back from her plate, "how long will you be staying?"

Larron looked to Annalla for the answer.

"Another day or two," she said. "The fairy should be arriving at the front lines within the week, if they are not there already. I want to go after a couple of the enemy supply or prisoner-work camps before they become accustomed to watching the skies."

"What do you hope to gain?" Tralie asked her.

She shrugged. "A bow does little without the arrow. I

am hoping we can make the retreat to regroup more challenging for Kahnlair's forces and press our advantage further."

"It could gain us additional soldiers as well," Larron said. "If any prisoners we find are in a condition to fight and help."

"We cannot take them with us, though. I can only carry one person and I do not want to slow our pace. Too much of Kahnlair's army is south and east for us to delay long."

"Send them to the northernmost camp," Tralie said.

"What do you mean?" Larron asked.

"The Woodland will be able to protect itself, for a while at least. I will take one of our remaining fighter groups and head south, to the northernmost camp. Assuming you have liberated it, we will take charge of and fortify the location, then man it with any additional allies you can free and send our way."

Annalla moved to grab one of the many maps tucked around his main room. She shoved her plate out of the way and spread the parchment on the table as Larron picked up all the dishes and moved them to the washbasin.

"These are far enough off the likely path of retreat. They would require a deliberate deviation for Kahnlair's forces to retake," Annalla said, smoothing a finger along the path in her mind.

Larron eased against his counter and watched the two women throw ideas back and forth.

"And we can pack enough supplies for a much larger group to live lean for a few months." Tralie leaned over the map with Annalla. "Which means we can support the people who survive to reach us."

"The survivors would need to hold this camp until you arrive," she said. "Likely a few weeks. We need to work out a signal to give you, in case there are no survivors. If we leave it empty, it would be too easy for Kahnlair to take it back and capture or kill anyone you send."

"Easy enough. We will send a pennant with you."

Annalla snapped her fingers. "And when the army is close, we can send a fairy unit to pick up anyone in fighting condition!"

Larron smiled as the two conversed, planning a mass liberation of the prisoners slaving away to provide for Kahnlair's army. The feral grins on their faces made him enormously pleased he would not be standing opposite either one on a field of battle.

***

Annalla screwed her face up in concentration as she mentally ticked through her list the evening after her energizing planning session with Tralie. She and Larron would be departing the heartwood after supper, spending the night at the southern edge of the Derou Woodland before continuing in the morning. As much as she would like to linger there, safe and resting, she worried every minute she spared herself another fairy life was sacrificed. She and the sanctuaries were meant to protect them, and she was failing.

"Everything is packed and ready for our departure," Larron said with a hint of humor in his voice. He had come and gone from the Derou so many times in his life that the task had become second nature. As a result, he found her fretting entertaining.

She sent a half-hearted glare at him over her shoulder to show him what she thought of his 'entertainment,' only to have him let out a full laugh in response. Her responding smile at his antics was hidden from him, as she had already turned to once more contemplate their packs.

How are they all so calm? She wondered. The Derou had lost so much. Their land was restored, but more than half of their population was known or presumed dead. Every elf present had lost someone close to them. Yet, they carried on, wearing their grief openly and supporting each other as they worked and did what was needed. Annalla found the level of inner strength or inner peace intimidating.

"Your family is here," she told him, hearing steps approaching outside. They took care to step loudly to give her a warning of their impending knocking. She wondered if they worried she might bring the Woodland down around them if they startled her.

"We brought your favorite," Tralie said, her eyes sparkling as she smiled at Larron. They set three covered dishes on the table and Annalla sidled up as they greeted Larron with hugs.

When the food was revealed, Annalla felt her eyes widen in anticipation. "That smells amazing."

"Thank you." Erro grinned at her. "I hope you enjoy it. The Derou sits at a convergence of natural diversity with the desert, mountains, and forest lands bracketing us here. We have the widest range of fruits, vegetables, and spices as a result, and therefore, the best food."

Larron paused in dishing up a plate to stare at his nephew. "When was it you learned to cook this particular dish?"

Erro maintained his smug expression. "Irrelevant. I stand by my statement."

"I believe the answer is while you fostered in Auradia," Larron said.

Annalla laughed and shook her head at their easy familiarity. She never had moments like that with her parents. Her childhood had consisted of training and travel, and they'd died before they could see her as an independent adult. She loved and missed them, but she would never recall them with the camaraderie Erro shared with his mother and uncle. Hopefully, they would all survive the battles to come.

"We have made two successful attacks against the remaining gilar," Tralie said in response to an inquiry from her son. "It should work well for our departure."

"To follow us south?" Annalla asked.

Tralie nodded. "Yes. The land between us and the camps is mostly flat and open. We should be able to make good time following you and arrive only a couple of weeks later."

"What about the hills further south on the map?" she asked.

"The paths through that rocky landscape are easy enough," Larron told her. "More like the low hills before the Palonian than the Claws." He shifted his attention to Tralie. "You remain set on this course, sister?"

"Larron." She sighed, done with the debate the two had the entirety of yesterday. "Your mission a year ago was considered a lost cause, this one is not. I am not going to my death if I can at all help it, and Zeris would be at my side on this one were he with us today."

He held up his hands. "Very well. I will leave the matter alone. But Erro—"

"I know." His nephew cut him off, a bitter note to his voice. "I must remain here safe and sound."

"*Do* you know?" Larron asked, staring at Erro until the younger elf ducked his head guiltily. "You *are* the Derou, Erro. Yet, you still left the Heartwood while gilar roamed our lands, risking yourself mere days ago."

"You—"

"No," Larron said. "No. You did not know I lived, and even if you did know, we were both at risk out there. You *cannot* do that again."

Erro hunched over the table, looking both frustrated and resigned. Annalla understood the feeling. Without thinking, she touched Erro's arm and waited until he met her eyes. "Dying is easy," she told him. "Living is the true struggle when everything around you is falling apart."

He studied her, considering her and weighing her words within while Tralie and Larron waited in their own silent contemplation. Finally, Erro gave a resigned huff of a laugh. He took another breath and sighed again. Sitting up straight, he looked Larron in the eye. "I made coconut cake as well."

Larron smiled at him. "That one *is* a Derou recipe."

CHAPTER EIGHT

Karasis Mountain Regions

In the desperate hours following the fight, Tyrus could do nothing beyond thinking 'weightless' thoughts and trying to remain still in his harness as the mass of fairy flew. Through the night, into the dawn, and on further beyond the next day, they remained in the air. As the sun began its final descent, his eyes watered from straining to sight anything even remotely indicating a human army camp ahead. He never wished for the eyes of an elf more than on that day.

A scout unit flew toward the leadership wing in the deepening dusk, the captain settling in to fly at Zara's left. He said something to her while pointing ahead and making broad gestures. Finally, Zara shifted over to fly between Ameris and Vela.

She shouted to be heard by Tyrus and Patrice. "They report a massive army ahead," she told them. "The numbers are well more than one army camp."

"Can you see the pennant?"

Her head shook. "By the time we see such a thing, they'll be able to see us too."

Two choices, he thought. *We halt here and scout the army in darkness, which will mean death to the seventeen still clinging to life. Or we press on, hoping to save them and risk exposing the fairy early.*

"Last I knew, we held these lands." Tyrus met her eyes. "I recommend we proceed."

She stared at him. He almost saw her mind working behind the gaze before she shifted her eyes to look above him. "Ameris, how are you feeling?"

"Well enough, Colonel."

Tyrus could hear the grin in Ameris' voice and saw the flash of Zara's own smile before she turned and started shouting orders. He heard none of them until the last.

"Yallista, maintain speed and course unless you receive orders otherwise. Ameris, you're with us."

With that, Zara and Ameris broke off and joined the scout unit ahead and above. They rose higher and arranged themselves in a 'v' formation like a flock of migrating birds. Tyrus felt his stomach flop as their speed increased, and he sensed the difference between raptors and papilio in that moment as he closed his eyes against the stinging of the air rushing past.

Periodically, he shielded his eyes with his hands—awed at the force pressing against his arms—and peered ahead and below to check how much closer they were. The army came into view, spread out in the distance. He saw no pennants or flags flying over the tents to tell him if they were friend or foe.

How? Why? he wondered.

Soon enough, their small flight closed the remaining distance and slowed at the edge of standard longbow range, though a skilled elven archer could probably hit them even there.

"Remain here," Zara told the scouts. "Fly back and inform Yallista if they attack."

"Yes, Colonel."

She and Ameris, with Tyrus, soared slowly down and forward, closing the distance by half before touching down. Zara watched forward, on guard as Ameris unhooked the harness behind Tyrus so they could walk the remaining distance together, Tyrus leading the trio. He closed in by another half and stopped, raising his hands to show himself unarmed. As the other two copied him, a lone man walked forward from the line of archers arrayed against them.

"They wear the armor of Ceru," Tyrus whispered as hope warred with fear in him.

The man, a captain of Ceru by his uniform, stared openly at the fairy, his eyes flicking between them as he practically ignored Tyrus and failed to challenge them. Tyrus forgave the captain his awe.

"I am Prince Tyrus of Ceru," he said into the waiting silence. "I bring allies, and we have wounded in need of healing."

"Prince Tyrus?" His eyes snapped to assess him in turn. "I will inform the Commander. Please wait here."

"I have a command code to give them," Tyrus told Zara as they waited, "but I'm uncertain if the commander here will know it to be able to verify my identity."

"Your name is well known. They seek to prevent infiltration, which is wise," she said approvingly.

"What would they think we are?" Ameris asked.

Tyrus glanced over his shoulder at the tall fairy. "Magai illusions. Fairy are a myth; only vampires can fly." Tyrus shook his head. "I'm more worried about them being the enemy, though, and capturing us. We can disprove illusion by touch, it'll simply take longer…"

A genuine smile split Tyrus' face at the sight of the man walking toward them as the troops parted to let him pass.

"Walsh!" he shouted, barely restraining himself from

running forward to embrace the man.

"Code, please, Your Highness."

"Celuna seven six," he said quickly; the short password was given to him when he'd left for the north. Walsh gave a signal, and the tension eased from the bowstrings pointed at them.

Another man came barreling forward shouting, "Tyrus! Tyrus!"

"Father!" Tyrus closed the distance and the two men came together in a crushing hug.

"What are you doing here?" they both asked each other at the same time, laughing with relief.

Tyrus shook himself, remembering their purpose. "Father, we have injured. There was a vampire attack, and we need healers and antivenin immediately."

"Yes. Yes, the healers were called," his father said.

Walsh, more composed than the reunited pair, addressed Zara. "Please, bring your injured here and we will see to them. Introduction can wait."

Zara bowed her head. "We have traveled far. Do we have your leave to set down and make camp?"

"Granted," Walsh told her.

"Ameris will remain to coordinate and translate," she told him. "I'll return for…introductions once my people are settled."

As Zara alighted and rejoined the scout unit and healers emerged from the human camp, King Garett spoke softly to his son. "I sent you for food and supplies."

Tyrus smiled at his father. "And I brought you an army instead."

***

Jarin rode up yet another foothill leading toward the

snowcapped Karasis Mountains ahead. He arrived a day late to the location at which he *should* have rejoined the army, only to find them already moved on and positioned closer to the mouth of the massive Karasis Valley, where Kahnlair's troops had laid siege to the southern dwarf clan.

The valley nestled between the enclosing arms of the mountain range. Every path into and out of the long swath of fertile land was easily defended from either direction. The dwarves had turned the natural cave system running beneath into a veritable warren, but they had been cut off from the rest of the world since Kahnlair's first strikes. He kept them penned in as he eliminated the mage academy, and left just enough forces to ensure they could not depart en masse or with supplies. Kahnlair could have overwhelmed the dwarven clan at any point, but the move would cost him dearly in troops relative to the cost of keeping them penned.

With his current plan, Walsh saw an opportunity to swell the ally ranks with the clan's forces. If successful, the move meant an influx of soldiers for which the allies were in desperate need. It could also mean additional food supplies if the clan successfully tended the farms within the range in excess of their own needs. The windani remained somewhere to the north. If they kept the vampires out of the fight until it was nearly over, the coming battle might become a rout in their favor, where they would only need to hold against a possible vampire wave to follow.

He urged his horse up the slope. The beast was another human-bred gelding made for hauling heavy things. Usually, that meant supplies, but Jarin and his weapons were enough to test a horse's tolerance and stamina. They plodded up, the fluffy hooves crunching against the gravel prevalent there. Jarin hoped the horse would not find one of the pebbles stuck in its shoe, as he was not the best at taking care of a horse's needs.

The slope leveled some as they drew near the top. Jarin

rose, hoping for a view of the army camp to be stretching out below him any moment. His horse seemed to sense his excitement—or it was simply glad to be nearly done with the upward trek—as it started clopping forward faster. Finally, tents came into view. He stood up in the stirrups, looking out with an enormous smile spread across his face. *Nearly there,* he thought, but the camp kept spreading. The tents were countless, far more than there should be for the size of King Garrett's forces.

Jarin drew up at the top of the rise, stopping to peer down at the military might arrayed below. As he watched, a group rose into the air and flew away south. It felt as though they took his hope with them as his spirits plummeted. *Kahnlair was waiting for them,* he thought. A mounted unit peeled away nearest him and rode in his direction. He had been seen.

Rather than wait for them in plain sight, he turned his horse around and rode back down until the slope steepened and there he dismounted, taking both weapons in hand. He readied himself. He would eliminate that unit and flee north, warning every camp along the way as he hurried back to convey the devastating news to Albertas. The sound of their horses grew louder as the enemy approached. Jarin adjusted his grip, crouching to attack.

The first man crested the hill and began his descent. "Lord Ja— Ack!" he said, falling from his mount, barely evading the swipe of Jarin's morningstar against his head and instead taking a slice across his shoulder as he fell.

"Lord Jarin! Stop!" another man shouted at him as the riders swung wide to avoid the combatants. "Stop! Commander Walsh sent us!"

"Lies!" he roared and swung again at the man, who scrambled away in a quick retreat.

"Hold!" The man barked the order at his men while holding his bleeding arm close. "Sir, why do you think we lie?"

Their behavior made him question what he had seen. They should be rushing for reinforcements to overwhelm him. Instead, the captain sought to calm and assure him. It had to be a deception.

"I witnessed the vampires leaving," he said, calling out the truth they could not refute.

He looked to be both relieved and frustrated, at a loss for how to respond. With every moment he delayed, Jarin became more sure they stalled for time.

"Captain," another man called out, "we can call the fairy here to show him. I've learned a couple of their codes."

The frustration left the captain's face, leaving only relief. "Yes," he said, then spoke to Jarin. "Not vampires, fairy. They arrived out of the southern sky not two days past. We can whistle one of their units here to show you."

"The fairy are gone."

"They came back. Somehow, they came back with Prince Tyrus to help us." He nodded at his man, who whistled a shrill three-note sequence.

The group did nothing more. They made no threatening moves and waited a safe distance from him even as Jarin darted glances around, keeping track of them while simultaneously watching the sky for additional threats. Soon enough, a squad of fifteen flew to the top of the hill, landing to walk cautiously toward the confrontation.

"Illusion," Jarin whispered in disbelief as he took in their varied wings, colorful and beautiful to behold.

The fairy-vampire in front took in the scene, then looked toward the injured man. "Ally?" he asked, pointing at Jarin.

"Yes."

At the man's reply, he nodded to another man, speaking in a language Jarin did not understand. He spoke as the younger fairy stepped forward slowly.

"We are not vampires," their leader said. "I'm told illusion does not conceal touch, and vampires have no feathers."

The young fairy continued his approach, stretching forward a wing the beautiful slate gray color of a northern nuthatch. He stopped an arm's length away, warily waiting for Jarin to close the distance. Transferring his weapons to hold both in one hand was simple enough. He reached his free hand forward slowly, prepared for any sudden movement. None came, and the pads of his fingers met the softness of feathers. Without thinking, he stroked down the wing almost reverently, tears forming in his eyes.

Jarin met the eyes of the young fairy, who smiled at him and extended a hand back toward the camp, inviting Jarin to join them.

"I'll take you to the healers," the lead fairy told the captain. "The others can see your ally to camp."

Watching the two glide off down the hill, Jarin felt lightheaded and had to sit down.

"Are you alright, sir?" one of the men asked.

"A moment, please."

They milled about, waiting for him with no sign of impatience. Jarin's eyes drank in the sight of the fairy waiting with them and speaking amongst themselves. For the first time in days, he smiled.

"Jarin!"

He turned, only to receive a mass of vibrant red hair in his face as Morena slammed into him. Without hesitation, he squeezed her tight and spun her around.

"Morena. Oh, how I missed you."

She leaned back from their embrace and laid a hand against his face. Her eyes saw too much. "Something happened," she said. "Before you left or on the journey here?"

Jarin shook his head. "During, but such events do not matter now."

Morena's eyes narrowed, and she scrutinized him.

He leaned in to kiss her forehead. "Let it go," he told her. "For now."

"Very well. For now." She looped her arm through his and led him away from his newly assigned tent. "We are due in a meeting with King Garrett anyway."

"So I was told. Preparation for the battle to free the dwarves, yes?"

"Yes," she said. "Walsh intends to attack tomorrow."

Surprised, he stopped and turned toward her. "So soon?"

"We are in position, hold information from the irimoten telepaths who escaped to the dwarven clan, and have scouted the area. The humans believe we only risk losing the element of surprise by delaying."

"And what of the fairy?"

"They are in alignment with the humans," she said, leaning toward him and lowering her voice. "Apparently, their orders are to press forward, leveraging the surprise of their presence for as long as possible."

Jarin winced. "The gilar adapt quickly. I hope such an approach does not cost more than it gains."

Morena raised her eyebrows at him. "Do you honestly believe *Walsh* will waste their lives in such a reckless way?"

"No." Jarin laughed. "Walsh is entirely too calculating. Even his bold strategies are heavily weighed."

"That man is entirely too intelligent for his own good. He needs to take some time for himself, so he does not burn himself out."

"He has you to worry about him, at least." Jarin grinned at her, and she elbowed him.

Everyone knew Commander Walsh thought of Morena

as a daughter of sorts, despite the elven woman having centuries on the human. He showed pride in everything she did, worried about her and the toll of reading their enemy, and often shared meals with her. For her part, Morena considered Walsh a close friend, second only to Jarin in the army camps. She took Walsh's concerns in stride and worried about him in turn.

They entered the command tent to find everyone else present, with the additions of Combat Mage Hephestar, Prince Tyrus, and a fairy woman. The mage used to be a frequent member of their strategy sessions, but the dwindling number of magai in their ranks had pressed him into service too much of late to spend his resting hours conferring with them. Prince Tyrus had rarely been present. His primary responsibility had been to oversee the supply lines, farms, and defense thereof.

"Welcome back, Lord Jarin," King Garrett said to him. "I'd like to introduce Lead Colonel Zara of the fairy."

Lead Colonel Zara's wings were also gray, like those of the young man from earlier, but hers were lighter toward her body and shading toward blue at her wing tips. She appeared around the same age as King Garrett, but he did not know what her appearance meant in terms of years. Every race's lifespan varied. Her stance was firm and erect. Her muscles strained against light armor, and she wore a variety of weaponry upon her. Weighted balls on a line, daggers with multiple points, and something on an arm sheath he could see part of.

"Lead Colonel," Jarin said, acknowledging her with a short bow.

She returned the gesture of respect toward him, addressing him as, "Enchantress."

The term gave him pause, and he glanced at Morena.

She grinned at him. "It is their term for those with essential abilities. They have an essential fairy."

"Here?" He glanced around, knowing he had not missed someone hiding in the shadows.

"No," Tyrus answered. "Annalla told Prince Darrin of the fairy that she headed for the Derou. We believe she'll be meeting the army from that direction later."

Jarin felt giddy again. *Fairy,* he thought. *Another essential. If only Kahnlair would disappear, they might find peace.*

Commander Walsh stepped forward. "Tomorrow," he addressed the gathering, "we attack the forces laying siege to the Karasis Valley."

CHAPTER NINE

Karasis Valley

Tyrus fidgeted with the buckles of the flying harness, trying to settle them comfortably around his armor. Despite having trained and worked with the Ceru army for most of his life, he had seen relatively little combat. Almost nothing compared to Albertas and Lukas, who spent their lives on the front line. Instead, Tyrus worked behind the lines. He had often traveled with minimal guards and moved from one place to another, directing local troops to eliminate smaller threats.

Harndorn, the gruff captain of his guard, remained behind in the Palonian when he set out to find the fairy, despite his vehement protests. During their time together, they faced two ambushes set by Kahnlair against their supply lines and participated in the fighting only twice more in planned counter attacks against forces threatening Ceru farmland. When they were sent north, most of the combat Tyrus saw was in surprise attacks along the river. That day would mark only the second major engagement in which he participated. Something planned out, prepared for, and executed according to a field commander's strategy.

The first had been Larron leading a cobbled-together group of peasants in a coordinated defense of their village. The next battle would exceed the scale of that confrontation by orders of magnitude. Fortunately, he wouldn't be one of only a handful of trained fighters, but the fact did little to settle his nerves. Against an ambush, there was no time to contemplate everything that might go wrong or wonder how many of the people preparing next to you wouldn't return from the field alive.

Anticipation is torture, he thought and reminded himself they held the advantage that day.

Ameris stepped up behind him and started connecting the buckles and safety lines to link them.

"Any advice?" Morena's jewel-like gray eyes sparkled in anticipation across from him as one of the papilio fairy captains hooked up behind her.

In the army camps, Morena stood out as a beautiful flower against the scraggly bushes that were the soldiers around her. Except in battle, she wore gorgeous jewel-colored gowns and shining ornaments in her hair. Her only concessions to the times were the number of ornaments and her sturdy boots beneath the gowns. That day, she dressed in light elven armor and covered her bundled hair with a leather cap to conceal the telling red color.

She would have two fairy units guarding her as she flew with them in targeted attack runs. The moment Tyrus shared how Annalla's essential abilities worked behind a mage's shield, she and Walsh shared a nearly maniacal glance. Jarin had immediately said, "No," pointing between them, but the majority had sided against him. Kahnlair's magai were the greatest threat. They could eliminate swaths of soldiers with each strike and protect too many against counter attacks. Even when Kahnlair wasn't directly bolstering them, they somehow drew on his strength to outmatch Ceru's magai on a mage-to-mage level.

The plan was to signal wherever a mage was found, have Morena fly in to strike with her essential ability, then retreat until the next was identified. Mage Hephestar, currently standing harnessed behind her, would shield the fairy unit in the sky and on the attack run. The second fairy unit with them would also run interference between ground archers and the attackers to provide an additional layer of protection. No matter the cost, they would protect the elven enchantress.

"Are you afraid of heights?" Tyrus asked in response to Morena's question.

She gave the matter some thought. "I do not believe so, but I imagine flying will feel different from climbing."

He laughed, thinking of Patrice. She loved climbing ridiculously high in trees, but hated flying. "It is. I guess my best advice is to trust the fairy and enjoy the ride."

Morena grinned at him. "I plan to. Oh!" she said and craned her neck to look back. "Can we fly over Jarin after the fighting is done so I can wave to him, Captain Luanna? It would be a marvelous image for him to carve into one of his pots someday, I am certain."

It seemed to Tyrus she restrained a smile at Morena's eagerness as she replied. "We'll see how the situation stands at the time, but it's certainly possible."

Colonel Zara entered and scanned the group. "Ready?"

Captain Luanna received nods from her units. "Ready, Colonel."

"Move out."

As they lifted off, Tyrus caught a glimpse of Morena once more. Gone were her friendly smiles and bright excitement. In their place, her visage became iced over, frozen, cold, and lethal. Woe to enemies in her path that day.

***

Jarin adjusted his grip on the weapons in his hands as he awaited the order to charge. Poised upon a rocky slope, he was well within range to make out the well-organized camp below. Throughout the morning, scouts and soldiers came and went to and from the pass leading through the Karasis Mountains and the valley protected within. They watched and waited for any of the dwarves to attempt escape. It must have been many years since any concerted effort to do so had been attempted by the clan, yet the enemy camp remained as diligent as if attacks happened every day. The discipline spoke well of their commander and represented unfortunate news for the allies.

For all their diligence, however, it appeared they did not expect an attack from the Ceru side, likely due to the vampires holding the mage academy. They posted a limited number of scouts to the east of the camp, and Garrett's hunters had already eliminated those they tracked on their scouting expedition over the two prior days. The commencement of their attack was set for midday, in mere moments, ensuring they attacked before the guard changed and the missing were noted.

Jarin's assignment was to drive forward, cleaving the enemy forces in two, and to create as much chaos as possible. Most of the enemy combatants were human or magai. Any gilar were to be killed, while surrendering humans or magai could be taken captive. The latter would be bound as necessary to ensure they did not cause additional damage later if held within the army camp.

Someone else would be responsible for sending up a signal if his group ran into any magai as they pressed forward. The humans carried torches and powder to color the flames an eye-searing white. A fairy patrol above would mark the flame, sight the enemy group and the mage, and move in with Morena to eliminate the threat with enough time for the allied forces to clear out from around the powdered torch. Jarin had his doubts, but those were overwhelmingly overruled.

Pushing aside his concerns, Jarin gripped his essence mentally and prepared himself for the rush as the final countdown began. *Moments now,* he thought. There was a collective intake of breath, holding and freezing a moment as the soldiers around him gathered themselves for the action to come. On the other side of the path, a group of men broke early, barreling down the slope. A few of them shouted a war cry and stones rumbled and clanked down the incline beneath their feet. Timing an attack never happened perfectly. Armies adapted, or they failed.

In response to the early charge, Ceru men poured out of their hiding places all around the enemy camp. Jarin ran forward, swinging his weapons menacingly as the surrounding men followed his lead and charged straight down the path toward a scrambling camp.

The enemy commander proved as competent as expected, and Kahnlair's men rallied to meet the wave bearing down on them. Rather than running before him, the wall of men flowed back and forth, sweeping aside Jarin's attacks rather than directly meeting them and holding him to more limited forward progress than he was accustomed.

This commander is wasted here, watching the dwarves, Jarin mused as another of his brutal strikes was redirected to the ground instead of tearing into his opponent.

A flare went up some distance to Jarin's left, and he ignored the mage signal as planned to continue pressing. The enemies before him backed off, and instantly Jarin switched to calling for a retreat. Many of, but not all, the nearby Ceru soldiers pulled back. The hesitation cost the rest. Beneath his feet, a blast of power exploded out, throwing Jarin and those around him into the sky and tumbling back to the ground in heaps of flailing and broken limbs.

Another flare to the right. Whether they were

identifying the mage who attacked Jarin or another, he had no way to know and no time to wonder. Even as he pushed to his feet, men rushed forward to stab at the groaning bodies of his allies. He pressed up, swinging his sword as he rose and ending one threat before the strike could land. A rage-filled shout clawed from his throat as he attacked again and again, driving toward the center of the camp.

A flash of chilled air washed over him, and he distantly thought, *Morena struck a nearby target.* She would eliminate the magai, Jarin would find the commander. Somewhere in the center of those ranks was the man behind their coordination. Shrugging off a blow to the back of his legs attempting to cripple him, he cracked his attacker on the head with bone-crushing force and moved forward.

***

The battle ended frighteningly quickly. Tyrus, with Ameris, remained at Zara's side throughout as she issued orders and adjusted her forces as the situation unfolded. Only about a thousand of the fairy fought that day. According to Zara, there was not enough air space over the battlefield to support more, and they would only end up in each other's way. Additional units stood ready, but they were never called.

Jarin led the charge on the ground, holding the line against the magai attacks. Bolts rained down on the camp from behind as the dwarves closed off the pass into the valley. In the first half hour, Morena dove down with her fairy guards and eliminated two separate magai. After the second mage went down, the rest stopped working their magic to keep from being identified. Left unsupported, the humans started surrendering down the line.

The entire engagement ended up being anticlimactic. By suppertime, the prisoners were securely restrained or restricted as needed, the site was cleared, any injuries were handled by the healers, and they had settled into the meal tent to eat on schedule.

"Why did we not do this sooner?" Jarin asked Walsh at the other end of their command table.

"We could never spare the forces. Today went…exceptionally smoothly for several reasons." Walsh set down his spoon and started ticking off fingers. "First, we coordinated with the dwarves thanks to the irimoten telepaths who fled to the clan. Second, with the bulk of the army here, we significantly outnumbered them. Third, you and Morena were here. Fourth, the vampires didn't have forces in the area. Fifth, and most significantly, we had the fairy on our side."

He tipped his head at Zara with the latter statement as he continued. "The fairy support was the reason we had men attacking from three sides rather than one, and they allowed Morena to target the enemy magai quickly and effectively."

"I cannot believe Kahnlair has not placed any of his magai in the air with the vampires before now," Morena said.

Her eyes retained some of the glow from her flight. Captain Luanna had held to her earlier promise. With the quick end to the threat and having lost no members of the two units under her command, Captain Luanna dove in low and fast at Jarin's position as he left the field. Morena had apparently cried out, "Jarin! I am flying!" as she passed overhead, and could be heard laughing in glee all the way back to the allied camp.

"Would you feel comfortable riding with a vampire, Mage Hephestar?" Zara asked the magai leader. "Thinking, of course, you were fighting with rather than against."

The combat mage chuckled and shook his head, but he gave the question some thought before responding. "I'll admit some trepidation at the thought of flying, but the harness helped me worry less about falling. The vampires might not be willing to wear such a safety device, or at least be less diligent with it. I think," he said, "that Kahnlair's magai would be less effective in the air because they wouldn't trust their bearers. Some of their attention and power would always be spent protecting themselves."

"Do not," Walsh said, cutting across the conversation, "allow your people to become overconfident. We were fortunate in every way today. Kahnlair will adapt, and we all know the numbers advantage is more often the reverse of what we faced today."

Nods of ascent met his sobering statement, and silence reigned for a moment as they tucked into their food.

"Oh!" Patrice said. "Do you have the names of the irimoten with the Karasis Valley clan?"

"We are working on updating our lists," Morena told her. "Why?"

"My son might be with them. He went across a few years ago."

Tyrus sensed the hairs on his neck stand on end as everyone at the table other than Patrice, Zara, and he pursed their lips and glued their eyes to the dishes in front of them. Patrice flicked her gaze from one to the other. The excitement and anticipation left her face, replaced by a terrified, frozen expression.

"What is it?" Tyrus asked for her. Beneath the table, he gripped her hand.

Walsh cleared his throat. "The reason the windani are so far north is that Kahnlair gave them orders to go, and to eliminate any irimoten they found in their path."

"There were no survivors in the camps south of here, and most of the guards from the one closest to our position were killed saving the telepaths," Morena said, tears brimming in her eyes.

Patrice's claws pricked the back of his hand before she ripped away from him, leaving the tent in a rush. A couple drops of blood dotted his hand from where she had not retracted her claws quickly enough and scraped him. Tyrus ignored the scratch and rose, feeling numb.

"Nedral is a guard," he told them. "She doesn't know where he's stationed."

"The irimoten are nearly done with their counts," Morena told him gently. "They will know."

His good cheer after the battle had vanished, and the food felt heavy in his stomach. Leaving his plate, Tyrus went to find his friend.

CHAPTER TEN

Scorcella

A week after his arrival at the magai city, Darrin sat in a dining room taking breakfast with Marto and Nurtik. The three of them had run from one location to another, meeting with leaders and workers in all the magical focuses. They inspected processes, tested products, and offered suggestions. Each day ended with a two-hour strategy meeting with the magai council, discussing who should go, how their magic would be used, and who would remain behind to guard the nearly empty city.

"The chemist magai have nearly exhausted their supply of the antivenin ingredients," Marto said. "I never thought they'd finish every batch in so little time."

Darrin gave a relieved smile. "It gives me hope. Braymis said we only lost three to the vampire venom in the battle's aftermath. The results of the conflict could have been so much worse."

"Hope Tyrus 'n Patrice are as lucky," Nurtik said. "They're flyin' right by that colony, an' likely won't see any magai for a while after."

"A known risk." Darrin feared the same, but there was

nothing he could do to help the other half of his army. "I only hope we arrive before their supplies run out."

A knock came at the door, and it opened to admit Mage Katira and Mage Setioral.

"Counselors," Marto said as he rose in greeting.

"Please, forgive our interruption of your meal," Mage Katira said. Today, her dark hair was pulled back from her face in a tight knot at the base of her skull, making her strong visage appear more severe.

"Nothing to forgive," Darrin said. "Please, join us." He waved at the open seats.

"We already ate, but thank you for the seats," she said, continuing once they were seated. "You're still certain of setting out the morning after tomorrow?"

He nodded. "Yes, we have an enormous distance to cover. I prefer not delaying."

Mage Setioral acknowledged his statement. "We voted and finalized our counts," he said. "We'll send just under two thousand magai with you."

"Clanlord Fwendilg'll be sending over three thousand soldiers wi't yer Colonel Braymis, 'cording to the last message I received," Nurtik told them.

"Yes," Darrin said to the dwarf. "I received the same information. "And that's wonderful to hear, Counselors. It's good so many will be joining us. This is what we hoped for when we kept so many fairy in the east."

"It'll take us a year to move so many across the continent," Marto said with a sigh.

"And I regret to say," said Setioral, "we won't have our supplies packed to move out for at least another week. We don't even have enough freight carts. We'll need to build more."

Darrin tilted his head in confusion, as they had just acknowledged his timetable. "We'll rejoin the rest of my people within three months, and you don't need carts," Darrin said, receiving disbelieving glances. He held up his hands. "I'm serious. Marto, you were in the meetings when we discussed the mobile pavilions. We planned, and hoped, for around five thousand passengers in addition to the fairy."

Katira leaned forward. "Please explain further."

"We use large pavilions during festivals," he said. "They're lightweight and easily convertible. We use them to transport supplies, and then they serve as platforms for audiences during performances. We already had about thirty-five and moved all of those to Essence and Thought before the connections closed. Those have been converted to transport approximately one hundred people each along with supplies, and another fifteen were in construction. They should be here tomorrow, and the dwarven forces, already using the pavilions, should arrive by tomorrow evening."

"You intend to fly all of us?" Mage Katira asked in disbelief.

"Yes."

"Tell me more about these pavilions," the architect mage asked him before he could respond further to Mage Katira.

"The framework is made of the same wood we use for our houses. It's sturdy but light, which allows us to carry more. We added hammocks for each person and netting around the outside for safety, and there are rope ladders throughout. While the next few months will not be comfortable, we'll arrive quickly."

"Hmm," Mage Setioral said, more to himself. "I have some ideas." He said no more, too deep in thought to respond to Darrin's raised eyebrow.

"How many fairy per pavilion?" Marto asked.

"Fifty each," he said. "They'll rotate every four hours."

The younger mage shook his head. "Carrying cargo? That will certainly slow you down, and based on the maps, we're at least five months away from the Ceru lines."

Darrin grinned at him. "This's why we brought in more raptors to the east. We can carry more and fly faster than our papilio counterparts. Our journey will be made in three-day cycles. Two and a half days of flying straight through, followed by a half day of rest. All the raptors will rotate between carrying, flying, and resting in overlapping shifts. The papilio with us will fly and rest, and when we stop for the third-day break on the ground, the papilio will be on shifts guarding us."

"Wait, wait, wait," Mage Katira said. "Are you saying that the two and a half days will be all in the air? Not even setting down at night to sleep?"

"Exactly," Darrin said. "We ran marathons and relays for games and festivals within the sanctuaries. This is similar, just…a grander scale. And we'll touch down briefly every four hours for the shift changes and to allow our passengers to relieve themselves and pass out food as needed."

The magai counselors made eye contact with each other, having a short, non-verbal conversation before facing the table once more. "If you'll excuse us," Mage Katira said. "We have some additional preparations to make with this information."

Darrin glanced between his two breakfast companions. "I thought I was clear that we were all leaving the morning after tomorrow."

Marto started chuckling and shaking his head, while Nurtik only grinned.

***

Marto stared at the pavilion in front of him with a combination of excitement, wonder, and dread. As they shifted supplies and packed the day before, Mage Goran, the counselor representing the combat magai, came to him and told Marto he would be joining the expedition. Mage Goran said the fairy knew and trusted him, so he made the perfect representative to work with them through the continuing war efforts.

"Ambassador," someone said loudly behind him.

"Hello, Karl." Marto smiled and shook his head at his friend's antics. "I'm not technically an ambassador."

"Close enough," he said with a grin. "Why are you staring at the pavilion as though it's going to bite you?"

"Ha," he said sarcastically.

Returning his gaze to the structure, he contemplated it again. About the size of two large rooms stacked on top of each other and held together by a frame of thin, flexible wood. The 'floors' were a combination of netting lined with plank walkways and the walls were only netting without any planking. The entire structure had a triangular orientation, with alternating rows of hanging hammocks hung in stacks over each other ten high. First one stack, then two, three, and four. According to Darrin, this reduced the drag and made the awkward structure easier to move.

At the foot of each hammock was a box stuffed with equipment, and more boxes lined the top edges of the structure for additional supplies. Most of the heavier items had been shifted to the magai pavilions to counter the weight of the dwarven armor. Each passenger was expected to carry with them a pack of personal items and food that would be replenished during each of the longer half-day breaks, as well as carrying their own cloaks and gear for inclement weather. All movement was to be kept to a minimum, with passengers expected to make the most out of their shorter, periodic breaks for stretching and exercising.

"I know what it's like to be stuck in bed for endless days in a row," Marto finally said to Karl's question. "This will not be a pleasant trip."

Karl joined him in looking at the pavilion. "No. There will be challenges for all involved. The added supports your architect magai put into the frame will help—a little—with comfort though."

Marto laughed, thinking about the arrival of the dwarves the night before. The frames had all bent back in flight, making the hammocks scrunch together more with every level toward the bottom you went. Dwarves on the lowest level ended up squatting curled up in beds that had become more like chairs by the end of the trip. When the fairy stopped, the entire structure swung forward and swayed back and forth for a time. A handful of the dwarves from every pavilion ended up sick every time at every landing.

The healers had seen to those most impacted, and their services would likely be needed throughout the coming journey. Mage Setioral must have already discussed possibilities about the pavilions with his fellows before anyone arrived, as they went up to one of the pavilions and started conferring and working with the fairy and dwarves. After they were done, the support beams and floor planks were stronger than before, while just as light as ever. It had the effect of helping the layers maintain the triangular structure without adding a burden to the bearers.

"I wonder…" Marto stepped forward with his crutches to run a hand along the lead beam.

"You wonder?" Karl asked after an extended silence.

He shifted to look at the man standing beside him. "We were in a storm, on our way to find the fairy—well, a few storms—anyway. You all speak of drag, wind, and airflow as though air has a physical presence like water."

"Very similar, actually," Karl said.

Marto didn't hear him, too busy processing his thoughts. "In one of the storms, I put a shield around our camp to keep the heat in, so we didn't freeze to death. That had to be related to airflow, right?"

"Possibly."

"Well, what if shielding can help with moving these things?" Marto waved a hand in a gesture encompassing the pavilion before him. "Darrin said the triangular shape helps. I wonder if we could experiment with some shielding today to see if anything helps or hinders."

Karl laughed and threw an arm around Marto's shoulders. "Let's go find the captain of your pavilion and ask."

Grinning with excitement, Marto led the way.

CHAPTER ELEVEN

South of the Derou

The first day of their departure from Larron's house in the Derou, Annalla flew them to the southern border of the Woodland. They planned to remain one more night within the protection of the elven land. She set down in one of the few clearings available.

No simple forest, the area was a jungle with a thick canopy, draping vines, clinging flowers, and thick undergrowth. A small shaft of light descended from a break in the canopy, highlighting the bright reds, yellows, and even blues of the petals and leaves interspersed among the predominantly deep green of the foliage. The temperature warmed considerably as they traveled south, and the humidity grew proportionally. A spring storm with heavy rain closed in as they landed.

"Was this area always like this?" Annalla asked Larron beneath the protective umbrella of her power holding off the rain. "Or did I ruin this part of the Woodland?"

Larron's eyes scanned the surrounding forest with a small smile on his lips. "You did nothing wrong here," he said. "The southern third of the Derou has always been a mixture of rainforest and jungle. There are deep reservoirs beneath these lands we believe feed the Oasis River to the southeast. The rain and water clash with the heat from the desert to the southwest, driving up the humidity. Until the gilar tore through here, the difficulty of traveling through this area was one of our best defenses."

He looked up, watching the raindrops halt mid-fall before collecting and streaming in arches all around them. The effect did not look like rain flowing over glass, but rather like water poured out of a pitcher. There was no surface pressing against the flow, simply her power redirecting movement through the air.

"Does this take much effort?" he asked and began unpacking for camp.

"No. Once the shell is established, it only requires a tendril of power to maintain."

Larron shook his head in apparent amazement. "How can you maintain a manifestation even in sleep?"

Annalla passed him dinner as they sat down on their bedrolls before she answered. "Do you remember how I told you about active and passive forms of manifestations?"

He nodded.

"Well, to maintain our campfire or the water dome above us now, I am consciously creating a link between the two forms. In this case, I am linking a specific, simple active sending of my water element to my passive receipt of information. As long as water falls, the dome is maintained. With our campfire, I link the flames to the passive perception to the portion of my will guiding and maintaining the level of the fire."

"And the connection is not distracting?"

"It was at first." Annalla thought about how she might explain. She snapped her fingers. "Think of the act like walking. You make a decision to walk from one place to another and your feet carry you there. You do not need to consider how and where to place each step and the muscle mechanics involved, whereas a toddler *does* put a lot of concentration into placing one foot in front of the other. Once you understand how to do something on a nearly subconscious level, the connection between thought and deed becomes so minor as to be imperceptible.

"I am better now at linking the active and passive forms, but it comes with experience. My lack of experience at the beginning is why I stumbled so many times, and still make mistakes with my abilities." Annalla laughed. "It does not always work this way though. My mother told me the story of another fire enchantress who came into her power without noticing. She was so good with flint and getting a blaze going that when her power emerged, it simply manifested through her mundane tools. The Protector at the time was at a loss as to figure out why her daughter had not manifested yet when she started a fire with wet wood in a massive downpour with just flint."

"So, she was not actually creating a physical spark?"

"She probably was," Annalla said, "but her will and her power ensured the fuel always caught. Once they understood the direction of her manifestation, she could learn to recreate the effect without the mundane tools. When dealing with essence, sometimes too much mundane knowledge in a subject is detrimental."

Larron smiled at the last statement and bit into his meat pie. Annalla set some of the rainwater to boil over her fire, and when it was heated through enough, she moved the liquid to their metal travel cups and Larron added tea leaves. She loved watching him move; the economy of every motion spelled out his training to any with an eye for it. In those small moments, she allowed herself to admire him briefly before shutting down that train of thought.

"When do you think your next ability will begin to emerge?" he asked as he passed her one of the cups.

Annalla sat up straighter. "The air element feels relatively…" She hunted around for the right word. "New, or maybe small? I suspect my elven side is slowing the progression a little. At twenty-seven, I should see the fifth element by now. Based on how air is progressing, though, I believe I will not see communication emerge for another couple of years." Her lips scrunched up. "At least it will be a normal emergence."

Laughing, Larron gave an agreeing tilt of his head and tipped his steaming cup in her direction. "At least."

That night was the last they slept without one of them on guard. Outside the Woodland, the jungle gradually gave way to savanna. Warm, dry grasslands spread far into the distance, punctuated by sparse trees and rocky outcroppings. Below them, on the first day flying over the open land below, Annalla saw a group of three enormous felines run down a gazelle. The massive cats were the first animals she didn't recognize from her schooling in Aryanna, and she had never been to that region in Elaria before. The cats had the build of lions, with muscular shoulders providing power, spots on their golden coats like leopards, and oversized top fangs like she imagined the extinct saber-tooth tiger might have had.

"What are those?" Annalla asked, pointing toward where the three crowded around their kill.

"Daraguar," Larron told her. "They are a relatively new species diverged from the savanna lions. With similarities to the jungle cats as well, they claim territory crossing the jungle and savanna border. We monitor their numbers, but we are not certain if they will continue to diverge, or merge with the lions once more."

"You won't try to save them?" Her surprise at the ease with which he contemplated extinction pushed her back into less formal speech, something that would have earned a raised eyebrow from her father.

Larron only gave as much of a shrug as he could while strapped into the flying rig. "Perhaps if we did something to bring about their end, but destruction and endings are as natural as creation and beginnings."

Annalla gave a final look back at the feasting cats before they were out of sight. They flew almost directly south. The remaining gilar reported were positioned southwest, so they assumed the southerly direction to be relatively safe. Annalla flew for a few hours, then they walked for a time before Larron rested upon the ground while Annalla guarded before the cycle began again until evening.

The effort to save the Derou set her recovery back, but not horribly so. With the frequent breaks, she regained her strength each day at a steady enough pace. They passed over the territories of the lions, passed beyond the southern edge of the trakin forest to their left. Eventually, the desert drew closer to the west, rocky outcroppings became more frequent, and the flat land ahead became clustered with craggy hills.

Almost two weeks of flying and walking later, as the noon sun began its descent, Larron pointed toward a silhouette drifting on the thermals far ahead. "Vampire," he said.

The figure remained too far to tell for certain, but there was little likelihood of it being a fairy in their location. Annalla turned them in a leisurely circle and backtracked another half an hour before setting them down.

"Let us see how far they patrol," Larron said, the same plan sitting in Annalla's head.

Setting up their fireless camp, they prepared to wait and watch.

***

They sat for one night at the initial distance, then closed in and waited for an hour, repeating the hour-long pauses between jumps until night began to fall. Larron took the first watch and tracked the progress of a vampire scout. The patrol passing overhead was the fourth they had marked in their observations. The intervals were not precise, but the timing was more consistent than vampires were naturally. Such a change in behavior might be Kahnlair's influence, or it might mean other races were at or in command of the camp from which the vampires came.

The camp sat against a short cliff with rock walls around its other sides. The cliff was one face of a larger rocky hill, where the other side sloped gradually down. With no other significant hills close by, those guarding the camp had relatively unimpeded sight of the ground for miles in every direction from the top. They had scouted only from the air and at a distance even Larron's sight struggled to discern details. Combined with the vampire patrols, there was little chance an armed assault could take the camp by surprise. Larron told Annalla as much the next morning when they sat discussing their options.

"What do they mine here?" she asked, ignoring his comment.

"Are you listening to me, Annalla? We have no hope of taking this camp."

She transferred her attention from staring at the speck of the camp far in the distance to looking at him. "I hear you," she said, "but I disagree. So, what do they mine here?"

Larron breathed out through his nose and stretched his neck in frustration, seeking some level of calm. "I believe the humans started mining this area for metals. The smoke may indicate a forge as well."

Annalla held up one finger, then another. "Metal. Forge.

Plus guards, means probably plenty of weapons inside. The question is how we reach the camp."

Weapons she could control. Fire she could manipulate. Larron set aside his familiar combat tactics and tried to view the potential fight from a different perspective. *She would not put herself at great risk because of her position.*

"Help me understand," he said. "What is your plan if you do make it into the camp?"

"You free the prisoners while I hold off the guards," she said. "I can hold off projectiles similar to how I held back the rain. I set up the 'shield,' then shift to controlling the weapons in the area to attack anyone closing on our position. You bring in more fighters, we fight, we win, they lose."

He knew well enough to know she had contingency plans built into her simplistic and glowingly optimistic recitation. "And if things go poorly?"

A shadow of regret crossed her face. "We save who we can, and I burn it to the ground. I will not risk capture or death, but a weapons forge is an ideal target."

Larron scowled. "Disrupting their food supply would be more impactful. Humans make up a majority of his forces."

"Such a camp would also have fewer weapons, fewer trained soldiers, and be less contained," she said.

All fair points, he conceded mentally. Taking another deep breath, he said, "I have an idea about gaining us entry, then."

"No," she said when he told her his part of the plan. "Now you are the irrational one!"

They hunkered down in hiding against a rocky outcropping as the next vampire patrol came near. Annalla bit her lip, deep in thought once more.

"Not without practice," she finally said when the threat of discovery passed.

Larron waved in the direction of the departing scout.

"We have a few hours now."

It was her turn to breathe out through her nose in frustration, but she started getting ready rather than arguing.

CHAPTER TWELVE

Prison Camp – South of the Derou

Larron brushed the dust kicked up by his latest practice tumble from his clothing. While he might benefit from further trial runs, they were out of the allotted time, and his landing proved steady enough to ensure he would not suffer debilitating injuries when he hit the ground for their assault on the camp.

"It is time," Annalla said, pointing out the silhouette of the vampire patrol in the distance.

He nodded and watched as she drew her fairy tré daggers before taking off into the sky alone. Her figure grew smaller as she rose higher and began a lazy spiral in the direction of the lone vampire. She attempted to give the appearance of a non-threatening bird of prey on the hunt. The day was well past the one marked for Darrin's assault on the gilar in the east, so there remained little chance of Kahnlair's forces remaining ignorant of the fairy's return. They hoped one lone figure would not raise suspicion until it was too late for the vampire to react.

Annalla rose higher still while the vampire remained closer to the ground, likely scanning for threats from that direction. The sun glared down on them, probably frustrating their nocturnal enemy on its assigned task. Larron absently wondered if the daytime shifts were used as punishment, or if they traded equally the less desirable jobs as the elves did.

With a burst of movement, Annalla shifted direction, falling toward the earth. The vampire did not react to her presence. She swiftly closed in above it. An instant later, well before she reached it, the vampire's limp form fell spiraling toward the ground. Larron followed it down until the body fell behind a slight rise in the land and shifted his attention once more to Annalla on her return flight.

"Did you throw your dagger?" he asked, thinking through the witnessed encounter.

Annalla gave him a small smile. "Yes, and directed the weapon with my power. I thought it safer since we have a limited amount of the antivenin with us and might need it after the coming fight." She cleaned the dagger in question, put it away, and opened her arms toward him. "Are you ready to risk injury and death in a daring rescue?"

Larron laughed at her eagerness and his own heart rate sped in anticipation. He stepped up to her, the fire in his eyes matching hers. "Let us proceed," he said as he wrapped his arms and legs tightly around her.

There would be no harness used for that flight. The plan was to hit the camp in a quick strike before the defenders had time to react. A harness would not only slow them, but it would also place them in each other's way. He needed to be able to disengage from her quickly, which left him using his own strength to hold on and to catch himself when they reached the ground.

As she brought them to a higher altitude, higher than they usually flew together, the air became thin. Larron never before appreciated the harness as he did at that moment. The rock structures below were nearly indistinguishable to his elven sight, and wispy clouds passed below them periodically. He concentrated on his breathing, keeping it steady and deep to keep from becoming lightheaded. The technique was one he learned long ago for a climbing expedition to the northern mountain range.

"Are you alright?" Annalla asked with her mouth at his ear.

He saved his breath and nodded. A quick glance over his shoulder showed him the camp quickly coming to the center beneath them.

Annalla tucked her wings, and they *dropped*. Larron's stomach tumbled and his head went giddy as they went into an uncontrolled fall, picking up speed with every second. Wind whipped strands of hair from his tight braids, and he felt one of Annalla's hands leave his back so she could move the strands out of her vision. He turned his face into her neck in an effort to keep her sight clear, affording him a view of the ground rapidly approaching.

Her wings peeked out. Larron understood the move would start to lower their speed of descent, but the change was imperceptible to him. They needed the speed to facilitate their surprise attack. Too early and they would be fighting in the air. Too late? Too late, and they would both be injured or dead. But they had practiced the maneuver, halting lower and closer to the ground with each attempt.

None of those attempts landed surrounded by enemies bristling with weapons, he mentally noted. *We have done this. This will work.*

The mantra played out in his head and the cold certainty of battle settled over him. Her wings began a steady progression outward, and he noticed the reduction in speed then as the weight of his body pulled against his hold on Annalla. She tightened her grip and spoke into his ear again.

"Ten." The countdown began.

Her fingers tapped against his back as he shifted his grip in preparation for his landing. Larron scanned the area, easily making out a group of elves for which she aimed. The angle made it difficult to tell, but he thought the ground angled slightly down toward the prisoners.

"Three."

Larron released his legs to dangle.

"Two."

He hung by one arm with Annalla gripping the back of his clothing in support.

"One."

She let go.

He bent his knees, released, and tumbled into a roll.

His momentum was too much. One roll continued into a second that sent him crashing into huddled bodies. He ignored the new bruises, rising to his feet and drawing his sword in one smooth motion.

"To arms!" he shouted, hoping they at least had tools at hand to use in a fight.

"Larron?!" a breathless voice called out in recognition. With more strength, the voice said, "You heard him! To arms!"

Zeris? He knew that voice, but he could spare no time to confirm as he engaged with a gilar guard bearing down on him.

***

Annalla released Larron with more speed than their plan had intended. As they were in freefall, she noticed a cloud of vampires incoming from the southwest and held off slowing their descent a little longer than their practice runs. She could have called off the attack, but they had already taken out the scout. As long as they started the attack on the ground before the cloud arrived, she could rise up and deal with the unexpected arrivals separately.

She dropped him near the group of prisoners she identified and targeted as they fell and turned herself toward the mass of gilar guards running at her. Behind her, Larron shouted, "To arms!" The call told her he survived well enough to fight, so she focused on the incoming attackers.

Annalla reached forward with hands and mind, noting the position of the weapons brought against them. She gripped the blades with her power and yanked them back. More than half flew out of their wielder's grips through the air. Most of the weapons slid past her, driven by her essence to arm the prisoners, while a dozen rose at her command to swirl before her.

Vampires swarmed up from the walls at the blowing of a horn deeper into the camp. Annalla pressed forward in a whirlwind of blades. She danced in the center, sword in hand. A gilar swung forward with a broadsword, aiming for her torso with a wide slice. Her curved wing deflected the strike upward as she ducked beneath it and rose to strike where its arm met its body. The blade sunk in. She twisted and pulled, drawing a spray of blood in the sword's wake.

Annalla kicked the dying gilar away and stomped a foot forward, pressing her essence into the ground with the movement. Thorny shrubs grew up from the cracked earth in the path of her opponents, tangling and slowing them.

Unfazed by the demonstrations of her power, elves and a handful of humans pushed forward in a battle line. Some bore the weapons she had stolen from the hands of the gilar, while others hefted whatever must have been at hand. Pickaxes, shovels, and even rocks were brandished and held threateningly against their captors. Even as they engaged, vampire guards started swooping down on the poorly armed prisoners.

A man to her right was picked up by a vampire. Claws pierced his sides as he left the ground, and his cry cut short when vampire fangs ripped out his throat. Another vampire dove in to attack as the first glutted itself on the dead elf's blood.

Annalla pulled her flying weapons in closer, fighting and striking with them to clear the area around her. She traded sword for daggers and took off, heading for the approaching cloud and drawing a dozen vampire guards with her. Bats, the vampires with bat wings, dove at her over and over, striking out with clawed hands as their flight path drew near. A flying sword took one in the chest and was ripped from her control as the dying vampire clutched its arms around the hilt as it fell.

The lost blade opened a hole in her defensive perimeter and the next attacking run closed in on her. Annalla banked to the side and struck out with the dagger in her hands, disabling one of her attackers at the forearm. It gave a piercing shriek and clutched at its bleeding limb, but not before the other hand sliced a claw line across her thigh.

Annalla cursed inwardly at the stinging wound. *Larron is going to give me* that *look now,* she mentally berated herself for letting even one close enough to mark her.

She ignored the pain and focused on the cloud of vampires ahead. Another breath and they would be around her. That was exactly where she wanted them—around her and high in the air. Her eyes locked ahead, gauging their attack pattern and preparing deflections to punch through their lines.

Two more weapons fell with dead or dying vampires as her blades struck a deadly line for her flight path. She caught the claws of another on her daggers and swept the vampire to the side, using its own momentum to push it past her out of range. The mass of enemies closed in, surrounding her.

Far enough, she told herself.

With a thought and a stretching of her arms, Annalla became an inferno. Flames licked at her clothes and skin without burning. The vampires caught in the firestorm were not so lucky. Piercing shrieks rolled across the sky as the essential blast consumed those around her in every direction. Her vision became spotted from the intense light, and she closed her eyes against it to concentrate on the reach of the fire.

The blaze wanted to run. It wanted to pour out of her until there was no more power within, but she held her essence in an iron mental grip. There would be no exhaustion or loss of self that day. She would not be responsible for the deaths of all the prisoners far below.

When she thought the fire's work complete, she pulled the power back, drawing the flames in and compressing them until she snuffed out the last between her clasped hands. Annalla turned from where she hovered in the sky and headed for the prison camp once more.

Battle continued to rage, but more of the prisoners had proper weapons, stolen from the corpses of their captors who fell. Annalla dove, striking out with her daggers at a vampire passing below on an attacking run. She gathered more fallen weapons into her swirling shield of blades and sent them flying toward one vampire after another, focusing her attention on the aerial attackers.

A blast struck out at the elven line. From the lines scored upon the ground, that was not the first such mage attack. Annalla turned toward the watchtower from which the strike had come to see another bolt of power headed toward her. She dodged to the right. A line of pain seared across her left bicep, but the brunt of the attack passed. Focusing her attention, Annalla reached out a hand to direct her power and the watchtower burst into flames, and the mage—who had not been shielding—went out in the blaze.

The attackers surged forward at the death of the mage, cleaving into the remaining gilar as Annalla steadily eliminated the quickly devolving lines of the vampires. They fell or fled, until only surviving prisoners remained below. She held herself ready, scanning the ground for movement or lingering combat, but there was nothing. Only the cries of the wounded broke the quiet descending over the camp.

"Gather the injured!" a dark elf called out.

His orders were met with immediate compliance, as elves scrambled to help their comrades. The elf and Larron directed the rescuers, and even before she landed, they had the beginnings of an area cleared to lay down those injured in the battle.

According to Sandrala, elves had hours before the antivenin had to be administered to be most effective. Annalla cut that down to a relatively safe half an hour with her more susceptible fairy blood. She had time to help a little before bothering Larron for treatment.

As she scanned the field for what to do, Annalla morbidly realized she sensed the bodies of the dead with her essence as she had not when they were living. Reaching out with air, she took hold of the gilar bodies nearby. Rising into the sky again, she drew the corpses with her and took them a fair distance into open lands to the west of the camp. After three trips, she grew sparse shrubs across the burial site, hoping it would be beneficial.

By then, her leg was starting to numb around the vampire scratch, so she walked over to Larron upon her return. His hands were bloody, but his face was calm as he sewed up a long gash in an elf's leg as the injured man winced and cried.

"Larron," she said. She hated to interrupt him, but she could not allow herself to be a secondary concern at that point. "Where is the antivenin?"

His hands froze and his head snapped toward her. His eyes scanned her body, lingering on the arm and leg injuries. "Tydair," he called out to another elf, who ran over. "Take over for me here."

The two elves passed the needle between them carefully. Larron rose, wiping his hands off on a rag as he approached her.

"Can you boil some water for us?" he asked as he grabbed his medical kit from where it lay on a rock.

She sensed a couple of barrels full against a wall. Reaching out, she brought the water to hover near them and ignited a fire within the floating mass. He was already inspecting her wounds visually as she executed his request. Soon enough, he was scrubbing his hands in water barely cool enough to touch without injury and pulling back the edges of cloth to see her injuries better.

"This is the vampire scratch?" he asked, pointing to her leg.

Annalla felt herself warming and knew a fever had begun. She nodded her confirmation.

Larron cleaned out the scratches before pulling out a vial from his pack. He set a clean cloth against the edge of one claw mark and dripped drops of the antivenin directly into the slice. Annalla's eyes widened at the stinging pain. She pursed her lips against a groan and looked away.

Her eyes met those of the elf shouting orders earlier. Black-brown skin and brown eyes with a hint of gold. He looked like Erro, with slightly thinner lips and nose. He stared back at her, measuring and assessing. His gaze shifted to Larron, and Annalla felt an urge to jump between them to shield him from judgment. Only Larron's careful ministrations held her back from acting on the urge.

"This will potentially give you vertigo," Larron said as he capped the vial, "so no flying again until tomorrow."

"Understood. Who is that?" Annalla asked, looking up and finding the staring elf had moved on to help another injured man over to the cleared space with ratty blankets.

Larron followed her gaze, and a smile broke out across his face, lighting it up as he turned back to her. "That is Zeris, my brother."

"I do not think he likes me."

A belly laugh burst out of Larron. "That is alright. I like you well enough for both of us."

She sent him an unamused, side-eyed glance and received an innocent grin in response.

"Come on," he said. "There is more work and more injured to treat."

Annalla might not have been able to fly, but she still had power.

CHAPTER THIRTEEN

Prison Camp – South of the Derou

Larron heard a splash behind him and someone shouted a word of caution. Glancing over his shoulder, he watched Annalla staggering as the ball of heated water obediently followed behind her. He resisted the strong urge to roll his eyes and growl her name in frustration. Tydair was already heading in her direction, holding out his arms as though to steady her but not touch her unless necessary.

A soldier once under Geelomin, Tydair had medic training centuries ago and served as one of two elves helping Larron treat the injured former prisoners. Raw umber skin with deep brown eyes and black hair, he stood close to seven feet tall and bore new scars across his collar and arm. Like all the rescued prisoners, his cheeks were hollow with malnutrition and shadows hung beneath his eyes. Despite the physical degradation, he was competent and capable, and he would see that Annalla rested.

Larron cringed internally at the grimy bandage tying off the relatively clean one beneath. There were no other options, so many of the wounds would need to be cleaned again once additional supplies could be boiled and dried. Annalla had filled buckets with heated water earlier, and elves worked around the cleared yard stringing up cloth and clothing from the then filthy water.

He rose, wiping his hands off, and scanned for the next patient. The labor camp had held around five hundred elven and human prisoners, guarded by an estimated two hundred gilar and vampire guards and one mage. With Annalla's help, most of the guards were eliminated. They lost just over one hundred prisoners in the fight and to their injuries after, and another hundred lay seriously injured.

The surrounding darkness did not surprise him. He often lost track of time when healing numerous people. It was, however, always unsettling to experience the sense of time loss. They'd begun their attack shortly after midday, and the sun had set long enough ago it was not even a pale glow upon the horizon. His work had to be almost complete; most of the survivors had already bedded down for the night.

"The rest are being taken care of," Zeris said as he approached. "You are done for the evening."

Larron washed his hands in a nearby bucket and smiled at his brother, at a loss for words with tears in his eyes. He had thought Zeris dead. Part of him had come to accept the loss and tried to move on, despite the pain in his chest. Seeing him there when the fight began had nearly cost Larron his life. He paused as his mind adjusted to the shock, giving a gilar bowman a momentary opening. Only Annalla's presence saved him then. She'd pulled at all the weapons around her with her power, and the arrow shifted course away from him according to her will.

"We thought you were gone," he said, swallowing thickly.

Zeris wasted no time. Larron's hands still dripped water as his brother pulled him into a crushing hug. He wrapped his arms around and gripped a handful of the filthy and tattered garment Zeris wore. The two of them devolved into rambling and back-slapping, ignoring the tears clouding both their eyes.

"So many sacrificed their lives for me and the soldiers here," Zeris said later as they sat together against a wall. He gestured with a hand across the sleeping elves stretched out before them.

"Our people are brave." The words felt inadequate, but they were all Larron had to offer.

"Tralie? Erro?"

A comforting smile lit his face. "Both are alive and well. Tralie will be here within a few weeks."

Zeris looked at him with concern at the latter statement. "What of the gilar and the Woodland?"

"That is a long story," he said with a huff.

The telling of all to have passed in the year since his capture took hours. As he trailed off toward midnight, Zeris sat staring toward where Annalla lay curled up, sheltered between another wall and bundles of supplies.

"I know you never wanted a bonding," he finally said. "You do not need to remain with her. There is no compulsion."

Regardless of their feelings, Annalla would eventually need heirs, but Zeris did not need to know that. He *could* not know the reason for such a requirement. The fact was also irrelevant.

Larron shrugged off his brother's apologies and worry. "I love her, Zeris. She is not someone to settle down either and will not tie me to one place. If we survive the war, we will figure this out."

"She is young."

"I have time," he said with a yawn.

"We all have a little more time now. Get some sleep, Larron. We can speak more tomorrow."

***

She curled up in a hot, wet sack. A thin film clung to her overheated skin and coated her tongue with a bitter taste. Weight pressed on her from every direction, as though the sack constricted around her slowly.

"Annalla," a muffled voice called to her from the outside. "Annalla."

A gentle hand rested against her forehead. She opened her eyes to see Larron's sympathetic face hovering and spinning above her. The world rotated and her stomach churned.

"Oh, no," she mumbled and rolled over as her gut heaved violently.

Larron held her hair back until she was done, then handed her a cup of water. She swished and spat a couple more times before drinking to soothe her parched throat. After only a few sips, the torture began again. He grabbed the cup from her before the contents spilled and kept his hold on her hair with his other hand.

"I am dying," she slurred later as he carried her away from her mess.

He chuckled. Annalla tried to glare at him but had to drop her head back against his shoulder as the sun pierced her eyes to stab right into her brain with painful intensity.

"You are not dying," he said softly. "This is a common side effect of the antivenin and better than suffocating when your lungs fail from the venom itself. You will be fine in a day or two."

Larron kneeled gracefully to set her down in the shade of an adjacent wall. The same elf to escort her to a sleeping spot the night before stopped at Larron's shoulder and handed him a steaming cup before continuing on his way.

"Drink this," he said. "We had some luck trapping this morning, and the broth should settle your stomach a bit."

Annalla grumbled, but took the cup and tested the

temperature before taking a small sip. It was mostly water with a little fatty flavor. Nothing offensive, and likely only minorly nutritious with how diluted the questionable protein seemed. That was fine. Better not to waste food on her if she might just be sick again.

"Zeris said he found some beets over there." He gestured to a space empty of all supplies. "We cleared it out. Do you think you could grow more food in that area? They have enough to wait if the effort would strain you, so do not push yourself."

She nodded and relaxed back against the wall. Her eyes drifted closed as she placed her hands palm-down against the ground and extended her awareness outward. The plant life there was nowhere near as plentiful and vibrant as in the Woodland, but there was enough for her to gauge what lived in the area.

Her body ached, but she was not dying or seriously injured. The amount of power expended in the largest conflagration had been minor compared to earlier experiences, and it had remained within her control. All of that meant she had plenty of power with which to work. Trees came first; she grew three of them to the point they began to fruit. Cacti sprouted up, growing up and out in numerous sections. Finally, she seeded a patch of the beets Larron had mentioned.

When she reopened her eyes, his eyes flicked to the cup in her hands. "How is your stomach?"

She grimaced and poked her tongue out, making him laugh.

"That well?"

"Mmm," she grunted.

Larron shook his head and handed her small portions of their jerky and travel bread to go with her quickly cooling broth. "I am assuming you want to depart again once you are feeling better, so eat these if you think you can keep them down."

"Yes, Commander," she managed.

He chuckled again and turned to walk away, calling over his shoulder, "And then get some more sleep!"

Annalla snorted, examined the food, and took a tiny nibble of bread to test the waters.

Two mornings later, they were back in the air. She had expected some form of interrogation from Zeris, but it hadn't come. Her entire final day in the camp was spent scanning her surroundings, expecting the elven king to pop out at any moment to pounce on her verbally to ensure his brother was safe with her. If the parting smirk he sent her way after bidding farewell to Larron was any indication, he found her constant vigilance amusing.

Another week later, Annalla scrunched her face as she inspected their cactus fruit dinner.

"You do not enjoy this dish?" Larron asked her from across the cooking fire she had created.

She sighed. "I guess I am just a little tired of the slightly sweet flavors and squishy textures of the plants that grow around here."

"So, no requests for berry pie anytime soon?"

Annalla huffed a laugh at the reminder of Thanon and her salivating over the possibility of pie. "No. Honestly, I would almost kill for something with garlic. And fresh baked bread." She paused and studied his face. A small smile graced his lips as he listened to her food dreams. "What about you? What are you craving?"

"Curry," he said without hesitation. "Spicy curry filled with vegetables over rice. Of course, at this point, any seasoning would be a welcome change."

"The drawbacks of traveling without pack animals," she said. "Did you take a pack animal with you when you traveled before the war?"

"Usually. It made the journey easier, as I could ride all the time without overtaxing my horse."

"Plus, seasonings."

Larron laughed. "Yes. That and better cooking equipment."

"Did you ever travel with others?"

He shrugged. "Sometimes. Travelers often paired up if they headed to the same area. Doing so made it less likely they would run afoul of trouble on the roads. The risks were less before the outside races came to Elaria, but most of the people are good and mean us no harm."

"Do you *prefer* to travel alone?" she asked, focusing on her curiosity rather than the underlying reason for it. "Like before the humans came?"

His smile softened. "I prefer to travel," he said. "Company is always welcome, though few elves ever joined me more than once or twice."

She considered that and thought the situation sad. Elves were drawn to their homelands. Few had a desire for adventure and discovery beyond learning new skills throughout their lives. It sounded like a rather boring existence to her thinking.

"Annalla," he said, drawing her from her contemplation. "I have been meaning to ask you: what is your plan for dealing with Kahnlair? I am assuming you intend to confront him yourself, as the magai have had no success against his power."

She nodded slowly and her gaze became unfocused as she thought. "Yes, I think either Morena or I have the greatest chance of eliminating him. We have proven that essential power can work behind a mage shield, at least to some capacity, and the two of us have the greatest ranged manifestations. We need the army and the fairy to get us close enough to attack him, but then the plan is relatively simple. I burn him as I did the mage back at the prison camp. If I can see him, I can kill him."

"That accounts for the shield," he said and looked pointedly at her healing arm, "but what about his offensive combat abilities?"

Annalla glanced down and pursed her lips. "Actually, I might be able to absorb the energy of mage attacks." The idea came to her as the mage's attack scored across her arm, blazing a trail of burning pain in its wake.

"What do you mean?"

"It felt like fire." She reached forward into the flames, scooping some out to cover her hand and dance around her fingers before closing her hand into a fist and snuffing them out. "I can handle fire."

CHAPTER FOURTEEN

Ceru-Auradia Front Lines

Blaring horns pierced the night, crying out a warning and call to arms. Tyrus jerked into a sitting position, ran his hands through his hair and down his face, and shook the lingering drowsiness from his head. He rolled out of his cot and scrambled into his light armor, belting on his sword as he flung the tent flap aside and exited.

Outside, people ran to their posts, some still in the process of arming themselves as they passed by him. Fairy took off into the air, followed by flaming arrows or dragging lines of torches with them. The sky above boiled. Bodies writhed in combat, shrieking out screams of pain and rage as they fought. Even as he watched, a body plummeted down, growing more distinct as it fell. The fairy crashed into a tent only a hundred yards ahead.

"Healer!" Tyrus shouted and sprinted to the demolished tent. "I need a healer over here!"

He pushed away broken supports and through the tangle of oil cloth until he found the broken soldier within the mess. One feathered wing bent in the middle, and bones protruded in multiple places along the man's right side. Bloody spittle bubbled from the corner of his mouth. He was breathing, but Tyrus could do nothing for him. Moving him might be the final death stroke.

"I need a healer!" he shouted again, hearing desperation in his voice.

"I'm here. I'm here," a woman said briskly. "Let me through." She reached his side, then her gaze took in the fairy and moved to him. "Watch my back in case they attack from above," she told him and kneeled beside the broken form.

Tyrus did as ordered, brandishing his sword and swiveling his head, watching for any vampires sweeping in to strike. More screams, shouts, and orders rang out as she worked and soldiers scrambled about, some on errands, others ducking and running in fear. One group passing by contained a captain shouting orders at his men.

"Captain!" Tyrus called.

Recognition lit his eyes, and he saluted. "Your Highness!"

"Where are we gathering?"

"Around the perimeter and the healer's tents, sir," he said. "We have orders to defend our archers trying to help the fairy."

"Thank you. Please send a unit to assist this healer with the injured fairy here," he said and dismissed the captain.

As Tyrus returned to watching the skies, small lights flew back and forth, illuminating those wrapped in aerial combat. It was impossible for him to make out friend from foe, and he wondered if the archers offered any real assistance to their new allies.

He needed to get to the defensive lines. Maybe there was some help he might provide or some information to share. As it stood, the fairy practically fought the battle alone. A group finally arrived to guard the healer with the injured soldier. His wings and bones were back where they should've been, but gaping wounds remained. The healer ordered the group around, but Tyrus was already running toward his assigned perimeter location.

They formed up, more heavily concentrated on the western side of camp as the most likely source of any attack. Walsh had them mustering in practice at all hours of the day during their long march north along the Karasis Range. After the latest attack, they would have nighttime drills as well. The exercises targeted a combined land and air attack by the enemy. While the fairy engaged above, keeping the vampires contained outside of the vertical perimeter as best they could, the Ceru forces pressed against any humans and gilar.

During the day, Tyrus continued to fly with the fairy units, but Walsh had still given him a ground assignment. The fairy could fight vampires without him in tow, but they were at a disadvantage at night, when the hearing and unique vision of the vampires reigned supreme.

He dodged through tents, around people, and barely missed being crushed by a falling vampire crashing to the ground with a visceral thump. Tyrus stumbled and looked back at the creature. Half of its chest caved in and a wing was broken. It struggled to rise, hissing and swiping at a soldier running around a corner into its path. Before it did more than raise its good arm, Tyrus thrust his sword through its back and twisted. The vampire died with a gurgled screech and fell still. Tyrus ran on.

When he finally reached his post, the vision was no better. The air raged with combat, but few arrows flew from the bows around him. Torches scattered among them simply didn't provide enough light to discern friend from foe. Patrice trotted to his side, her knives out and bloody in her hands.

"I wish Annalla were here," she said to him, her wide feline eyes still clouded by grief, scanning the sky as he had.

Tyrus agreed with her thinking. Annalla would have lit up the night sky with fire, burning away the darkness and her enemies alike. He was also glad to hear more from his friend than a one-word response. Since receiving confirmation of her son's death, the warmth he associated with Patrice had fled, replaced by cold indifference. The marked change was understandable, but he worried, nonetheless.

"Can you see what's going on up there?"

Her nose scrunched. "It seems the vampires are thinning, but it's still hard to tell. Irimoten archers are the ones firing up. The fairy are circling up and back toward camp so they fire outward on their descent."

"And others should be pressing down from above to close them in toward the ground," Tyrus said. He had heard the planning and hoped the fairy had the numbers advantage expected.

"No ground troops," Patrice said. "This is him testing us. Testing the fairy."

Tyrus nodded grimly at her logic and wondered how long they had before Kahnlair's tactics adjusted sufficiently.

"Irimoten!" came a called order. "Clear the camp!" The ambush hunters were being released to hunt down any vampires within. Tyrus allowed himself a sigh of relief, as it meant the fight above was nearly over.

Patrice's eyes lit with a vengeful fire at the order. Rather than warmth and caring, the fire burned with a cold rage he saw for only a moment before she stalked off, disappearing between two tents. Pursing his lips against his worry, he returned his attention to the night sky.

"We need better lighting options," King Garrett said the next day. Tyrus' father was not happy with the response the previous night to the attack on the camp.

Walsh shook his head. "The larger constructs used with our trebuchets are not feasible for a mobile force."

He was referring to the collections of mirrors stationed at the well-established army camps along the front lines. Four groupings of eleven mirrors interlocked into a concave shape were stationed around large, oiled, and prepped fire pits. The mirror groups sat on a platform able to rotate one hundred eighty degrees, sending a relatively significant amount of light from the fire into the sky in any direction, depending on the orientation of the four mirror sets. Those fire pits were positioned strategically between the trebuchets, allowing better night sightings of any attacking vampires.

In theory, the mirror system should successfully illuminate their enemies and enable effective nocturnal combat against an aerial opponent. In practice, most of the materials they had for the fires didn't burn bright enough to provide sufficient light. Select elven units under Captain Lesyon manned the trebuchets because the limited light the setup *did* produce was enough for them to target more effectively than humans firing blindly.

Walsh was unfortunately correct; the methods they had for aerial engagements did not translate to an army on the move.

"Not good enough," Garrett said. "We were impotent out there last night, incapable of helping our allies at all!"

"Carrying torches and lanterns caused more problems than it solved," Zara said. Circles beneath her eyes attested to a sleepless night. "If there is more combat at night with the vampires, I think the best course is if you leave them for us to handle. Too many of my people were brought down by friendly fire."

"Oh!" Tyrus snapped his fingers and sat forward. He wiggled his fingers, trying to grasp onto the forming thought before he pointed at Mage Hephestar. "When we were running from the windani, Marto did something. He lit some brush on fire and hovered the flames in front of the horses so they could see their footing ahead of us. Can the magai do something like that in the air?"

Hephestar pursed his lips in thought. "Marto is a combat mage?"

"Yes."

He scratched his jaw. "He likely started the fire and then used a shield to make the burning brush hover within. It worked well for your situation because the shield could be maintained at a close, static distance from the mage and held constant without risk to his allies. Unfortunately, the amount of fire we are talking about here and the distance from the mage required mean we would burn through the magai too quickly for it to be a viable option."

Tyrus' shoulders slumped, and he murmured his disappointment.

"What about an artist?" Patrice asked quietly into the ensuing silence.

She had been attending the meetings at Tyrus' request since they rejoined his father's army. Even if her heart was broken, her mind remained sound. She knew as much about the fairy abilities as he and often thought in unique patterns. Tyrus might not like her current mental state, but with all her other responsibilities passed to others, destroying Kahnlair had become her focus and remaining goal. It was the one thing keeping her engaged.

At her question, Hephestar's head tilted and raised as a hunter sighting prey. Walsh was the first to respond. The small smile on the commander's face told Tyrus he was already moving along Patrice's line of thought.

"What do you mean?" he asked, likely wanting to hear her version before contributing his own.

"They deal with sight and sound," she said with a shrug. "When Marto related the story his mother showed him when he was young, he described the figures as 'glowing' in the fading light before bed. Can an artist create light?"

"Yes," Hephestar said, grinning. "Light is one of their primary duties within Scorcella. They maintain the street and building lighting, but anyone can replenish the power on an existing light construct. However, it's usually no more than the glow of a torch or lantern. What we need here is grander in scale." The mage rubbed his eyes. "We also don't have many artists with the army. A few for distraction and detection with larger camps, but that's about all."

"Determine what can be done and pull artists from posts to join us as needed," Garrett ordered him. He then tipped his head to Lesyon. "Argent's forces will be joining ours in a matter of weeks, but even the elves need to see what they are shooting at, and that means having light."

Tyrus turned to grin at Patrice, receiving a weak smile in response. The light didn't reach her eyes, but it was something.

CHAPTER FIFTEEN

Ceru-Auradia Front Lines

Jarin bounced on his toes and stretched up to peer once more into the distance. The action remained as futile as the last dozen times he made the move, but he could not contain his excitement. Before that day ended, the elven army would join the armies of Ceru and the sanctuaries. As with the humans, strategic posts would continue to be manned, but the majority of the allied armies' forces converged.

Xochima would be with Argent. Jarin's king would not prevent her from contributing to the war, but he and Xochi coordinated to keep her far from the fighting as a concession to Jarin's sanity. His essential power was invaluable, and no one wanted to face the repercussions should he lose his love. He wished all loved ones had such protection, and he fought for them as well.

"Standing taller is not going to allow you to see over the rise," Morena said with a teasing smile.

Morena and Lesyon waited with Jarin at the front of the elven unit fighting with Ceru. While most of their forces remained with King Argent under his command, a select few had been assigned to work under King Garrett. Kahnlair's attacks often more heavily targeted the humans, so the two essentials transferred with the unit.

"I am waiting for him to mount a horse and ride out to meet them," Lesyon told her as though Jarin were not standing between the two.

Jarin refrained from rolling his eyes. "The two of you are as excited to be reunited as I am," he said.

Lesyon laughed and tipped his head in subtle agreement. "I like our new friends well enough, but I do miss those of old."

"Oh! Look!" Morena pointed ahead. "Movement!"

There they were. Over the crest of the hill, heads bobbed steadily into view, followed by the bodies and the horses they rode. At the top, Argent kicked his mount to a faster pace, and the rest followed suit. The hill hiding the army from view until that moment was close enough that they had no trouble discerning individuals as they crested and began their descent. Jarin avidly scanned the growing line.

No. No. Still not Xochi, he noted to himself. *She will be with the supplies in case something broke along the way. Just a little longer.*

With so many soldiers, Argent would reach them before most of the carts became visible. Jarin stretched his shoulders to relax and focused his attention on his approaching leader. Argent smiled and waved a greeting at the waiting elves.

Jarin once heard a human soldier describe King Argent as a dandelion. It must have been a derogatory reference, as the soldier's captain responded immediately and harshly with words and punishment. If considering strictly color orientation, then Jarin understood the comparison. Argent's gray skin held a distinctly moss green tone and his hair was a brown-gold with subtle hints of green, like a field of dry grass. While the hair color came from a distant Palonian relative, the greenish-grey skin was common enough to Auradian elves, as were his striking emerald eyes. Those eyes moved across the three of them at the front and settled on Jarin.

A smirk crossed Argent's lips as he dismounted. "Xochima is well, but I am afraid she will be at the rear of the line. We had some misfortune with a few carts this morning and she stayed behind to assist with repairs."

Jarin sighed. While disappointed at the additional wait, he felt no surprise at her decision and did not begrudge it. "My reunion can wait. It is good to hear she is close, and to see you again."

"You as well," Argent said, setting his hands on the shoulders of the other two. "I have missed you all."

Lesyon gave a small bow of his head and swept his hand back toward the waiting soldiers. "Everyone came to help you all settle," he said, "and King Garrett wishes to confer with the broader council when you are available."

"We may as well go now, if it is convenient," Argent said. "It will take some time to integrate our camps."

Garrett had been hoping Argent would say exactly that, so Lesyon led the four of them through the gathered troops and into the camp proper. Even with Argent stopping frequently to greet his people, it took them relatively little time to arrive at the council pavilion.

"King Argent." Commander Walsh bowed low to the elven king and held the tent open for them. "Please, after you."

Humans were often so formal. The elves smiled at, laughed with, and even embraced their friend and leader, while the humans stood on formalities as though King Argent was *more* than other people. His connection to the Auradia Woodland made him important, but even Argent would acknowledge he was simply another elf among many. His position required him to receive specialized training in combat and governance, but anyone could gain those skills if they desired.

"King Garrett." Argent greeted his counterpart, who stood at their entry and came around for a brief handshake. "Prince Albertas sends his regards. He is preparing all but a small guard to depart the camp and join our forces as we pass to the west of his current location."

"No doubt he intends to come with them. And us."

The king's voice indicated he wished his son would make any other decision. Thinking of Xochi traveling with their army to confront Kahnlair directly, Jarin could relate to the feelings of worry. There were, however, reasons Garrett kept his eldest with the army, and those reasons also supported his presence on the upcoming aggressive endeavor.

Everyone other than the elves was already inside. Garrett, Tyrus, and Walsh for the humans, Hephestar for the magai, Clanlord Guldrith for the Karasis Valley dwarves, Patrice for the irimoten—though Morena continued to serve in her role as representative as well—and Zara for the fairy.

Argent's eyes fell upon the fairy colonel. "I remember when we lost touch with the fairy. We mourned your loss from the realm. I thank you for your aid in this conflict, and I hope our efforts now serve to strengthen the bonds between our peoples, so none of us fight alone again."

As one of the eldest elves alive, Argent had been alive when the fairy conflict with the vampires reached its peak. He was one of the few living people to have seen a fairy before their recent return to the world. The eldest among them held some guilt in their hearts at the fate of the fairy. Seeing them in the world once more helped ease some of the old, lingering pain.

Zara gave Argent a soldier's nod, softened with the hint of a smile. "I appreciate your caring words. I am sure my prince and our protector will give longer-term alliances all due consideration."

The four elves settled into the open seats, and Garrett resumed their discussion from the previous days. "I'm concerned at the lack of additional attacks from Kahnlair," he said. "Since the second nighttime assault nearly two weeks ago, we've seen no sign of his forces."

"We continue to thwart raids from the base he established at the south end of the Claws," Argent said, "but they have not changed pattern or approach. We have had reports of the windani slowly returning south, though. A few of our patrols were recently overrun. Some went missing entirely, but most were able to escape back to our defensive lines and report the attacks."

"Kahnlair is consolidating his forces as well," Walsh said.

Argent tipped his head. "So we believe, but it will take time, and the windani are exhibiting no signs of rushing their progress."

Walsh stalked along the far edge of the table, tracing the markers with his eyes. "Until last year, our lines were nearly straight south from the eastern edge of the Claws. The spring push nearly gained the Oasis River."

"And we just took back the southern half of the Oasis," Guldrith said.

Since freeing the dwarven clan, the army had been marching up the eastern banks of the river, expecting to have to clear out enemy soldiers from all along its length. Instead, they'd found it abandoned. Indications of long-standing military camps spotted the way, but all that remained when they arrived were scattered posts and refuse piles amid empty lands.

"The question is, where is he regrouping?" Walsh muttered as he continued staring at the map.

"He wants one of the fairy women," Morena said into the thoughtful silence. "His people have orders to find and capture the 'powerful winged woman.'"

Zara leaned forward. "Explain further, please."

Morena rubbed a hand across her forehead. "I believe it was a couple of months ago now, I picked up thoughts from Kahnlair's forces about targeting a 'powerful winged woman.' We did not know about the fairy at the time, so there were thoughts it could mean me, or one of the women leaders among the elves or magai. But I am now confident that the 'winged' part means one of the fairy."

The fairy colonel had concern on her face, but it was Tyrus who spoke. He shared a worried look with Zara and Patrice. "Annalla."

"What would he want with Annalla?" Patrice asked.

"Perhaps he thinks to turn her to his side?" Hephestar wondered.

Zara vehemently shook her head. "That would not happen. The protectors are raised to uphold their oath."

"He has corrupted more magai than I ever thought possible," Hephestar said. "Perhaps he has some magical means of influencing thoughts or personality."

Tyrus grimaced. "The intent was for Annalla to eliminate Kahnlair. Maybe we should try to keep her away from him?" The latter was said with a distinct lack of confidence to Jarin's ear.

"It might be best to keep more of the fairy women out of combat," Garrett said. While the human leader was more open-minded about women than most of his kind, there was a reason beyond qualifications that Lesyon and Hephestar had been sent to represent their people over others. Zara and Garrett continued to grate on each other over his ingrained notions. Jarin could see Zara's jaw clench at his latest comment as she bit her tongue.

"I do not know that we have a better option," Morena said to Tyrus, ignoring Garrett's addition. "I am the only other essential who can attack from a distance, and I do not believe I can get close enough. The magai cannot penetrate his shields."

Zara swiped her hand out before her. "This is a discussion for when the Protector joins us. She makes her own decisions. We should focus on the potential attack upon this army."

Neither Tyrus nor Patrice looked happy to Jarin's eye, but they both pursed their lips and shrugged.

Walsh looked at Tyrus. "Your Highness, you said she was expected to join us coming from the Derou?"

"That was the plan she mentioned to Prince Darrin before she and Larron left the sanctuary."

Walsh nodded, and Jarin could see the calculations going on behind the man's eyes. "If I were Kahnlair and was targeting Protector Annalla, I'd want to test her and her army against me and my army before the main confrontation."

"You believe he has spies among us," Morena said.

"They'd have to be magai protected in a previously unknown way for Lady Morena not to have discovered them," Hephestar said grimly.

"Not necessarily." She shook her head. "Others can discipline their minds to avoid focusing on any incriminating thoughts. There are too many individuals for me to scan beyond the surface."

Walsh waved off their concern. "Spies are to be expected, as are scouts," he said. "He may attack us again, testing our defenses as a combined unit, but I believe a larger attack will come after Protector Annalla joins us. If she's the one he wants, he needs to learn how she fights and how we defend her."

"But you don't believe that this major engagement will be his full might," said Garrett.

"I do not," Walsh said. "If his attack results in her capture, it would be a win, but the objective is more to test us and wear us down. In his place, I'd draw us all the way to his desert stronghold with strategic attacks along the way."

"But..." Tyrus had a look on his face as though he bit into something disgusting. "That *is* our plan. To drive into his stronghold and eliminate him. Are you saying we're playing into his hands?"

"Our best chance would be to draw Kahnlair to us," Walsh said, "but waiting only favors him. He has never been taunted into reckless behavior before, so we can assume he wouldn't now. His options are to wait for us to come to him, drawing us in as he is now, or come to us. The latter option has no upside for him. That leaves us with either waiting and hoping we can increase our army faster than him, or pressing our attack now.

"Both sides know we're going into the desert," he said. "He'll want to bleed us as much as he can along the way, and our goal is to arrive at the final battle with as much strength remaining as possible."

"So," Argent said, peering around the tent, "we maintain our vigilance, despite the recent lull in attacks, and we keep the fairy protector out of Kahnlair's hands. A major attack is likely to come after she joins us."

"I believe so." Walsh nodded at the summary.

"We will drill together in preparation," Argent said. "I will also send messengers with some fairy to bring as many artist magai from Auradian lands as will join us, if the fairy can spare some of their people to transport them. Many settled in our perimeter farmlands, and I was recently informed of the need for their skills."

Zara smiled. "I'll assign some raptor units."

Garrett nodded to Walsh. "Integrate the elves into our drills and adjust our plans for the northward march."

"Yes, sire." Walsh turned to Argent and Lesyon. "Will the two of you join me?"

"Of course," Argent said, and turned his gaze to Jarin as he rose. "Go find Xochima, she should be arriving soon."

Despite the grim atmosphere, Jarin grinned at his friend. "Thank you. I will."

They would bring him into their plans soon enough. Jarin quickly left the tent, not missing the delighted and amused laughter in Morena's eyes as she watched him go.

CHAPTER SIXTEEN

Yaziren River – South of the Palonian

Geelomin stood patiently upon the cliff-face, waiting for their enemies to pass below. Oromaer gave him command of a hodge-podge patrol primarily made up of those from outside the Palonian. Harndorn, Prince Tyrus' guard captain, stood as Geelomin's second in command of the unit, which included all seven of the men who'd arrived with Tyrus. The rest of his patrol consisted of him and the other two Derou elves, eight Palonian elves, four irimoten, and two magai.

After the poorly organized siege around the Palonian was routed, Oromaer executed his plan to move down the Yaziren River and eliminate the bandit threat. According to the detailed reports from Harndorn, there were multiple places along the river where humans loyal to Kahnlair had set up ambushes. Tyrus lost most of his guard during his journey north last year, and it was presumed the fall harvest deliveries had been taken by those same bandits.

Spring planting was complete in and around the Woodland, so Oromaer packed up as much of their remaining supplies as they could spare and led the procession downriver.

Skilled scouts ranged ahead, seeking to identify the bandit camps for swift elimination ahead of the barges. A team of irimoten had found the camp assigned to Geelomin. Estimated at just under one hundred men, he planned to use the terrain and diverse skill set of his people to overcome their numbers disadvantage.

Harndorn had command of the ground team. The four irimoten were infiltrating the camp with the goal of eliminating several of the bandits' sentries before gaining their attention through an *apparent* mistake and fleeing. Harndorn and his men were stationed just past a turn in the rocky landscape that would naturally limit the number of attackers passing through at once. The irimoten would join them for the melee, while the combat mage further back shielded the group from ranged attack.

The elves and the artist mage with them hid, positioned at the top of the steep slope leading up to the cliff rising behind them. Once the battle engaged below, they would begin firing arrows from above into the trailing bandits. While the artist could not shield the archers, she would be visually cloaking them. To be able to see who was firing at them, the bandits would need to climb the precarious slope past her false image.

They might still fire blindly in the direction from which the arrows were fired, so Geelomin and the rest of the elves selected positions well-guarded behind large rocks or outcroppings while still allowing the range of motion needed to shoot. Geelomin scanned to the left and right again, checking on his people. Thanon observed his movement, and the prankster managed to convey amused exasperation with a smirk while remaining battle-ready.

By the sun's position, the fight should begin soon. He set the time of their attack for just after dawn, early enough that some of the men might not be as alert, and with the benefit of the sun peeking over the cliff at their backs. The irimoten would already be working through the sentries, eliminating the tired watchers. Those on the morning shift to replace them would be looking out, waiting for them to return to camp only to see an irimote kill someone at the perimeter.

Shouts rose to the south. The alarm went out. Geelomin rolled his shoulders and checked his weapons a final time before staring down the trail. Sherval ran by on four legs, shifted into his fighting form. He pulled up by a tree, shifted back, pulled a crossbow from his back, and waited. Three more ran around the curve. Trichelle stopped, flung a dagger back the way they'd come, and resumed her sprint. The cry of pain accompanying the movement told of her accuracy.

The three irimoten ran past Sherval and around the far bend in the trail where Harndorn waited. Sherval aimed, waited, and fired at the first man to emerge in pursuit. He was already running by the time the bandits fired back. The mob flowed around their archers on the irimoten's tails, shouting their fury. Geelomin and the elves took aim and waited.

Hold, he mentally willed his people. *Patience.*

The men rounded the corner. Geelomin knew there were cries of pain as men were cut down by the first volley of arrows from Harndorn's back line, but they could not be heard over the noise of the mob. He counted the attackers progressing and waited as the line became congested at the bottleneck.

Now, he thought and released the arrow, quickly drawing another from the quiver positioned conveniently before him.

Ten other arrows flew near-simultaneously from along the wall, striking down bandits where they fell. Men turned, confusion lighting their faces as arrows rained down from a seemingly deserted slope. A few returned fire while others fled, falling down the far slope or running back around the initial bend. Someone called out from the rear, ordering the group to charge the hill. An elven arrow took him in the neck, but the order was already heeded.

Bandits rushed toward the elves, more heavily concentrated toward the end of the trail where Harndorn engaged with others. Those at the rear weeded down quickly enough to not come close to reaching the top, but Bealaras' and Clarsimara's positions were becoming overrun. The bandits charging had been too clustered for them to eliminate all upon the slope. Geelomin's elven line turned their fire forward up the line, helping thin the trailing attackers still below the mage's illusion.

The sound of steel on steel rang out nearby. Geelomin buried his concern and continued firing. His patrol was better armed and trained than the bandits, and they had the superior position. Thanon emptied his quiver first and drew his blade as he dashed down their line of archers, disappearing behind the next position. The men thinned. Harndorn and his squad emerged from their position and set upon the back line, while the irimoten sprung up the rocks with a nimble lethality.

When the last man fell, Geelomin called out, "Sherval, I want the four of you to hunt down those who fled. Surrender is an option, but do not put yourselves at risk."

The irimoten nodded and disappeared silently back down the trail. Geelomin looked toward his remaining troops.

"Thanon, report," he said as he made his way toward their end of the line.

"No serious injuries," Thanon said. "We remain in fighting form, but most of us are out of arrows."

They would retrieve those unbroken, some of the elves were already doing so. "Harndorn?"

"Law took a cut to his calf," the man said as he signaled five of his men to take up defensive positions. "He's down, but it's not life-threatening."

There was an undercurrent of amusement to Harndorn's tone, giving Geelomin pause. He smiled as a thought came to him. "Is it the same leg the bear trap hit?"

Harndorn grinned up at him. "It is indeed! Man is muttering words not appropriate for polite company right now. I think he's feeling more incensed than pain."

"We will head out as soon as the irimoten return," he told his second in command as he reached Bealaras' position.

His Derou comrade had a minor cut on his left bicep. Thanon and Clarsimara already had his shirt off and the injury cleaned for a quick bandage. Unless there were no injuries from the other teams, the wound was small enough to delay having a healer mage look at it until later. He nodded at the three elves and started downslope to assess Lawrence's injury for himself, signaling Pearaltar to join him.

Clarsimara and Pearaltar were the two in his patrol with medic training. The latter caught up to Geelomin in time for them to round the corner together. At first, they saw no one. He suspected Harndorn had ordered the man to hide in case any enemies made it around to this side while he and the others had moved to render assistance to the ongoing combat. His guess proved correct when Lawrence hopped out from behind a bush, nearly toppling over as he did.

Pearaltar hurried forward, taking one arm to help the man sit while Geelomin grabbed the other. He watched as his medic raised the soldier's pant leg to reveal a relatively deep slash. Geelomin tilted his head and stared at the wound curiously.

"How did they cut you so close to the ground?" he asked. *Was he kicking out with his leg?*

Lawrence flushed. "One of them toppled toward me after Franklin killed him," he said reluctantly. "He fell with his sword flung forward. I was blocking another sword strike and couldn't dodge the dead man."

"Did you eliminate your foe?" Pearaltar asked, pausing his ministrations.

With a snorted laugh, he said, "I did, yes."

"Assessment?" Geelomin asked Pearaltar.

"Nothing serious, as Harndorn said. I do not want you walking though." His last statement was directed at Lawrence, who grimaced but nodded in agreement.

Geelomin looked up as the rest of his patrol made their way around the corner and joined them. He looked at Sherval for confirmation.

"No surrender," he said to the unspoken inquiry. "We eliminated all those we found and tracked. Most returned to their camp."

He nodded and did another quick headcount. "Let us collect our gear and return to the fleet. Lawrence will be taking the sling. Standard carry-guard rotation. Scouts, move out."

No other bandit camps were known to be in that area, but he would take no chances by becoming complacent. The irimoten ranged ahead and behind, silent and invisible stalkers in the wilderness. Everyone else stood turns either carrying the sling with Lawrence—muttering to himself—and in a guarded marching formation. Every ten minutes, one of the irimoten flashed by, signaled no enemy contact, and melted into the shadows once more.

Knowing the way, and the obstacles between them and the main river, the group made good time on their return. If more of them were injured, it would have taken longer, but they did not need to stop for any extended breaks carrying only one sling between them and returned to the supply fleet before the evening meal would be served. Geelomin gave Harndorn orders to see their patrol settled while he reported in to Oromaer.

Entering the cabin, however, only the king's bonded stood within. The pair were leading the expedition, and Orion was left in charge of the Palonian. "Arbellie," he said in greeting.

She smiled at him, setting down the ledger she had been studying. "Geelomin, you return early. Was your raid successful?"

He tipped his head. "It was. We suffered only minor injuries. I am certain the healers can address them without undue strain."

"Faerladie's patrol ran into trouble," she told him with a frown. "They dealt with the ambush itself, but Oromaer went with the healer magai to help carry the wounded if needed. We will be camping here for the night and continuing in the morning instead of floating for the evening hours."

"Do you need my patrol to render assistance?"

"No," she said, waving a hand. "They should have enough hands for the necessary tasks. I would appreciate it if you could assign half your people at a time to perimeter duty, though. He took more with him than usual, hoping one or two of you would be able to assist."

"I will give the orders immediately."

Arbellie stepped toward him. "Allow me to join you," she said. "I have been cooped up in here all day and could use the fresh air."

Geelomin smiled as he held out his arm, allowing her to precede him. "How are we progressing?"

She brightened. "Better than expected! It helps to have Mage Gregry with us. I hate to think of how many more would have died without him here. Though, I worry for his health."

He nodded in understanding. The ancient mage was fading. His skin seemed almost paper-thin and brittle. "As do I."

As they descended the barge to the shore, an elf messenger came striding toward them. "Lady Arbellie, we—" His words cut off mid-sentence as he stared into the distance behind them, head tilted to one side.

Geelomin and Arbellie turned as one, hands on their weapons, to see what had caught the man's attention. In the distance, he made out an odd flock of birds.

"Something is not…" Geelomin was trying to figure out what was wrong with the image.

"Larger birds do not flock like that," Arbellie said, then turned to the messenger. "Spread the word quietly. Abandon the barges. Hidden defensive positions."

The man nodded and ran off, starting a chain reaction as he issued the commands.

"Vampires?"

Geelomin pursed his lips, thinking. "There are no colonies this far south."

He felt her gaze settle upon him. "Larron?" she asked when he met her eye.

His stomach churned as he thought of his friend and commander out there somewhere on another desperate mission. He did not know how to respond to the hope in her voice. "Let us prepare. We will know soon enough."

CHAPTER SEVENTEEN

Ceru-Auradia Front Lines

Annalla tensed up more with every mile they flew. After freeing the camp where they'd found Larron's brother, she shifted their path further east to reach ally territory again based on the maps they studied back in the Palonian so long ago. At the first elven encampment, they were notified of the main force shifting south with King Argent in response to movement by both the Ceru army and Kahnlair's windani. Three camps later, they met with the first fairy messengers flying between allied holds.

Since the return of her memory, Annalla believed the right course of action was to call the fairy army out to fight against Kahnlair. She still believed the decision to be correct, and King Delon concurred with her. He would not have given the order and sent his only son into combat otherwise, no matter the prophecy swirling around her existence. The line of fairy kings had made a promise long ago to fight when the protector called. To not do so would spell disaster.

While in the sanctuary, she had not realized how much playing the role of both a politician and legend weighed upon her. The responsibility piled on top of her returned memories.

She had to set aside grief freshly uncovered and face derision and disbelief. Eventually, it turned to respect and admiration, but the change was almost worse. She felt like an imposter, inadequate for the tasks before her. All she wanted to do was run to Larron and have him make the decisions and handle all the important people.

It would be even better if he made those decisions safe and secure behind the full strength of the army and guards. Annalla had not lied to him when she said she didn't know if she could handle his death. Another weight of sorrow piled upon the loss of her parents and a significant portion of her life might break her resolve and threaten her hold to the oath she swore as a nine-year-old child.

Limiting their relationship to friendship helped. He gave her someone to rely on with a I of distance between them. For a while, as they traveled, she pretended they were once more simply Derou traveling together on a mission. Then, her fairy responsibilities began to reemerge, and she started to wonder and doubt.

The sanctuaries were never intended to be permanent. Their temporary nature was the driving force behind the significance of the military and the ability for the protector to request aid. Each step, when viewed together, inexorably led to the conclusion that the sanctuaries would end. To assume one family could forever survive alone and protect an entire race of people spread around the continent would be either hubris or folly.

She wished Protector Dahlia would have included specific instructions or expectations in her long-ago prophecy. It was no longer some far-off day. Annalla walked the steps foretold. Evil cloaked the world. The fairy had returned. Prophesy had become reality, and there were no longer any guideposts.

One thought Annalla kept returning to with every fairy

messenger they came across was: if this was the path to the end of the sanctuaries, then she would not survive the war. It might be that her destiny was to fail. If her death meant the fairy won, would it be worth it? Would that be the correct path?

The entire purpose of the sanctuaries was to protect her people. There was now an antivenin and they would have allies. Saving herself and the sanctuaries at the cost of losing would only delay the inevitable. Winning the war was more important...right? It was the only way to hold true to the purpose and intent of the sanctuaries and the role of Protector as Solaar had reminded her.

Her thinking circled around and around. *No matter the cost, I must ensure an end to this war.*

She could tell no one. They would try to protect her, thinking her a risk to herself, but she was not. There used to be no higher priority than her survival and the continuation of the sanctuaries. There, at that moment, in that war, there was one thing more important. Annalla would not risk the success of her mission.

"Is everything alright?" Larron asked as they set down for a night at another camp.

Annalla forced a smile as she looked up from removing her half of the harness. "It will be nice to eat another meal in camp," she said. Her smile eased as she focused on something she genuinely enjoyed.

Larron's brief frown conveyed his skepticism, but he left it alone for the time being. "Are you ready to report in?"

She rolled her eyes. "You mean 'ready to be the center of attention for all the fairy within flight range?'"

"Yes. That." He laughed. "You cannot blame them for wanting to meet their hero."

"I am no one's hero, Larron."

"You are my hero," he said with overwhelming sweetness.

Annalla sent him an unamused eye, one eyebrow raised and lips pursed.

He laughed again, drawing attention and waves of greeting from the elves they passed. "No?" he asked innocently. "You have saved my life a time or two."

"And you and the Derou saved mine," she said. "It is what friends do."

Grinning, he turned toward the elf approaching. "Faeneela!"

"Do you know every elf by name?" she asked under her breath.

He flicked her a glance and gave a twitch of his eyebrows, but otherwise ignored the remark. The woman had soft olive-green skin and deep forest-green hair. Her apricot eyes shone with joy as she came forward to embrace Larron. The various weapons they wore clanked together before they held each other with stretched arms. Faeneela's eyes raked over him as though measuring and assessing.

"It eased my heart to hear you and your brother were safe," she told him.

"Relatively, anyway." He shrugged and turned toward Annalla. "Faeneela was a friend of my mother's. They grew up together in the Auradia Woodland. Faeneela, this is Protector Annalla."

Smiles and nods were exchanged, and she swept the two of them up to follow in her wake. "Let us get you settled."

Everything happened in an ordered and efficient manner. They entered a moderate-sized tent used primarily for briefings and reports between leadership. A tray with enough dinner for the two of them followed shortly after they arrived. Faeneela left them alone after that, but it was only a matter of time before a mass of people descended on them once more.

Larron leaned forward, setting his elbows on the table, and held a piece of bread in his fingers. "The fairy will not think less of you," he said and popped the bread in his mouth.

Annalla studied him. "For?"

"Not being whatever it is you think they want you to be."

She took a moment to follow the logic of that sentence. "The Protector is a legend. My role is that of a mysterious, powerful being who periodically visits for brief instruction before disappearing again. My position means safety and hope. It is easier to maintain such a I for a handful of days than for the extended duration they will interact with me now."

"Perhaps." He shrugged. "But what they *need* is a warrior; someone trained and capable of fighting with and for them. That is a role for which you are uniquely suited."

She gave a non-committal grunt in response, but took time to ponder his assertion. Fighting *was* something she understood. Her training made her one of the best in the realm, and her power elevated her to a force of immense destruction on the battlefield. The open question was whether she tipped the balance against Kahnlair and the power he commanded. They ate in silence until Faeneela returned with a fairy captain.

The man, Captain Hashiko, was a raptor with beautiful wings. They began with a soft bluish-white at his shoulders and grew progressively darker until reaching the midnight blue wingtips. His black hair also seemed to have a blue shimmer to it, but that might have been the light reflected from his wings. Hazel eyes smiled at her, brimming with excitement, but he remained professional.

"Protector. Prince." He greeted them with a salute. "I have instructions to fly with you on your next leg. If we leave at first light tomorrow, we should arrive at the main army before the end of the day."

"Where are they expected to be?" Larron asked.

"Kings Garrett and Argent intend to begin crossing the Oasis River tomorrow."

Larron nodded and pointed to a spot on one of the maps lying about. "There used to be barges here. Draft horses would pull them upriver on each side, and the flow of the river helped guide the vessels across. I cannot imagine Kahnlair's troops left them intact after withdrawing though."

Captain Hashiko grimaced. "They did not. Carts are being modified to function similarly, and Colonel Zara is coordinating the transfer of troops and supplies by air as well."

"That will be a multi-day endeavor," Larron said before looking at her with a raised eyebrow.

Annalla laughed. "Yes," she said. "I can probably speed that up. Which means we should get to bed in preparation for an early morning."

They were led to a tent with shared cots, and Annalla fell asleep quickly, waking only when Larron woke in the morning and shifted into a sitting position on his neighboring cot. A quick wash, then breakfast, and they were off for another long day in the air. Most of Captain Hashiko's unit were raptors, so Larron rode with one of them, rotating between bearers with each break throughout the day.

The Oasis River became visible long before they could make out details. Descending behind the river, the sun glinted off the water's surface. Annalla estimated they would arrive about an hour before sunset. She and Larron were able to discern the form of the army well before then.

"Annalla," Larron called, concern in his voice. "Is that smoke, do you think?" He pointed ahead.

She peered into the distance, squinting against the sun's obscuring glare. Annalla shook her head. "I cannot tell. It could be distortion from the sun." She looked to where Captain Hashiko flew, observing their exchange. "Send scouts, please."

Two raptors pulled ahead on his whistled order. Annalla continued staring in the direction they flew, trying to make out any additional detail as worry gnawed through her. Smoke might mean a large campfire or a bonfire. It was not an unreasonable occurrence for a location they would be at for the multiple days of the crossing, but it would be an egregious waste of fuel.

"Definitely smoke," Larron said after some time. "Multiple fires. And the scouts are returning."

Captain Hashiko blew an inquiring whistle. The message pattern sent in return dropped her churning stomach to the ground. *Battle.*

"Can you increase your speed?" he asked her, seeing she understood the message.

Annalla nodded and did so. The adrenaline spiking in her system pushed aside the weariness from flying all day, lending her wings strength. The group rushed forward, closing the distance and bringing the raging fires and battle into view. Carts in the middle of the river burned, abandoned by all personnel. Skirmishes engaged on both sides, with those on the western bank pinned against the water's edge. Flights of vampires and fairy fought, weaving in and out over it all with bodies dropping into the water or onto the ground below.

As she watched, an elf swung a massive morningstar, sending a group of men flying back into the gilar closing. A wave of the river lapped at the bank behind him, forming into a bubble and rising. The mass of water crept forward. Men shouted in alarm behind the elf, but he was engrossed in the combat before him. The bubble closed over him. He struck out and men pounded on it from outside, but the suffocating construct remained intact.

A familiar swell of essential power rose from the battlefield, one she had experienced only once before, when she was a child. *No,* Annalla internally denied the implication even as she acted.

She pointed at Larron. "Get him to those in command!" she ordered Hashiko and pressed her wings further, straining for

every bit of speed she could muster.
 The power spiked. An essential was about to die.

CHAPTER EIGHTEEN

Oasis River – Ceru-Auradia Front Lines

They had known the river crossing would be a vulnerable position, so they reasoned it would be better to attempt it before the fairy protector joined them based on the assumption Kahnlair wanted to time the next major attack for when she would be involved. They had gambled that he wanted to test *her* more than he wanted to take advantage of *their* vulnerability. They were wrong.

Everyone gathered together presented a unique opportunity to leverage their varied skills to accelerate the crossing. Magai would assist with the modifications to the carts to turn them into barges. The fairy would shuttle soldiers across to establish a defensive perimeter for the anticipated camp opposite. While horses pulled the cart-barges upriver on the departure side, Jarin would do the same with the empty ones on the arrival side. A crossing normally requiring a week or more would be done in two or three days.

They were almost parallel to the northernmost peaks of the Karasis Mountain Range off to the west. Rolling foothills eased off northward from the mountains, and the elves could make out the southern tips of the Claws far to the north on the eastern side of the Oasis. The river wound between hills on its way south, skirting closer to the mountains in some areas with sheer cliffs between the Karasis Valley past and their position. Those cliffs had kept the army on the eastern bank until they reached the planned crossing location.

Throughout that morning, they had established a camp with an efficient path for loading supplies and hauling barges. While the architect magai and crafters had worked together to modify the carts, the fairy began shuttling the soldiers assigned to the west bank. Jarin had worked with the men and women to position the initial tents and clearings that would eventually become the army camp. The afternoon had grown late, settling toward evening, and they took turns resting for a final meal.

Jarin had sat down on a boulder and brought the spoon to his lips. It felt good to be off his feet and not have the enormous ropes digging into his shoulders. The weight of the barges pulled differently than fighting, and he felt his muscles protesting the novel treatment even with his essence having taken most of the burden.

He stretched and wondered if he might convince one of the fairy to return him to the opposite bank that night. Maybe Xochi could be convinced to trade back massages. She had likely been working as hard today as he, if only in a different way. Jarin smiled at the mental reminder of his bonded so close, and then his world exploded.

A blast of fire struck the central campfire in the clearing where Jarin sat, sending him and all the other soldiers in the area flying. Burning air punched him, and he landed with a splash in the river, his weapons dragging him down beneath the surface.

His lungs struggled to regain the breath lost in the strike, and Jarin fought the instinct as he crawled toward the light of flickering flames barely visible through the muck-churned water at the river bottom. He called on his power, giving his arms and legs strength to push faster against the confining water. Lungs burned. Vision clouded. Cold air brushed the back of his head, and he flung himself into a standing position, coughing and gasping.

Jarin's chest heaved as he peered wide-eyed at the chaos on the shore. People and animals screamed, charred bodies littered the ground and floated on the water, and fires burned through the tents and supplies gathered on the riverbank. Captains ran past, shouting for the soldiers to form ranks. His vision followed them to a battle well met.

How long was I down there? he wondered.

Despite no enemy in sight when the first strike hit, men and gilar fought against his allies well within the defensive perimeter. There was no time to consider the inconsistencies. Jarin trod through the water, out of the river, and ran to the line, hefting both weapons as he approached. A soldier went down, and Jarin stepped into his place. The morningstar crunched into the arm and side of the gilar, sending the creature flying.

***

The initial blast shook the ground beneath Tyrus' feet and he staggered in the direction of the attack. Across the river, a pillar of smoke rose from what had been a peaceful campfire only moments before. Another mage strike hit, exploding in a ball of fire and bodies thrown back from the assault. Most did not rise.

Fire attacks were coming out of thin air, which had to mean an illusion. Magai were already grouped at the edge of the water. Mage Hephestar and a handful of others stood in a line facing the opposite shore, their hands held up as though against an invisible wall. The combat magai shielded the others, who conferred a moment before assuming a similar pose with only one hand raised.

Tyrus didn't know how their magic worked, or if it even *was* working. Nothing immediately changed, and he needed to find a fairy to take him to the other side so he could help the soldiers under attack. As he turned, a shadow seemed to pass over the setting sun. When it faded, a massive army appeared, charging forward from the foothills. A crowd of fairy rose all around, shooting forward to aid the humans and elves under attack.

They were, however, not alone. From behind the two near mountain peaks, a swarm of vampires alighted, filling the sky and darkening the sun once more. Tyrus ran. Morena and her fairy unit took off at the same time he arrived at the command tent, too late for him to join them.

"Walsh," he addressed the man giving orders without seeming to pause for breath. "I need to get over there. Our people will never last against that."

The commander held up a hand, telling Tyrus to wait. He swore and paced, but held off further interruption. Patrice ran in. Rather than joining his pacing, she stood frozen, staring at Walsh as though the man were a bird she hunted for the night's dinner.

"Go," Walsh told a human soldier. "Tell the fairy colonel the elven archers need to be established at the south end first."

Tyrus and Patrice stepped forward together into the void left by the man.

Walsh addressed them without pause, the next item on his agenda. "Their majesties are headed over with the second round of fairy. Go to the receiving dock and wait there. We only have two units serving as transport. The rest are engaging the vampires."

Fear spiked in Tyrus as he emerged from the tent with Patrice at his side. Their forces were nearly surrounded by enemies and another battle raged in the sky above. To the south of the combat, hundreds of fairy dropped off additional soldiers. The elves took aim skyward, trying to thin the airborne enemies as the humans formed around them in defense. At least one mage should be with them, but Tyrus couldn't discern whether his assumption was correct or not. They reached the makeshift dock and lined up.

"Do you think they'll hold out? Maybe we should evacuate them instead," Tyrus muttered to Patrice as he stared uselessly at the fight while another mage strike exploded.

"We would lose more fairy in the attempt than the number of soldiers they saved." She shook her head. "Jarin is with them."

A blast shook the air, a flare went up deep over the enemy lines, and even from there, Tyrus made out the ice spikes shooting up where Morena attacked an enemy mage. Too many fairy dipped in and out over the enemy soldiers for him to identify where she flew, carried by her guards.

Another group of fairy dropped. A force strike swatted them out of the sky, and that time there was no resulting flare to call out from where the mage attacked.

The transport fairy returned, spreading out among the waiting soldiers. Tyrus clung to the first person to stop in front of him. There was no time for a harness. He hopped into the woman's arms and held on to her as she wrapped her own arms around his back and threw them both into the air.

He turned his head away from the wind, looking upstream. Patrice had her head tucked against the chest of her bearer and he saw claws in her hold. Past Patrice, on the far shore, a gilar body sailed backward at the powerful swing from an elf. Behind the elf, an odd construct rose from the water. It looked like a glass jar meant for a fish, and it moved steadily, drawing closer to Jarin.

Tyrus narrowed his eyes and tipped his head in confusion, wondering what the odd sight meant. As the bubble of water closed around Jarin, Tyrus' heart pounded in his chest. *Jarin can drown,* he thought in terror. If Kahnlair eliminated Jarin, they would lose every soldier there.

The woman set Tyrus down and started to take off, but Tyrus grabbed her hand. "Wait! Stop!" he shouted at the departing fairy. "We have to save Jarin!"

Tyrus waved and pointed, shouting for attention. *What can we even do?* he wondered.

"Get a mage," he said to the fairy woman, gripping her shoulders and staring panicked into her eyes. "They need to break whatever is holding the bubble. Get a mage!"

Her forehead scrunched in frustration, her eyes filled with incomprehension, and she looked around in a panic of her own. She shouted in the fairy language at other passing fairy, and the realization dawned on him: she didn't understand Market.

***

The lines formed up, and Jarin pressed himself into a forward wedge, holding a swath of the enemy back all on his own. Fairy flew overhead, engaging with vampires coming in from the mountains. Arrows from the south arched over them and struck the enemy forces, meaning the rest of the army was establishing a second foothold from which to support them.

Another mage strike exploded to his left. Less substantial than the prior attacks, it still left a hole in their defenses that had them withdrawing once more to plug the gap. That time, though, a flare went up over the source of the strike. Jarin felt both the blast of freezing air and the echo of essential power as Morena lashed out at another enemy mage.

She rode by overhead on the wings of her fairy guards, skimming over the enemy toward the river. Her bright dress was hidden by the quickly donned armor, but some of her red hair streamed behind her, not completely concealed by the leather cap. Another blast from Kahnlair's magai rang through the air like thunder. The force strike hit Morena's unit, driving them to the ground.

"Morena!" Jarin cried out, swinging fiercely at the enemy before him to clear his way. *They were close,* he thought. *Nearly to the river, right? I can reach them if I rush the line.*

The thought barely crossed his mind when a wave of river water crashed over him. Rather than receding, the wave surrounded him, submerging him despite the fact he stood upon the bank. He tried to walk forward, but the water and whatever barrier held it remained stable. He tried striking out with his weapons, but the water slowed his strikes and softened his blows.

Fear overwhelmed him. Jarin kicked out, swimming for the top of the bubble. He tested every surface and started flailing about wildly. The pressure built in his chest, his lungs burning once more. He could not escape, his strength failed him. All his power and he would drown upon the shore.

I am sorry, Xochi. The thought passed through his mind as he continued struggling, continued holding out against the urge to open his mouth and pull in the breath that would kill him.

Deep inside, he felt a building of power. Jarin closed his eyes and peered within, seeking the core of his essence. Unlike Morena, whose essence flitted upon the surface of her self, Jarin's ran deep within. The growing power tingled against his essential senses, warning him of a devastating impact. Perhaps it would free him in the end, or maybe the only result would be destruction. He did not fear the power; that essence was known and familiar.

The power struck out, and the bubble around Jarin burst. Water shot forward, blasting gilar and enemy humans off their feet with crushing and deadly force. No longer supported and floating, Jarin's body fell to the ground with a wet thump.

CHAPTER NINETEEN

Oasis River – Ceru-Auradia Front Lines

Annalla dove. The power accumulating below became blinding to her essential senses. When her mother sacrificed herself to save Annalla, she had been standing within arm's reach. The release of her essence was the essential equivalent of the sun shining right in your eyes. Her world became blank of everything other than the glare surrounding her.

Looking at the same effect happening on the ground from the outside proved just as blinding, but only for a contained area. The battlefield below was bathed in the glow from the essential's power. She felt the desperate will behind it, swelling the power and pressing it outward to execute one final act before the physical body failed.

Annalla remembered the moment that physical connection broke for her mother as her body lay on the ground, unmoving. The pressure had built to an almost painful point until there came a snap. Shock from the sensation drove her breath from her and made every muscle seize. An instant later, the pain of her forced transformation hit. It was nothing compared to the devastation of watching her mother's prone body stop breathing and the color seep from her skin.

She braced herself for the snap of the essential's release even as she raced to prevent it. There were likely only seconds before it was too late. Annalla had neither the manifestation nor the skill to recall one's essence to their physical form. All she hoped to do was save the person before the final manifestation concluded and hope they pulled back on their own.

Annalla reached forward with her mind to grasp onto the water surrounding the elf below. She pushed and pulled, trying to free the drowning man, but only succeeded in moving the whole. Within the bubble of water, he thrashed, striking out at whatever held him.

Her thoughts reeled, crashing through options. It had to be a mage's shield. She could work through a shield, but water could not pass through one. That meant she needed to overpower the mage. She had the strength, but time was a problem. The man had stopped moving.

Setting down behind the bubble, Annalla stabilized a plane of water close to her. Its position became fixed in her mind, immovable. She mentally gripped the rest of the water and pushed. The bubble held at first, then rippled as she threw more and more essence into the effort. The front of the bubble warped, stretching and thinning until finally, it burst. Water shot forward in a spray under the pressure of her power, knocking the first three rows of combatants off their feet.

Annalla winced as the body flowed forward with the water, knocking into others caught in the deluge. As he fell to the ground, she rushed forward, rolling him over to listen for breathing. Nothing.

"Form up!" She heard the shout as men surged around them to defend their position in the area cleared by the wave.

The power buildup snapped and Annalla's heart fell. She whipped her head up in time to witness a winter storm fan out into the mass of the enemy army. Snow whirled into the air.

Soldiers froze in mid-motion. Biting cold wind blew out in all directions, nipping at exposed flesh.

She had focused on the wrong person and an essential had died because of it. Tears gathered in her eyes and fell upon the man's face. Swallowing past the lump in her throat, Annalla worked to get him breathing again. Closing her mouth over his, she pushed air back into his lungs. His heart fluttered beneath her fingers. Another breath. Another. She listened, then leaned in again, but pulled back when he coughed.

"Help me turn him on his side!" she shouted at a nearby soldier.

He was heavier than he appeared, and it took three of them to roll him to a position where he would not breathe it all back in again. Annalla kneeled in the blood and mud. The footing at the bank of the river had become treacherous with the fighting on top of the water bubble. Shaking off heartache, she pushed to her feet, pulling out of the squelching mud.

"Stay with him," she ordered the younger-seeming man. "He will need a healer."

Annalla rose into the air, picking up the massive weapons the elf had wielded with her power and joining the melee. About a quarter of the enemy forces had been caught in the essential blast. Frost covered the center area entirely, and reinforcements struggled to traverse the slick ground clogged with bodies frozen in upright positions. She ignored the iced section and dove in to attack with the still-overwhelmed allied line, sweeping out her new weapons with crushing force.

***

Larron watched helplessly as Annalla flew ahead and dove for the battle lines. Half the fairy followed her, rushing in to help their fellows engaged in aerial combat over the river while the rest remained with the one carrying him. Pressure built in his head, battering against his senses. Annalla knew something about what was taking place, but she had not shared her insight before departing. Larron had to focus on what he saw before him.

Fairy and vampires filled the air, fighting with weapons both natural and created. They fought primarily over the far side of the river. The bulk of the enemy arrayed north and west, surrounding a much smaller group of allied soldiers. Larron could identify Jarin helping hold their lines, but some sort of magical attack crept up on him. Annalla headed in his direction, so Larron dismissed the position. She would save him if she was able, and he could do nothing to aid her.

South of the fighting, allied archers assembled. Fairy took off from the group and headed back toward the east bank, showing Larron the plans to gain a supporting foothold. His escorts could help in that task easily enough.

"Take me to that group," he told his bearer. "The rest of your unit can help bring more fighters across the river."

From the corner of his eye, he saw the woman's assessing gaze. He did not have to wait long to determine if she needed more convincing, as she nodded and issued orders. Their flight path peeled south, and Larron groped at where his weapons were tied off. He would need to drop his supply pack, but there was nothing irreplaceable inside.

The sound of combat grew as they approached, most of it shouts and screeches from the fight on the wing where the fairy worked to keep the vampires from attacking the elven archers below. Arrows flew up, striking vampire targets or arching northward into enemy ground troops. Larron's heartbeat kicked up the closer they came. He and his fairy circled safely around to the back line, landing, and removing their harness as quickly as possible.

Done, Larron took a step forward when the pressure inside his head popped and a blast of frozen air punched him in the chest. He staggered, falling to his knees, his vision spinning. Something in him broke; like leaving the Woodland only immeasurably worse. A man kneeled at his side, leaning over to meet Larron's eyes and giving him something to focus on other than the dirt beneath his hands.

"Sir!" the soldier shouted. "Sir? Are you injured?"

Human. He had skin as dark as Zeris' and brown eyes full of concern. Larron gripped his arm as he turned away, likely to call for help.

"No," Larron said. "I am uninjured. It's alright."

The man appeared unconvinced, but helped Larron back to his feet regardless.

"Go. I am fine."

Larron judged himself steady enough. He stood firm and reached for his bow and quiver with smooth, efficient movements. That, more than his words, served to assure the soldier he was not at risk of fainting or falling. He moved up into an open position, took aim at the sky, and let fly an arrow. From the back, he could not see the battle lines, so the vampires received his full attention where they engaged with fairy allies above.

Most of the archers with him were elves. They took their time firing, knowing an errant shot might harm a friend. Fairy continued bringing in additional fighters and ammunition from the eastern bank, and human soldiers positioned themselves throughout the field to attack any vampires falling or diving within reach and protect their ranged attackers.

Larron's world narrowed to his quiver, bow, and the target sighted at the end of his next arrow. Shaft after shaft flew skyward. Some brought down enemies, some injured. One flew wide, and he hoped it did no harm to his people. He reached down to find himself without another arrow and peered around. Behind him, a familiar face listened to an animated fairy.

"Tyrus," he said. "How can I help?"

His friend's eyes lit, but they exchanged no further greetings at the unanticipated reunion. "They have catapults incoming and are moving to surround our position. We can't bring over reinforcements fast enough, even with whatever Lady Morena did."

Larron wondered at the last statement but did not question it. "Annalla was heading for Jarin's position. She may be able to clear enough space to regroup."

Tyrus looked at the fairy. "You know where to look for her?"

He nodded.

"Good. Go. Ask her."

***

Bones crunched beneath the weight of the massive weapon, and another enemy soldier went down. As with all the men before him, another took his place as soon as she eliminated that one. One after another, Annalla killed and killed in an endless stream of bodies and meat for the slaughter. With her support, the line held. She could not do much more though, with the mass of fairy engaged in combat above them. Fire would destroy allies along with enemies.

Air and earth were her weapons of choice for that field. She steadily added blades to her swirling cloud of death, and the vines and brush she grew under the feet of Kahnlair's soldiers tripped them up, spread them out, and slowed their forward progress. It meant the small group with whom she fought held their own against the larger force, but provided little additional help. In her mind, Annalla had no doubt he would order his people to shift their attack to the support group to the south. She needed a new approach.

"I need to get back in the air!" she shouted at a human warrior. He had issued orders that were quickly followed, so

Annalla assumed he had some level of authority. Whether it was from rank or earned respect, she did not care.

His gaze raked across the immediate area before he slid forward to stab at an attacking gilar before it reached another man engaged with an opposing human soldier. The blade slipped neatly beneath the gilar's raised arm, punching into its chest from the side. Fresh blood dripped from the gleaming metal as the gilar's body fell to the ground.

"Can you do those spikes again?" he asked her. "Give some breathing room to regroup without you?"

"What about the arrows?"

The first time she spiked the perimeter, enemy archers had taken the opportunity to fire into their suddenly wide-open group, cutting many down. Losing so many again to distance strikes would prove more detrimental than her departure alone.

"Give us some brush cover just behind the spikes?"

Annalla smiled as the two of them shifted forward together to meet the attack of another two humans charging forward. While her cloud of weapons continued fighting, she met that attacker with the sword in her hands. An upward slash threw the man's strike wide, and she reversed her swing into a killing strike. In her mind, Annalla promoted her new battle buddy to a field captain, despite the fact she still did not know his name.

"One moment," she told him as she stepped back and kneeled upon the muddy ground, pressing her fingers into the muck.

Weapons flashed around her, protecting, and the captain took a defensive position in front of her. Annalla kept her eyes on the surrounding threats as she sent her power forward. Her essence hovered beneath the surface, waiting for an opening when the fewest number of allies might be caught in her attack.

"Disengage!" her captain shouted, and the order went down the line.

Annalla smiled and pressed her essence to action. Allies up and down the line struck and retreated in a wave following the progress of the order, and her manifestation followed in the wake of the wave. Brush grew up to provide moderate cover before her people, while spikes erupted out of the ground on the enemy side. Most dodged the new threats, but not all. When the crescent was complete, encompassing the entirety of the small ally force on the riverbank, Annalla stood and pulled water from behind her to clean off her hands. Arrows flew, but most of their people huddled behind the brush, taking a much-needed break from fighting.

Her captain looked back at her. "Go," he told her.

She took off, wondering if she would see him again.

CHAPTER TWENTY

Oasis River – Ceru-Auradia Front Lines

Annalla took off, leaving the besieged soldiers to hold their position alone. Her cloud of weapons rose with her in a lethal, protective nimbus. She scanned the broader battlefield and frowned.

The river separating the two main armies meant they would not *lose*. Neither side could completely overwhelm the other with the positioning. They would, however, sacrifice everyone on the enemy side to the combat if she did not finish the other essential's work and break Kahnlair's forces enough to press them into a retreat.

Vampires dropped fire onto floating barges, meaning it would be suicide for any armored soldier to attempt a crossing that way. Catapults approached from the north and would soon be in position to fire at the small clusters of the Ceru and elven fighters holding the bank and potentially at the tents across the water. To the south, enemy troops closed in on the archers and their meager count of melee defenders.

The fairy slowed the enemy's progress, but forays deeper over Kahnlair's army were met with mage strikes and the loss of fairy units. Annalla could try to eliminate the magai herself, but she suspected that is what the other essential had been attempting when he or she was eliminated. Until she knew how to defend against mage strikes, that was not an option.

Annalla observed the catapults rolling forward and settling. She wanted to scream in impotent rage. All this power and she could do nothing without killing friend along with foe, possibly doing more harm than good.

Studying the two allied groups under attack, she tried to do the math in her head. Annalla knew about sacrifice. In her first moments as Protector, she allowed her own parents to spend their lives protecting hers. She could bring herself to sacrifice allies, but only if it meant saving more. Her lips pursed in a grimace as she considered her options and hoped the ally leaders would understand and agree.

Decision made, Annalla plummeted down. The water reached up to embrace her and pull her to the bottom. Looking up, she saw the flickering red glow of the fading sunlight glinting on the surface, but the river was so deep there that the light did not reach. The muck or silt her boots sank into was beyond her vision in the darkness.

It did not matter. The river was all around her, and she claimed it when she sent her power pulsing out. She felt the current, and her awareness spread upstream and down. Annalla spread her arms wide and stopped the flow above her. Water levels rose, concentrated on the west bank where she wanted it, building higher and higher with the water continuing to flow from upstream.

Eddies formed, churning up and back on themselves where the forward progress stopped. Waves formed, lapping at the land and the people standing and fighting there. Annalla's lungs started to protest holding her breath, but she held, needing more. The waterline grew, pulling at people until they had to swim, and drowning those unable to float to the surface under the weight of their armor.

The ground beneath the catapults softened. The waves swished around the dirt until the wheels of the cumbersome structures became mired in the mud. Her lungs burned as she propelled herself upward and angled toward the northwest. A swell of water followed in her wake, growing and reaching up and out over the shoreline. She shot out of the bloated river, drawing a massive wave after her dripping form.

The river surged up and over the catapults, flowing over Kahnlair's forces. It reached the frozen section of the battlefield and melted the lingering frost.

Exhausted, Annalla released her hold on the river. It rushed back, flowing along the easiest paths and taking men and machines with it. Waves splashed up onto the opposite bank and white water led the charge downriver to rejoin the natural flow. Screams of terror were drowned out by the crashing of water. Horns blew, sounding out orders the panicked people caught in the current were unable to follow.

An arrow pinged off one of the weapons still surrounding Annalla, and she tightened the circle of them as she turned toward her lines again. A mass of fairy floated in to surround her—protection from any attacks that might follow. She needed it. Her breath still gasped out from holding it for so long, and her wings felt heavy. Her body was giving of itself for the massive extension of her essence. She hoped it was enough because she was done. The rest of the army was on its own.

**

Larron and Tyrus watched the fairy depart on his mission to find Annalla. They started to turn; Larron intended to join those protecting the archers if he could not resupply his quiver. He was stopped by a hand grabbing his arm, and he glanced back to note Tyrus staring out over the river, his head slowly tilting as his eyes narrowed.

Tyrus' hand rose to point. "What...?"

Larron's brow furrowed in confusion. He shook his head, glancing between Tyrus and the river, attempting to discern what held the man's attention. "I don't— Oh, no."

A shelf was forming as though a great barrier were being lowered across the span of the massive river. On one side of the barrier, the river drained slowly, exposing more of the riverbed with each passing moment. On the other side, the water rose higher, swelling further on the western shore like the world was a bucket tipped to one side. The distinction, so subtle at first, grew more pronounced.

They looked at each other, and Larron thought it likely his eyes were as wide as those staring back at him.

"Is she losing it again?" Tyrus asked.

Larron gave a slow shake of his head. "No," he said. "This is too controlled."

Tyrus peered out at the river, then north to where the bulk of the fighting continued. "She is going to drown them out. We need to get away from the shore."

His thoughts followed the same path, so he turned and shouted out orders in Jularian. "Form up front lines! Prepare to charge! We must gain ground clear of the bank!"

He ran in one direction while Tyrus took the other. They had no time to coordinate, so when he reached the end, he ordered the charge and rushed forward. His sword rang out, stabbing and slashing at enemies in their path. Men went down before their blades and were crushed beneath their feet as the men and elves ran forward in only slightly disjointed effort. Some of their own fell. Larron did not stop to determine if they might be helped or if they even survived. They needed distance or, he feared, they would *all* perish in the blow about to fall.

The initial attack was silent at first. In his peripheral vision, Larron saw a wall of water rise like a gentle swell upon the surface—if it could be considered a swell when taller than the trees in the Heartwood. Then the screams started. He heard shouted orders to 'run' called out and followed without any control or discipline. The lines broke and scattered on both sides as the wave crashed down with a roar.

No one fought. Men, elves, gilar, magai; all sprinted in panic away from the flood rushing toward them. Larron grabbed those running past. "No." He pointed to his left. "Up, away from the river, not south." Some of them shook him off and continued their panicked flight, many followed.

Soldiers started trailing him. Larron picked up a fallen elf with a broken leg, slinging him over his back and running on. Others helped more injured to their feet or continued lending a shoulder to someone limping forward. The gravel of the riverbank gave way to grass and vegetation, and a few scattered trees. Larron halted them among the trunks, trying to forget the image of the uprooted tree lying on a bank far downriver from where Annalla caused the flood on the Nierda River months ago.

Tyrus found him there, and they observed together as the surge crested and rushed back. It moved south and east, flowing over the easiest paths and drowning everything in its way. With another crash, the deluge plunged back into the riverbed and up over the other bank. Larron's elven sight allowed him to witness the allied fighters jumping and rushing away from the fury. The vast, calm river became white water as it filled back in, tearing downstream at a breathtaking pace.

Larron let out a sigh of relief. "It is not going to reach us here," he murmured to Tyrus as he scanned those around them still staring in awe. "We need to regroup and capture the enemy soldiers among us before they regain their wits."

Tyrus nodded, and the two of them set off together, quietly and efficiently gathering the attention of the soldiers they discerned as theirs to carry out their orders. They passed quickly through the gathered people, taking known enemies into custody and finding soldiers who vouched for each other. With a majority of their fighters in that group being elves, distinguishing ally from enemy proved easier than expected, and they rapidly formed up, once more looking to the north.

The catapults were useless, either destroyed or disabled by the flooding. More than half of Kahnlair's army was dead or struggling after the attacks of Morena and Annalla. Rear lines were breaking off, retreating from the river.

"Look!" Tyrus shouted with a broad grin. "Our people are still there!"

Enemy fighters continued to harry the beleaguered troops, and arrows flew in from range, but the fighters took cover within a ring of brush and spikes holding their attackers at bay and likely saving those individuals from being washed away. He shared another smile with Tyrus, and the two of them worked to order their respective units. The remaining arrows were consolidated with a line of elven archers who would remain in the back, working in pairs to ensure one scanned the skies for vampire attacks. The rest, elves and humans together, prepared for an assault on the southern flank of the remaining enemy forces.

They swept forward, shields leading the way. The archers stopped first, releasing the first volley and gaining the enemy's attention. Some attacks shifted in their direction. Most of the incoming arrows struck the shields, but a few made it through. People fell on both sides, and they charged. Gilar rushed to meet them, closing the distance and taking away the potential for ranged attacks against them.

A woman ahead of Larron lunged forward, but the gilar dodged to the right. It reached forward and struck back with its elbow, and Larron watched impotently as the forearm spines pierced her neck. With an almost dismissive gesture, the gilar ripped out her throat and raised its sword to face Larron.

He met the gilar's strike with an arching block, using the gilar's momentum to drive its blade tip into the muddy ground. He spun closer, within its guard, and slashed up with his curved blade, opening a long gash along the underside of its off hand, drawing it out as he extended the spin back out of reach. The gilar roared in pain and yanked its weapon up with a jerky motion.

A second gilar closed in from Larron's right, and the two worked to strike at Larron from opposite angles, but the first one was already slowing from the steady loss of blood dripping down its arm. Larron blocked and parried, maneuvering himself closer to the first. The second lunged, and Larron dodged. He hooked his sword onto the gilar's arm spines and pulled, increasing the force of its thrust to impale the already injured gilar. With a forward jump, Larron pulled his blade across the second gilar's throat and moved to the next combatants.

The battle ended quickly. Those at the back fell into the retreat, leaving their fellows already engaged to fall or surrender. Soldiers from the initial foothold poured out to pincer the last of the enemy fighters between the two groups, and more fairy shifted to bringing over additional reinforcements as the vampires also left the field.

A young human man issued orders to the men pouring out of the protective brush. He had black hair against pale skin. While his gray eyes appeared tired, he remained focused. His men took up defensive positions with the rest of those with Tyrus and Larron before he approached them and saluted Tyrus. "Sir. Lieutenant Seamus reporting, sir. The other officers didn't make it."

Without the royal honorific, Larron suspected he did not recognize the youngest Ceru prince.

"Jarin? Annalla?" Tyrus asked.

"Sir, Lord Jarin was evacuated by the fairy after an

attack knocked him unconscious," he said. "That was before the…flooding. I don't know of any Annalla, sir."

"The fairy woman with essential powers," Larron told him. "She was fighting with you."

The man smirked, as though at a fond memory. "I didn't know her name, sir. Lady Annalla departed before the flood as well, but under her own power."

Tyrus thanked him and ordered him under another officer arriving to sort out the post-combat necessities. More soldiers were landing every minute, as well as healers and medics.

Larron shook his head. "We will discover nothing here."

"Agreed," Tyrus said, scanning the area once more in case she had fallen nearby. "Let's request a lift back to the command. We need to find out what happened."

"And how much we lost," Larron said under his breath so Tyrus would not hear. He had a heaviness in his heart he could not explain and dreaded discovering the source.

CHAPTER TWENTY-ONE

Oasis River – Ceru-Auradia Front Lines

Jarin crested a hill and peered out at the battlefield before him, stretching as far as his eyes could see. He turned slowly. The fighting raged all around. A sea of pain and death, encompassing and unending. Above, the sky boiled with vampires where they fought and felled his new allies. He took a breath clogged with the scent of blood and bowels. Over the din of clashing blades and cries of pain, a scream ripped out.

Who is that? He wondered. His head whipped back and forth, trying to identify the origin of that scream.

"Jarin!" the voice screamed. "Help me!"

A woman, maybe. Perhaps a child. "Xochi? Brai?" he called out. Over there, he thought. That direction.

He rushed down the hill to enter the battlefield. Gilar engaged with Ceru forward units, and figures from the sky dove to attack both sides of the line. Weariness melted from him as he dove into the fray, driving enemies back and cutting a wide swath around him. Blows glanced off him ineffectively as enemy humans, gilar, and vampires tested his defenses and tried to back away before he countered. None of them could harm him, yet every night they came en masse, pushing and testing endlessly. It was a suicide mission at the order of Kahnlair, but there was never a lack of those willing to follow his orders and pay for that loyalty with their lives.

Not right! Something screamed at the back of his mind. Constant fighting? Yes, but not with the fairy.

It made no sense, but that fact did not make the gilar cleaving through his allies to the right disappear. Jarin swung his greatsword, clearing the space in front of him and sending bodies to the ground. The move was one he had made thousands of times before, but the momentum was too much for him that time.

Jarin's eyes widened. The weapon, one he usually wielded as though it weighed no more than a feather, was suddenly beyond his control. His blade continued on its path, making the circuit, and he helplessly followed. His back turned toward the enemy. This is what they had been waiting for, the reason they would not leave him alone despite how many lost their lives to him time and again.

A hot, searing pain lanced up his back, making him cry out. The pain shifted to his chest; a long cut from abdomen to shoulder. His lungs burned. Changes flickered through his awareness. Back? Chest? Lungs? He was so tired; it hurt so much. He found it difficult to concentrate.

Jarin shook his head, fighting through the overlapping images. He dropped the mace and put both hands on the hilt of the broadsword, bringing it up to meet a killing strike aimed at his heart. Eventually, his efforts would not matter; he was a good swordsman, not great. They had his scent now, and all those he killed and drove back were replaced and doubled.

It did not sink into his mind that not all of those around him were enemies, not until one of the men fighting with him stepped in front of a sword meant for him. A gurgling breath left the unarmed man in a spray of blood before he slumped to the ground. Another blow caught on a friendly blade while he stood frozen by what had just happened.

Time seemed to slow when he spotted a familiar face off to his left. Xochi? Morena? Brai? The face of the figure would not settle, flickering between those he knew. The figure had a long carving knife and was stabbing and slicing between the men he fought beside, oblivious to danger.

Jarin saw the shadow stalking his friend, with wicked, bloody knives of its own, darting between the defenders.

"No!" Jarin screamed, pushing forward. "Watch out!"

He was too late. Brai's face took on a gaze of confusion and shifted to Morena's before the pain set in. She grabbed at her belly as the blood and guts spilled out and fell to the ground. Jarin wanted that man dead, but he was not the only one. Frost licked at his fingers and encased him in ice before anyone took another step. A fiery anger blazed in Morena's eyes—Morena? —as she stepped through the clustered fighters, and one-by-one the enemies around them turned to frozen statues. She made her way toward him, looking and motioning toward the sky, but she might have already frozen him too, for all he felt. His head spun, but the rest of him went numb. The world fell on its side, covered in blood and turning black.

"No!"

Jarin bolted upright, his eyes blown wide as he looked around, unseeing.

"My love. Jarin, please."

The soothing voice penetrated his lingering horror. He blinked, clearing the visual fog, and took a stuttering breath. "Xochi?"

Her face resolved before him, dark like smoke on the wind. With skin a dark gray edging toward black, she had hair the light blue gray of a rainy spring day. Worried blue eyes stared into his, full of love, sorrow, and concern.

"Yes, my heart," she said. "I am here. How are you feeling? The healer mage said you would recover quickly."

Jarin felt fuzzy, like his mind had wrapped in wool before bed, but otherwise fine. There had to be a reason for the concern in her eyes, though, so he tried to think back about what may have happened to worry her.

We were...crossing the river today, he thought. *We made steady progress throughout the day. I remember that.*

"We were attacked," he murmured. "At the river."

"Yes." Xochi nodded encouragingly. Her tone and gestures remained gentle, as though he would break. "The attack came earlier than expected. You were caught on the opposite side with too few soldiers when Kahnlair struck."

"Right." Jarin's memories gradually cleared. He recalled the water closed in around him, unable to escape. Early in the war, Kahnlair's magai had attempted to kill him with fire. An enormous blast burst on an area centered on him. Everyone in the vicinity other than him died, but it showed him to be impervious to fire. "They tried to drown me. How did I survive?"

"The fairy essential arrived in time to save you. She broke the magai's hold on you." Xochi shifted on her knees beside the cot on which he sat, maneuvering to face him fully. She gripped his hands and bit her lip—a nervous habit of hers. "Jarin, something else happened. I need you to listen to me."

His heart pounded. A recognition burned deep within his chest that he refused to accept and vehemently denied. He did not want to hear her next words.

"Jarin," she said, "Morena is dead."

He shook his head. "No," he said, pushing to his feet. "No."

Xochi and Morena were his life. The two women held the halves of his heart. Morena was the only person who knew what it was to grow up to discover powers beyond your control. She understood what it was to be afraid you might hurt, even accidentally, the people you loved and were meant to protect.

The two of them had spent decades moving back and forth between their two Woodlands. Morena had come south to visit him. Sometimes they lived together, other times Morena stayed with lovers or other friends. Jarin did the same on his travel to the northeastern woodland. She teased him when he found Xochi and celebrated with him when they fell in love. He would do the same for her. He was supposed to do the same.

Jarin left the tent, stumbling. The air carried the chill of morning, damp with the moisture coming off the river. A quick scan of the area indicated where the command tent should be set up. He bullied his way through the people and tents between him and his objective while Xochi called his name. He registered none of it, his vision clouded in a fiery haze seeking an outlet.

He stalked, a cat on the hunt. Rage built. Someone would answer for what happened.

The tents stopped to reveal the larger pavilion. Voices could be heard within, though he could not make out the details. *Talk, talk, talk.* He threw back the flap, stormed inside, and scanned the room. New faces among the familiar, but only one unknown to him.

"Lord Jarin," King Garrett stepped forward. "I'm so—"

"You!" Jarin shouted and closed in on the stranger.

"Jarin," Larron said warningly as he shifted to intercept.

Jarin flung the Derou prince to the side with little effort. The woman stood defensively, but hesitated. She would have been unable to stop him regardless.

"You!" he yelled again as he shoved out with both hands, striking her in the chest and sending her flying backward.

She plowed into the wall of the tent. The force of her

movement ripped out the tent spike, and she tumbled out. Jarin followed, ripping the treated fabric with ease.

"You killed Morena!" he said as his eyes landed on her once more.

The woman crouched, a flaming sword in one hand as the other reached out toward him in a grasping motion. "I did not," she said with a surprising amount of calm.

"You killed her."

Jarin's next step was halted by a tugging on his leg. Looking down, he saw a thick vine wrapped around his ankle. It was easily torn up, and he ignored the other vines stretching upward.

"I saved you," she said, closing her hand into a fist.

The vines shot up and tightened around him. Jarin's forward momentum had him toppling forward. He dropped to his knees to avoid ending with his face in the dirt. His anger flared as he struggled against the plants, ripping through them again and again while she replaced them as fast.

His vision became distorted, watery. "You saved the wrong one. It should have been me."

Xochi darted into sight between Jarin and the stranger. "Stop, my love. Jarin. Stop."

He held still before Xochi's pleading, no longer fighting the restriction. As her arms closed around him, Jarin shattered.

CHAPTER TWENTY-TWO

Oasis River – Ceru-Auradia Front Lines

His arm broke. The bone in Larron's upper arm snapped when Jarin shoved him, sending him tumbling into Colonel Zara. Despite her efforts, the two of them collapsed to the ground in a mass of limbs. He hissed in pain as she helped him to his feet, both hyper-focused on Jarin's target.

The level of pain and anger on the man's face when he entered the command tent…Larron could relate; he had felt the same when Zeris had been taken and presumed dead—but he had not *also* faced a near-death experience before hearing the news. Jarin and Morena had been a solid pair for as long as Larron could recall, well before he was even born, in fact. They had rarely spent time in the Derou, but stories of their friendship spread far and wide.

Morena had been the troublemaker of the two. She'd dive into Jarin's workshop in her brightest gown to pull him out wearing a stained tunic and trousers so she could drag him along on more mischief. They'd played matchmaker, made a mess of Oromaer's community kitchen with random baking experiments, dodged combat training, and had gone on countless other adventures together within their Woodlands. Larron wondered if Jarin would have ever bonded with Xochima if Morena had not been in his life.

Then she was gone, and Jarin's mind wanted a focus upon which to vent his rage. For some reason, it had focused on Annalla, and there was nothing Larron could do to protect her. He raised his head from his fall in time to watch him shove her with enough force to send her shooting backward like an arrow off the string.

Larron and Zara scrambled to their feet and went in pursuit, stepping through the ripped fabric of the tent wall. Annalla stood defensively, flaming sword in hand, and faced her attacker. She was hurt. No one else would notice; she hid the pain well. Larron saw it in the tightness of her jaw, how she held her sword a little low for an ideal guard, and her posture remained slightly too stooped. Her breathing was shallow.

He had seen her stand tall under significant pain before. The difference may have been that she was surrounded by allies there, but he did not think so. Those around them were allies, but she did not know most of them, and they were not her friends. She needed a healer, quickly.

Zara took aim at Jarin. Larron rested a hand on her arm and shook his head. "It will have no impact against him," he whispered to her. He needed to find a means of calming Jarin and redirecting his grief and anger.

Xochima darted around the command tent to position herself directly in front of Jarin, and Larron felt his fear ease a notch.

"Stop, my love. Jarin. Stop," she said, holding out a hand in a calming gesture as she approached slowly.

With Jarin focused on Xochima, Larron crept around the perimeter of the scene toward where Annalla remained standing, holding her vines against her attacker. When Jarin's bonded enfolded him in her arms, Larron darted in to close the distance remaining to his own lifemate.

"Healer!" he called out. "We need a healer!"

The flames licking along the length of her sword snuffed out, and Annalla dropped her arms to her sides. She took a stuttering, shallow breath, likely to speak, and coughed. Bloody froth collected at the corner of her mouth.

"Annalla!" He tried to reach out to help her and hissed in pain. His broken arm protested, driving a spike of fire through him and causing a spell of vertigo.

"Protector Annalla!" Zara was a half-step behind him.

Still dizzy, Larron took a breath in through his nose, then out through his mouth. "Help her sit," he told Zara as he stabilized his right arm with his left.

Annalla was sweating by the time Zara eased her to a supine position upon the ground. She turned her head, coughing again and spraying her cheek with blood. Larron dropped to his knees, ignoring the jostling of his arm. He gripped her hand, squeezing it briefly before pulling back her wings and reaching beneath her leather tunic to feel up her torso to where Jarin had shoved her.

Zara stood and faced where Kings Garrett and Argent stood in the growing crowd surrounding the scene. "If she dies," she said, pointing, "by his hand, then this alliance ends here."

"That is not your decision, Lead Colonel Zara," Annalla said roughly, holding back against another cough.

"Attacked!" Zara spat out and started pacing. "In the middle of camp by an ally!"

"This way, quickly," Mage Hephestar ignored the tension as he led another mage through the crowd toward them.

"Here!" Larron called. He continued when the second mage kneeled on Annalla's other side. "I think her lung has been punctured."

She was a thin woman with medium brown skin and a cloud of dark hair. The puffiness beneath her eyes stood testament to how overworked the healer magai were there, but she showed no signs of slowing. She placed her hand on Annalla's chest, just below her collarbone. "Yes," she said after a moment, and pulled out a knife. "I need to cut into her. Please make sure no one attacks me in her defense."

Larron gestured for Zara to remain calm as the mage pulled out a small—and obviously sharp, as it made quick work of the tunic laces—knife, sliced a hole in her shirt, and followed that by deftly cutting a thumb-width size hole in her skin, just beneath Annalla's left breast.

Without hesitation, she slid a finger into the cut and returned her free hand to its initial place upon Annalla's chest. Larron watched as a depression filled in, reforming her healthy ribcage outline. Blood trickled from the cut, but stopped shortly after the finger was removed.

Annalla took a deep breath. "Thank you."

"That was close. You are lucky." Her brown eyes shifted to pin Larron in place. "Your turn."

People shifted positions as Larron's arm was healed. When his awareness returned, Annalla stood over Jarin and Xochima where they still kneeled on the ground. Zara stood behind her left shoulder, a menacing shadow of support.

Annalla's gaze sent a chill down Larron's spine. Cold. Unyielding. There remained no sympathy or acceptance within her. The person standing at the center of attention then was no longer Annalla, his friend and lifemate. She was the Protector of the Sanctuaries, the embodiment of the oath taken by her and all her forebears.

"You will not touch me again," she said.

"No." Jarin gave a slight shake of his head, his face tilted up toward her. "Never again. I can never express the depth of my regret."

Annalla ignored Jarin's words and turned her eyes on King Garrett and King Argent. "No one will," she said. "From this moment, I consider myself in hostile territory at all times. You will order your people to maintain a respectful and safe distance from me. Anyone closing in will be considered an act of aggression, and I will respond accordingly. The alliance stands, but if these terms are unacceptable to you, then I will leave now. Do you understand and agree to my conditions?"

They had an audience. Leaders and soldiers from every race in the alliance stood witness to a fairy leader giving the human and elven monarchs an ultimatum. Larron could guess Argent's greatest concern at that moment: Jarin's mental well-being, and Annalla's too.

The human king was more difficult to predict. While the Ceru royal line attempted to raise their children to leadership with a generous moral code, humans were less consistent in general. Larron was also less familiar with King Garrett specifically, but his experience with Tyrus gave him hope.

"I am sincerely sorry you were injured," Argent told her, holding out a hand but not stepping any closer. "It will be as you say. This will not happen again."

A man pressed forward through the crowd opposite Garrett, his red hair a flame against the drab background of an army encampment. His eyes were puffy and bloodshot, his shoulders stooped with the weight of the world—or that of great sorrow. He skirted the perimeter and approached his king. The two men said nothing, but some unspoken exchange passed between them.

Garrett placed a comforting hand on the man's shoulder and bowed his head. He brought his attention back to Annalla. "We will spread the word," he said. "I would ask that you attempt non-lethal responses if at all possible."

Tyrus stepped forward as Annalla tipped her head in acceptance. "Would you accept a guard to run interference?" he asked her. "We could place our tents around yours."

"Our?" she raised an eyebrow, a fraction of Annalla's

unique personality returning with the gesture.

"Patrice, Larron...me." He gave his patent charming smile and gestured back to where Zara hovered. "And your own people, of course."

Garrett looked worried but did not gainsay his son as Annalla snorted an abbreviated laugh. "Very well, my friend," she said. "If you believe it will help."

Larron's muscles unfroze as the tension eased. He took a deliberate step forward into the open space, capturing the attention of the crowd. "Please return to your assigned activities," he said to those watching. To the leadership who had been gathered in the command tent before the excitement began, he said, "and perhaps it would be best if we reconvened after mid-day?"

"Agreed," Garret said. His eyes darted around, taking in the troubled forms of Annalla, Jarin, and the red-haired man whom Larron guessed to be Commander Walsh.

Leaving others to deal with their own heart-wounded, Larron moved toward Annalla. Argent sent him a concerned glance, but Larron waved him off. He was in no danger from her fully awake and alert. She knew him even in sleep. She turned her head, glancing from him down to Jarin and back. Message sent and received.

He placed his hands upon the backs of Jarin and Xochima. "Jarin," he said softly. "Let us return to your tent now and clear this area so everyone can get back to work."

"Yes, love, come with me now." Xochima eased up and pulled her taller lifemate with her.

Annalla stepped back. "I will do the same," she told Larron, "and see you later."

Everyone moved at once. Annalla and Zara turned away to leave. Tyrus took a step in Annalla's direction but was immediately called back over by his father, who waved him and their commander into the broken tent. As the others cleared out,

Argent made for Jarin's position. Soon enough, they were the only four lingering in the clearing.

"How much danger are our people in from her, Larron?" Argent asked. "Is she capable of killing Jarin?"

Larron sighed. "We now know Jarin can drown. So, to your second question, the answer is 'yes.' The answer to the first is more complicated. Respect her boundaries, and there will be no problems. No one should enter her tent without a verbal confirmation from her, and do not attempt stealth. She is as reactive as any soldier too long in combat and a hundred times as lethal."

Argent pursed his lips as he looked toward where she had disappeared into the camp. "Understood." He turned back. "You are safe? And Prince Tyrus?"

"We traveled together. Familiarity helps, but even we are cautious if we need to wake her."

With Xochima on one side of Jarin and Argent on the other, they started a slow walk, speaking softly and casually to put him at ease.

"Larron." Jarin spoke for the first time since standing. "I am so very sorry. I never meant to hurt you, or anyone. It has been ages since I lost control of my strength in such a way, and now I have ruined—"

He reached across Argent to grasp Jarin's hand. "No, Jarin. You own your loss of control, but the rest was bound to happen sooner or later. As far as our alliance with the fairy…I cannot say you have endeared yourself to Colonel Zara, but Annalla knows loss. You are not alone in your pain."

Something in Larron's voice must have piqued Xochima's curiosity. She stopped and studied Larron with narrowed eyes. "You stepped in front of Jarin to protect her?"

He felt his brow furrow. "Yes?"

She sent him a smirk and started walking again. Larron ignored inquiring glances from the other two men and followed.

CHAPTER TWENTY-THREE

Oasis River – Ceru-Auradia Front Lines

"Annalla!" Patrice called out from where she walked between tents and hustled over. "You're bleeding!"

"Nothing to worry about, Patrice. I am healed now."

Zara snorted her disagreement. Annalla ignored her, but Patrice caught the gesture and scanned her again from head to toe.

"This isn't 'nothing.' What happened? We heard about a conflict within the council."

"Jarin stormed in and *attacked* Protector Annalla," Zara said, "screaming accusations about her killing Morena. She was coughing blood, and the healer had to cut into her chest."

Well, she thought, resigning herself to a lecture, *Patrice and Zara certainly bonded during their trip.*

Shock lit Patrice's face, but it was quickly followed by grim recognition. "Come on," she said. "Let's get to your tent so you can change."

Annalla looked down at the blood speckling and staining her shirt and the hole cut in it. She grimaced and groaned. "Ugh, I like my fairy shirts. They have the better wing slits."

Zara picked at the shirt she wore. "I'm sure we can find you an extra in our supplies, Protector."

She considered the beautiful feathered wings floating at Zara's back and laughed at herself. "Yes, I suppose so."

They reached her shelter and Annalla began to change, uncaring of the other two women with her. She grabbed for another shirt, sniffing it to see if it was the clean one she had remaining. A washcloth flew at her from the side, and she caught it with her power.

"You still have blood on your face and side," Patrice said sardonically. She continued speaking as Annalla wiped herself down. "We—the irimoten—were holding a remembrance for Morena when word of the dispute reached us. My people called them 'the twins,' her and Jarin. As opposite as night and day in most things, but as close as family. He lost one of the most important people in the world to him."

Annalla was unsure if her loss could compare. Her parents had been the most important people to her, but the care and affection shown to her had been tempered by their knowledge of what she would become. They had not been the parental figures she knew many held in their hearts.

"While I sympathize," Zara said in response, "that's no excuse for attacking an ally. He nearly killed her and Larron both."

"He nearly died, Zara." Annalla sighed. "He died and came back to find his best friend dead in his place. I should have reacted quicker and more aggressively, but I saw an elf ally first and a traumatized man second. It is not a mistake I will make again."

Zara and Patrice went back and forth a moment before Annalla interjected once more. "How did it happen?" she asked. "How did Morena go down?"

A look of pure frustration crossed Zara's face before she bowed and shook her head. "We don't exactly know," she said.

"The entire unit—both of them—went down with her, so the best we have are distant eyewitness reports and speculation."

Annalla plopped down on a cot, washcloth in hand. "So, what are we speculating?"

The fairy colonel paced as she reported. "Mage strike," she said. "No one saw any enemies in the area, and Kahnlair's magai have been dropping too many of my people every time we face them. But we had two units with her running interference and a magai of our own in the mix. She should have been shielded."

"We lost the mage too?" Annalla asked.

Zara nodded. "His body was found with the rest of them. Mage Hephestar believes the mage shielded Morena enough to ensure she survived the strike and the fall. Healer magai have said it appears most of the fairy died on impact—whether from the initial strike or the fall to the ground, they couldn't determine. Those who didn't die immediately were frozen to death when Morena used her essential abilities."

"She focused her power out toward Kahnlair's side, but those close to her were all hit, regardless of affiliation," Patrice said.

Annalla leaned forward with her elbows resting on her knees as she ran her hands through her hair, scratching at her scalp in frustration. "Which means our magai are not enough protection. At least, not on the wing."

Both of the other women put up their hands, at as much of a loss to offer a solution as Annalla. Marto had told them all how Kahnlair's magai were reported to overpower the allied forces. She would need to figure out a safe way to test more things with the magai.

She sighed aggressively through her nose. "Maybe we can learn something from her death, but I wish we had not lost Morena."

"As do I," Patrice said. "Morena will be missed by

many. She brought a fire and light to the camps with her energy that cannot be replaced. The irimoten here considered her one of them. She acted as a representative for my people, with the humans and their leadership."

Annalla's words had been more in regards to having a backup plan if she failed to eliminate Kahnlair herself, but she allowed Patrice's words to take the conversation in another direction. That, and more details about the attack she had interrupted, would come up again when the council resumed. "They did not want a matriarch on the council?" she asked.

Patrice's muzzle scrunched. "We have no trouble with the elves, but humans often find the irimoten...unsettling. We're too different from them in appearance, and it disturbs many of them. As a result, we've encountered an elevated level of hostility, disrespect, and even violence from human groups and leaders."

Annalla stopped with the clean shirt in her hands to stare at her friend. "From Ceru? Tyrus' people?" she asked incredulously.

"The royal family interacts with outsiders more frequently and are trained to withhold their initial reactions to avoid political ramifications with the realm's caretakers. To be fair," she said with a shrug, "most of the humans here seem to have become so accustomed to other races that they don't react any differently to us."

"Hmm," Zara huffed. "A small clearing in the storm of this war."

The three women fell silent as Annalla finished changing.

"You're not due back until after luncheon, right?" Patrice asked, continuing when they nodded. "Come back with me. You can share the meal with us and share in the continuing remembrance." She glanced at Zara with a smirk. "Maybe it'll help you be a little less angry with Jarin."

Zara chuckled in response, but quickly sobered. "Even for the brief time I had with her, I know I could have come to consider Morena a friend. It would be an honor to participate."

Annalla said nothing and followed to observe the memorial for another essential woman she could not save.

***

Tyrus didn't want to have the coming conversation with his father. King Garrett was one of the more open-minded kings of Ceru in a fair number of generations. He pressed his advisors and lords for changes, drove cooperation with their elven neighbors, and was the primary reason for the unprecedented integration of forces during the early stages of the war. The soldiers loved him, because when you belonged to him, you knew he would take care with your life. Even with the death and destruction, his people believed in his purpose.

When Jarin and Morena came to be under his command, he brought them into his fold. They became his. His responsibility. His to care for. At that moment, one was dead, and the other had been threatened by someone he would see as an outsider.

For all his talk of gender equality, King Garrett still held older prejudices, despite his best efforts. Morena, exuding femininity whenever she could, had not threatened tradition, so he could accept her without much hesitation. Lead Colonel Zara was another matter altogether. She was Walsh with wings and breasts, her presence commanding and her bearing direct.

He tried to integrate them as well, but Zara grated upon his underlying assumptions at a subconscious level he had to fight against constantly. As a result, the fairy were not yet *his* in Garrett's mind. Out of nowhere, one of them presents herself—another dominating female personality—as a threat to someone who *is* his. The emotional tug-of-war taking place in his mind had to be painful.

"I don't like her threatening our people!" For all that his exclamation lacked in volume, his statement was nonetheless emphatic.

"Father..." Tyrus tried for patience. "She saved Jarin's life, and then he nearly killed her in the middle of our command tent. Annalla is an important figure to the fairy people, and I believe she's our best hope of defeating Kahnlair."

"So, she's entitled to kill our people on a whim?"

"To defend herself? Yes. As much as your guards would to defend you."

"My king." Walsh spoke for the first time, his hoarse voice cutting through the family argument. "Morena is gone, and her power with her. We need this woman, and her demand for safety is not unwarranted."

His father pinched the bridge of his nose and rubbed his eyes. Walsh, and select others, were the few his father respected enough to listen to when they disagreed with him or offered an alternative opinion. Albertas had earned such a position. To that point, Tyrus had not.

Walsh turned his tired eyes on Tyrus. "Will she work with us, Your Highness?"

He considered her personality and position. "Work with? Yes. Obey? No. You should treat her as equal to a king."

"She commands Zara now?" his father asked.

"I don't believe so. Not exactly. Prince Darrin will command the fairy army when he arrives. Annalla is an army all on her own."

Walsh chewed on that a moment. "What can you tell us about her abilities?"

Tyrus appreciated the way he phrased the question, and he could see by the dip of his father's head that he approved as well. He would not betray his kingdom, but they also knew he would not betray any trust he had gained with their allies.

"Her essential abilities are no secret. You've seen all of them already. Plant growing, like the vines she used against Jarin and in defense of our people across the river. Water…that one is obvious. Fire control as in the flames she placed on her sword just now. And air is the origin of her ability to control the weapons flying around her."

His father drew a hand down his face. "Are they all of the magnitude we saw with the river?"

"Yes."

"An army indeed," Walsh muttered thoughtfully. "I'll request a meal be brought. We should discuss your stance and order, my king."

His father studied him when Walsh departed. "What would you do in my position, Tyrus?"

The earnest question caught him off guard. Garrett still tended to treat his youngest son as a child, despite him being old enough to have begun a family of his own, were times different. "May I speak freely, sir?"

Garrett tipped his head.

"Despite your efforts to change our society," he said gently, "you still view the world through primarily human expectations and societal constructs. The other races know this and intentionally avoided sending any female leaders onto your council. Mage Hephestar. Captain Lesyon. Both are skilled leaders, but their people selected them for this position rather than a woman as equally skilled because their people did not believe you would listen to a woman as you would a man. The irimoten took it a step further and elected to trust someone to be their voice powerful enough that you could not ignore her, but they are a matriarchal people. That, and their vast physical differences, leave them as outsiders to humans.

"The fairy did not consider your inclinations when deciding who to send in command of their forces here. They could have sent Colonel Braymis, but Zara is better at understanding politics. While she has a brash demeanor, she is highly logical. Her threat to revoke the alliance just now is a perfect example. Annalla may be correct that she doesn't hold that authority, but we don't know that. Zara didn't attack, she didn't take her people and leave. She threatened and imitated to show a position of strength.

"If I were you, I'd stop treating Zara as a female subject and start seeing her as Walsh's aggressive counterpart. As for Annalla, rely on the fact that your goals align. Do not order her around and do not threaten her. You can't control her, and she'll make no promises. The best you can hope for is to remain aligned and communicating."

Garrett chewed his lip in thought as he sat down in his normal camp chair, contemplating what Tyrus had told him. Walsh returned then, twitching his head to indicate having heard most of Tyrus' speech. The food came, and King Garrett sent orders to leave Annalla alone as requested. Despite Walsh wanting to discuss additional orders, they instead spent their time supporting the commander in his time of loss. Walsh had loved Morena. In his own way, he was as devastated by her loss as Jarin. The 'daughter he always wanted' was gone, and he had to continue the fight without her.

By the time the others started filtering in again, Walsh was composed—if still red-eyed—once more and back to studying his maps. Patrice, missing earlier, entered with Zara and Annalla. The elves were the last group to return. Larron left King Argent's side to stand with Annalla, while Argent took his place beside Garrett, Captain Lesyon trailed him and took up a position at his shoulder.

"Jarin will rest further today," Lesyon told the group. "We will fill him in on any tasks requiring his specific attention later."

Walsh stepped forward to speak as Argent took his seat. "Our first order of business is to move the army across the river.

This is still the best location unless we want to travel another month to the north, but we can't be certain another attack won't come as our forces are split again."

"We estimated a two or three-day effort utilizing the barges, correct?" Argent asked and received confirmation. "Colonel Zara, could the fairy take more of our people across at a time?"

"Yes. We would want to hold some units in reserve on guard, so the entire effort would be close to twenty trips, more if we're pulling the barges across," she said. "That's at least a day or two."

"Some of the artists should cross with the first wave," Mage Hephestar said. "That will help mitigate the possibility of the same surprise tactic Kahnlair used this time, hiding his army with illusion."

"How long to just move the people?" Annalla asked.

Zara juggled her hands. "Most of a day," she said after a moment.

Annalla nodded. "Line up the supplies at the edge of the river and pack the animals in the carts blindfolded with a handler. I will move the supplies and animal carts over when half the army personnel have made it. Each person should carry their personal items and supplies with them when the fairy take them across to minimize my load."

"What are the repercussions of you doing so?" Walsh asked, unfazed by her statement.

"It is unlikely I would be able to assist in a night attack, potentially being out through the next night as well."

"Zara," Walsh said, looking to her, "will your people be available to defend if needed during that time? You'll be doing most of the work."

"Not a problem," she said. "I'll plan the shifts accordingly."

"Alright, next up, I've been thinking about entering the

Kalachi Desert." Walsh grimaced. "We won't be entering it in the best season, but waiting only allows Kahnlair time to wear us down. We need better information about desert travel than I possess."

"Send out a call through the ranks for the desert refugees to come forward," Garrett said. "Enough of them joined our ranks at the start. They might not want to become Ceru citizens, but they want to be part of a gilar herd even less."

Walsh bowed his head. "I'll send the request with the rest of the orders this afternoon. We should be able to prepare today for a river crossing tomorrow. Any other more immediate matters?"

"I need a combat mage the fairy trust," Annalla said.

Mage Hephestar sat forward, curious. "Depending on the task, I can assist you or provide recommendations."

"I need someone to attack me with mage strikes in a controlled environment," she said.

Tyrus saw Zara's lips purse, but she didn't interrupt or contradict her protector.

Annalla continued. "I must understand what strikes I can absorb and how to counter those I cannot. Until I have this information, I cannot risk flying over our enemy to eliminate their magai. It must wait until after I recover from tomorrow's work, though."

"Yes," he said, blinking in thought. "Yes, that makes sense. May I coordinate this effort with Zara?"

Annalla nodded.

"Anything else?" Walsh asked. "Very good. Have the first portion of your people based on Zara's estimates packed and ready to depart at first light. Thank you all."

CHAPTER TWENTY-FOUR

Oasis River – Ceru-Auradia Front Lines

Annalla sat on a hill overlooking the camp as it was quickly dismantled, Patrice at her side. A fair portion of the first shift woke early to tear down their bedding and pack for the initial fairy transportation across the river. The rest would be in the second wave, while those soldiers established a defensive perimeter in preparation for the camp supplies to arrive later.

Patrice and Zara bunked with Annalla the night before, consolidating into one tent so the others could be packed ahead of time. Her only job that morning was to rest and conserve her strength, with the hope of accelerating her recovery after the day's efforts. From what Annalla had observed in the short time since her arrival, Patrice was a nomad within the army camp. She would borrow a different bunk each night and go where she pleased and attend only the meetings she wanted.

Patrice stared out over the activity below. "We're going to defeat Kahnlair, right?" Her voice was low and raspy with buried emotion.

From condolences given to Patrice when they lunched with the other irimoten, Annalla knew Patrice's son had been killed in the windani raids. She had spoken often of him during their journey, so proud of the man he had become and his desire to contribute to the fight against Kahnlair. To discover his death must have been heartbreaking, and it had left her alone in the world.

"That is what I am here for, my purpose," she said.

"He took my son, Annalla." Her voice quavered. "He took everything from me."

"I know." There was little comfort to offer.

"I'll be on the team going after him. I'll kill him if I can."

"I do not believe I can uphold my oath to protect the sanctuaries if we do not eliminate the threat he represents," Annalla told her, voicing part of what weighed on her own mind for the first time. "Kahnlair is my target as well. I will not hold you back."

She felt Patrice turn her head to study her. The weight of the scrutiny grew, developing into a near-tangible pressure as she continued to stare without speaking. Annalla wondered what she saw, what she read into her words or tone.

Can she read anything into it when I am still uncertain myself? she wondered. *I do not even understand where my own lines are anymore. Or maybe she thinks I'm lying to placate her, that I will try to stop her mission of vengeance.*

Eventually, Patrice shrugged. Annalla glanced over in time to see a shift in her demeanor. Her lips turned up in a smirk that did not reach her eyes.

"I think that large fairy guard has been flirting with Tyrus."

She blinked at the change of subject. "Ameris?"

"Uh-huh." Her amusement was only half forced. The grief lingered, but their small group had bonded during their desperate quest. "Tyrus did say he was drawn to strength."

"Heh! Wow," she said as another round of fairy ferries

took off. "Serious?"

"Eh." Patrice angled her head. "I think Ameris was earnest in his overtures, but they haven't spent much time together since we joined with the army."

"Understandable."

"To be fair," Patrice added, "I don't think Tyrus is prepared for a relationship, if that's what Ameris was interested in."

"Maybe he was only looking for a distraction," Annalla said dryly.

Patrice snorted. "Aren't we all?" They shared an amused grin before Patrice scrunched her forehead and asked, "When are you supposed to move all of this?" She made a wide gesture before them.

"Soon." Annalla squinted toward the sun. "About…"

She paused before turning back, staring into the sky to the northeast. A trio of raptors raced toward the camp, the standard number for a scouting group. Annalla rose to her feet, shifting her body around as she did to watch the approaching fairy without straining.

"Scouts are returning with speed," she said and pointed for Patrice.

"Northeast," her friend said. "It could be Albertas. There was a report earlier about him heading to rejoin the main army with reinforcements. Shall we go find out, or do you need to stay here to move the stuff?"

Annalla shook her head. "No. Whether this is Albertas or something bad, it will likely require changes to my plan. We should check in."

They arrived just after the scouts, having elected to walk down the hill to appease Patrice's fear of flying. There was also no point in rushing ahead when no information would be forthcoming before the messengers got there.

King Garrett stood alone with them in the largest tent

still standing. All the maps and documents were packed and waiting along the riverside with the tables and chairs. An imposing man, he was a version of Tyrus more aged, more weathered and worn. He laughed less and growled more, and he possessed none of Tyrus' suave, easy-going demeanor around strangers.

Tyrus had said he was often used as an ambassador due to his being the youngest. Annalla wondered if that contributed to his social skills, or if his skills simply made him great at his assigned role. According to Zara, who heard from Patrice, who had it from the other irimoten, Garrett had always been less polished, but he became even less so through the years of war. Annalla didn't mind; she enjoyed being able to be just as direct and not have to worry about being considered rude. They could be rude together.

Garrett acknowledged them as the two women entered and faced the scouts. "Problem?"

The lead raptor started to shake his head, stopped, then shrugged. "I don't know if it will be a problem for you or not, Protector," he said to Annalla first, then faced Garrett once more. "Prince Albertas and his forces are close, but they will not arrive until later this afternoon."

The human king turned to her. "What does this mean for your part of the plan to cross the river? You and the rest of the fairy are doing most of the work on this endeavor."

Annalla pursed her lips and asked the messenger, "How many people?"

"I estimate nine thousand. No more than ten."

"A marginal increase," she said. "Depending on the timing, it may mean the last flight or two of people will camp over here tonight."

"I'll have Walsh make sure the last few contain enough soldiers to defend the group should it become necessary," Garrett said. "What about the supplies and livestock?"

"We will need to convert more of the supply carts for livestock," she said, thinking out loud. "Some of the supplies need to be transported by the fairy as well, I think."

"There are a few of the modified carts remaining," Garrett said. "The ones that can float. What if we use a handful of them to move supplies throughout the day? It would only divert a small portion of our forces to work the river while the rest continued as planned."

Her eyebrows rose and her lips turned in an expression of impressed approval. "That would help minimize the impact on me, yes."

"I'll see to it and let you know when we have them separated so you can begin your work," Garrett said and thanked them all before seeing himself out of the tent.

Patrice stared at Annalla with her forehead scrunched in exaggerated confusion.

Annalla dismissed the messengers and faced her friend. "What?"

"That was a rather civil exchange."

"With King Garrett?" she asked as they made their way toward her staging position from which she would begin her individual efforts. "I like Garrett."

Patrice raised a disbelieving eyebrow, then the other eyebrow raised in consideration. "I suppose you have not had much interaction with him. Zara has been here longer."

"Has she been having trouble with the king?"

Her nose twitched as she frowned. "I wouldn't say trouble. Before you arrived, she was frustrated, often enough, when her voice was respected only with Tyrus' or Walsh's support. She made some progress against that, though."

Annalla grinned. "Flexed her wings a bit, did she?"

Patrice flashed her fangs. "Not until we started the march north. At one point though, she gave them a flat 'no' and told them exactly how the fairy were going to proceed and that they were free to accommodate and follow or go their own way. I think Walsh talked Garrett down after that discussion, then Argent arrived as a buffer. Now you show up and drown a massive portion of Kahnlair's attacking army to save his men. I think he's experiencing a major shift in his thinking."

"Ha! I love it." Annalla laughed as a human soldier called her over.

"Ma'am," the soldier said as she approached, and she recognized him as the one who'd fought with her the other day.

"My captain!" she called out. "Shouldn't you be on the other side already?"

"Uh." His expression became surprised for a moment before he continued. "Ma'am. His Majesty, King Garrett, assigned our unit to assist you with the supplies. We have a unit under us to do the work while we coordinate for you. He indicated it would be a restful break."

His tone indicated the break was either not needed or not appreciated in the way Garrett had intended. She was uncertain if she agreed with him or his king. Downtime allowed them time to remember the fight and everyone who did not survive. Many of the men there had friends who'd died across the river the prior day or might not recover from their injuries. However, the assignment also allowed them to bond together and acknowledge their grief in some small part.

"How did you know about my promotion, ma'am?" he asked. "I would think such a thing not worth noting to you."

Annalla winced. *Does that mean he considers himself not worth noticing? Was he simply commenting on the difference in rank?*

"I did not actually know your rank," she said. "I started calling you that in my head yesterday."

He grinned and offered her a salute. "I appreciate the compliment, ma'am. Captain Seamus, reporting for duty. What are your orders here?"

Patrice touched Annalla's forearm. "I'm heading over with the irimoten soon, so I'll see you later." She paused. "And thank you."

Thank you for letting me pretend, for allowing me to bury my grief and act like I'm not changed, not dead inside. Annalla understood. Patrice had one purpose, and she would forgive no one who got in the way of her goal. Before the end, either Kahnlair would be dead, or Patrice would. That was not the time to attempt to convince her friend there were other options, and she was not sure it would be right to try.

"Of course, my friend," she said and gave her a tight smile before turning back to Captain Seamus and the carts arranged near the water's edge.

Everything stood as she had instructed. The carts were parked close together with a second line staggered behind the first. Most of those in the second row were empty, with their back wall open and a ramp attached. Some of the supplies were actively being unloaded and placed on the handful of barge-carts floating on the water, but most remained for her to move.

"Alright." She bit her lip and scanned the line once more. "We need to get the animals into position behind the carts in which they will be riding. I want to be able to load them all quickly before I am ready to move out, and they will need to be blindfolded. This only applies to the northernmost two-thirds of the carts. I plan to leave the southern third to take with the supplies Prince Albertas will be arriving with, but I want to pack as many of the animals into the first round as possible. Can your men handle all of that?"

"Yes, ma'am. We can have the horses in position in about a half hour. Will that be sufficient?"

With her confirmation, Seamus nodded and started barking orders. The men there had been almost begging for something to do rather than sitting around waiting. They scrambled about, gathering up other workers in their wake, and had the animals ready to ascend their respective ramps in less time than Seamus' estimate.

"When do you want us to load them?" he asked, standing at her side.

"Let me take a look from the air and decide where I will be drawing the line."

She unfurled her wings and took to the sky. Her air ability did not require visibility for Annalla to move objects. Basic testing with Larron during their journey showed she could set up a general 'catch' order to halt objects coming toward her. She could also put out a general 'move' order that would grab everything in an area. Both took additional concentration and effort on her part, so it made more sense to limit her reliance on such blind applications, although she was practicing more with the first one to protect herself from projectiles while in combat.

That being the case, the carts were lined up cleanly where her elven sight distinguished them well enough. By fixing the objects in her mind—or rather within her awareness of her essence, which was a concept she was still working through—lifting the massive cumulative weight of everything became easier. The benefit would be nowhere near the level she gained within the Derou by working through her Woodland connection, but it would be enough to complete her promise.

Annalla scanned the line, reaching out with her essence as she did so, starting from the south and moving north. The horses and other livestock would add weight to the empty carts, so she tried to estimate how much she could take in the first trip without overextending and keeping the second move in mind. When she reached the stopping point, she descended to that place in line and told the men to the north to hold those animals for the second trip later in the day.

She returned to Seamus. "We can begin. I do not believe I will take all the carts we are going to fill. If any are left behind with animals, they can be unloaded for the next round."

Seamus nodded and moved back before waving a blue-gray flag. Horses to her right and left were deftly blindfolded and led up the ramps onto the waiting carts. More flags flew up and down the line, starting a wave of similar actions. He returned to her side. "It should be done shortly, ma'am. If you want to get into position in the air, you will know it's done when all the flags are switched out for this darker color here. Then you can do…whatever you're going to do." The last was said with a hand flip.

The carts remained locked in her mind. As she took off again, she pressed a small amount of power to them for a fraction of lift to gauge the weight being added. She mentally placed her power on one side of an imaginary scale, weighing it for the amount she wanted to use. To the other side of the scale, she hooked the weight of the carts held within her control.

Closer. She monitored the balance as it tilted. *Closer. Too much.* When the weight tipped, she dropped the furthest cart. Then she let go of another and scanned the lines as the weight increases slowed, then stopped. Dark flags waved below.

Annalla tightened her hold on the remaining carts and lifted. Horses shifted nervously, goats screamed, and wood creaked as the platforms rose smoothly off the ground. Wheels spun in the air leisurely, no longer held in place by the weight of their burdens. Clumps of mud and dirt dropped off to splat upon the riverbank and splashed into the water as the mass floated out over the river in her wake.

Work stopped as people stared. The barge-cart below floated down the river soundlessly as the two handlers riding looked up with open mouths. Fairy hovered in place for a moment, admiring the power displayed by their protector.

Annalla tuned out their reactions and concentrated on her burden while scanning forward for enemies. They would lose half their supplies if she were attacked at that moment and dropped everything. With the prospect of a long trek through the desert ahead of them, they could not afford to lose any more than what had washed away in her flood during the battle. Her jaw clenched and her hands fisted. The effort involved was not physical, but it presented physically, nonetheless. She took her time, moving slowly and steadily forward to avoid panicking the animals.

She reached the other bank and brought the supplies over beneath her, moving them far enough from the water to allow room for grooms to guide the horses and others from their mobile pens. Breathing heavily, she worked to settle the carts back on the ground gently, but she had not accounted for the uneven terrain. Some bumped and jostled, and animals cried out once more, but they landed and became someone else's responsibility.

Annalla breathed a sigh of relief and headed back toward the eastern bank to find her cot and take a nap. One down, one round to go.

CHAPTER TWENTY-FIVE

Oasis River – Ceru-Auradia Front Lines

She rested for two days after the river crossing. On the first, Zara coordinated the movement of the final troops across the river. A small contingent had slept out under the open sky, most of them members of Prince Albertas' group having arrived later in the afternoon than initially estimated. The delayed arrival pushed back the coordination of supplies, which had delayed Annalla's second shipment until well into the evening. After her work concluded, she dragged herself to the tent indicated by Zara and Patrice on the western side of the river—once again sharing with them—and crashed.

    The next day and night she slept, guarded by her friends and fairy around her while they finished bringing everyone else over. Even such an extreme level of protection was not enough for her to sleep soundly. She roused each time at the sound of approaching footsteps, but her exhaustion drove her back under quickly enough. When she woke the second morning after their river crossing, the bulk of the army prepared to depart. Another small contingent planned to remain behind to support the third of the fairy who would also stay with Annalla for one more day.

It would be easy for them to catch up to the caravan when they could fly straight there.

Mage Hephestar remained behind as well. Zara trusted him most of the combat magai, mostly from having interacted with him more than any other in the weeks of travel together. She might not be completely comfortable with *any* mage attacking Annalla, but they sought the path of least concern. Annalla rested physically as she and Hephestar sat with Larron, Patrice, and fairy captain Karlo, the Dean of Combat from the school in Essence for a planning session. Tyrus and Zara had departed with the rest of the army.

"I'm still trying to get my head around what you want," Hephestar said, squinting at her with a hand to his temple. "You *want* me to attack you? What can you possibly hope to gain, other than injuries and my death at the hands of Colonel Zara?"

Annalla chuckled at his exasperation. "I hope to avoid both serious injuries to my person and your death," she said. "I need to test myself against mage attacks in a controlled situation to know my options and limitations. Before we left the sanctuary, I worked with Marto to determine how and if my essential manifestations can work around magai shielding, but we did not test my defenses against attack."

Karlo held up his hands, palms out. "I'm also under orders not to harm you."

"None of us like this any more than you do," Larron told Hephestar, "but we *need* this to avoid another loss as we experienced with Morena."

Hephestar frowned and took a sobering breath. "Do you think we could've helped her? We never thought to run any tests."

"No," Larron said. "There was never a need before. The enemy magai would have never considered bringing themselves within Morena's range. Then, once the fairy arrived, you sent multiple magai with her, protecting her in the air except in this last battle. It was chaos."

He nodded thoughtfully. "So, how do we do this safely?"

"If I understand correctly," Annalla said, "all mage strikes fall under either force, fire, or magic energy categories."

He grimaced at the 'magic energy' description but did not press a distinction. "More or less."

Annalla bit her lip in thought. "I think we start with fire. I have direct control through my own manifestation, and it is the form I will most likely be able to counter."

"Energy second," Larron said. "The attacks appear similar to lightning strikes, and the resulting injuries look like burns."

She met his eyes. "You think I can potentially counter it the same as fire hits?"

"Theoretically." He shrugged. "It is a good place to begin."

His thoughts followed her own line of thinking. She had some additional scientific knowledge from her time and studies in Aryanna. Fire, lightning, electricity. All were related to energy and its creation, results, and consumption. Perhaps she could leverage the combination of her power and education to find a solution. Then again, the influence of essence on Elaria might mean scientific rules would be inconsistent at best. The only way to know for certain was to test.

"What about force?" Patrice asked. "That's the one you're worried about, right?"

"Yes," she said. "Air is the obvious choice, but I do not directly control force; I exert force upon objects."

"You are able to catch objects I throw at you blindly," Larron said.

"Believe me," she said, tilting her head in his direction, "I will be trying that, but I do not think it will be as straightforward of an answer."

When she caught objects, her power created a barrier of force through which objects did not pass. The limitation was that she *only* influenced things and *not* life. Their livestock had to ride across the river in the carts because of her inability to lift the creatures directly. At one point, when traveling with Larron, Annalla tested a theory and found greenwood more difficult for her to manipulate than seasoned wood. It was dead, but not dead-dead.

"I think I should start with some demonstrations before we try any direct attacks," Hephestar said, shaking his head in a manner implying his disbelief at their thinking.

Annalla pointed at him. "Not a bad idea. If I have an understanding of how you work, I might be able to come up with a counter." If she failed to find an answer, Kahnlair's magai would swat her out of the air like she might smack a bug.

"As long as you are willing," she told Hephestar, "I would like to linger behind the army every other day to train and practice until we have a solution."

He looked grim, but bowed his head in agreement.

***

Larron bared his teeth and hissed an indrawn breath as the blast struck Annalla's side and sent her spiraling through the air to her left. He winced in sympathy at the bruise she was likely to have when they finished there. Annalla promised everyone she would proceed with caution and was holding to that promise.

Scouting units had reported Kahnlair's forces having retreated to the desert camps and strongholds as far as they could tell. While the army remained on guard, the general consensus was that their enemy had learned and accomplished what he desired at the river. He would wait, regroup, and plan additional surprises for them as they moved into his long-held territory.

They spent the initial week of travel working through fire strikes, which proved as straightforward as she had expected. When they finally tested direct attacks against her, nothing hit. The flames broke around her and became absorbed by her essence, shifting to her control immediately. Part of Larron rejoiced at the ease with which she'd conquered that threat, but the rational part knew the true tests were still to follow.

The first week of her work on energy blasts ended, and they moved to active testing. Hephestar became more agitated each day as they progressed, but he said he "refused to subject another mage to the emotional trauma."

Larron would have preferred if they kept with the initial testing approach, where she attempted to modify the trajectory of each strike. Every attempt resulted in failure, and she determined the energy was not similar enough to fire for her to gain control. Rather than deciding that would be the end of the experimentation, Annalla said she needed a closer understanding of the *feel* of magic energy compared to her essential energy.

Another week later, and there was a healer mage assigned to her. He remained behind with their party for the training exercises and dealt with her injuries after she called a halt for the day and before they took off to catch up with the army. Larron and Dean Karlo, along with his unit of fairy, continued to stay with her, watching and supporting as much as they were able. After the first few hits, the fairy started to run patterns beneath her in case she fell and needed to be caught. The precaution was smart, and Larron shuddered at the need for it.

"I feel as though part of me knows the answer, but my brain is getting in the way," she said as she landed where Larron stood with Hephestar.

"Are we done for today?" Mage Sholdray asked as he

strolled over to join them.

Healer Mage Sholdray was a thin, balding man in the middling years of his life. He kept what there was of his long black hair tied back and wore the faded shirt and trousers of a kitchen hand. His eyes remained tired at all hours, and his head hung. Mage Sholdray was the least disturbed by the injuries Annalla sustained.

Hephestar had brought him on that assignment because he was talented, and he was close to burning out. They hoped by taking him away from the constant fighting and death of the front and showing them working on something and making progress would help. When a mage burned out, it was psychological, but lasting. Their concentration failed and they could no longer effectively apply their magical powers, despite retaining all the knowledge and training.

"No," Annalla said. "I want to try a couple more things, but I want to think first."

"May I?" Sholdray asked, gesturing at her side.

Another new hole seared into the cloth of her shirt, Larron thought. The garment was more patches and darning stitches than original material at that point. He eyed the hole before Sholdray reached her to heal her wound. "You are less burned this time," he said.

There were blisters, but the skin was a seared red rather than black and dead around the injury site. As always, she did no more than wince when she moved the wrong way and pulled at the tight skin. He wondered if she even registered pain the same way anymore.

Sholdray placed his hand over the wound, his face flashing into and out of the magai aspect of concentration. "Your elf is correct. If this injury had been made by a physical weapon, I'd describe this as more of a glancing blow."

"Okay. Okay," she muttered to herself.

As much as he hated the war and hated watching his

bonded allow herself to be injured over and over again, he loved watching her think. Her eyes became unfocused, flipping through a myriad of facts and data he could hardly fathom within her mind. Her lips twitched and words were breathed out every once in a while so softly he could not make them out. She relaxed, her posture softening as she considered things beyond her immediate surroundings.

What if we had met in different times? He wondered. *Would we have been able to travel and contemplate puzzles together, or would she have continued to hide from the world as her forebears?* He wanted an opportunity to journey throughout the land and live together without fear.

"I'm mitigating the effects," she said, lapsing back into less formal speech and tapping at her skull in a fidgeting gesture. "I should burn, but my essence innately understands fire. It doesn't understand *this* burning, so it has to convert the sensory input."

Larron saw where the line of thinking was taking her. He took a deep breath and sighed it out. "Practice," he said.

Hephestar glanced nervously between them as Annalla nodded in response to Larron's statement. "What do you mean?"

Annalla's lip turned up in a sneer, irritated by the implications of their discovery. "Protecting myself from fire is an innate reaction linked to my essential connection to the element. Because your energy strikes cause the same physical effect—burning—I can also protect myself from those, but it is not innate." She paused. "If I want to be able to get better at preventing injuries, I need to practice."

The combat mage visibly wilted. "So, I must keep hurting you."

She smiled gently at him. "No, not yet. I think I have enough 'training' to keep myself alive. I want to shift to the force attacks. How do those work?"

He looked relieved to Larron's eye and gestured for them to sit down. Only when they all settled did he relax and begin a lecture.

"Our force strikes are like a physical hit executed with our power instead of a fist or weapon," he said.

"Does the force always emanate from your position?" Annalla asked.

Hephestar shook his head. "Any point of our choosing, but the force away from us will naturally be stronger because of the mental element in how we use our magic. This is true even if we're using an omnidirectional strike from an alternative source."

Larron's brow furrowed. "An omnidirectional blast from any point seems useful. Why is it not used more often?"

"The attack is unreliable in combat," Hephestar said. "Unlike the other magic concentrations, the environment in which we work is constantly changing, so we can't focus wholly on manipulating the magic. If we did, we might put ourselves at risk or potentially injure allies moving into the target area. Without that concentration, natural reactions take over. That most often means we push and less frequently pull.

"Either reaction could result in disaster, which is why we train to push out from ourselves. The mage selects a location ahead of them and throws the force forward to that point. Everything is forward movement. Consistency. Repetition. It keeps the damage we cause where we want it."

Annalla tilted her head. "So why mention the other methods?"

"Because Kahnlair's magai use them when he is supplementing their power," he said, "and we found them easier to use and most effective against the vampires."

"And therefore, against fairy as well," Karlo said.

She leaned back and looked away in thought. "Okay. So, any direction?"

Hephestar tipped his head.

Annalla hopped to her feet and clapped her hands. "Okay," she said again. "Let us set up my bag of dirt."

Her 'bag of dirt' was a grain sack loosely stuffed with dirt and gravel. It weighed about fifty pounds and stood about three feet tall. That was the object Annalla decided to use as a test model. They walked or flew the bag out a hundred feet and found something elevated to set it upon.

Annalla returned to the group and nodded at Hephestar. "Show me."

Larron watched as the combat mage planted his feet and raised his arms, stretching them forward with palms forward and fingers spread. His lips pursed and his eyes squinted as he focused on the target. A brief muscle twitch, a pulse of movement. The bag ripped at the seam and shot backward, a trail of dust following in its wake. Larron clenched his jaw and fought to hide his wince.

CHAPTER TWENTY-SIX

Oasis River – Ceru-Auradia Supply Route

Marto jolted as the flying pavilion set down. He breathed out a sigh of relief and felt his body relax for the first time in days. That night was a rest night, meaning all the fairy would take a much-needed break and no one would be in the air.

He had flown with Karl often, and for days at a time, but riding in the flying pavilions was an altogether different experience. The wood swayed and creaked at all hours. There was no shelter from wind and rain, as any coverings increased the drag and made them more difficult to carry. Travel was miserable for everyone. Sleep took forever to come and remained fitful throughout. The fairy worked themselves ragged with continuous flying while carrying twice their weight.

"Ugh," Franklin, one of Tyrus' former guards, groaned. "I'd rather be dead."

They had stopped and picked up another two thousand troops from the Nierda River, including King Oromaer, Larron's fellow Derou elves, and the guards Tyrus had left behind in the Palonian. Oromaer had left his bonded with those on the river, clearing it of the bandits plaguing it and continuing their mission to bring supplies to Ceru. He and the rest had come with the fairy to join the main fighting.

Franklin was one of many who discovered they became nauseous in the air. Less than an hour into their first trip, at least a hundred people were leaning out of the pavilions over the rails, expelling their last meal. The wind caught the sick and sprayed it on levels below, causing more people to be ill. They set the structures down and lost a good four hours of travel cleaning up, recovering, and formulating a plan.

People prone to airsickness were shifted to the lowest levels to prevent the disastrous mess from happening again, and two or three healer magai were assigned to each of those levels. They took turns healing the physical effects, but their magical stamina ran thin by the time the fairy called a halt. As time passed, they tired more quickly on each trip. Rarely were they available to help relieve the symptoms for everyone anymore.

"We're closing in on the army." Harndorn patted his man's back, eliciting another groan. "Another run, maybe two, and you'll be back on a horse instead."

Franklin stumbled to his knees and plopped down onto his backside. His hands caressed the grass beneath him. "Sweet earth, embrace me."

His companions laughed at his misery, and Marto smirked at their familiar antics.

Geelomin dropped down to stand beside Marto. He shook his head and pursed his lips in disapproval, but his eyes sparkled with amusement. The elf lieutenant kept his hodgepodge command. All of them signed on to rejoin their leaders, the ones who went on the mission to find the fairy with Marto.

"Alright," Geelomin called out. "Everyone except Franklin start helping set up camp. The fairy have done enough of the work carrying us."

"You heard him," Harndorn shouted. "Let's get to work!"

The group moved out, giving Franklin pats on the back, head rubs, or gentle shoulder squeezes as they passed. Geelomin was correct about the fairy. If the journey was difficult for the passengers, it was near torture for them. They were worn thin by the constant flying, and adding nearly half again as many people to their burden did not help matters. The fairy drooped. Wingtips brushed the ground and feet dragged.

Marto jolted at a thump behind him and nearly toppled over, despite his hand braced on one of the pavilion supports. He hopped in place to turn himself around. Prince Darrin stood uneasy on his feet. His short, dark hair stuck to his forehead with sweat, and his cheeks were gaunt, the shadowed indents matching the dark circles beneath his eyes. He looked ill, and Colonel Braymis following behind was no better.

"Darrin," Marto said as he grabbed his crutches from the shelf on which they sat and hurried to his side, "you can't keep going like this. We should take a week down for you and your people to recover."

Darrin started a slow shake of his head in the negative.

"Mage Marto is correct, Your Highness," Oromaer said, approaching from Marto's left. "Your fairy soldiers will help nothing if you are all close to collapse when we arrive. A week of rest, and then we are no more than two of your marathon flights from joining our allies."

The fairy prince forced his posture straighter and his jaw set, preparing to argue.

Oromaer held a hand forward in a motion for him to wait. "Three days," he said. "We can spare three days."

Darrin sighed and raised a hand to rub his tired eyes. He glanced over at Braymis, who shrugged a shoulder and twitched his hand in a gesture that effectively meant anything from 'it's your decision' to 'it couldn't hurt.'

With another deep breath in and out, Darrin said to Oromaer, "Very well, three days. We could use some help defending the camp."

His fellow monarch smiled and placed a hand on his shoulder. "You have some of the greatest soldiers remaining in the east with you here. Rest, my new friend. We will keep you safe."

***

Geelomin perched atop a pavilion and scanned the night. His group was one of the many on night watch while the fairy slept below. For most of the last two days, the fairy had rested, eaten, and little else. The next day would be their last planned ground day, and Oromaer coordinated with the dwarves and magai to help ensure their new allies were cared for.

He felt his throat choke up again at the wonder of a fairy army. When the sight had become clear over the river those months ago, Thanon had let out a whoop of joy and ran down the line of people hugging everyone he could reach. Bealaras had leaned back against a tree with a contented smile on his face. Geelomin had thought it only a matter of time before the Derou became lost forever when either the royal line or the Woodland itself died out. Instead, Prince Larron had survived and brought new hope. He would do what he was able to protect the source of that hope.

That morning, most of the fairy looked healthier than they had in weeks and so were the healer magai who had been wearing themselves out helping stave off the frequent airsickness. It would take more than three days of rest to return them to full strength, but they would not be near death when they finally linked up with the main force of the army. They had already passed by multiple army camps reduced to the minimum number of defenders. Ceru and Auradia had sent their full might forward in a final, desperate strike.

Those camps then served as wayposts and supply camps

from which critical resources would be sent forward to the ever-progressing front lines. As such, they were not immune to attacks from enemies lingering in the area. All reports received from the fairy messengers assigned to the routes told of Kahnlair retreating into the Kalachi Desert to draw the bulk of the army further into his territory, but there had been a few attacks on allied camps in the interim, and a couple of messenger groups had gone missing.

Vampires continued making forays into allied territory, and scattered clusters of ground troops hid behind the lines and harried the forces left behind. To the north, King Argent also relied upon the Derou territory and the natural barrier of the Claws to limit the threat from that direction. Doing so, however, meant that small groups trickled in gradually to pose a consistent threat. All provided reasons for maintaining a diligent watch at night, even so far from their main opposition.

"Yes, Thanon?" he asked the elf who had been creeping up behind him for the last ten minutes.

He was prepared for the conversation for some time now. Both Thanon and Bealaras were gentle souls, even for elves. While they were highly skilled soldiers, they wanted and needed to talk through their thoughts and emotions. Usually, they spoke with each other, but periodically one or both came to Larron—and then him—for some form of validation.

They were so young. Everyone around him was so young. Geelomin did not have to wonder when he became one of the elven elders. In conflict, the eldest always threw themselves forward in defense so future generations would have their time. Never had they lost so many so quickly; not until the war with Kahnlair.

"Bealaras and I were talking about the Derou Woodland," he said, "and how Prince Darrin said Larron and Annalla were headed there." Thanon paused, almost as though he was afraid to ask and hear the answer. "Do you think they helped? With as much as we had lost already?"

"What do you and Bealaras think?" Geelomin asked.

"We think she saved them. The messengers say she is already with the army, so she either succeeded or decided it was a lost cause, right?"

"I like to believe they accomplished something with their journey," came his noncommittal agreement. "We will see them soon enough, in a week or—"

Geelomin cut his statement short as Thanon's head perked up, coming to attention and staring out into the night. They made ready their bows, and Thanon let out a warbling whistle like a screech owl. There existed no doubt in Geelomin's mind something was out there. Thanon was one of the best scouts and hunters around.

Shadows flitted through the sky, barely discerned from the moonless darkness by his elven sight. He followed one shadow with his eyes, leading the target as he always taught his trainees. His arrow flew, and the shadow dropped to join the deeper black of the dark below. There was no sound or cry of pain to tell Geelomin whether or not his shot had found its mark. He sighted again.

More whistles echoed through the night, and the sky lit with the burning of a hundred torches as magai threw light into the air. The area to the north boiled with bodies. Vampires poured forward, nearly upon his pavilion. Their claws stretched forward, and the sheen of venom glistened in the light and spittle flew from slicing fangs in their overly large mouths.

"Keep firing," Geelomin told Thanon as he released another arrow and then traded for his blades.

The first vampire arrived. It reached forward in an attacking move toward Thanon, and Geelomin intercepted the claws, diverting them to the left and shifting to slam his pommel into its face. It reared back, screeching, and Geelomin slashed deep across its throat. Arrows bolted past him as he shifted to engage the next enemy swooping down.

Other pairs worked similarly across the tops of the pavilions; not all escaped unscathed. A man screamed in pain and fear as he flew past in the clutches of a vampire retreating northward. Thanon's next arrow hit the vampire in the shoulder and the pair tumbled over the side.

A raid, he thought to himself, *not a full attack.* The strike by the vampires was specifically to cull their numbers and bring in food. Such a hunt was much more of a traditional attack by the vampires than the structured and targeted strikes during the war.

It made no difference to their defense, but the fight was more likely to end quickly. Their goal would be to limit the number of captives with which they allowed the vampires to escape. Another man was flown over them and disappeared into the night. They would not be able to save everyone.

Geelomin focused on the people around him. He darted back and forth, striking out at grasping claws as his unit fired into the sky. He took the hand of one as it clawed Fremya's back. She hissed and arched away from the pain. The arrow in her hands clattered to the boards at their feet.

"Get below!" he shouted the order.

Her eyes, gray with a burst of bronze around the pupil, flashed in defiance a moment before she resigned herself to go. With barely a wince, she swung down off the top, leaving him one less person to shield. He turned in time to glimpse Thanon duck away from another attack. Geelomin shouldered in, shoving the vampire away and receiving a scratch down his arm for his troubles. The cut stung, but it wasn't deep enough to warrant his own retreat.

"Lieutenant!"

He and Thanon turned at the panicked shout. His eyes widened and his heart pounded.

"Bealaras!" Thanon cried out.

Their friend was lifted off his feet. Pearaltar lay dead or unconscious where the two had been positioned. Bealaras dangled. His legs thrashed and his arms flailed as he fought against the vampire's hold.

Thanon fired, but another vampire making a diving run intercepted his arrow after only a few feet. Geelomin jumped forward again, eliminating the second attacker following the first, but he lost sight of Bealaras in the melee.

"Where is he?" Thanon called frantically, his eyes darting around in growing panic. "Where is he? I do not see him!"

No. No, no, no. The thought became a mantra as he battled.

"Geelomin, I do not see him!"

The vampires thinned as they departed. The magai-powered light began to fade.

"Geelomin?" Thanon asked in a breathy, panicked voice.

"Go down," he said. "We will search. Now."

No. Please, no, he repeated over and over again as they made it to the ground and ran north.

CHAPTER TWENTY-SEVEN

Kalachi Desert Border – Ceru-Auradia Front Lines

Annalla slept inside the tent while Larron sat with Patrice out front. They watched her turn in early every night after enduring repeated magical beatings. At that point, Larron was close to knocking out Mage Hephestar or having the fairy fly him far away to put an end to their fruitless exercises. He would never do that—take her choice from her—but he desperately wanted to find some reasonable alternative.

"She's running out of options," Patrice said softly to him. "There will be no reason to keep trying when she is out of ideas."

He grunted. "Perhaps. At least this problem will mean a day or two off while she comes up with new things to try."

She chuckled under her breath, but her amusement ended too quickly. The kindly maternal figure she had embodied on their quest was still present, under the surface, beneath the grief. He hurt for his friend and wondered if she would ever find solace.

They sat in silence together, staring up into the starry night. Patrice took a breath as though to speak, but no words came. He heard her sigh deeply. She took another audible breath in.

"Larron," she said, then paused again.

He waited. She had something she wanted to broach with him, and she would come to the point in her own time.

"Larron, you need to watch her," she finally said.

"Who?" he asked. "Annalla? I will always watch out for her."

Patrice sighed and shook her head. Her muzzle tightened as she pursed her lips. "No. It's more than that. Larron, I see so much of myself in her."

He saw many common, positive qualities echoed between the two women, but he did not think those were to what she referred.

"She changed," Patrice said in an apparent change of subject, "after her memories returned. She withdrew from us, became distant with a wall of professionalism. We all assumed she simply had a lot to deal with. The memory of her parents' deaths on top of her responsibilities to her people would give anyone pause."

"Yes," he said. "We have had discussions around this. She wants space to focus on the war and her role as Protector, but she is not pushing us away any longer."

Her eyes glistened. "I'm glad you talked, and I hope it's enough." She swallowed. "I have lost everything."

He reached for her hands. "Patrice, I am—"

She cut him off. "No. Listen. I lost everything; everyone who means the most to me in this life. As much as I love you all, as much as I love my people, this life will never be as it was before. I have…one purpose left, and that is to end Kahnlair. I will see him dead, or I will die trying.

"She is the same, Larron. Annalla has one purpose, as she sees it, and she has sacrificed everyone who has ever been close to her for that purpose. She will not stop, and she will destroy herself to accomplish her mission. Give her a reason to want to live. You love her. I know you do. Don't be the next sacrifice she has to make. Don't force an eternity alone upon her."

"Patrice," he said with a gentle tilt of his head, "I would—" He stopped before finishing the thought, recognizing what she was saying. His lips pressed together in a line and he held his fingers to them, as though he physically held back the words.

"Die to protect her?" Patrice finished the sentence for him. "Without hesitation, I would have given my life to save my son. I will willingly go to my grave attempting to avenge his death. What I don't know is if I can live without him."

She glanced up and stared into his eyes. "I'm free to make this choice. Annalla doesn't have the same freedom. Her life has been turmoil and duty. Her friends have been in her life for mere months, and they could leave as quickly. All I'm asking is for you to be there for her."

Larron, too, had responsibilities. To his brother, his people. He had also promised to help her hold to her oath. None of those responsibilities required his survival, but if she was immortal and he died, he likely doomed her to a never-ending obligation.

"I promise you," he told her, squeezing her hand, "I will keep in mind all you have shared."

Patrice visibly strained to swallow. "Good. I don't want to lose any of you either."

***

Annalla grit her teeth against a groan. She hurt. The ache permeated from her skin down to her bones and across every limb and muscle. Mage Sholdray told her the repeated healings had diminishing returns based on the frequency required. The strain placed on her body also drained her essentially. She would need to take multiple rest days soon, regardless of making progress or not.

The lack of progress against the force attacks frustrated her. It felt like there was something obvious she was missing, but whatever that something *was* continued to elude her. *Today,* she thought. *Today will be the last attempt for a while.* If nothing came from the attempts, she needed time to think.

She took a deep breath and let it out with a dejected sigh.

"Heh." Patrice snorted where she sat on her cot. "You can take an extra day off, you know."

Annalla laughed. "Tomorrow. I will let this go for a few days if nothing jolts loose today." She chewed on her lip in frustration. "I just wish we could have found some answer. I cannot fly over enemy forces when this is a threat to my safety."

Patrice patted her forearm. "I know," she whispered. "We'll think of something."

"Protector," Karlo called from outside the tent, "the magai are ready to depart."

"We will be out in a moment," she said.

Zara, of course, had already left for her morning patrol check-ins. Annalla and Patrice finished cleaning up and dressing in quick order. They joined Karlo and Larron outside and began the short walk to where Karlo's unit waited.

"Karlo," Annalla asked, glancing over at the fairy captain, "why is Crastus not assigned to me?"

The former school dean chuckled. "The privilege of rank," he said. "Crastus was returned to command of his guard unit and the honor of serving you has fallen to me and mine." Tongue in cheek, he continued. "Unless you wish his company for other reasons, Protector."

Annalla rolled her eyes dramatically and did not dignify

the comment with a response.

"What are you thinking of trying today?" Larron asked, changing the subject.

He wore his half of the flying harness, but Karlo carried him. When her injuries started slowing her, he asked Karlo to help to minimize the strain on her.

She gave him a knowing, slightly teasing smile. "You will be happy to note, I want to work with the bag again today," she told him, rubbing her eyes. "I feel like I have lost ground with this one, so I want to go back to the start."

Without turning her head, she sensed the weight of his eyes staring at her. When she stole a glance over, she noted concern, sympathy, and understanding in his gaze. He restrained himself from reaching out, but she felt the intent of a hug regardless and a corresponding flip in her stomach. His presence continued to impact her, despite their agreement of distance.

"You will find a solution," he said with complete confidence. "We have time before we reach the desert city Kahnlair claimed."

He meant every word. While she doubted herself and wondered if they would ever find an answer, Larron believed. The day before, he'd said as much to his brother when they'd discussed strategy. Zeris, who arrived with his bonded and additional Derou troops about a week prior, had asked about alternative tactics now that Kahnlair had learned to counter the use of an essential with the fairy targeting his magai.

Unless she could figure it out though, they were relegated to relying on flights of fairy with a combat magai carried along. The hope was that they could work in concert to break an enemy's shield and eliminate them. Not a bad plan, especially if Kahnlair was not strengthening his magai during a battle. They remained overpowered, even without his direct aid, but were closer in strength, at least.

"I'm off," Patrice said and closed in for a hug. "Have fun with your flying."

She laughed, as her friend intended. "We will. See you later."

Their flight was not long, they simply moved to a safe distance in the mornings and let the army move away from them as they embarked. Once settled in an open area, Karlo and the others helped her set up her bag, which earned a relieved sigh from both magai companions.

"Working with the bag again?" Hephestar asked. "What kind of attacks are you looking for today?"

"I want to go back to what we did the first few days with force," she told him. "I felt nearer to an answer then than I do now. Start with some directional demonstrations and we will go from there."

An hour later, Annalla was floating the bag into the air for Hephestar to attack. She was no closer to breaking through whatever mental block had her unable to find a solution. *If a solution exists,* she muttered mentally and cracked her neck.

"Anything?" the combat mage asked.

Annalla growled low in her throat. "No." She ran her hands through her hair and pulled at the strands.

Larron walked over to stand in front of her. He reached up and placed his hands over hers, gentling them down to her sides before reaching back up to smooth her hair. He frowned. "You ruined your braid."

She snorted and rolled her eyes. "You thought it was ruined from the start."

His lips twitched in a smirk. "You know me so well."

"Larron." She said his name. Two syllables. The first came out exasperated, the second conveyed exhaustion. She wanted to cry in frustration.

"Love, talk through what is happening." He trailed his hands down her arms. "Let us help you."

Annalla forced herself to ignore and dismiss the term of endearment. "Okay." She blew out a breath and looked out over his shoulder, trying to organize her thoughts. "I…" she stumbled over the words and tilted her head. "What is that?"

He shifted to stand at her side, his left hand slid to and lingered on her back. His eyes narrowed as he stared into the distance. A smile spread across his face as he glanced toward her and again to the east.

"Your prince is here," he said with a growing grin.

Her heart thudded. "What?"

His smile faded at her apparent confusion. "Our reinforcements. We were expecting them anytime over the last few days." He snapped, a look of realization on his face. "Right. You missed that meeting. Messengers reported Prince Darrin and the forces from the east were close."

Karlo gestured at his group and half the fairy took to the sky, heading for the approaching dots in the distance.

Annalla turned her head toward Larron, a genuine smile stretching her cheeks. "Marto and Nurtik?"

"Both came with." He shared her grin. "They also picked up Oromaer's force on the Nierda River, including Geelomin, Bealaras, and Thanon."

Her eyes watered and she choked up. She put a hand to her chest, surprised at the overwhelming emotions tumbling through her. The Derou were the closest she had to family. She had grown closer to them than to her parents at that point. Childhood was so far removed from that day, and responsibilities had always lingered between them.

"We will wait for them," she said decisively.

At her words, Karlo bowed his head and sent another two fairy soldiers in the direction the army left. They were likely assigned to inform the other leaders of both the arrival of

Darrin's forces as well as their own delayed return.

"So?" Larron said to her when they settled onto the ground to wait.

Her brow furrowed. "*So?*" she asked in turn, unsure of what he sought.

He gave her a cheeky grin and waved at the bag of dirt. "We have plenty of time now. Talk to us about what you are thinking regarding the force strikes, and maybe we can come up with something together."

Right, she thought, *the problem at hand.*

"You found a solution for energy strikes, even though it was not immediate," Hephestar said. "Where are you running into trouble with force? What's the difference?"

"Good thinking." Annalla bit the inside of her cheek as she considered his questions. "Fire was easy, and energy I sensed through the fire element. The problem, in that case, was that I had no control at the beginning."

"And with force?" he asked.

She threw up her hands. "I cannot even feel it. I thought I would be able to sense whatever power is at work through at least one of the elements."

"You were hoping you would sense it through the air element because that is how you move objects yourself," Larron said, following her logic.

Annalla nodded and grimaced.

Karlo frowned over at the bag with which she practiced as he picked at his fingernails with one of his daggers. "Do you sense the force when he attacks the bag?"

"No," she said with a slow blink. "Nothing. I definitely feel the hit when it happens, to me or the bag, but not whatever is doing the hitting."

"Then why did you switch back to the bag today?" He pointed at their target with the dagger.

She reached her arm up and around to scratch at the

back of her head. "I don't know."

"Something must be different," Larron said. "Hephestar, can you hit the bag again? Annalla, describe to us what you sense as he does."

Karlo flew over to set up the bag, and Hephestar struck when he was at a safe distance.

"I see and hear it being hit," she said, "but nothing leading up to the impact."

"Only see and hear?" Hephestar asked.

"*Yes*," she drew out the word as a thought occurred to her. "I experience the sequence of events just like everyone else. Could you hit it again while I float it?"

He nodded, and Annalla raised the bag using her power, letting it hover a few feet high. The strike hit as always, ripping the target from her gentle hold and sending it shooting backward.

"Anything different?" Hephestar asked.

"It feels like you would expect if someone were to punch a bag out of your hands."

"But you feel the bag get hit?" Karlo asked.

She shook her head. "No. I feel it ripped from my hold."

Larron threw aside a piece of grass he had been twirling in his fingers while lounging and sat up straight. He met and held her eyes as a triumphant smile spread across his face. "You feel the force working against your hold?"

"Yes."

"Like you are holding it in your hand and Hephestar physically strikes it. The same feeling?"

Annalla's eyes widened with excitement. "Yes." She smiled back.

"Can you hold the bag tighter?" he asked, knowing the answer.

She turned to Hephestar. "One more time?"

This time, when she floated the bag into the air, her

mental grip firmed like steel. She held the cloth and the dirt within and planted them in place within her mind. Hephestar took his mage stance, calmly exhaled, and struck. The attack hit with an audible *whoomp*, but the bag held. All their heads whipped around to stare at her.

"You did it!" Hephestar said. "How?"

"Heh, opposing forces," she said, simplifying the fact that she would need to hold something in place to shield herself from a force strike. She stopped to meet and hold the eyes of the two magai in turn. "The *how* needs to go no further than those of us here. I need everyone, especially Kahnlair and his magai, to think I am neutralizing the energy behind these strikes the same way I do the others."

Hephestar held up a hand. "You have my word."

"I have no reason to object," Sholdray said. "Your health is my concern."

"Good," she said, "because I have to meet force with force. It is going to be draining if they attack me in unison while Kahnlair is amplifying them."

"How draining?" Larron asked, unamused.

"Survivable as long as I can intercept," she said, "My main concern would be the impact on my ability to contribute offensively in the field. The more hits I deflect, the less power I have available to attack. I also cannot protect all of me if I want to be able to see and contribute to the fighting."

"You want them to think attacking you is a waste of their time and energy." Hephestar nodded in thought. "His magai will start to hide rather than take the risk of attacking when you fly over."

"Exactly, which is why—as far as everyone else is concerned—I found a way to neutralize force with my essence as well."

"Start pulling shields," Larron told her. "Ease into it, but start using those in your floating mass of weaponry. The shields will provide a better surface upon which to counter the mage strikes."

That was by no means the perfect solution she hoped for, but they could make it work. She had an entire army backing her. The army was why she'd requested help from the sanctuaries, and it would help her reach Kahnlair to end the conflict. She only needed to rely on them and not try to do everything herself.

"It looks like they are setting down for a shift change," Karlo said and pointed his dagger once more, that time toward the east where the dots had grown to distinct structures being carried by hundreds of fairy each. "Should we go meet your friends?"

"Yes," she said with a smile and accepted Larron's hand helping her to her feet.

CHAPTER TWENTY-EIGHT

Kalachi Desert Border – Ceru-Auradia Front Lines

By the time they approached the mass of people, it looked to Larron's eyes like the group was starting to pack up again. People filtered toward and into the multitude of spindly wooden structures spread across the rocky terrain. The army he traveled with was larger than that group, but the magnitude of the forces spread before him, knowing they had traveled from the other side of the continent, carried on the wings of the fairy, was astounding. People. Equipment. Supplies.

A group waved from in front of the leading structure, and Karlo began a gliding descent, circling around to land before them. Once they touched down, the group walked over to greet them. Larron smiled as he waited for Karlo to finish disconnecting the final harness connections.

"Oromaer!" He raised a hand in greeting toward his long-time friend.

Before he responded, Annalla called out. "Darrin, you look terrible!"

Darrin stopped, and the way he rolled his head and sagged his shoulders told Larron that was not the first time he had been told as much. Oromaer barked out a laugh. He patted the fairy prince on the shoulder and murmured something to him as he passed.

Oromaer faced their group again, standing at Darrin's side. "Larron. Annalla. It is good to see you both again. You are not the first to point out to the fairy how they are pushing themselves too hard." He grimaced and continued. "I am afraid the tardiness is our fault, in part. They did not anticipate carrying additional people from the Palonian."

"We'd be exhausted regardless," Darrin said dryly.

"They at least rested for a few days. Though, we did run into some trouble with a vampire raid not two nights ago."

Larron grinned at the easy interplay between the two but came up short when his gaze passed over Annalla. He snapped his head back to her. She was biting her lip and squinting at the closest structure. "No," he said, holding up a hand as though he stood in front of a horse ready to bolt.

"What?" She looked offended.

"I see you assessing those." He gestured in the general direction. "Annalla, they are carrying thousands of people and all of their equipment."

"Which is less than last time," she pointed out in a perfectly reasonable voice.

He felt less reasonable with every passing moment. "That was across a river, and you were down for days. The army is hours away."

"That must be Annalla," a familiar voice said. "She is the only other person who can cause such irritation in our steady commander."

"Thanon!" Annalla lit up and ran to hug her friend. "I missed you." She held him at arm's length and looked past him to where Geelomin stood. "You too, Geelomin. Where is Bealaras?"

Their smiles faded and Larron's heart dipped to his

stomach.

Geelomin held up his hands. "He was injured during the attack," he said. "Mage Gregry said he will be fine, but the healers are also overworked, so the healing is taking place in stages. His injuries remain fragile, so the healers ordered him to stay in his cot."

Annalla had a hand pressed to her chest. "I thought you were going to tell me he was dead."

"It was close," Geelomin told them. "A vampire had him, nearly beyond our range. Had Fremya not followed on the ground—against orders—he would not be with us today. She shot the vampire out of the sky, and they both fell—far. He was broken when we found him."

"I can take a look at him," Sholdray said, "and any others who need help. I haven't done much healing in the last few days."

"I'm certain the magai with us will appreciate the help," Darrin said and held out a guiding arm. "I'll show you to them."

As Darrin led the healer mage away, Geelomin faced Larron once more. "So, what are you opposed to Annalla doing?"

She sighed and answered for him. "He thinks I was going to carry the platforms for the fairy."

"You were not?" he asked.

At the same time, Thanon asked, "You can do that?"

"Yes," she said to Thanon.

"No," Larron said at the same time.

They stared at each other a moment before Annalla's eyes softened and a smile tugged at her lips. Thanon laughed and threw an arm around her shoulders.

"I *can*," she told them both, "but I was only considering how I might *help* the fairy with their burden. I do not need to do all the work to lend a hand."

Larron understood that, and he *knew* she would not risk

her well-being by overextending. While she was impulsive at times, she thought through issues that might impact her oath.

"There is a long road before us, Annalla," he told her. "The demands placed upon you are only going to grow and compound."

She reached up and took hold of Thanon's hand, but her words were for Larron. "I know. It is going to be a balancing act, and I am going to get the balance wrong. We must hope I get it right *enough*."

***

Annalla leaned back in one of the cots in the flying pavilion. They were converting the structures to mobile healing wards. The medically trained fairy would be responsible for carrying them, and the injured would be installed in one with a set of guards. Those people would remain behind with healers until they recovered enough to travel, and then that pavilion would rejoin the army. Unused pavilions became filled with supplies to free up additional mounts.

The empty pavilion they lounged In would be the first one used for healing, and Annalla Invited her friends there for a reunion supper while the leaders held another meeting. Larron, Tyrus, and Nurtik were all attending that meeting with Darrin and Zara. Marto skipped it with her, and so did Patrice. The three of them relaxed with Geelomin, Thanon, and Bealaras.

Bealaras was doing much better since receiving steady treatment from additional healer magai. He was on an exercise regimen to regain the strength lost with the damage his body had taken. The slow progress of those exercises was making him as irritable as Annalla had ever seen the usually serene elf.

"I am surprised my captors allowed me out of bed rest," he said grumpily.

"Ha!" She laughed as he flopped down into an adjacent

cot. "I have some influence here."

"So we noticed," he said. "Would you care to fill the three of us in?"

She shrugged. "The fairy have one essential each generation, and I am she. We used to be the only ones able to leave the sanctuaries. My family found themselves cornered at the beginning of the war, and my mother used her abilities to send me to Aryanna.

"Coming back to Elaria landed me in the situation in which you all found me." She held out a hand. "Yes, there is more to the story, but I do not want to talk about that now."

"Very well." Geelomin leaned against a post. "Then allow me to say 'thank you.' Thank you for saving our home and rescuing Zeris. None of the Derou will ever be able to repay you for your help in our time of need."

Annalla grimaced, uncomfortable with the demonstrative gratitude. "I took a chance," she said. "There was no guarantee I would succeed."

"Aww," Thanon gushed. "She is blushing."

The group spent the next few minutes enjoying her discomfort, taking time to laugh and remind themselves the others were still alive.

"Maybe you disagree, Patrice," she said as they settled once more, "but I feel like we are missing something. Kahnlair is not fighting for any ground. Other than the battle at the river, we are moving through without opposition, and it bothers me."

"The lack of more attacks could be because the windani are still far to the north," Patrice said.

"Yeah," Annalla said. "Why is that?"

"They are roaming the Claws now," Geelomin said. "The Derou or the Palonian are the most likely targets. Kahnlair may have given them orders to attack either one."

"Orders," Patrice said with a snap. "When my son—"

She stuttered to a stop, and both Annalla and Marto

reached for her hands. She squeezed, and Annalla visibly witnessed her balling up her grief and burying it deep within. Her eyes watered, but no tears fell.

With a deep breath, she continued. "One of the last irimoten guards to escape the base in the Karasis Mountains overheard the windani. He told of how they talked about Kahnlair ordering them north and seeking out the irimoten strongholds, no matter how much it cost them.

"The guard said it sounded like the creature was complaining, and that its tone implied it knew where the escape tunnels were. He *swore* the windani was angry and intentionally defying orders. Some of the irimoten think they're being compelled in some way to obey his orders."

"To clarify, you mean not by choice?" Marto asked her.

Patrice shrugged and raised her eyebrows. "It's a theory."

Annalla considered her position with the fairy. "Blood and power connections matter in Elaria. A leader's submission could potentially carry over to his subordinates."

Understanding spread across Geelomin's face. "Like our connection to the Woodlands."

She nodded. "And the fairy connection to the sanctuaries."

"I know our bonds are more limited because we remain in smaller, more isolated groups," Patrice said, "but even the elves are not compelled to obey."

Geelomin lifted a shoulder. "Submission and control are not as integral to elven societal structure as they are within our counterparts. My understanding is that strength allows for disobedience, but those who are weaker are beholden to their masters."

"But the implication is that they are compelled to follow Kahnlair's orders, not their leader's," Bealaras noted.

Patrice slowly shook her head. "It's simply a theory

floating around among the irimoten. As is"—she stared down Annalla—"a theory that *you* are the reason he's allowing us easy access to his territory."

All her friends sat up straighter.

"What do you mean?" Thanon asked.

"Apparently," Patrice said, settling in to share irimoten gossip, "before the fairy arrived, Morena intercepted some orders to Kahnlair's troops. They received instructions to watch for the 'powerful winged woman.' He wanted her brought to him rather than killed. At the time, they thought the description might have referred to Morena, but..."

"But..." Geelomin echoed.

Scanning their faces, Annalla saw pinched and worried expressions. Bodies held tense, ready to act against any threat to her. Their behavior was sweet but unnecessary.

"Good," she said, earning a few raised eyebrows. "No, seriously. Good."

"Annalla," Geelomin said patiently, "you are powerful. If Kahnlair wants you, there is something we are overlooking."

She waved a hand. "It changes nothing. We have this one opportunity to press our advantage and eliminate him. Any delay sacrifices whatever momentum we gained with the emergence of the fairy. Whether or not he has some agenda concerning me makes no difference other than allowing us to reach him with greater numbers than we could otherwise."

"It might change nothing about how the army proceeds, but his attention does matter," Marto said as he stood and crutched over to her. "This man possesses magic beyond any the magai have known, even those as strong as Mage Gregry."

"So, what do you suggest?"

"That," he said as his shoulders sagged, "I don't know."

"You remain cautious," Patrice said. "Don't go off on your own. Ensure a fairy unit always has eyes on you. I know they can't remain with you, but they can be nearby."

"When we find Kahnlair," Thanon said as he too stood, "and we will reach him. You do not face him alone. That may be the exact confrontation he is hoping for."

Annalla gave no response to that and schooled her expression. A direct confrontation with Kahnlair was exactly what she wanted while the allied army distracted his army and magai. Such a situation was the best she dared hope for. Larron would have seen the intent in her features, but no one present had the bond necessary to see through her.

"I promise," she told them, meeting the eyes of each of her friends in turn, "I will take no unnecessary risks." And she wouldn't. "But we are at war."

"And there are no guarantees," Geelomin finished her thought.

Thanon slapped his knees as he pushed himself to his feet too. "Well," he said, "perhaps we can break whatever compulsion he has over his minions and it will not matter."

Everyone stopped and stared at him, dumbfounded.

Annalla huffed out a laugh. "Oh, how I missed your optimism, my friend," she said and drew him into a hug.

CHAPTER TWENTY-NINE

Kalachi Desert – Ceru-Auradia Front Lines

Horns sounded, waking Annalla from a fitful sleep. Their quiet travel ended when they entered the grasslands at the edge of the desert. The last week had been filled with frequent attacks and depressing discoveries as they traversed the lands holding most of Kahnlair's former work and supply camps. Prisoners held in those camps were found murdered, but only after the retreating guards joined forces to attack the traveling army.

Those were not surprise attacks. They knew the enemy was there, waiting for them. Unfortunately, there was little they could do to avoid the confrontations. Their destination was known, and sneaking their full might in from another direction would be impossible, not even taking into consideration the time required to try. Kahnlair was throwing small units against them from advantageous positions and letting them do as much damage as possible before they fell. They became sacrifices to his will, fighting to the death and leaving more emotional destruction in their wake.

Annalla groaned as she rolled out of her bedding and pulled on her boots from the ground.

"Need some help?" Patrice asked dryly from where she stood, buckling her dagger belts.

"Ha. Funny." She finished with her shoes and rolled to her feet. "We cannot keep up this pace if they attack every night. There is no rest."

"I think that's the point," her friend said as she led them out into the cold of the open air. "Stay safe, Annalla."

As Patrice sprinted off, Annalla rose into the air and headed for the main fairy line. After the first such confrontation, they held back in a defensive perimeter rather than move forward to attack. It kept vampires from striking the ground forces and allowed those troops to focus on their own battle. Jarin and Annalla fought on opposite sides, right or left of center, to try to balance and spread their influence.

"Hold fire! Hold fire!" Annalla could not tell where the call originated, but it spread up and down the line.

"What is it?" she asked Karlo when she arrived at his side. They usually wasted no time eliminating enemy troops before they closed in to present a risk to allied soldiers.

Hovering, he gestured at the humans running toward the defenders. She blinked and squinted down, confirming her initial assessment. The men held no weapons.

"We think they're escaped prisoners," Karlo said. "They're trying to give them time to reach safety before their pursuers catch up."

Not all would make it. The prisoners were injured and stumbling, while those chasing were armed, armored, and gaining quickly. She eyed the lines and made an assessment.

"Cover me and whistle for a ground guard," she said and dropped below.

An infantry unit moved to surround her while Karlo's people circled above. While the guards were not technically necessary, it was the smarter move. She could have executed her plan from the air, but using earth was always easier while in contact with the ground, and it saved energy if she also dove into the element mentally. Those factors lowered her defenses, so she added to them by leveraging those around her. After days of increased combat and decreased sleep, she wanted to preserve her strength as much as possible.

Annalla already placed the position of her attack in her mind, estimating how far each side would run by the time she acted. Her feet touched down, and she kneeled, putting her hands against the dry ground.

Her power reached for examples of local seeds, roots, and shoots, and a line of enormous trunks erupted amid clusters of woody shrubs. Though she had understood something of their general size, the trees still came as a shock. Caps of branches and leaves topped massive, bulky trunks much larger than appeared necessary for the smaller canopy. Handfuls of people hurled into the air with each full-grown sapling while the rest stumbled through the new underbrush.

Some of the fleeing prisoners faltered as the ground shook beneath the impact of her power, but most kept their feet and carried on. Annalla rose to see the lines close up around the prisoners as support personnel helped the escapees move away. The enemy recovered, most of them, and continued their charge, plowing into the reformed defenders.

Arrows arched over to strike the next wave and fairy shot down at targets visible from above. Annalla scanned the skies along with other assigned fairy for any sign of vampire support. More air support peeled off to aid the battle below with every moment that passed without sighting their aerial opponents.

"It explains how prisoners escaped from this camp," Karlo said as he paused beside her as the fight waned.

She nodded. "Kahnlair either did not leave as many guards behind here, or the prisoners were able to overcome and eliminate a good portion of them."

He gave her a skeptical grimace at the latter option.

"Yeah." She frowned. "I do not believe that one either."

Karlo laughed and dipped his head. He caught sight of something that had him giving a jerk of his chin in that direction. "It looks like you're wanted."

Annalla glanced down to see Argent and Garrett waving her over.

Karlo shooed her away. "This is under control."

She took him at his word and headed back to the ground. By the time she joined the two kings, Commander Walsh and Captain Lesyon stood at the sides of their monarchs. Lesyon scanned the air, looking for someone or something, but he shifted to face her when she arrived.

"This is wrong," Walsh said without preamble.

"What is?" Argent asked.

Walsh's lips tightened. He threw a hand toward the battle. "This. All of this right now. The entire engagement is full of mistakes, and Kahnlair does not make this many mistakes."

"Obvious mistakes, too," Lesyon said in agreement.

"Exactly!" Walsh said, becoming more agitated. "For the last week, he has effectively thrown some of his least valuable tools against us, diminishing our resources and leaving camps filled with murdered prisoners for us to find. What happened here? Did half of his guards rebel?"

Annalla felt her stomach twist into a knot. "You think this a trap?" She turned her head toward the dwindling fighting.

"Yes." He ran a hand up over his face and through his hair, making it stick up at odd angles. "But for my life, I can't—"

"What?" Garrett asked when Walsh cut his words short. "What is it?"

Walsh paled and his already light skin became chalk white. "The prisoners. Where are the escaped prisoners?"

"The new medic pavilion," Lesyon said as the two of them turned together and started running, leaving Argent and Garrett behind.

Annalla did not hesitate or waste time running. She shot into the air and over their heads. Her fear spiked with her pulse and she tasted bile when a shrill whistle sounded ahead. The emergency alert call cut short mid-note.

She landed to carnage. The body of a healer mage lay broken in a spreading pool of blood. Above, the guardrail from the third floor was busted as though someone had been thrown through. Annalla rushed into the structure, sword in hand. She passed more bodies, ignoring them and continuing forward.

Lamps swung from the support beams between cots and hammocks. Shadows swayed, highlighting the macabre scene punctuated by low, pained moans.

A blade flashed from her right. She grabbed the wrist holding it as she dodged, noting the clothing dirty with grime and crusted blood. He was dressed like a prisoner and coated in damning evidence. With her hold on his wrist, she broke his arm over her knee, slammed her elbow into his face to break his nose, and kicked out to destroy his knee. The man dropped to the ground shrieking, and she kept going.

Another man struck at her, and she made his tattered clothes for a lie. Not threadbare, they had been torn and dirtied intentionally. The bruising on his face was superficial and the cuts elsewhere were minor. Everything was staged. Well enough to bring them into the heart of the camp, but not enough for the scrutiny that would come after a battle.

His clumsy attack, effective against distracted healers trying to help him, was no threat to her. She dispatched him with a flick of her blade and moved on to the next. They came, creeping through the dark like vermin, and she exterminated them as such. One after another. Squash, squash, squash.

"Help me." The terrified voice came from the deeper

shadows beneath a cot ahead to her left. "Help me."

A child. She noted the age when she approached. He was scared but had enough awareness to differentiate her from the attackers. Below, she heard guards entering the structure. Her backup had arrived. They would have reached the first man by now.

"Go down," she told the boy. "Go now and keep your hands in the air so they do not mistake you. Help is on the way."

His jaw trembled as he crawled out of his hiding place. She took up a protective position and waited until he rose and settled. "Be careful," he whispered before he fled.

Annalla moved on, heading up another level. She found an injured human holding off four attackers with a short sword. He looked like a Ceru soldier, and six people huddled behind him. Three magai, one unconscious fairy, and the other two appeared to be Ceru soldiers as well, either injured or dead. One of the enemies lashed out, and another slash opened the man's pant leg, drawing blood, as he shifted to avoid that strike while parrying one from another.

She rushed forward, taking advantage of the distraction provided by their attack. With a quick jab, she punctured the heart of the first man with her blade, spinning as he fell to slice across the back of the second. The third went down from a pommel hit to the back of his head. By the time they were down, the fourth moved to defend. The effort was too late. His sword was not even up by the time she scored a cut across his throat.

It took seconds, and the startled survivors stood frozen a moment before their defender sank to his knees, breathing out a stuttered breath of relief.

"Thank you," he said. "We couldn't stop them."

"Come over here," one of the magai shifted to his side and tried to get him to lie down. "You need treatment."

Annalla shook her head. "You are not safe here. Can you carry them?" she asked, gesturing at the unconscious figures.

"We can." The soldier nodded as the healers muttered exasperatedly behind him.

She ignored the healers. "Good. Go," she ordered and moved on.

Their victims fought back—enough of the false prisoners were already dead to tell her such. It appeared the existing patients and the support medics had been the primary active defenders. The only magai they left with the injured were healers. Despite living in a war zone for decades, most of them had no training to defend themselves.

Annalla turned another corner and felt her breath catch. She sprinted forward and dropped to her knees beside the prone figure. His face was turned toward her. Old. Gray hair and a thin wiry frame, his clothes bagged around him.

"No," she whispered, light-headed. "Please, no."

Steps shuffled behind her, creeping forward. Her blood ran cold. The tears welling in her eyes dried beneath the onslaught of her rage. She turned her head, slowly, and stared down the man preparing to stab her in the back as she held an old man who had been kind to her, who had become her friend in so short a time.

The attacker jerked into motion, striking, attempting to reach her before she could counter. The attempt was wasted. She had more weapons at her disposal than the sword lying forgotten at her side. After one step, no more, he burst into a pillar of flame. He shrieked and ran, batting at himself and bouncing off support beams as he went. His screams rang in her ears long after he disappeared.

"Annalla," a voice called to her from beyond the abyss. A hand reached out.

The flames were gone; the darkness returned. Her focus

shifted a fraction to the side. Green eyes full of concern stared.

"They killed Gregry," she whispered and took a deep breath. The tears returned and her vision blurred. "He did nothing but heal, and they killed him."

***

Larron ran toward the medic pavilion, but he was well behind the initial response. He pushed through the crowd, coming out into an open space where commanders directed a rescue effort. Someone shrieked within and he saw the flicker of flames. A figure ran out, crashing violently through the thin rail to fall to the ground, dead.

The frightening level of control displayed—to burn the man but prevent the fire from catching on anything else—sent a shiver down Larron's spine. He hurried toward someone directing people in and around the structure. Some headed for the still-burning corpse.

"Has the area been secured?" he asked.

"Yes, sir," he said, "but teams are still securing the floors of the structure."

"Keep everyone else out for now," Larron ordered as he rushed inside.

He hurried to the fourth level, from where the burning man fell. A ring of people stood frozen, staring toward where Annalla knelt. Her gaze was unfocused and glassy-eyed, but furious. There was no doubt in anyone's mind you faced your death if you breathed wrong.

Larron moved forward and noticed the face of the mage lying dead behind her. *Oh, my love,* he thought. *So much loss. Patrice is right.*

"Annalla." He knelt before her and held out a hand.

Blue eyes full of pain shifted to meet his. "They killed Gregry." Focus returned, and with it came tears. "He did nothing but heal, and they killed him."

Annalla collapsed against him and buried her face in his chest, silently crying. "It's all my fault," she stuttered. "They killed them all, and I helped them do it. I helped them do it, Larron."

"No," he said. "*Shh*, no. None of this is your fault or doing."

She raised her head, looking so defeated. "I helped them. If I had not helped them on the field with their fake escape... I killed him."

Larron felt his heart breaking for her. "You made the right decision; the only decision."

"I should have left them."

"We should have assigned additional guards to the prisoners," he told her, "and that failure will haunt every leader among us. But helping them escape will always be the right answer, Annalla. You are a defender and protector in more than title alone."

"Gregry is dead," she said bitterly, not believing his words.

Larron sighed. "This place was nearly empty tonight. His power, his work here, left fewer victims for this deception. He saved countless people in his life, and he saved more tonight with his mere presence. He died a hero, and he would not want you to become less of one for your grief of losing him."

Annalla tightened her lips, shook her head, and turned her face away from him. *Stubborn,* he thought, but considered his words enough for now. She needed time.

She sat up, discreetly wiping her eyes as she shifted. Taking a deep breath, she cleared her throat and spoke roughly, still staring out over Mage Gregry's body. "Is everything secured?"

A human off to the side gave him a slow nod. Before Larron could answer her, Oromaer stepped into that section of the structure. He took in the scene: dead healers, Annalla sitting and staring blankly, and Larron crouched awkwardly at her side. His lips pursed, and he took a step forward.

"The soldiers have everyone in custody who is alive," he said to them both. "Let us depart so the fallen can be taken care of."

He held out a hand to Annalla, helping her to her feet when she took it. Smooth as ever, Oromaer kept a gentle hold of her hand and positioned himself so they linked arms as he escorted her through the dimly lit passages and down to the ground level. They remained quiet on the descent, with Larron trailing in their wake.

"He was dying," Oromaer finally said as they moved out into the open night. "Gregry was. He told me before we left the Palonian that his organs were beginning to fail. The injured had not made it to us last year—lost with the barges—so he wanted to join us for our journey and help as many as he could in his time remaining."

Annalla leaned away from him and gave him a flat, raised eyebrow look. To Larron's eye, it said, 'and that makes any of this better?'

Oromaer must have read something similar in her face. He stopped and turned to her. His free hand gently smoothed her hair down and stopped to rest holding her cheek. "Gregry's presence here was his choice. What happened tonight? This is war. Nothing about this is right or okay, but he made a difference with us, as he intended, as was his final wish."

"And what is your wish?" she asked him. "What is it you hope to achieve here?"

"That by my actions, I can help to free my son from this war," he said. "Even our immortality is not forever. We live and we fight for the generations to follow. Always." He shifted his hands, placing both on her shoulders and giving a comforting squeeze. "Rest, even if you cannot sleep. Both of you." He shot a parting glance at Larron.

They stood in silence, watching Oromaer walk away. When he was no longer in sight, Annalla twisted her lips into a wry grimace. "He was including me in the 'generations to follow' comment, wasn't he?"

"Yes, but do not look too deeply into it." He forced a smirk. "He includes me in the statement as well."

Head still hanging heavily on her shoulders, she raised a questioning eyebrow.

Larron shrugged. "Elven generations are complicated."

CHAPTER THIRTY

Kalachi Desert – Ceru-Auradia Front Lines

"Are you certain?" Larron asked Argent, standing in front of him, holding a flying harness.

Argent was too dignified to roll his eyes, but he gave Larron a blank stare. He took the harness and held up the tangle of leather with a question on his face. Larron reached out to help him into the straps for his pending flight.

A day after the deception where they lost twelve healers and twenty of the injured who had still been receiving treatment, a fairy patrol had returned with news of another camp ahead. An elf scout went out with them the following morning to scout from a safe and undetectable distance. Two days away from the main army, they were still in camp.

Early summer produce was available, if a little under ripe, and Kahnlair's people whipped and drove their prisoners to bring in as much of a crop as possible. The chances those prisoners knew how close the army was were slim unless someone recently taken had been added to their numbers. They would die, likely the next day, not knowing help was near.

Zara had decided there was no reason to allow those

murders to proceed as planned. They possessed the location and basic scouting of the area, and they had the means to do something about the situation. Larron was certain Annalla had no direct influence on Zara's position—he had remained with her all that first night to ensure she slept as soundly as possible—but he was less certain of indirect influence. Regardless of her influence or lack thereof, Darrin agreed with Zara that the army needed a victory. The deception used by Kahnlair had hit straight to the heart. After the hope of the fairy's arrival and Zeris' rescue, using prisoners against them had been especially heinous and devastating.

"I can go," Larron said. "I have made this run before."

"No," Argent said. "First, any prisoners are more likely to recognize me or Lesyon than they are you. Second, we have plenty of soldiers on the mission already, including Jarin. And third, you will remain safe here where your bonded will not worry over you while she has responsibilities elsewhere."

For the first time in centuries, Larron's patience waned in the face of overwhelming frustration. He was an elf and a leader among his people. He was one of the most skilled sword masters in known history. He was valuable, useful, and skilled in his own right. Larron of the Derou did not exist solely for the benefit and consideration of another person.

Larron sighed and grit his teeth. "Very well."

Argent chuckled. "Is my daughter any less important for remaining within the Auradian Heartwood?"

"I am not the heir, Argent," he said. "The lives of the Derou do not depend on my survival."

"No? What of those of the fairy?" Argent shook his head at the blank look spread across Larron's face at the last statement. He waved him off. "You do not need to share details. We elves know well enough that titles in Elaria are not without obligation and connection."

Larron swallowed thickly and looked out over the

horizon. "When Zeris rose, before he found Tralie and before Erro was born, times came when he had to leave the Woodland. He waited patiently for me to return and kept his travel as brief as possible. I chafed. I ached. I am not made for inaction." He paused. "And I had no compunction about leaving Zeris to endure what I could not."

"Zeris loves his life." Argent smirked at him. "He is content within the Derou, and he understands that you are not. I believe your fairy understands this too. No one is holding you here, Larron. We are assessing and utilizing our resources as best we can, and you are not needed on this mission." His smile grew. "No matter how you worry over her leaving your side."

Larron ran a hand down his face. "You make me sound so…"

"Young?" he said. "In love?"

"Impulsive and selfish."

"They are not so far removed as you might think."

"Come here." Larron took back the harness and started explaining it. "She will drop down before the attack to unhook the harness, and you will need to hold on to her. Be prepared to roll when she releases you. Plan on it being like falling from a horse and a second-floor landing at the same time."

Argent nodded, taking in every word.

"Prepare yourself for the fire," he said. "It is…beyond anything you have experienced thus far, especially because of the proximity. Do not get in her way, keep her safe, and save as many as you can. The fairy are right: we need this victory."

"We will do this, and then Annalla and Jarin can rest," he said, resting a hand on Larron's shoulder. "The Kalachi will not be kind or easy on us after."

No, Larron thought. *The desert and Kahnlair both will do their best to weaken and drain us with every step taken toward our opposition's stronghold.*

***

"This is highly disconcerting," Argent said as they soared so high in the sky that the landscape far below was a blur. "Do not misunderstand me, I find flying to be an exhilarating experience, but I much prefer flying with the harness connected."

"Even if you slip," she said, "I have plenty of time to catch you."

His grip on her armor tightened. "Let us not speak of falling, please."

She couldn't resist a chuckle. "Right. Of course."

They flew with five hundred papilio fairy assigned to the mission carrying fifty additional soldiers skilled at combat without heavy armor. They were selected for their ability to engage in ground combat after a swift trip to reach their target.

Everyone would drop to the ground in the same maneuver she and Larron had used previously. The scouts had identified vampires on the premises, so Annalla would take to the air when they did and eliminate as many as she could in one initial blast. Fairy captains would assess whether they should remain grounded after or join her in the sky. Her attack would also signal the support wave following behind to move in, bringing medics, healers, and reinforcements.

Since the attacks from the camps began, the vampires had been splitting their forces to minimize her influence in any one engagement. It would be nice to have a clear field again. If it happened to not work out that way, their backup plan was to grab as many prisoners as they could and flee. Annalla's task then would be to deal with any pursuit.

"If you need to scream or vomit, please do so away from me," Annalla told Argent as Karlo gave the signal for final preparations.

"I…" He paused, taken aback. "I will do my best."

"Here we go," she said and dropped.

Her stomach dipped as the sensation of falling gripped her. Argent let out a closed-mouth sound of startlement as he squeezed tighter, but he restrained himself from the shrieks of fear a couple of others could not contain. Down and down, the air rushed past, and the ground grew closer.

Annalla was nervous, but apparently the rest of the fairy loved those types of freefalls. They practiced and competed in aerial combat on a regular basis within the sanctuaries. Some of it was exercise as a youth, some was training for their military service, and some of it was for fun during competitions. The other fairy possessed lifetimes of experience flying, diving, and making extreme landings, while her experience was limited to the training and prior mission with Larron.

The nerves did not outweigh the thrill of the drop, though. She was also more comfortable with the logistics of it that time, not only because of practice, but because she was improving her control over the essential manifestations as well. She could compensate for many errors in flight.

Just below, the lead fairy began the spiral, starting the slowing of their descent. Annalla placed a mental wall before them, moving as they did and prepared to halt any projectiles fired up at them should the guards notice their rapid approach.

"Prepare for landing," she warned Argent.

He shifted, adjusting his grip as instructed and focusing on their objective. After the initial shock, he took to staring around, trying to take in everything during the experience. She wondered if he would, after the war, invite the fairy to the Auradia for a repeat performance.

Annalla back winged and set down. She and Argent sprang apart, weapons at the ready, and dove into the combat. His primary task was to work with the other ground troops toward where the prisoners were held while she, Jarin, and a few fairy established a defensive line. Others landing after them would position themselves to take her place if she took off.

Screams emanated from the back. Prisoners panicked and started to scatter. The elves with them stepped forward, waving for attention and shouting.

Argent moved to the fore with Lesyon at his back. He shouted, "We are here to help! Gather around!"

A wall of vampires rose, screeching into the air, and dropped down like a dark wave cresting over the camp. With so many targets, she wondered if they would follow her or fall upon the ground forces.

Only one way to find out.

"Go!" Jarin shouted, succinctly echoing her thoughts.

She took off, lighting fire along the edge of the sword in her hand to call attention to herself. Perhaps if they still had orders to target her, it would draw more to her. Either way, acting quickly was her best option. She needed enough altitude to ensure the heat radiating from a circular blast would not injure those on the ground.

Annalla plowed through the curtain of leathery wings, slicing as she went. Claws stretching toward her met with her floating blades and shields. None reached her. She danced through the air like a fish in water, sleek and agile. Attacks fell short of her while hers struck with deadly precision.

She spiraled up, slashing out and drawing more attention. Vampires followed in a frenzied whirlwind of wings and snapping fangs. They trailed her, and as she halted, they surrounded her, closing in. A feeling of claustrophobia settled into her bones. The mass of bodies blocked the daylight, wrapping her in shadows and a flurry of eyes hungrily watching and waiting.

Her power exploded. Despite the violent results, using fire was like exhaling a deep breath. It was a release. She held tight for so long, and then, she just let go. Choosing the direction and holding to it was the most complicated aspect, much more so than increasing the damage.

The shadows melted, replaced by the light of the flames. She pulled her weapons tight, wrapping them in the protection of her essence. They floated with her at the center of the maelstrom, coated in a blanket of fire. Nothing could reach her, not until her power ran dry and she became helpless. The feelings coursing through her were of comfort, security, and surety. And they could not last. They were not real, not there.

Annalla reigned in her essence and pressed out on the floating weapons, once more forming a swirling defense around herself with them. The fire became nothing more than a second skin around her form, and she peered at the fighting below. Prisoners huddled in a mass of people surrounded by defenders who had shrunk their defensive circle to prevent too many of the prison guards from coming at them at the same time. Jarin, meanwhile, waded through the enemy forces, cutting himself a path of death back and forth.

With a vicious smirk, she dove to cleave her own path through their enemy. As Jarin swung, sending three men flying back to land unmoving, she engaged another three at once with separate weapons. She circled around, fighting all the way, and eventually met with Jarin. They paused, staring at each other with weapons held mid-strike.

His gaze flicked behind her and she swept one of the shields she carried across the space. A satisfying *thunk* and a groan greeted her ears, and Jarin relaxed a fraction. He tipped his head in a salute, and they turned away from each other to begin another circuit. The enemies dwindled until many of those remaining threw down their weapons in surrender.

Argent turned to the rescued prisoners. "Are there any areas where more people are held?"

"There," one of the women, dirty and malnourished, said as she pointed toward some rickety...buildings would be a strong word for the thin structures referenced. "They took the younger women there."

"Jarin, go. Check," he ordered. "Annalla, if you would be so kind as to watch over us from above?"

Her feet had barely left the ground when screams and shouts came from the building. A crash sounded, and the structure Jarin had disappeared within only moments before wobbled. Another fear-filled scream pierced the general noise.

"Annalla!" Jarin shouted. "Hold the building!"

His extraordinary strength would do nothing to save the women if the building collapsed on them. From the shouting, it appeared he faced attackers who had hidden from the initial assault for a last stand within. Annalla suspected they hoped to eliminate as many soldiers as possible, but Jarin's presence counteracted that goal. He would survive a collapse, even if the hostages would not.

She reached out and flooded the exterior with her power, stabilizing it. The interior would be more of a challenge. Invisible from the outside, she had no idea of the configuration or existence of any support beams within.

Another crash sounded, like someone hitting a beam with a hammer. Screams followed, and some of them were cut short. A warrior's battle cry sounded, wood creaked and groaned, and Argent looked up at her from where he stood holding back other soldiers trying to enter.

"Do you have it?" he asked.

Her power crawled forward. She felt it wrap around more. Rooms formed within her mind. Enough. It had to be enough. Her jaw clenched. She looked down at Argent and nodded.

CHAPTER THIRTY-ONE

Kalachi Desert – Ceru-Auradia Front Lines

Annalla lounged against a large rock heated from the sun's rays as she watched the sun setting over the desert horizon. They were at the edge, camped where a natural spring bubbled up, protected from the force of the sun by well-positioned rocky walls. That night was the first night there, and they would remain another full day to stock up on water and let the closest supply carts catch up. It would be the last rest they would see for some time with the desert looming.

She stared out over the landscape, awed by the magnitude and beauty. Thin clouds drifted like pink wisps against the darkening blue of the sky. Dunes cast shadows stretching toward her across the golden sand, making it seem to move hypnotically. It looked warm and welcoming, but their guides warned them not to take the dangers of the desert lightly.

"You appear relaxed," Thanon said as he crested the hill and walked over to sit next to her. "Are you still basking in the glow of your prison escape?"

She thought of watching Jarin and Argent carrying those young women out of the building before it collapsed, and smiled. Her efforts had been enough to support the structure long enough for them to get everyone out.

"I am resting, as ordered," she said.

He bumped her shoulder with his. "And basking in recognition of your greatness?"

"Ha," she said dryly. "No... But it was nice to save those people. Too many of the camp prisoners before them died before we could do anything."

Thanon sighed.

She held up a hand before he could reply. "Not my fault. I know."

He studied her a moment before leaning back against the rock again. "Good."

After a breath of silence, Annalla smirked and peered at him from the corner of her eyes. "I met Sandrala while we were in the Derou. He is...stunning."

Thanon grinned. "Body and mind," he said. "We did not lie, you know."

Annalla patted his knee. "I know. So does Larron, even if he was not happy with either of you initially when he found out."

His face shifted to an expression of guilty stubbornness.

"But Sandrala reminded him that you are one of the best at what you do."

He raised a skeptical eyebrow. "And that worked?"

"Ha!" She laughed. "Well enough. I helped by distracting him with my crazy antics, fainting spells, and massive displays of power."

"Remind me to thank you for all of that sometime," he said as they exchanged cheeky grins. "Does this 'Protector' title help you worry less over Larron's position with the Derou?"

She frowned at him and rolled her eyes. "As you and your paramour have well demonstrated, this is no time to be concerning ourselves with the complications that come with relationships."

"Annalla!" he cried out, as though she was speaking nonsense and frustrating him. "You cannot continue to—"

"Did you hear that?" she said, cutting him off.

"Annalla—"

"I am not making something up to get out of the conversation," she assured him. "Someone is shouting for help."

There were no accompanying sounds of fighting, but the shouts sounded panicked. When they peered over the camp, it was difficult to pick out, but the activity around the support tents was elevated, and perhaps around the medical pavilion.

"Fly me down?" Thanon asked with a mixture of concern and anticipation. The latter reminded Annalla of his desire to go flying with her from before the search for the fairy.

She stepped in front of him and held out her arms. "Hold on."

He jumped at her and wrapped around in a frontal bear hug. "I love you! Best friend ever!"

"How old are you?" she asked as she lifted them off the ground. "And was there no opportunity to fly during your journey to join up with the army?"

"We rode in those contraptions. This is much better. You will have to take me flying when there is not a potential disaster looming."

A huffed chuckle escaped. "Deal."

She landed at the edge of the growing chaos, and they waded into the frantic people. At the edge of a mess tent, someone stumbled between them. He fell to his knees, holding his stomach, and retched violently. Thanon leaned over and stroked the man's back.

At least a half dozen others were throwing up in various places and positions within that small intersection of tents. Friends knelt at their sides, some calling out for help. Soldiers out of their armor milled about, heads turning as though looking for an enemy to fight, but they could not attack an illness. Annalla's stomach churned; she missed Gregry. That was a battlefield designed for him.

Karl dropped down into a small clearing, his feathered wings kicking up dust before he tucked them back. He carried Marto in his arms, and the two set the young mage on his leg and crutches in what appeared to be a well-practiced maneuver. They scanned the scene, concerned. Karl went to the closest sick man, feeling his head, leaning closer to sniff, then peering around again.

"Any ideas?" Marto asked him.

"Stop everyone from eating or drinking anything for now," he said. "It could be an illness, but I suspect something they ingested was tainted."

Poison? she thought.

No one asked the question; they rushed into the nearest tents to do as ordered. Answers and details would come later. At that moment, they needed to minimize the damage.

Most of the tents set up with stools and rickety tables for eating stood concentrated in the same general area, with the cooking fires and apparatus in the center. The arrangement made it convenient for the packing and set up as well as for grabbing a quick meal. It was convenient at that moment because they did not have far to move to reach anyone who might still be eating. She split from Thanon and Marto, taking a different tent.

"Everyone stop!" she shouted. "Eat nothing! Drink nothing!"

Half of the people, mostly men, were already standing away from their seats. They wore looks of disgust and held their hands over their mouths and noses. Annalla's nose also wrinkled with her next breath, recognizing the stench of vomit before the sight of more victims registered.

"Not a problem," one of the standing men said between gags.

Whatever affected their people, it happened quickly after exposure, if she were to judge based on those she had seen thus far. Even a few of the men hovering around the periphery held their stomachs. Whether the gesture was sympathetic, caused by the smell, or from a delayed reaction, she could not tell.

She stuck her head out of the tent. "Karl, we have more sick in here!"

Ducking back in, she had to hold back a gag of her own. The stench was pervasive, and she was losing the battle-hardness insulating her against it. There was no fight there, only illness. Turning, she took the tent flap and tied the entrance open. It could not hurt to get some fresh air inside.

She scanned the tent again, focusing on more than the people. The usual tables and stools were scattered about, some of them dirtied with spilled or regurgitated food or overturned. The space was cramped and disgusting. Ten men still milled about, wanting to get out of the tent, but unwilling to leave their companions.

Annalla pointed at the two men looking the least green and the only woman present. "You three, get the sick people into relatively clean spaces and roll them onto their sides so they do not choke. You four"—she pointed at a cluster of men at the back wall—"move the dirtied tables outside and out of the way so the healers have a clear area to work and travel. The rest of you, bring empty buckets and one or two with clean water and some clean rags."

Years ago, she'd helped her foster parents take care of other sick children. She hoped at least some of what she'd learned back then might help.

The woman approached her. "I'm one of the cooks," she said. "I haven't eaten yet, so I can stay with the people here.

You can go check the others."

Annalla nodded and turned to leave as two others entered, both magai. She nimbly jumped out of their way. The man went to kneel at the side of the closest victim lying on the floor, while the women went to one of the two tables remaining upright and undisturbed.

"I'm strengthening them and healing some of the damage," the healer said as he left the side of the first man and moved to the next, "but we need to know what this is and create a treatment if we're not to lose at least some of them."

The female mage started sticking her fingers in the food and drinks. "I know. I know," she said. "The ale is clean. I'd need more time to check the soup because of all the ingredients, but the water has something in it that shouldn't be there."

So, she is likely a chemical mage, Annalla thought.

"We cooked with the same barrel of water they were drinking from for this batch. It'd just been refilled," the cook, who had also been observing the magai, informed them.

The chemist pierced the woman with her gaze. "From where?"

"Uh, f-f-from the spring. I-I think," she stammered, taken aback.

"Separate any food and drink that used the new water supplies," she ordered the cook. "Anything you even *think* might have used water from the spring. Go. Do it now and tell your fellows."

"You think the water was poisoned?" Annalla asked as the cook rushed out.

She shrugged. "It's a place to start. Will you take the soup and water to the central area? We're bringing anything suspicious there to start trying to discern the specific cause of this."

Not wanting to touch them and get a potential poison on her hands, Annalla wrapped the bowls and cups in her power and floated them out after her. In the short time since she entered the tent, the immediate area outside had become a frenzy. Medics, healers, and doctors from all races converged on the scene. Sick people were carried off by fairy and on stretchers as more professionals arrived.

"Over there," Marto said.

He approached her from the left while she looked around for the place she was supposed to put the food. There was a growing pile in the direction he pointed, and she sent hers to add to the pile with a thought, not bothering to try to maneuver through the crowd.

"They think the spring might be the source of the sickness," she told him.

Marto nodded. "So I was told as well. Chemical magai are heading down to the spring to see if they can identify what it might be from there."

Annalla's gaze slowly slid around the area. So many people were sick and moaning in pain. Medics worked diligently, some having to ignore where their clothing had been soiled by someone throwing up in the wrong direction. The rank air hung about in a noxious cloud around them. She grimaced and put a hand to her stomach, feeling nauseous herself.

"Was this intentional?" she asked, not expecting her companion to know more than her, but the question came regardless.

"I overheard some of the cooks," Marto said. "Apparently, after an incident early on, they started being very careful about food storage and preparation. They were vehemently saying this couldn't have been a mistake on their part."

She pressed her lips into a worried line. What if someone had poisoned her? She could fail everyone by eating something tainted without knowing until it was too late. She couldn't protect herself from everything, despite her power, and it was another example of that fact.

"So, probably intentional," she murmured.

"Probably."

She pinched the bridge of her nose. "I am going to join them at the spring. I have power over water, maybe I can help in some way."

Marto nodded. "There is little either of us can do here, anyway. I'll tell the others where you've gone."

As she took off, the last piece of the sun slipped below the horizon.

CHAPTER THIRTY-TWO

Kalachi Desert – Ceru-Auradia Front Lines

Larron looked at the tired faces around him.

"What have your people been able to discover?" Garrett asked Hephestar.

The mage breathed deep and rubbed his eyes. "The spring was indeed poisoned. Unfortunately, the poison was a biological agent, so our chemists can detect it, but we can't remove it."

"Why not?" asked Lesyon.

"This pollution is technically alive," he said. "Our healers can help the bodies of those who ingested it fight off the infection and repair damage, but chemical magai cannot separate out organisms."

"So, what can we do?" Garrett asked.

"We boil it," Walsh said with a sigh.

Argent's face was grim. "We need a great deal of water," he said. "The risk of entering the desert without an enormous supply is too great. This is going to take days."

Larron bit his lip and considered their options. Could they afford the additional time? Each batch of water would need to be boiled for a period, then allowed to cool enough to store. The barrels would also require washing before they were refilled. At least a day of work in addition to the work already planned. He frowned at the waste.

"Can we not ask Annalla to do it?" Zeris asked the group.

Larron stared at his brother. "No," he told him. He understood the desire but disagreed with the approach.

The Ceru king tilted his head. "Why not? She controls both water and fire. She could probably have it done in no time at all."

Walsh beat him to the answer. "Because we're going to be relying on her heavily for nearly two months to get everyone through the desert."

"And at the end of it," Argent said tiredly, "we will need her and Jarin to face Kahnlair."

Garrett wiped a hand down his mouth and scratched his beard. "Okay, we keep resting our main weapons." He turned toward the newest member of their meetings. "How does this impact our travel plans?"

Vaseer was one of the first Kalachi Desert residents, the Istali, to escape and defect. His skin was a deep burnished bronze, which had to be his natural color after living for over fifteen years away from the searing desert sun. He still covered his head with the wrap common to his people. Since the human migration to Elaria and his people's separation from Ceru, the necessary head cover had become traditional as well as functional.

Through the Istali, the allies knew most of the Kalachi humans were coerced into fighting for Kahnlair with threats against them or their families. Within the desert city of Var Istal, Kahnlair had gradually gathered bandits and others bitter with Ceru and its catering to elven limitations. The forces grew and took control of Var Istal through fear and violence. Gilar from the south and vampires to the north guarded the desert passageways for Kahnlair, ensuring no word of his growing army escaped the harsh landscape before he struck.

Vaseer had only a sister. When he'd received notification he would be shipped off to fight, she'd told him to run if he saw the chance. She would have done anything she could to sabotage Kahnlair's supplies, working against him until she was caught. There was no way to know if she had been successful. He suspected she would take her own life before allowing herself to become part of the gilar herds or some other atrocious end.

The desert might have held Kahnlair's stronghold, but the Istali held no love for him and wanted to see him brought down as much as anyone. At that moment, they had the opportunity to lead the army through the lands they knew best. Their chance to free their people from Kahnlair stood before them, and they were determined.

"We were already planning to split the army," Vaseer said. "I propose we begin the separation earlier than originally planned and reverse the order."

"You mean to break off a smaller portion to proceed rather than leaving the small portion?" Walsh asked.

Their plan had been to hold a quarter of the army there for an additional three days. At the next water source, they would separate another quarter of their forces, which would linger for two days, and the final half of the army would again split at the third source. According to the Kalachi residents, the water sources diminished in size as they entered the desert proper, so they could not handle the full scope of the army. By splitting into smaller, balanced groups, they could better utilize and stretch their resources.

Darrin had proposed using the converted supply pavilions to haul additional water. The fairy would transport pavilions from the rear group to the forward group, supplementing with natural sources and allowing each to fill the water supplies a little during their stays. The medical pavilion was also to move from the oasis furthest back to the forwardmost one each time, allowing the injured to heal for extended periods at a place where water would not be an issue.

"I do," Vaseer said. "Refilling our water here will now take more time, but we can supply the forward quarter and send them off as scheduled tomorrow. The remaining three-quarters would remain here, working on the sterilization, and send off another group each morning. With this approach, we wouldn't lose any time."

"I still want the leading force, and the second, at full strength," Garrett said. "We'd need to shuffle personnel to compensate for those injured by this illness."

Argent turned back to Hephestar. "How quickly do the healers estimate it will take for the people who took ill to recover?"

"They'll be fully recovered by the time the last group leaves," Hephestar said. "Thanks to the efforts of the additional magai brought with the reinforcements, there were few injured left to be treated, so we can focus on this without overtaxing the healers and medics."

Thanks in large part to Mage Gregry, Larron thought, feeling another pang of mixed pride and loss at the memory of the elderly mage who had first healed Annalla. While he had not personally felt a deep connection to Gregry, the man had made an impression on Annalla. For her, his loss was more than losing a powerful ally.

"That'll help fill out the final group," Walsh said.

"Chalise and Yallista were working on the disposition of the fairy support lines," Zara said. "I'll tell them the implementation will be moved up. Braymis and I had already given assignments to the fairy soldiers."

She glanced at Darrin as she spoke, receiving a discreet,

confirming nod from him. The two had settled into an easy partnership. They conferred regularly and Darrin spent most of his time within the fairy encampments. Zara retained authority over their tactical decisions, and Darrin had yet to override her, though he offered thoughts and opinions whenever a new disaster presented itself.

Garrett nodded at Zara. "I guess this is it then," he said, and looked around, meeting the eyes of his counterparts and people.

Along with the army, they planned to split the leadership. King Argent would lead the first wave, bringing with him Annalla, Commander Walsh, Controller Nurtik, Mage Jesmin, and Matriarch Patrice to represent the other allies. King Garrett would lead the second group with Lead Colonel Zara, Captain Lesyon, Clanlord Fwendilg, Hephestar, and Matriarch Ambergine. Clanlord Guldrith would lead the third with Colonel Braymis, King Oromaer, Leader Donistor, Mage Alastair, and Prince Albertas. Finally, Prince Darrin was placed in charge of the final group and the supply lines to follow. With him would be Prince Tyrus, Mage Marto, King Zeris, Controller Zendisha, and Matriarch Sonara.

The next day would be the last time they would be together until they neared Var Istal.

Argent smiled across at Garrett. "We have some water to boil, friend."

***

Annalla spiraled down and circled Larron, signaling to him she was incoming. He rode in the second row with King Argent. She glided up behind them, stepped upon the horse's flank, wrapped her wings, and dropped down behind Larron.

"I was thinking," she said to no one in particular. "Will we not simply find the next water source destroyed in some way as well?"

There were nods all around, and Walsh said, "Quite possibly."

"And you already thought of this," she said, based on their unconcerned reactions. "Of course you have."

Argent chuckled at her wry tone. "Commander Walsh brought it up first. This is why Mage Jesmin is with us instead of another. She is one of the best chemical magai we have."

"You flatter me, King Argent," Jesmin said, then grinned, "but you aren't wrong."

Annalla grinned, enjoying the mage's confident tone.

"Thoroughly exploring the spring will be our first task," Walsh said. "This one is another natural spring rather than the artificial wells we'll find more frequently later. I suspect if it's been tampered with, that we'll find a similar form of contamination."

"What d'ya think they'll do to the wells?" Nurtik asked.

Walsh shrugged. "There are more options for him to use there. Bodies or feces are potential contaminants. Filling or destroying them are additional possibilities."

Annalla pursed her lips, considering. "You will need me for those, right?"

"Likely," he said. "Unless they do a shoddy job of destruction."

"They're good at destruction," Nurtik mumbled under his breath. Annalla could not disagree with the sentiment.

She had at least a week before she would be needed, based on that information. Needed from a water perspective, anyway. At each oasis, she would be proliferating the local edible vegetation. The first three groups would fill their storage and leave what was left for those following. That included filling the containers in any of the pavilions as they shifted forward each time, brought by the fairy assigned to the task.

Each day, they were also going to be shifting their travel

patterns further for desert travel. They would leave a little earlier and continue later, expanding the break in the middle of the day until there were two rest periods during the hottest and coldest times. That was on the advice of Vaseer, who rode with the front line, guiding them based on no landmarks she could discern.

He was an interesting person with a story as sad as hers and many others. His only remaining family, his sister, was likely deceased. He had no one. He was also loyal to no one and nothing other than his quest for vengeance and freedom for his people. The Istali swore no oaths to Ceru, and those in the army followed Garrett's orders and those of his commanders voluntarily.

Some people expressed concerns about following such a person into a deadly environment, but Annalla did not think a volunteer was any less trustworthy than someone conscripted against their will. According to Patrice, the irimoten and Garrett had no concerns about the men and women guiding them because Morena had read them when they'd arrived all those years ago. They wanted their land back. They wanted freedom.

Vaseer remained stoic most of the time. He gazed out at the desert as though it could tell him secrets or give him the insight he desired. She wondered if he looked for answers about his sister, or perhaps wondering how their campaign might end. The latter was something she too contemplated as she soared high above, staring off into the unknown, burning distance.

A day later, Annalla stood overlooking a small body of water, hiding her wrinkled nose behind her hand. It did nothing to alleviate the stench. She tried to breathe shallowly and fought against gagging.

"Did they use the spring as a refuse pit for the whole of Kahnlair's army?" Jesmin said. Her nose twitched in disgust as well, but she appeared to handle the stink better than Annalla. Her petite frame, large eyes, and button nose made her look almost childlike in the voluminous mage robes bunched up beneath the leather flying harness she wore.

Her statement was accurate enough, as far as Annalla could tell. Whatever had been done to poison the first spring had been undetectable visually. Maybe they had put something contaminated in and weighed it down. Maybe it had been something liquid, but either way, no one saw it. That next one left no doubt about contamination.

Walsh's guesses of corpses and feces were only the start. Entrails, rotting food, tattered and bloody clothes, and broken pieces of equipment were among the trash clogging the water or floating on the surface. She would not be surprised to learn they had, indeed, used the spring as both a latrine and trash pit. Between the water and the desert sun, the rot progressed to the point where the miasma of vomit and defecation from before was almost a pleasant memory.

One of Karlo's teams, the one led by Crastus, had found the spring in that state during their regular scouting patrol. They returned to request additional eyes on it, so Annalla and Jesmin came along to assess the situation and report back. She regretted her decision to come herself rather than holding back and letting Argent assign the second person to go.

Karlo made no attempt to conceal his disgust. His undershirt was bunched upward under his leathers far enough so he could hold the fabric over his mouth and nose. "It's wretched no matter how they did it."

Crastus chuckled. "Is the unshakeable Armsmaster bothered by"—he coughed—"a little decomposition?"

"How did you ever fool people long enough to be selected as my companion?" Annalla shot him an incredulous look.

The grin he sent her way was only a little strained by

their circumstances. "I'm *that* charming."

Karlo snorted, then groaned when it caused a larger intake of breath. "The deans of the schools also have influence in the selection process, and most of us had different criteria than the council you faced." He waved a shielding hand at the water. "Can we move away from this now?"

The mage had moved to crouch at the water's edge. Her arm reached down to dip her fingertips in the dirty water. She scrunched her nose and stood up to make her way back toward them. "Yes, we can leave," she said as she approached. "I'm done here."

"Oh, thank you!" Crastus breathed out and crouched down to reach for the first harness hook to connect to her half.

"I want the two of you to land with us to update Argent and the rest," Annalla told Crastus and Karlo. "I think we are going to need some of the fairy to start working on the spring before our main group arrives, and that will require a guard rotation as well."

Karlo nodded. "We'll join you."

The flight back to where the ground army rode was relatively quick. They were about midway through the afternoon portion of the day's travel. Annalla set down ahead of the army with Karlo, Crastus, and Jesmin. There was enough time for Jesmin to remove her harness before the first rows of travelers arrived and flowed around them.

They walked their horses at that time of day, trying not to overheat their mounts in the blistering sun. Even in the late afternoon, the temperature was hot enough to have even the elves sweating profusely. On Vaseer's advice, they had prepared as much of the lighter cloth material as they had available as head covers and other garments to keep the sun's rays at bay. Despite the preparations, those with fairer skin were turning pink and red in places they could not cover.

Larron, with his Derou heritage, was tanning to a deeper

brown than his natural olive skin tone, while Argent "tanned" to a darker gray paired with his strong green undertones. Everyone else looked like they were baking a little more each day. Vaseer had also told them about some of the compounds used by his people as sun protection. The chemists, medics, and support personnel were working on creating more during any downtime they could eke out.

"Was it as bad as reported?" Argent called out to Annalla and Jesmin as they connected.

Annalla and her companions started walking with the larger group. "Worse. It is disgusting."

Thanon, who happened to be traveling behind them as part of the guard unit, snorted at her comments. As she glanced back, she saw Geelomin glare Thanon into silence, bringing a smile to her face.

"Annalla isn't wrong," Jesmin said. "We'll want to camp well upwind of the spring, and I don't believe we will get any clean water out of this source; not during our stay."

"We cannot boil it as before?" Argent asked.

The chemist shook her head. "Not until it's cleaned out. They used the water as a dumping ground. All the refuse will need to be removed before we think about first filtering it, then boiling it."

Argent chewed on his bottom lip and peered forward over the open sand in thought. "So, we clean it as much as we can and leave the empty containers for the next groups."

"That won't leave us enough on hand to reach the next source," Vaseer said. "We'll be dependent on the expectation of supplies from the rear line."

"We suspected as much after the first contamination," Larron said.

Argent turned back to Annalla. "Can the fairy help begin the cleaning efforts early?"

"That is my intent," she said. "We have nets and can

add weights to drag the water and carry most of the larger items well away from the spring quickly enough. I want to send word back to request a few fairy units be moved forward though."

Karlo and Crastus nodded in agreement as Karlo said, "Agreed. We'll want additional units to assist with the scouting."

Annalla looked back at Argent. "With your permission."

"Granted," he said and tipped his head. "Please proceed."

She and Karlo were the two nodding that time.

"Crastus," Karlo said, receiving a salute. "Coordinate the dredging of the spring. Take three units and set up a temporary camp."

He wrinkled his nose, but otherwise gave no indication of his distaste for the assignment. Maybe she could reward the fairy assigned to clean up with a shower structure of some sort after it was done. She started making plans as Crastus took off to give his orders.

CHAPTER THIRTY-THREE

Kalachi Desert – Ceru-Auradia Front Lines

Annalla stood with the rest of the group as Vaseer paced back and forth, stopping frequently to look up at the stars before pacing more or moving a few steps to one side or the other. He stopped, muttered to himself, shifted, muttered. The frustration emanating from him became more palpable with every moment.

They were about two hours into the evening, close to the time when they should halt to set up a hasty camp for the freezing hours. The plan was to stop early at the next water source. Vaseer described that location as an old well protected by a stone wall built up around the perimeter. It was a small, stable location that often became covered by a thin coating of sand, but some portion of the structure was always visible.

That night, in that place, nothing broke the smooth, sandy landscape. Graceful dunes flowed out across the desert for miles in every direction, and little drifts floated leisurely on air drafts. The moon hovered just above the horizon, three-quarters full, and its silver light reflected off the golden sand.

Vaseer kicked the sand, then stood with his back to them, running a hand over his face. Annalla imagined he rubbed his eyes, but she couldn't see it. He turned to face them, spreading his arms wide. "It should be here. I swear to you."

Argent gave a gesture of assurance. "You have not been wrong before. Mage Jesmin, do you think an architect might be able to locate the stones beneath all of this?"

She asked for a minute and moved off, likely to call forward a fellow mage to do a quick search. When she returned, two magai trailed her. They moved to stand near Vaseer, each taking one side with about ten feet between them. The two knelt together, placing their palms against the ground. After a few moments, the magai rose and conferred with Vaseer. The others likely did not hear what was said, but Annalla knew their news was mixed.

"The well is there," one of the magai pointed about five feet further out from where their guide had stood. "It's buried about fifteen feet down and feels as though the cap was removed, so the whole of it is filled with sand."

"Can you recreate it?" Jesmin asked.

His face scrunched up in a wince. "Not based on how deep he says the well was to begin with. It'd take weeks because of the distance and safety requirements needed to ensure it wouldn't collapse on top of the magai working within."

"Can you tell if there is water down there?" Argent asked. "Or is the water blocked as well?"

The talkative mage shrugged and raised his eyes to where Annalla stood. "We can only sense the solid matter. What about you?"

Annalla closed her eyes and reached out with her essence. If she could pull water from a mile upriver, she should be able to sense it at the well's source. Her essence stretched down until the cold dampness tickled her senses.

"It is there," she said.

Jesmin sighed. "So, we can't get to it, but we know it's

there… Can we bring the water up to us?"

"It would just soak back into the sand," Vaseer said with a shake of his head. "Water does not last long on the surface here."

"What if we turned this into a solid base like a pool or bath?" the architect asked.

Move the sand or move the water? Annalla asked herself as she considered what he proposed. Both required significant effort because she would be working blind. She might be able to clear the well, but that risked a complete collapse of the aquifer. Moving the water like they asked would be as much effort, but safer.

She moved forward, sliding between people and out into the open space until she was past Vaseer and the magai. Pointing, she asked, "Is this about where the well is?"

The architect nodded.

"I would need a solid surface about ten feet across and maybe three feet deep?" she asked. "But, I would want this spot under me to remain loose sand as wide as the well below."

The magai nodded and conferred, looking around and gesturing to each other before confirming they had enough people to make her request a reality.

"What are you all thinking?" Argent asked.

"I will pull the water up through the sand and fill the pool the architects create," she said. "You will need to work fast to fill as many of our containers as possible. I also want Karlo to send the fairy to bring forward as many of the empty barrels as they can carry before we leave. Even with the pool, the water is unlikely to remain long enough for groups to use it after us, so we will need to provide supplies for them."

Argent scanned his advisors, receiving nods or shrugs in answer to his unspoken question. There was little choice. They needed water, and that was the only source for at least six days in either direction. He too nodded and began issuing orders while Annalla and the magai got to work.

Her eyes snapped open at the sound of a horn blowing in the distance. It was still too dark for her rest to be over, but the sound of the horn had her scrambling for clothes and weapons. She was still not feeling recovered from pulling up the water a few days prior.

"Run!"

"Form up!"

Orders and screams competed in volume, punctuated by the panicked crying of the animals and growls all too familiar.

Gilar.

"To arms! Wake Annalla, we need her!" She barely heard Argent's voice over the terrified shouts of surprise growing between them. Fighting occurred right outside of her tent.

"How in all hells did they get so far forward?" Patrice said to her as they tightened the final buckles.

Annalla wrapped her power and physical defenses around her, stepping outside first. A gilar struck, but his blade stopped short, caught in her essential hold over air. One of her own weapons swept up, stabbing through its chest. The gilar snarled and lashed out, clawing the air with its hands before it died. The blade pulled out and flew to her side to join her other swords in a flurry of movement, ending the fighting in the immediate area.

They were between oases. After Annalla had worked throughout the night to bring up the water, the following two nights were interrupted by attacks against their camp. Both were quick. Their enemy darted in, dealing as much damage as possible before darting out again.

Regardless of the duration, the incursions woke them and had the guards on high alert through the remainder of the night. She was exhausted. Resting helped her recover from massive expenditures of power, and that was something she lacked. It would be the third night in a row of interrupted sleep, and it sounded like the attack would not end as quickly as the prior two.

Artist magai already had lights in the sky, and Annalla added a massive circle of fire. Dark forms of vampires became further silhouetted by the blaze. It seemed they had learned from the fairy's involvement in the war. Many carried the forms of other people. Rather than victims being carried off into the night, they appeared to be additional attackers the vampires dropped in the middle of the sleeping army.

No fairy had yet taken to the sky. It could not have been more than a handful or two minutes since the attack began, but they were not slow to react. They waited for her. She would either clear the air or give the signal to engage, but their patience ensured no fairy died in any counter-attack she executed.

Annalla took off, slashing out at vampires and their passengers as they flew by on her way to assess their disposition. They were too low, too close to her own forces for her to risk a full blast. She decided on a brief burst, hoping it would injure and disrupt their attack.

She gathered her power, pulling it up just beneath the surface. Focusing on a ring around her, she exploded, sending searing flames in a devastating ripple expanding from her position. Vampires screamed and dodged. Gilar and humans fell as they were dropped. One section of her attack broke against the shield of a strong mage. She pulled the floating weapons and shields tighter around her and attacked the defended position.

The mage saw her coming. A mage strike hit hard, and one of her shields shattered under the blow. That was not Hephestar gently tapping to test different defenses. A hit like that landing would mean broken bones, or worse. With a glance down, Annalla grasped and pulled additional arms up to swirl around her.

Another strike. That one hit a short sword, bending the sword toward the hilt end and dispersing most of the force. Two more attacks followed in quick succession, both energy blasts. They were trying to blast through her defenses and knock her down with power. Her pulse spiked, and she hissed in pain. Despite hours of practice, she remained slow to convert energy into something she could absorb. Her arm blistered and bled.

Part of her wondered if a healer mage could regrow eyeballs, or if those were like limbs, where they could not replace what was lost. Annalla fought against a shudder at the thought and told herself to avoid taking a hit to the head. She was nowhere near skilled enough with her abilities to only use them blindly.

Annalla threw out a fan of fire ahead that broke once more upon the shield less than a hundred feet away. Another force blast clipped a sword, sending it spinning to the side. She braced herself, prepared to dodge an energy strike that never came. Instead of a mage strike from the fore, something slammed down from above, sliding off a floating shield and knocking into her.

Clawed hands grasped at her, spinning her to the left and down. Her mind wheeled. *Something got through!*

From the corner of her eye, leathery, green-skinned hands clung to her leathers. While the gilar's armor, weapons, and clothing did not penetrate her essential barrier, its naked limbs passed through without issue. Agony sliced down her back beneath her wing as something stabbed into her flesh. Panicked, she flexed her protection, shoving the gilar away using what he wore as leverage.

Her attacker shot away, but whatever he'd stabbed her with must have caught on a rib. She heard and felt a *snap*.

Every movement of her wings became torture. The pain churned her stomach and sent a wave of dizziness through her head. Two successive force blasts hit; one shattered another shield, and the second shattered something in her leg. She swallowed back a scream and fought against tunnel vision.

That place was familiar to her. The point where everything hurt. There was only one path: forward, through.

The magai were the greatest threat, but she needed to account for attacks from above. She pressed her barrier out far enough to stop objects further than arm's length away. They would do no damage if they could not reach her. It did not stop the next two mage strikes. Both were energy—they likely suspected fire would be useless—and they hit mid-body, burning through her clothing and into her skin before she neutralized the power.

Annalla gritted her teeth and glared. They might be strong enough to shield against her fire—and somehow prevent her from starting a blaze within—but they probably could not see through the flame. She focused her vision on the point from which she thought the magai were attacking. Her hands formed claws that squeezed into fists as she gathered her power for another explosion.

A ball of light took shape and grew, swelling with the force and growing under the strength of her pain and anger. What started small grew swiftly; from the size of a horse to the size of a wagon, the size of a pavilion, and larger still. The flames swept out. People below scrambled to clear the area as her fireball expanded.

Mage strikes shot out of the flames, roughly in the direction of where she had been when the fire began. Annalla had moved, though, up and away from the fighting below until she hovered over her inferno. Easing herself down, the heat embraced her, and she began a slow, methodical search for her enemy.

There. A bubble defied her, pressed back against her power. She squeezed and increased the temperature. A mage strike passed by her close enough to sense it disrupt the winds of her firestorm. Despite the proximity, they remained blind. Staying where she was, she threw more power into the blaze until the shield flickered.

One moment, one instant of weakness, was all it took. The heat engulfed her enemies and consumed them in a blink. Annalla closed her eyes, reveling in the comforting warmth of the fire. She was injured; it hurt to breathe. A battle raged below; she was needed.

Taking careful, shallow breaths, she pulled the fire back into herself and took stock of her surroundings.

***

Larron and Argent split turns at watch, with Argent allowing him to sleep at night. He and Walsh used the same small tent used by Argent and Nurtik during the day. That night was the third in a row their sleep had been interrupted. Walsh shared a look of tired frustration with him as they slammed their feet into their boots and rushed out into the night, neither having removed their leathers.

His heart slammed against his ribs, battle awareness raging to the fore as he glanced up and had to dart to the side. A gilar crashed silently to the ground where he'd stood a moment before, swinging its weapon in a deadly arc. Larron brought his weapon up to meet the strike, forcing his opponent's sword into the sand.

Against another enemy, he would have slid up to strike their nose with his elbow, but the maneuver would leave him vulnerable to the gilar's arm spines. Instead, he kicked out, forcing it to stumble backward. He followed with quick, offensive strikes to eliminate the gilar before it recovered its footing and scanned the area.

Fighting raged all around. Vampires flew over, illuminated by magai light and Annalla's fire. They continued dropping additional combatants in the midst of the camp. It could have been chaos if not for the experience and discipline of the defenders.

Another gilar plunged into their clearing. Before Larron reacted, a body flashed out of the shadows. The blur leaped, closing the remaining distance in a blink and landing on the gilar's back. Claws grasped, and a knife sunk into the back of its neck. Patrice held on as the body crumpled to the ground.

"Annalla's in the air," she said moments before a fiery explosion rolled across the sky.

More bodies fell at once, some injured, while others joined the fray. Larron charged in with Walsh and Patrice at his side. They fought, killing enemies and defending their own as they cut paths forward and split in different directions.

He did not notice the ball of fire at first. No one did, but it grew distractingly large. Then it kept growing, threatening part of the camp turned field of combat. Shouts of fighting became screams of panic as fighters from both sides fled the area beneath the flames. Larron took advantage of the confusion to eliminate fleeing gilar and other enemy soldiers.

Injured allies went to the healers. Geelomin's team had been assigned to protect the ten magai traveling with them, so Larron trusted they were safe enough amid the chaos of the attack. His people were well coordinated and leveraged their complementary strengths. Anyone reaching them would receive treatment.

Larron fought on until the essential miniature sun started to shrink. It collapsed in on itself rapidly, disappearing in a moment and leaving him blinking at the sudden darkness enveloping them. The disorientation and spots in his vision nearly resulted in his death as a gilar, better adapted to the dark, chose that moment to strike.

Their blades connected awkwardly for Larron as he threw his out in a desperate move. The edge sliced a thin trail along his side, but he avoided most of the damage and recovered in time to meet the next attack with a solid parry and counter strike. A soldier cried out, and another gilar freed itself to attack Larron from the other side.

He dodged and blocked, positioning himself so his enemies would be forced to attack him where they would be in each other's way with their longer reach. Most of the tents had collapsed into a tangled mess of dangerous footing, but a few remained standing. One of the gilar caught its swing on a lone tent pole perched naked in the sand. It proved little barrier to the creature's strong blow, but the fraction it slowed the movement was enough.

Larron spun in on the other with his sword held close. Inside its reach, he jabbed, cutting its throat before spinning out to block the interrupted attack swing. The dying gilar gurgled as it toppled into its companion, and Larron kicked at the gilar's legs as it did, sending them to the ground together as he danced behind them. Their end was swift, but another soldier emerged to take their place.

There had to be an end to their attacks. They could not have brought many more close enough to camp before Annalla's first aerial attack.

So why are there so many? he wondered, then froze. *The command tent.*

The thought hit him as a human soldier struck. They set up a larger tent each time and left it empty at night. During the day, it served as a shelter from the sun for some of their smaller animals. The use of a command tent for leaders had become standard for the allied army, and Walsh thought it might offer an enticing false target for Kahnlair if he attacked. At that moment, Larron was nearly in the center of the false command area.

Reinforcement poured in behind him, and it started to feel as though they had a relative handle on the situation. A distinctly dwarven battle cry rang out, and Nurtik charged past Larron at a group of three. His swing batted aside their weapons bared in defense and sunk into the belly of one as the armored figure crashed into the other two. Their weapons were pinned beneath the bulk, and Nurtik pummeled the two not bleeding out into unconsciousness.

He rose, pulled his axe free, and stormed up to Larron. "Annalla's injured again." His head moved in a gesture telling Larron to go.

Larron retreated, doing so cautiously in case of lingering threats. There was no reason to panic. 'Injured' meant she would be with the healers, and they could heal most things. He knew that, and he should have remained fighting to see it through. Instead, his legs carried him quickly and efficiently to the area staged for treatment.

Crastus came into view first. The fairy captain paced in a tight line at the foot of a cot near the far edge of the row. As he drew closer, he saw Annalla lying down on her side with her wings flowing over and onto the ground. Bone protruded from her back, her visible clothing and leather were drenched in blood, and her leg appeared severely swollen. A mage held his hands over her.

"Deal with the bones and anything serious," Annalla's voice came out clipped and shallow. "Save the rest of your strength for others who will need it."

The grip his concern held on his heart was not known until it released at the sound of her conscious and aware. She had protection against weapons and magical attacks, defenses no one else could match or counter. Massive injuries were not supposed to happen to her, not anymore. Closing his eyes, he took a deep breath and used the moment to collect himself.

"It was the magai," Crastus told him, shaken. "We need a better answer to the threat they represent."

"They are not—" Annalla grunted. "I just need them marked. I should be able take them out from within if I know where they are. It simply takes too much energy otherwise."

"As you expended tonight?" Larron asked. He looked at the mage as he knelt behind Annalla. "I can finish her back if you are done with the serious injuries."

The man looked him up and down, noting the blood and grime coating him. "Not until you clean those hands, you won't."

His hands went up, and he smirked. "Fair enough. I promise I will wash first."

A raised eyebrow was his initial answer before he smiled back and gave a minute tip of his head. "Soon. I have dealt with the threat of infection, and we have supplies prepared by the fairy doctors over there."

Larron could not hold himself back from stroking Annalla's hair before he left to wash his hands while Crastus continued to watch over her.

"Did I hurt any of our people?" she asked him.

The question was likely in reference to the fireball that grew large enough to reach the fighting on the ground. He shook his head as he began to stitch the cut along her back. "It does not matter," he said. "You should have done it sooner."

Her head jerked to the side to stare at him in question.

"Sooner, Annalla," he reiterated his statement. "How did this happen? The magai? Gilar?"

"Both," she muttered.

Larron shot a look at Crastus that had the man politely walking away before he continued their conversation. "We are coming to the end. You have an oath to keep, and you are our best hope of victory. Act sooner, regardless of the consequences. That is for Argent to deal with, and he is well aware of his responsibilities."

Annalla sighed as he worked. "I know," she said. "I already know. It will not happen again. I learn more with every encounter."

For all their sake, he hoped she learned her powers quickly enough.

CHAPTER THIRTY-FOUR

Kalachi Desert – Ceru-Auradia Front Lines

Food, water, fight. Food, water, fight. Throw in injuries and recovery, and those few words encompassed Annalla's entire world.

The air was sweltering as they set up tents for shade during their day break. It was hot everywhere, but at least the cover offered some minor relief. She would gladly strip down to her undergarments, regardless of the fact their tents would have the sides rolled up to allow better airflow.

Maybe I can take a nap in a water bubble, she thought. *I probably wouldn't drown, but I wonder if it would boil.*

"Why are you poking your cheeks?"

Annalla's head turned and her vision focused as she looked up at Thanon and Patrice standing over her. She moved slowly, her reactions more lethargic than usual. Her head hurt, too. The headache was not like when her powers were emerging. Those earlier headaches were a stabbing sensation starting at her temples. That day, it was more of a low throb behind her cheeks and ears, making her fuzzy-headed.

Two faces staring at her started to look concerned.

Right. One of them asked me a question, she reminded herself. *I should answer... What was the question?*

"I'm fine," she said, mentally congratulating herself on a logical guess and response.

Judging by the way their frowns deepened, it had not been an appropriate answer. She pulled her hands away from her face and smiled at them as innocently as possible.

Thanon snorted.

"Annalla, what are we going to do with you?" Patrice asked as she knelt at her side.

She lifted a shoulder in a half-shrug. "I am just tired. Not dehydrated. Not injured."

"Good news, then," Thanon said cheerfully, the torturous temperature having zero detrimental impact on his good-natured optimism. "We have come to keep you company as you rest this afternoon!"

"Larron asked you to check on me?"

The snarky elf shot her an amused grin. "Larron is smarter than that."

"He'd check on you himself," Patrice said. "Argent was the one to send us this time. He wants us to make sure you stay out of any combat today, no matter what."

The three of them shared a look that said it was a nice thought, but there was no chance Annalla would sit on her hands if any attack turned against the defenders. They pretended otherwise, however, and sat together, trading innocuous comments as the soldiers finished setting up the tent. She felt bad not helping, but they were more likely to get in the way than they were to offer any meaningful assistance to the men.

Annalla tried to sleep once they'd finished and her friends had left, but her mind continued to churn. Perhaps it was the heat, or maybe she was on edge waiting for the next crisis. She still struggled against the magai Kahnlair sent on the attacks. While she kept the gilar off her, force strikes continued making it through, and their shields protected them against fire unless she started it within. That meant she needed a location. Even then, sometimes that also failed, for reasons she could only guess but likely having to do with Kahnlair. It was her desperate hope the failures were the result of inaccurate information and *not* from Kahnlair bolstering those particular magai.

She was stronger than them, but overpowering their shields took too much energy. It was like throwing herself against a door over and over again to get it open rather than using the handle. Possible, but heavily draining. An added frustration to the situation was that she was unable to determine if, or how much, Kahnlair was supplementing the power of the magai she had faced.

If he made them even stronger, then she and Jarin might not be able to turn the tide. They might burn out against his magai before having a chance to face him directly, which would leave the rest of the army to face the most powerful mage in the history of the realm without essential support. She needed to get close to him without draining herself.

There must be something he wants, she thought. *Some way to draw him out.*

Her tired mind kept ramming against the hypothetical first line of magai. Every scenario played out in her mind like a series of recent battles back to back, leaving her exhausted and dead on the field. Part of her was becoming resigned to her death and failure, but she did not want that to be the future of all of Elaria.

"Annalla... Annalla."

She must have dozed or drifted off to some extent. The voice calling her name insistently roused her to some semblance of awareness. Her eyes were gritty, but she avoided rubbing them. The sand had taught them the error of such a gesture early in their desert travels.

"Mmm...what?" she mumbled, blinking to clear the sleep from her eyes.

A blurry form condensed into Karlo standing out in the sun, squinting against the glare. Sounds of combat would have woken her immediately, so it was not an attack. Karlo appeared subdued, sad, and almost guilty. The last woke her up and made her weary with a sense of dread growing in the pit of her stomach.

She licked her dry lips. "Karlo, what happened?"

"Protector." He swallowed thickly. "I regret to inform you that Crastus has been captured by our enemy."

"What?!" She was on her feet in front of him before consciously making the decision to stand. Captured? No one had been taken alive since...she could not recall when. "What happened?"

"His flight was scouting," he said. "They encountered a group of vampires large enough for a full attack and heading in our direction. His second reported that another group was waiting for them on their return, and Crastus ordered them to scatter and fly fast. Most evaded them. Two were reported killed, witnessed by others, and three are missing and presumed captured."

Her fingers brushed her lips, which seemed numb. All of her felt numb. Gregry. Crastus. Annalla wondered if her world had become large enough to include so much loss, or if, perhaps, she was bad luck in some way. Did knowing her become a harbinger of a person's doom, as she was a harbinger of war to the fairy?

Is my life worth so much loss? She wondered.

"Protector Annalla?" Karlo said as he reached out to her hesitantly.

"What—" She cleared her throat. "What did Argent say?"

Before he answered, Larron ran out from behind a

corner. He looked warm. You could not avoid a little sweat in the heat of the day, but relatively speaking, he seemed relaxed and unbothered by the daily temperatures. The flowing robes of the desert wrapped his strong, lithe frame, but he had forgotten the protective head cover in his rush.

He did not speak, only walked over and wrapped her in his arms. Crying would be natural, but she instead felt tired and weak. For moments, minutes, Larron's hold was the only thing keeping her upright as she borrowed his strength. His hand cradled the back of her head as she closed her eyes and buried her face against his chest.

Too much. She wasted away under the pressure and wondered how she ever thought she could save anyone. Their interpretation of the prophecy had been wrong; her existence was not a warning to act, but a harbinger of the end.

Larron eased back until he cradled her face in his hands. His eyes roved her face before returning to hold her gaze. She could tell he wanted to speak, to reassure her and offer comfort or words of wisdom.

"Rest," he said instead of the words he truly wanted to convey. "There is no action we can take at this moment, and we must continue our journey soon enough."

He helped her settle down in the shade again. As his steps departed, a shiver trembled down her spine. Despite the heat, she felt chilled.

***

Larron did not wake Argent until it was time to pack up and move. He set additional guards, ordered heightened patrols, and allowed the night watch to sleep. He wished Karlo had not informed Annalla of the situation, but he understood why the man had done so. She had command of the fairy with their group, with Karlo as her second. The problem they'd found after so many weeks of travel, where she supplemented their food and water and fought against massive attacks daily, was that she tired as anyone would. Despite her extraordinary strength, she remained only one person.

Argent shook his head and pursed his lips as Larron brought him up to speed on the day's events. "How is she doing?"

Larron's jaw tightened at the question. His instinctive response toward protecting his lifemate rose forward and blanked his expression.

"Allow me to clarify," Argent said with hands held forward in a calming gesture. "First, as your commander, is our asset stable and healthy?"

Taking a deep breath through his nose, Larron calmed himself before responding. "She needs more sleep. We have been able to rotate everyone else, but no one can take her place, and we continue to rely on her for other needs as well."

"Coordinate with Karlo. I want her grounded tonight if there is any combat, so the fairy will need additional units on shift."

Larron nodded, taking note of the order.

"Second, and I do not mean to pry. But as your friend," Argent said, placing a hand on his shoulder, "how are you and your lifemate doing, and can I help?"

He rubbed his neck and looked around. Chairs, couches, walls. What he would not give for something to slump against at that moment. Instead, sand. Sand for beds. Sand for pillows. Sand difficult to walk in. Sand finding every clothing seam and rubbing skin raw in unmentionable places.

There existed no doubt in his mind that the traveler in him would find the beauty in the landscape and adventure in exploring the desert, but he did not have the luxury of that mindset then and there. They pressed forward, stretching themselves thin to minimize the strength brought against them in the coming battle. All of them, the entire army, were rocks tumbling down a hill with no way to halt their momentum. They had to hope they reached the bottom still in one piece.

"She is so young, Argent," Larron finally said to his friend. "No elf her age would be sent out of the Woodland into a combat situation."

"The fairy brought their young adults, and because of her position with the fairy, she was raised more in their culture than ours."

"I am not certain Anor did her any favors by allowing her isolation." His anger flared at the deceased elf. No child should consider their worth only in terms of some unnamable obligation to the world. Anor should have brought them both to the Derou.

"You can go," Argent said. "The two of you. You can leave, run, and hide. If you stay in this fight, we will use you, both of you, but you know we will never force you. That is not our way."

"That would only break her heart quickly instead of destroying her slowly." Larron shook his head. "I wish I could help her."

"You do. All her friends help," he said. "You understand as well as I that walking alone is not healthy. Even travelers make connections and come home. You give her that, my friend, and she will need it more than ever when this is over."

If she accepted him, and if she did not end up broken beyond healing. *If we both survive,* he thought, but recognized everyone there was in the same position. Many of them would not live to return home to their loved ones. He could not save them all, but he firmly believed Annalla was the key to saving more.

"We need to pull additional combat magai forward with us," he told Argent. "If we do not relieve some of the pressure now, she will have nothing for the main confrontation."

Argent nodded. "Darrin has suggested merging the rear two groups. Combining those forces will free up some of the defenders and allow us to rebalance. I will send a missive back with the next messenger group to depart." He paused. "She is not alone, Larron. I think both of you need to remember that."

CHAPTER THIRTY-FIVE

Kalachi Desert – Ceru-Auradia Front Lines

Marto had soon realized he was given command of the magai traveling with the final portion of the army for two reasons. First, his relationship with the fairy was the best established of any magai. Second, despite his injury being as healed as it ever would be, they still saw him as impaired, so they left him with the healing pavilions.

They weren't wrong. He couldn't walk with the soldiers. Desert sand was not conducive to easy passage using crutches. Bitterness churned at first, but Tyrus and Darrin threw so many things at him so fast that he had little time to wallow. Their faith in him and utter lack of sympathy for his missing leg did more to bolster his confidence than almost anything before. 'Almost anything' because Karl remained his staunchest ally and supporter.

"He *does* know how to rest!" said the subject of Marto's thoughts.

Grinning at Karl, he said, "Resting is easy. Feeling rested is the challenge in these temperatures."

"Hmm," Karl grunted in agreement. "Darrin is looking

for you, by the way."

"Speaking about people who don't know how to rest..." They shared a significant, speaking look before Marto continued. "He wants to move one of the healing pavilions forward. We're ready for it to go tomorrow, and the soldiers will be able to return to duty by the time it arrives."

Karl smirked in his direction. "You're becoming quite the efficient administrator."

He huffed a laugh. "I'd prefer to be helping Annalla, but at least they asked for more combat magai to be sent forward."

"Including Alastair when we merged, which put even more onto your administrative plate!" Karl sobered. "I worry you're pushing yourself too hard."

Marto shook his head. "Darrin and Clanlord Guldrith do most of the work...and speaking of again..."

Darrin's golden-bronze wings circled down to where they sat. He looked like a god of the desert with those wings. His tan had deepened and his dark brown hair sported new golden streaks. Their fairy prince turned the heads of more than just the fairy when he passed through and over their camp.

As predicted, he inquired about the status of the healers upon landing, and Marto conveyed the same information given to Karl only a moment before. The dark circles beneath Darrin's eyes worried Marto, probably more than *he* worried Karl. Darrin was hardly much older than Marto, yet the fate of his entire people rested upon his shoulders.

"Sit," he said. "Join us for a moment. I have something important to ask Karl, here."

He tried to beg off, but Karl deftly maneuvered his prince to a seat next to them. Based on his efforts, he noticed the signs of exhaustion too. You could almost see the mantle of authority shed from Darrin's shoulders as he sat with them and softly smiled.

"So," he said, "what's this question you have for him?"

Marto grinned mischievously. "It's actually a question from your Protector, so keep that in mind," he said. "Along with Tyrus, I've been trading messages with Annalla and Nurtik via your messengers, and we had some confusion when I mentioned Karl. She asked if we were talking about Captain Karlo. Tyrus said he was armsmaster of the school, but *Annalla and I* wanted to ask if you two are related."

"I don't know what you're talking about," Karl said.

His innocent expression was ruined by Darrin's belly laugh. "They are, indeed!" he said. "What is it, Karl? Cousins?"

Karl appeared resigned to the conversation as he nodded. "On my mother's side, yes."

Darrin pointed at him and focused on Marto. "There was a mayor before my time," he said. "She was staunchly pro-Protector. She led the shift in governance when Reyna didn't return on schedule. My father fought with her constantly and was half in love with her."

Karl had a wistful smile on his face. "Karalonia. My mother practically worshiped her. She and my aunt argued over who would get to name their daughter after Karalonia. Then they both only had boys."

A messenger arrived to find the three of them laughing. Marto listened as the two fairy traded stories and reminisced about relatives and their childhood.

"Sir," the messenger said as he saluted and passed Darrin a note.

Darrin broke the seal and read the short missive. Marto watched his smile fade, his face fall. Whatever the note said, it wasn't good news.

"More trouble from the front?" he asked as the two fairy seemed to hold their breath.

"No," he said with a slow movement of his head in the negative. "King Delon is dead. My father passed away a couple of months ago."

And so begins the reign of King Darrin, Marto thought with no little sorrow. *Hopefully, he will not be the last fairy monarch.*

***

Annalla wanted a bath and a bed—a real bed—for just one night. And a room with cooled air. And an ice-cold drink. Anything to make her feel like a person again instead of a sweaty, smelly mess of caked-on dust and sand finding its way into every crack and crevice. She lay beneath her tent for their midday rest, fanning herself with her wings and praying to anything that might listen there would be no attack that day.

Since the day Crastus and two others from his team were taken, Argent had worked with everyone to keep her out of combat as much as possible. Grounding her completely would cost more lives than they could afford to lose, but the additional rest allowed her to regain some of her energy, and some of her sanity.

She felt embarrassed about that day. The depression and fatalism always hovered around the periphery of her thoughts, but she had promises to keep. Exhaustion had her so muddled in her head, she had swum within mental wool and not thought clearly. Her emotional stability had been paper thin. Thinking back, she understood her state of mind more, and their changes allowing her to rest likely saved her life. She would not have made competent decisions on the battlefield, which would have been good for no one.

It was impossible to sleep in the heat, but she needed to try to regain more of her strength. Every day out there was more draining for everyone, and they often settled for the foggy, half-dazed rest during the hottest part of the day. They maintained their increased guard constantly because Kahnlair's attacks had shifted without a clear pattern. His kidnapping strike had been the first deviation.

Attacks started coming during the day, as they traveled, during rests, and some still at night. Sometimes his vampires dropped attackers in their midst, sometimes they took prisoners. Some attacks had larger forces arrayed against them, while others were small suicide runs to inflict maximum damage. Then they stopped. For two days, there had been nothing.

People wondered why no attack came, and many began jumping at shadows. Having been kept more in reserve, Annalla was one of the least paranoid people in camp at that point. They were settled at the final oasis, another small spring protected from the sun by the foliage surrounding it nourished by its waters. Fairy brought forward empty containers for them to resupply as they waited for the rest of the army to catch up and consolidate with them. The second group would arrive that day, and the other half of their forces another two days later.

From there, as a combined force, they would travel for five or six days to reach Var Istal. One week. It might all be over in that time, and she wondered if she would be around to see it.

"Protector Annalla."

She rolled over and looked at the man calling out. Her brow furrowed in confusion. "Prince Darrin! You are here early. Welcome!"

He smiled at her as she stood. At least, he imitated a smile. The strained gesture had her own pleasure at seeing him melt away.

"What's wrong?" she asked.

Darrin's eyes closed, and he turned his face away as his jaw trembled. She had been in his place before. Larron had shown her what to do then. Without asking more, she gathered him up and let him cry.

She dropped the sides of the tent to give him privacy. They slowly sank to their knees as his grief took him down, her strength insufficient to hold them both up. Eventually, his shaking subsided, and he leaned back. By then, her feet were feeling cramped from crouching awkwardly, but she ignored it in the face of his heartache.

He wiped his eyes, hissing as sand particles scraped across his cheeks and lids with the movement. The abraded skin added to the flushed complexion and puffy red eyes. His shoulders slumped, and the sigh sounded like it accompanied all the remaining energy leaving his body.

Darrin made an aborted gesture to wipe his eyes again, stopped, and grimaced at his hands. "How does anyone get clean around here?" he asked, his voice harsh and raspy.

"Scrub with clean sand and pat dry, do not rub," she parroted the advice given to them weeks ago, receiving dramatically rolled eyes in response. "Come on. We can talk more somewhere else. I will have Karlo assign a guard rotation."

He shrugged and pushed himself to his feet as though the weight of the world sat on his shoulders. His wings hung limp and dragged along the rug. Annalla guided him outside and made the arrangements before they took off, a canopy and water in her supplies.

They did not go far. Doing so would put them at too much risk, and it was not necessary when all she wanted was privacy to talk more freely than they could in the middle of camp with fairy ears listening. She ordered him around when they landed, making him help her with the tent and earning a grudging smile for her antics.

"So," she finally said as the still warm sand heated their behinds, "what happened?"

Darrin cleared his throat and swallowed thickly. "My father…"

It was easy enough to guess the end of his unfinished sentence. "Has passed away?"

His head jerked up and down. "A couple of months ago. The news took that long to reach us. We knew he was not well, but..." He stopped and knuckled his brow.

"Loss can be tempered," she said. "Knowing it is near can help you address your grief in advance and bolster yourself mentally, but nothing negates the pain entirely. Do not berate yourself for your emotions."

"I feel like crying more, but," he huffed, "there's nothing left."

"I am so sorry, Darrin. I wish I could fix this for you."

Taking her hand, he squeezed it as they watched the shadows shift across the sand dunes. Neither of them rushed; they could catch up. Darrin made a few comments and shared a couple of stories, but there was little conversation until late in the day.

"Tyrus asked me if the sanctuaries would be open to hosting vulnerable people from our allies," he said much later.

"It is your decision now," she said. "What do you think?"

The smile he sent her was half pride and half smirk. "I already have orders in place to do so. If I give the signal, the people assigned will take the children supporting the army here. They will make for the elven Woodlands and extract the royals and grab any other innocents along the way."

His answer warmed her heart, and she hoped her expression conveyed as much.

He continued before she could respond. "The fairy are my responsibility, and none of our people could live easily if we did nothing to help. A more important question is, do you plan to flee if the battle goes poorly? Otherwise, my orders and generosity will be for naught."

"Honestly?"

"Always."

Annalla bit her lip and looked away. "I do not know,"

she eventually said.

"Did your mother have a chance to tell you the story of the origin of the Protector?" He continued when she nodded. "Then you know we are distantly related. Our royal line unites us in a way similar to the elves, but less intense.

"The eldest child used to be the heir until your ancestor changed that. She disappeared for years, leaving her people to fight without her. When she returned, she offered her father a deal. No one knows how she did it or figured it out, but she relinquished her title and all claims to the safety she promised others. She committed herself to upholding the protections with an oath, and as long as her descendants held to the oath, her people would remain safe."

"I know the story," she said. "And that is why the royal line is male and the protector line is female."

Darrin snorted a laugh. "You may know the story, but you are missing my point."

"What would that be?"

He shifted, turning and moving to kneel in front of her. The eyes meeting hers remained bloodshot and red-rimmed, but his gaze was firm. "I govern the people, and you govern the sanctuaries," he said. "But the entire purpose of your oath, at its root, is to protect the fairy *people*. *You* protect the fairy people."

She turned her head, unable to maintain eye contact longer. "I don't know."

"You will," he said. "Whatever you decide, whenever you decide, I'm behind you completely. I trust you, Annalla."

"You do not really know me," she said dryly.

A hand lightly shoved her shoulder, and he plopped back down on his butt. "We're family!"

She laughed, relieved at the banter. They both were.

"Your elf is on my list," he said in a seeming non sequitur.

Annalla blinked. "What list? And he is not 'my elf.'"

"Absolutely your elf," he said, grinning, "and I refer to the list of who our people are to rescue and sweep off to safer lands. If you protect our people, I can help protect you."

"Now *I* am going to cry."

Darrin's smile softened, still filled with grief, but a grief shared. "Thank you, for today."

Annalla nodded and reclaimed his hand. "We both needed it," she said, thinking about the challenge to come.

CHAPTER THIRTY-SIX

Kalachi Desert – Ceru-Auradia Front Lines

Annalla and Karlo touched down in one of the clearings in the fairy section of the massive encampment. Their supplies had been restocked, and the army was once again whole. An air of anticipation and dread permeated the camp. The knots churning in her stomach were not unique, but everyone remained determined.

"Annalla, good," Darrin said as they joined him, Braymis, and Zara beneath a canopy.

Grief shadowed his eyes, but it no longer dragged on his shoulders and wings or pulled his head low. He appeared healthy and confident, a marked contrast from their stolen moments of conversation days prior. The thought that he would be the one soon fighting a hasty pairing to produce heirs made the corners of her mouth turn up, but she avoided a full grin.

"Will you be at the planning session tonight?" she asked.

"Zara and I will, yes," he said. "I'd like you to be there as well, Annalla. That's not what I brought us here for now, though. I already sent the report to the kings, but I thought we could take a flight closer to the city and see for ourselves what we'll face."

Deep breaths came from all around. Annalla wondered if seeing it would make it real. Maybe they could hold off reality if they closed their eyes to it.

"You don't want to take any of the others with?" Karlo asked, implying Garrett, Argent, and the rest.

"Not this time, no passengers," Darrin said, slashing a hand for emphasis. "I want to be mobile in case any vampires rise against us. There and back, quick and quiet."

With her papilio wings, Annalla was the most likely to slow them, but she had defenses the others did not. A guard of raptors lifted off with them, rising to an altitude at which the temperature became marginally more reasonable, and headed west.

After a couple of hours of flying, Zara pointed. Annalla's eyes tracked in the same direction and scanned the horizon. A few of the advanced fairy guards were ahead, but the sky looked relatively clear of everything else. The ground, however, was a different story. There were rock formations scattered across the desert, and they had passed plenty of them on their way there, but what she had originally taken for another cluster was the city Kahnlair controlled.

It didn't stand out from the desert. Instead, it blended with it in a way serving both form and function. There were a few tall buildings. The layout was more of an open honeycomb pattern she could just pick out thanks to the short shadows cast by the walls. Without those differentiating colors, the entire city faded into the desert well enough to be a cluster of rock until you were on top of it.

The city had a harsh beauty, like the desert it nestled in, but Annalla's gaze did not linger long. Arrayed between them and the city, growing more distinct with every moment they flew closer, stood the army they would face. Already, it looked to be ten times the size of their ground troops, and she could not see the vampire forces. It was likely they holed up in a true rock formation not far away and would be called in when needed. Humans mostly, with the gilar a close second in numbers. Worse, they had war engines the allies could not bring with them through the desert.

"This is...ugly."

Darrin's laugh was resigned. "I'd say that's an understatement. This is very bad. I sent a report to the other leaders, but I thought you might want to see it for yourself before we discuss how to approach the coming battle."

"Yeah." She sighed. "And you can bet there are more we cannot see that he is holding in reserve—on the off chance he needs it."

"Agreed. What do you think? We'll arrive in a couple of days?"

"Sounds right, depending on how we time it. We should head back." They completed a lazy curve to head back the way they had come. "He might let us be the aggressors to see if we break ourselves on the wall he formed."

"Maybe he's the one who will break!" Zara shouted to be heard over the distance and wind generated by their speed. Silence met her fierce statement, but hungry grins soon followed. The fairy were ready, despite the odds.

By the time they returned, the ground leaders had already pored over the detailed reports from the scouts. A map was sketched onto parchment, with markers added to represent opposing forces. From the sounds rolling out of the general area, the reaction inside was less optimistic.

"We can't close unless we take out those catapults," Garrett said firmly.

"And we can't eliminate the catapults without closing," said Clanlord Guldrith.

"What about Annalla?" Lesyon asked.

"No," Larron said. "We are already too reliant on Annalla and Jarin, and sending her so far in advance would expose her too much to the magai."

She entered with Darrin and Zara and peered around the tent as Jarin spoke.

"Find Ambergine and Donistor," he said. "We need the irimoten here. Morena would be the first to tell you all to leave the catapults to them."

"Why are they not here already?" Annalla asked.

Walsh shrugged. "We passed along the information. They said they would be back in time for us all to meet."

"And so we are!" said a female irimote with gray fur, shifting toward red along her head and back like a squirrel's. Ambergine was followed by Donistor, whose fur was light gold with darker gold rosettes. While Patrice often attended the meetings, it was those two who officially represented the irimoten forces with the army with Morena no longer acting as their voice. "What did you need from us?"

Jarin smiled at the pair. He had spent more time with them since Morena's death. Annalla thought it was to be around others who had been her friends. "We are discussing what to do with the catapults, and I suggested we ask you."

Ambergine flashed her fangs in a vicious grin. "It would be our pleasure."

"You think you can get to them?" Garrett asked.

"With some help," she said, looking at Darrin before moving over to the map. "We want the fairy to fly us over there in advance of your arrival. My people will work our way into the city and behind their lines to disable as many of the weapons as we are able."

Lesyon grimaced. "That is suicide," he said. "Your people will be discovered as soon as they make a move."

She sobered, her grin fleeing in the wake of something filled with grief and sorrow. "The risks are being taken into account."

Patrice, Annalla thought, *and people like her.* They would take volunteers for the mission, and those individuals were likely to be alone in the world. Were she in a different position, Annalla might have volunteered herself.

"How many do you think you can eliminate?" Walsh asked after a moment, acknowledging the gravity of the prior statement.

"All of them," she said, "if we have help. Ideally, we would strike during or just before the first action. That means you need to engage and potentially withstand multiple hits before we end the threat."

He tipped his head, trusting they knew their own capabilities. "We assume the irimoten take care of the catapults, at least most of them. Jarin holds the middle. Hephestar?"

A pinched expression graced the mage's face. "I suspect we'll be of little assistance offensively. We have more combat magai with us here than there were at the academy, but that won't matter if Kahnlair supplements the power of those on his side.

"We might...*might* be able to shield against his magai if we merge our efforts. If he's distracted and focused elsewhere, then we should have more magai than him."

The last line was said with a glance in Annalla's direction. She might be a distraction for Kahnlair, based on his standing orders, but putting her in play would be challenging.

"I have a similar problem with his magai," she said. "They know to use only force and energy against me, and I have not yet determined a counter that is consistently effective. My plan is to gain his attention by eliminating some of his magai, draw him out, and engage in a direct confrontation."

Larron's face, always a visual draw for her, took on an expression of mixed disbelief and vexation. His jaw went slack, his eyes closed, and his brow furrowed. Their bond told her part of him thought she was crazy. Another part wanted to tell her to run away. Yet another thought it might be fun to run headlong into danger at her side. She smirked in his direction, waiting for him to open his eyes once more and return her smile.

Zeris cleared his throat. "Yes, well, what if that plan does not work?"

She shrugged. "Then I keep attacking until I can reach him."

Half the people circled around put their heads in their hands at her statement.

Walsh waved her off. "We'll set your part in this aside for the moment. Prince Darrin, what about the rest of the fairy?"

"Unfortunately, we haven't been able to gain reliable intelligence on the number of vampires in and around the city," he said. "Most of our people will be assigned to engage with them in the air. We have units assigned to disengage if their numbers are low enough and provide additional support for your ground combatants, as we have previously."

If nothing else, the regular assaults during their journey had improved the coordination between their disparate forces. They had become better at working together, taking care of their area while offering effective support to each other. Each had learned the strengths of their allies and figured out where they fit.

"So," Walsh said, "we're going in with the expectation that the fairy will keep the vampires from us, and the rest of us will face the remainder of his army. We need to time our arrival and attack for the morning, which means traveling through the night."

"We should stage our medics where we would camp for the night shift," Ambergine said. "It'll be far enough to have relative safety while remaining close enough to retreat to."

"And we need a better plan—no offense to Annalla—or at least some contingencies, for dealing with Kahnlair," Garrett said to a round of agreement.

They talked for a while, sharing more details from their most recent scouting, but no one could answer the key components of their preparations. Could Kahnlair harm Annalla, and could she penetrate his defenses? Until they tested each other, any planning was guesswork at best and wishful thinking at worst. No one could make any promises.

Annalla sought out Patrice after everyone was released for the evening. The fairy assigned to carry the irimoten passengers to the point from which they would embark on their stealth mission left soon. If she did not take the time, she might never see her friend again.

She had to ask around before she thought herself on the trail of the elusive irimote. Away from the irimoten camp, away from the soldiers' training, she followed the latest guidance over to the healers, not far from her starting point where the leaders congregated. Patrice sat talking quietly with Marto.

A gentle smile spread across her face. "Annalla," she said in greeting. "I wondered if you would be joining us."

"I heard about the mission," she said, taking a seat on Patrice's other side.

"They placed me in command."

"Then the machines are as good as gone," Annalla said with good humor and no little confidence.

She had seen Patrice fight, and her stealth was enough to defy fairy hearing. The irimoten trained to become some of the greatest ambush hunters in the world. Many of them had lived for years in the lands behind enemy lines, gathering and providing intelligence on Kahnlair's army movements and those of his supply lines. No better choice existed for the mission.

"We'll see it done," she said. "And while we're willing to die for our cause, not one of the people going is treating this like a suicide mission. I'll get as many of my people out as I can."

"What about you?" Marto's voice remained soft, almost as if he was distracted or afraid of asking the question because he did not want an answer.

Patrice did not respond right away and instead peered out over the camp. From where they perched atop one of the remaining pavilions—those not left behind to lighten the load—they could see most of the camp and make out the individuals milling about below. Sentries flew above and patrolled the perimeter, while others finished storing materials, taking care of the animals, or any number of additional tasks required to support an army on the move.

Her eyes seemed to catch on one particular spot, and Annalla followed her line of sight. The meeting had gone long, and it seemed many of the leaders had gathered with loved ones for a late meal. All three elven kings sat together. The lifemates of Argent and Zeris joined them, as well as Larron. Garrett laughed with his three sons, shoveling in bites, as though this were his last meal, between bits of conversation.

"They don't understand," Patrice said finally. "Not like us. Those they love surround them, and they live in constant fear of losing those people. But fear is not grief. We have, each of us, at some point in our lives, lost everyone who ever mattered to us. We know…what it is to be alone, and alone with our pain.

"I hope they never understand. I want every one of them down there to live through this, for those families to remain whole and unharmed. My wish will not be granted. More people will lose everything, and I can only try to minimize the damage."

"So, instead, you choose to leave us. To be another person *we* have to say goodbye to." Marto's heart was in his voice.

"Oh, Marto," Patrice said, turning her back toward Annalla so she could face the young mage. "Marto, I'm so sorry. I know. I know how much it hurts, and I know how unfair it is for me to ask this of you when I'm doing the opposite."

"You want us to fight, be strong, and live," he bit out, "when you will not do the same for us."

Her head dipped. "You're right," she said. "You are absolutely right, but I ask anyway. I've lived my life, had friends, a family. You, both of you, have lived war, but you have not lived *life*, and I want that for you."

Marto shook his head and turned away from her. Patrice dropped her forehead to her bent knee, and they sat once more in silence. Laughter rang out below, making it to Annalla's ears and drawing her attention to Garrett again. Tyrus sat with them, but positioned a little apart, a wistful smile on his face as he took in the sight of his brothers and father together. *Does he contemplate who he will see again?* she wondered.

Larron, too, sat apart. *Will he sacrifice himself to save one of the elven kings? Does his duty lie with them, or with me? Can I ask him to remain safe for me, when I am not certain I can promise the same to him?*

"You know," she said to Patrice through the silence, "that we cannot promise you anything. You want to go into this battle, believing you will be keeping us safe, that we will live the beautiful lives you envision for us. None of that is guaranteed. Marto and I are not running from this fight. We will be there, in it, and we might not emerge."

Patrice swallowed and knuckled her eyes. "Don't say that."

"Why not?" Marto asked. "It's true."

"Because I need you to live," she said. The last word came out choked. "I need you to *live*."

Tears rolled down Marto's youthful face as he looked at Patrice and gripped her shoulders. His cheeks were blotchy, reddened, and pain hung in his eyes. "Then promise you'll *try*. Promise me you'll go in, execute your mission, and then you'll try to escape."

"Marto—"

"I need to know you'll try."

She gripped his hand in both of hers. "I promise you. I will not waste my life; I will not throw it away for grief."

Marto placed his free hand on top of hers, only wobbling a little due to his missing leg as he shifted weight.

"Will you be here if I return?" she asked him.

"I'll try," he said, accusation in his voice. "I promise I'll try."

CHAPTER THIRTY-SEVEN

Kalachi Desert – Ceru-Auradia Front Lines

The last encampment had been left behind hours before. They had then walked through the night after an extended rest the previous day. Little light shone down from the sky. The moon was a sliver touching the horizon. Stars littered the darkness above, twinkling in mesmerizing patterns and clusters. Nothing broke the vastness around her, and she remembered how small and powerless she was on that grander scale.

There would be one morning rest before they closed the final distance to their enemy. A few hours, maybe a handful, and Annalla would be standing before her ultimate purpose. Most of the fairy had flown ahead, setting up a small forward camp in preparation for their arrival. It should make for a quick and simple settling. No one thought their rest would be as easy, but some time down was necessary before the battle to come.

By the time they reached the site, the sky eased toward dawn. Sunrise remained hours ahead, but its hints began to hide the faintest of stars behind the veil of growing light. Annalla allowed herself to go to a quiet tent, sit on the rug laid out for her, and send her awareness out.

No earth, no water. Both elements were too far forward or below for her to use effectively without draining herself. Being limited to fire and air would be nothing new in the desert. It gave her at least one primarily offensive and defensive ability at her disposal. She tested her reservoir of power. Moderate. Getting the army to their destination had been a constant, subtle drain on her resources. Were it not for the limitations placed on her fighting, she would be drained to near uselessness.

Part of the problem stemmed from the fact she had yet to regain her full strength. Air was a new ability, and she estimated she would not achieve her full potential in it for another year. For the rest, she suffered from the way those abilities emerged. As she fought for control, essence blasted out of her. Every time, she faded a little more until the effort nearly cost her life.

Annalla suspected Larron was aware of her continuing limitations, despite having never specified the extent. Essentials recovered rapidly, but her well ran deep, and she suspected few had ever become as depleted as she and survived. They would have to hope her power was enough, though. Delays only benefitted Kahnlair.

Returning to herself, Annalla noted the time based on the growing daylight outside. Her heart pounded. *So close.* One last thing remained for her to do before the end began. It might be cowardly, but she wanted a time limit on her humiliation.

She donned her armor and strapped on her weapons. Stepping out into the already warming air, she took a deep, bolstering breath. Her steps carried her steadily toward the elven warriors. Row upon row of elves sat or stood checking and preparing quivers of arrows, testing bowstrings, and sharpening blades. Weapons gleamed in the dawn light, and the armor was so well made and maintained it did not make a sound of protest at any movement.

With their hair pulled back in tight braids and fighting

queues, their lean faces seemed lengthened by their pointed ears, making them look more fierce. The elves were devastatingly beautiful and stunningly dangerous. She wanted their lethal grace, but her own form was more muscular and compact.

"Annalla," Argent said from her right. "Our preparations are nearly complete. Did you need something from us?"

She scratched at her head, pulling some hair loose from her relatively sloppy braid. "I was hoping to borrow Larron for a moment, if possible."

"Of course," he said and looked around with a furrowed brow. "I believe he is at the end, two rows down." He pointed.

Nodding her thanks, she moved on and down the rows of archers, scanning for the familiar face. She found him laughing with a group of eleven others as they repaired damaged arrows together. Back in his 'Commander' personality, he remained a touch more removed than his companions, but their trust and comfort with him was obvious.

"Larron," she interrupted, "could I have a minute?"

The smile on his face softened when he looked at her, and she could not stop the returning smile even if she had tried.

"Of course," he said. He sent a questioning glance at another of the elves, who replied with an easy, "We have this."

"Is there somewhere private we can talk?" she asked when he joined her.

For once, she found it difficult to read his expression. Perhaps curious with a dose of good-natured patience, but it could as easily be distraction or acceptance. The coming conversation had run through her mind countless times, and she tried to go through her options once more as she followed him the short distance to one of the few closed tents.

Limited open space remained inside, as most of it held supplies they wanted protected from the sun and scouring sand.

Boxes, crates, and barrels carried with them since before they entered the desert, clustered in stacks with close aisles between. Larron turned in the middle of the main aisle and gave her a lopsided grin.

"I am afraid this is the best I can offer," he said.

Annalla allowed her eyes to roam the walls boxing them in, avoiding meeting his eye and giving herself more time. *Maybe this was a bad idea.*

He tilted his head and reached out a hand to hold her forearm lightly. His thumb made gentle strokes meant to calm that only stoked her nerves higher.

"How can I help?" he asked.

She stared into his forest green eyes, darkened by the tent's shadows, and what came out of her mouth was not what she intended. "Would you braid my hair?"

His thumb paused, and the joy in his eyes at her simple request startled her.

"It would be my pleasure," he said, gesturing for her to have a seat on the only lone crate around them.

A strap was placed in her hand, and she closed her eyes when his hands threaded into her hair, touching her scalp. With gentle strokes and firm holds, he wove a masterpiece she might be able to achieve if she dedicated herself to years of practice. His warm fingers danced and took her pulse with them. She forgot, for a moment, how intimate that could be.

Her fuzzy brain scrambled for something to say.

She swallowed. "I thought Geelomin and the others would be with you."

"Hmm? No," he said, and she could hear approval in his voice. "Geelomin will retain command of the team he has led since they left the Palonian. Oromaer spoke highly of his integration of the different people and skills assigned to him."

"I thought Tyrus' guards would have been returned to him."

"Oromaer requested otherwise, and Garrett left the decision up to his son," Larron said. "It is my understanding that Tyrus asked his men if they would prefer to return to a human unit, and all of them declined 'unless their prince thought it necessary.'"

"So, where will they be positioned?" she asked.

"They are assigned as Jarin's support unit."

"What?!"

Annalla started to turn in panic, only halted by Larron's hold on her hair and his hurried, "Hold still."

Jarin's position would literally be front and center. He was meant to hold the line with his immeasurable strength and endurance. Kahnlair's forces would throw everything at his position to see if they could break him, or at least break through. While Jarin might be invulnerable, her friends were not.

"Larron..." She was unsure what to say, and did not want to voice her concerns, fearing that speaking them might conjure them into reality.

"I know," he said softly. "Geelomin and Jarin have a plan, and there are magai in their group. He believes they will be as safe as anyone else today."

She grunted her displeasure as he held out a hand and said, "Tie, please."

He tied off her hair while she continued fretting over her friends. Thoughts and plans for how she might help protect them during the battle flitted by one after another, each one more untenable than the last. Saving one might lose them all.

Larron circled around and crouched down in front of her, placing his hands on her knees. "You cannot help them."

"I know," she said. "I came to the same conclusion."

He smiled and gave a comforting squeeze that she found far different from comforting. "And you trust them."

"And that," she echoed. "Larron..."

Her gaze dropped again, but the sight did nothing to distract her. He seemed bigger in that small space, with his knees bracketing her and his hands touching. His head dipped, catching her eye.

"What is it, Annalla?"

"I wanted to..." Her breathy words faded out and her eyes drifted lower, low enough to see his lips quirk up in a slow, knowing smile.

Larron shifted smoothly, dropping to his knees and leaning forward. One hand trailed up her arm, and the air left her lungs. His hand cupped her cheek. His fingers dug into her hair.

One moment, she thought. *We can be for one moment.*

Annalla did not realize her eyes had closed until Larron's lips brushed hers. She closed the remaining distance between them and kissed him as she had longed to for the eternity of the last year. And, to her delighted surprise, he kissed her back as fiercely.

The world melted away. Fears. Responsibilities. Nothing mattered beyond the man holding her. She heated from within. As she ran her palms down the leather covering his chest, she regretted waiting until the last minute.

A second hand gripped the back of her head. Her butt hit the crate, and she pulled him closer, grasping at his hips, his back. *Yes.*

"Larron," a voice called from down the lane outside, "we are on final count."

No! Everything in her screamed as the two of them broke apart at the interruption. Annalla looked anywhere but at the entrance or Larron. His hand remained on her cheek, though, and he brought her face back.

His eyes were heated, and he watched the movement of his thumb tracing across her lips. "I guess we should go," he said softly.

She allowed herself one more moment, leaning her cheek into his palm before pushing herself back. "We should, but—" Annalla stopped at the pained look on his face. "What?"

The pained look turned pleased and amused. "I messed up your hair. Allow me to fix it?"

Annalla rolled her eyes but sat on the crate, still regaining her wits. When he finished that time, she stood and faced him, placing her hands against his chest. The move served to maintain some distance while reminding her he lived through the beat of his heart against her palm.

"Larron," she said firmly, speaking to his collar instead of meeting his eyes. "I am going to pretend this meant absolutely nothing. And, even more unfair to you, I am going to ask you for a promise."

He reached up to where her hands rested and covered them with his own. "So, ask."

Struggling against herself, she bit her lip and forced her eyes to meet his. She swallowed and drew in a breath. "Don't die." The words came out a whisper, a bare breath, but he heard and understood.

His hands squeezed gently, and he smiled. "I will be with the archers, in the back," he said as he drew her in for a hug.

Something inside her chest burned as she laid her forehead against him.

"Do what you need to do, Annalla," he said, speaking against her hair where his cheek rested. "I will be here."

CHAPTER THIRTY-EIGHT

Var Istal – Kalachi Desert

The interrupting elf waited for them only a short distance away, surreptitiously peeking in their direction while scanning the area. At least none of their clothing was disheveled, and Larron had fixed her hair to a better state than before they'd entered the tent. Her lips felt kiss-swollen, but that could just be the memory forever engrained upon her mind. The still-pounding heart might also be regret and nerves rather than lingering excitement.

Larron, the picture of cool and undisturbed confidence, waved the other elf over to convey whatever message he had been assigned. He had rosy spots on his tanned cheeks, hinting at a usually paler complexion than his current tone. The tan went well with hair the deep brown of rich topsoil. His brown eyes, glowing in the dawn sunlight, also lit with humor as they flicked between Larron and Annalla.

Amusement faded as he focused on Larron. "We are preparing to move into position, sir. They are waiting on your return."

"Go," he said. "Tell them I will be right there."

They watched the man depart before Larron turned to her once more. "I do not believe you have faced Kahnlair's true strength yet. Be conservative and hold as much in reserve as you can. The army is here to support you, not the other way around."

Her lip curled in disgust, but she did not refute his assertions. She wanted to say more, but her words were used up, gone. With tight lips, she nodded abruptly and left, forcing herself not to look back as she walked away and took to the sky. The entirety of her attention and effort would be required on the field. If she knew where any of her friends fought below, they could become a lethal distraction.

A whistle blew off to her left, drawing her attention to where Karlo waved her over.

"Kahnlair is calling us out," he informed her when they met. "Apparently, he wants to talk. Argent has asked for you."

The elf king must have left for the front almost as soon as she left him to find Larron. That, or he'd requested a ride from a passing fairy. Karlo led her to where Argent waited with Garrett, Zara, and Hephestar.

"Where are Darrin and the others?" she asked.

Garrett shook his head. "They are all with their various assignments," he said. "Listen, we need to prepare you quickly for what is about to happen."

"Normally, we would avoid this confrontation," Argent said, "but this is an opportunity for you to test yourself against Kahnlair's power when we know it will be active."

"Zara," Garrett said, taking over again, "we will need three fairy to carry the three of us out there with Annalla. They need to be people who can restrain themselves from any emotional reaction and follow orders no matter the provocation. This is not a physical battle, but psychological torture, and whoever you send must be able to endure."

She gave an acknowledging dip of her head as Argent

spoke to them solemnly. "When we meet with his representative, they will kill someone they have taken prisoner. We believe that, for many reasons, this time it will be one of your people they sacrifice. Your friend will die, and Kahnlair will take over their body.

"There will be words of threats and promises and the appearance of negotiations," he said. "In the end, the attack will be ordered. Kahnlair will use the body of your friend to fight and kill until the corpse is beyond effective movement. Your friend will be gone, already dead, so do not hesitate to strike."

"The Derou told me about this tactic," Annalla said. "I will see what I can do, but there have already been instances in which I could not penetrate their shields."

Zara assigned other fairy to their group and remained behind. Annalla and Hephestar would shield them from any surprise attacks while the fairy extracted the leaders as quickly as possible. As she flew the short distance to where a dozen of Kahnlair's people clustered, she tried to brace herself mentally. Whoever they had with them remained hidden from view by the milling bodies surrounding their captive.

A gilar stepped forward and called out. "Lord Kahnlair wishes to speak with the fairy essential."

Blood chilled at the same time hope flared in her gut. If he knew she was there, then he became more likely to be drawn out to face her. The gilar stared, but they did not wait for a reply. Two more gilar moved forward as the first stepped aside, revealing the man held between them.

Annalla met Crastus' eyes as his bloody, excised wings were thrown to the ground, their beautiful colors muted with the death of the limbs. Tears welled in her eyes, and panic spread through her as her mind reeled. She had mere seconds to save him.

Air and fire. She thrust her essence forward, reaching for clothes, weapons, anything she could use to throw his captors clear and maybe burn them. Instead of finding purchase, her power ran into a wall and left her reeling. If it had been physical, the damage from running headlong into it as she had might have been permanent or at least required magic healing.

Fighting against a reaction that would show her desperation and frustration, her eyes darted around for other options. Her brow furrowed and her lips tightened as her eyes snapped back to Crastus'. His gaze held no recrimination or anger. He stood tall and stared into her eyes as one of the gilar raised a dagger.

"I'm sorry." His lips formed the words, but he said it silently, for her alone.

Pain burned in Annalla's chest as she could not even respond with her own apologies lest she give away the depth of her reaction. She couldn't save him, and she couldn't even tell him it was her own inadequacy at fault and not his value to her.

The blade punched home, straight to the heart, and it took her breath with it. Something wet hit her cheek and rolled down as she watched the light fade from Crastus' eyes, only to be replaced by a new awareness. His sagging body stood upright once more, and he brushed his hands down his body, straightening his bloody clothing as the gilar released his arms.

Annalla felt dizzy with the spinning of her emotions. Pain and anger churned with her disgust at the facsimile of life before them. The corpse of her friend smiled at her as the desert air dried the escaped tears on her cheeks.

It pulled the dagger from its chest and spoke in a voice still familiar to her. "Welcome, Annalla. It is a pleasure to finally meet you."

"But we have not really *met* yet. Have we?" she asked, leaning on her anger to bury the rest.

The regal smirk—full of derision, on Crastus' lips—did not belong to her friend. "I suppose there is truth in your words," he said, "but a meeting in person is part of my proposal, if you will hear it?"

Drawing on some of the more petulant behavior observed during her teenage years, she crossed her arms and cocked a hip. "I'm listening."

A twitch in his cheek hinted at his displeasure with her insouciance. "I will allow your entire army to leave the desert unmolested. No interference. No attacks. The way will be clear all the way to the other side of the Oasis River."

Reversing all their efforts from the past two months did not seem like much of an offer to her, but she refrained from saying so aloud. "And what are you asking in exchange for this *generous* offer?" she asked.

"You," he said as his eyes studied her. The look was not sexual or possessive. He didn't *want* her, or perhaps the better emphasis would be that he did not want *her*. His study felt more curious or covetous, so there was something *about* her drawing him.

"I want you to submit yourself to the custody of my gilar," he said, "who will ensure you are not conscious as you are brought to me so that I may meet you."

I wonder if I would ever regain consciousness in this hypothetical scenario, she thought, doubting the answer would be a positive one.

"Why would I agree to this?" she asked.

"Because you recognize what is at stake," he said with a patience both derisive and patronizing. "I am being generous in asking for only one life, in exchange for all of theirs. You destroyed my work camps and dwindled my forces, and I would allow everyone else here to survive to fight another day. I do not crave so much death, but sometimes sacrifices are necessary.

"If you do not take my offer, I promise you I will make it so no one leaves here alive, who is not a part of the gilar herds. They will take their pick of anyone remaining after the battle, and everyone else will face summary execution. No exceptions. No mercy. Your people will never recover to again threaten my purpose."

Annalla wondered if she'd read him wrong. She would never commit herself to his cause, so what did he want from her? Perhaps he thought he could bind her in some way, as the irimoten thought the windani were bound. Perhaps it was not greed, but fear driving him to push for the exchange.

Afraid she might tip the balance, he could be seeking to eliminate her there and then, so he could return to his slow and steady domination of the realm later. Yes, he had lost many in their recent offensive push, but so had they. The advantage provided by the fairy would wane as their numbers dwindled and he would return to his dominant position.

He was ignorant of her position among the fairy, though. She could run and hide or stay and fight. Sacrificing herself so everyone else could fight another day was literally the one avenue denied to her by the oath she had already spoken. The deal, the conversation, was irrelevant.

She stepped forward, walking toward the body Kahnlair had stolen. Her companions did not protest, but the sharp inhalations indicated a strong desire to object. Whether they thought she intended to submit, or were afraid she placed herself in too vulnerable of a position, the move would make anyone nervous.

Kahnlair studied her through eyes clouded with death. He waved a hand to stop the gilar from moving and stood alone, waiting for her. A smile tugged at his lips, giving an impression of smug satisfaction or superiority, while the body posture became predatory.

The changes were nuanced, subtle. His chest tightened and his spine curved as his hips angled. None of the adjustments were extreme or overt, but he went from 'waiting for an answer' to 'waiting to pounce' in a moment. Dead eyes widened with an almost crazed hunger.

When she stopped before him, Annalla raised a hand slowly, reaching out until she gently grazed his cheek with her fingertips. His skin retained some warmth. Crastus' death had not been long enough ago to yet lose it.

I am sorry, my friend, she said the words in her head to the man who had helped her and made her laugh. He had supported her and accepted her without question when she'd been reeling from her power and renewed memories.

"Do we have a deal?" The cheek beneath her hand moved as Kahnlair spoke.

She shifted her gaze, meeting his eyes briefly before moving her vision back to her hand, which began a slow descent. Her fingers trailed down his neck and came to rest against his chest, where she trailed one finger in a circle around the bloody hole left by the dagger still held in his hand.

Annalla stared a moment, taking a deep breath before looking into his eyes once more. Calm, her expression blank, she opened her mouth to speak.

"No."

As the word left her lips, fire erupted beneath her palm, consuming and turning the body to ash in seconds. The gilar and magai tried to react, but the moment her flames touched Crastus, her power swept forward to engulf the area in front of her. Screams rent the air in a short burst, quickly silenced, and she snuffed out the pillar of fire with a thought.

Turning her back on the distant enemy army, she took in the wide eyes staring at her. Garrett sent a fierce grin in her direction, while Argent and Hephestar appeared shocked at the sudden violence. She didn't care; her friend's body would not be used to harm his allies and companions.

"We should go," she said. "They are bound to respond quickly, and this might trigger the irimoten to action."

"How did you get past the shield?" Garrett asked as he

turned toward the fairy assigned to carry him.

Giving him a smirk still filled with her anger, she replied "They had to drop the shield to allow me through."

He glared out over the field and let out a vicious laugh. "Ha! Let's battle!"

CHAPTER THIRTY-NINE

Var Istal – Kalachi Desert

Jarin stood, weapons in hand, at the front of the mixed army and waited while his king went to parlay with the enemy. Geelomin of the Derou watched the distant exchange at his side while their people spread around them. As usual, Jarin would be left to defend a larger swath, but that time he had been assigned specific backup.

The day grew hot. Even at the early hour, the desert heat made itself known. Sweat collected in droplets at his hairline and ran a trail down his back. It had to be worse for the humans in their armor and lower tolerance.

Fighting in the heat of the day was a gamble, but they believed the superior night vision of the vampires and gilar was too much of a risk to do otherwise. They planned the attack for sunrise, which would place the glare of the sun in the eyes of their enemy for hours over the dunes behind them.

"You know Annalla," he said to the lieutenant. "Do you think she will forgive me for my imprudent actions when we met?"

Geelomin stepped closer and put a hand on his shoulder.

"I think she already has. Annalla is no stranger to excessive power and imprudent actions. She once held Larron hostage after we saved her life."

"Larron?" he asked with surprise, knowing how close the two were.

"Hmm," Geelomin hummed in confirmation. "It was back when we first encountered her."

A blast of fire scorched the earth ahead and sent a wave of heated air to wash over them. The flames raged like a tornado, rising into the sky before they were cut off as suddenly as they'd begun. At least half the people who had been standing there were gone.

"Prepare to move out!" Geelomin shouted.

"Do you think they noticed!?" Thanon called out to a chorus of chuckles.

Jarin smiled as Geelomin sighed and closed his eyes. "You have a good group," he told their leader.

"Yes," he said as whistles sounded and horns blew. "Just do not tell them I admitted it."

Shouts and war cries rose on both sides. Geelomin called for their march, and Jarin led the line forward. Sand shifted beneath the force of so many feet. Light gleamed off tens of thousands of unsheathed blades.

A *twang* thumped in the distance, followed by a second, and two boulders soared into the air. Their arcs carried them up and over Kahnlair's forces until they began their descent toward the allied lines. Jarin ignored them; they would fall past him. His enemy approached.

***

Marto rode with Karl in the air over the battlefield. A handful of magai were selected to provide protective shielding for the fairy against any magical attacks from below. His limited mobility combined with his experience flying and in combat made him an obvious choice.

Every fairy went airborne as soon as Annalla took off with the rest of the negotiating party. Such an exchange would traditionally require no attacks from either side, but Marto suspected Kahnlair had forfeited the claim the moment he'd murdered a prisoner to open proceedings. Regardless of his opening, Annalla's closing point was unmistakably final.

One figure stopped ahead of the rest, while the others continued to rejoin their troops. Annalla pulled her mass of shields and weapons up to her from where they had been positioned ahead of time.

A roar grew as the two armies moved. Catapults fired. Behind the city, a dark mass swarmed into the air, blocking the horizon. *Vampires.*

"We have the numbers advantage," Karl said.

Marto looked again and tried to estimate for comparison, but he could only see a swirling shadow growing larger and closer. "Really?"

"Yes. Keeping the magai from interfering will be key to winning the skies."

"Right," he said. "No pressure. I can handle this."

Before Karl replied, two boulders hurtling through the air toward their army made abrupt turns. It was like they hit a wall and bounced off with enough force to shoot in another direction. Instead of hitting his allies below, they dropped at odd angles, crushing some of Kahnlair's people as they hit and rolled.

Annalla. He grinned.

She hovered, a symbol of might and protection. There could be no doubt of her hand in redirecting the boulders. As she moved, sounds of destruction came from Kahnlair's back line. Another stone flew into the air, but the force was wrong. Instead of soaring forward, the rock went only a short distance before crashing into the middle of his army.

Another catapult creaked and cracked until it collapsed on itself. A third swung all the way around to slam its cargo into the ground. On and on down the line, war machines broke and toppled. Not all were eliminated, though, and projectiles soared toward them ahead of the vampires. Annalla again redirected the two closest to her, but one penetrated beyond to crash into their forces.

"Here we go," Karl said.

That was his first time seeing vampires so close. They had taken his home and killed his parents, but the children had been sent away before the attackers had arrived at the former academy. He noted the fangs and claws first, natural daggers designed to pierce and tear open flesh.

Pulling his eyes away from the weapons closing on them, he noted they appeared almost…burned. Their skin was a dark gray to black, and something about it seemed flaky, like they had been cooked and charred. He thought it more likely to be their sparse, bristly fur, but it was not distinguishable as such from that range.

Marto snapped his shield into place around himself and Karl and struck out ahead of them with force. A dozen vampires dropped as though smacked by a giant hand. Other blasts hit from his fellow magai, and then they were zipping between vampire bodies.

He had been in combat before, back in the human town and again against the windani in the mountains. Those experiences were nothing compared to the mess he flew into with Karl. Prior encounters had him working behind the lines, holding defenses, or shooting from a distance. As frantic as those battles had seemed, he knew at that moment how insulated he had been.

Everything narrowed. Blood pounding, eyes wide, his own breath fell loud in his ears. Grunts of effort punctuated twists and turns and jerks of movement. Marto shifted his shield below and extended it wide, trusting Karl to see them safe, as he couldn't follow the fighting raging around them.

His head jerked back and forth, and he fought to hold himself relatively steady rather than flopping erratically and slowing his bearer. A strike hit his shield. The power of it was like a punch to the gut, driving the air from his lungs. Another handful like that, and his shield would shatter.

Before he could follow the line of the strike to pinpoint the enemy mage, Karl whipped around. He twisted and dove to avoid a vampire's grasping claws. Feathers obstructed his view as they spun, leaving him dizzy when they leveled off and rejoined the fighting.

Marto blinked to clear his vision and felt for his shield, making sure it remained oriented correctly rather than spinning with him as Karl kept them aloft and unharmed. A break in the constant movement came when they shifted to regroup.

Bodies from both sides littered the ground, painting the golden sand red. Another mage strike blasted against Marto's shields as they clustered together in an easy target, drawing a groan of effort from him. He traced the path of the magic that time, though, and flicked his hand to send a flicker of energy out to hover over the point of origin. Once it was in position, he pressed more power into the mark and it lit like a beacon of blue flame against the reds and yellows of the desert day.

Their group dove back into the fray before he could see if Annalla had latched onto or responded to his marker. He fended off another strike against his shield and hissed as the pain radiated back to him, making his fingers tingle.

His eyes watered from the speed of Karl's movement. Left, right, spin up. There were some ponds with little fish in the Palonian Woodland. Growing up there, he had watched them dart in and out as they grabbed food and swam back to hide whenever a shadow moved overhead. Such was the speed and agility of Karl's flight, despite the additional weight of Marto hooked to him.

The rest of the fairy in their flight, unburdened by passengers, moved with blinding pace and precision. Karl needed to stay close to keep Marto in range to protect them, while the rest fought dagger-to-claw with the vampires. Unlike on the ground, providing support in the air meant being well within the mess of the fighting.

"Hold on!" Karl shouted a moment before something impacted them.

It came from above and to the left, far enough that Marto had not seen their attacker. Karl's arms went limp, dangling at Marto's sides, and they began a rapid, spiraling descent. Turning his head, he saw Karl was unconscious, the wind caught in his silky blue-black wings was not slowing them enough with one bent awkwardly, likely broken.

"Karl!" he shouted, reaching back to try to tap the man awake. "Karl!"

They continued falling, trailing a line of feathers. Marto frantically looked around, seeking anything that might save them. The sand below might be loose, but it was nowhere near soft enough to break their fall safely.

Not force—he couldn't push himself with the attack. They needed stopping power. Shields? He thought he might have an idea. A ridiculous idea, but their only option.

As quickly as he could manage, Marto threw shields below them, layering one on top of another. They slammed into the first, and he let it go almost instantly, allowing it to shatter beneath them. The second clung a moment longer, and the third. He tried to hold on a fraction more with each layer, but not so long the shield impact broke them rather than breaking under them.

With each hit, he felt more tired and strained, and then the ground was there. Their connected bodies crashed, sending a spray of sand and dust into the air. Marto cried out in pain as his arm snapped with the landing.

Tears filled Marto's eyes from the grit and pain as he struggled to move. Dizzy and aching, he reached around with his good hand, seeking the knife strapped to his thigh. He struggled to free it, but eventually held the weapon and cut at the harness bindings holding him together with Karl's still unconscious form.

A head turned in his direction, pausing a moment to study him. The figure made a motion, gathering attention, and pointed at them. "Oh, no." He doubled his efforts to get free, sawing as fast as his awkward reach could manage. The gleam in the eyes of the people coming at them did not appear to be one of concern for their health.

Arm throbbing with every rapid beat of his heart, he felt the last connection snap free. The sudden lack of tension sent him toppling forward, face-first, into the sand and onto the broken arm cradled against his chest.

Marto fought against blacking out from pain and snorted a noseful of sand as he tried to settle himself with a deep breath. He coughed and cried out in equal measure as he pushed himself to his knee. Blurry figures closed in, weapons raised for an attack.

A knife, thrown forward, sank into his side and he cried out. His breath became shallow, but he gathered magic to him as he threw his stump of a leg over Karl's limp form to straddle the fairy. Marto closed his eyes and threw an energy strike in every direction before he fell into darkness.

***

The massive boulder Annalla didn't deflect crashed down hardly a thousand feet away from where Tyrus charged forward with his brothers. Valdas would kill them again if they all died there, but his brother would have worse things to address if such a disaster happened. His group was positioned with the last melee line before the archers and would serve in a support and reinforcement capacity.

"Tyrus," his eldest brother called and pointed toward where the stone fell. "Take your men and shore up the line there."

Nodding his head, he called up the captains under his command and moved with them to where Kahnlair's troops pressed around the boulder, where it lay amid the carnage caused by the line of its impact.

Their melee forces were primarily human, supplemented with the smaller number of irimoten assigned to watch their backs. The elves were better with ranged attacks, primarily because of their superior vision. That left the magai to be threaded between the lines, hopefully in a manner concealing them to some extent.

His people swarmed forward, falling on the men preying on their injured companions. The surprise of their entry into the fight lasted only a moment, but they made it count and pressed their attack well past the obstruction. Tyrus' blade sang as he fought, but only a few opponents made it far enough to face him. Most were stopped well ahead of his position.

Their line firmed, and Tyrus stepped back to order new captains and their soldiers to replace those who had been lost. The rest, he pulled back to return with him to their overwatch position at Albertas' side. His brothers looked at him as though confused about something.

"What?" he asked.

"That was efficiently done," Albertas said with a regal tip of his head.

Tyrus raised an eyebrow. "You sound surprised."

"Don't look at me like that." Albertas scoffed. "You know what I mean."

He did. When the war began, Tyrus had still been a child and treated as such. The responsibilities and training given to him had changed over the years, but he hadn't been trained for military leadership specifically. While he could advise, he'd never had to issue orders likely to end with the deaths of those following his commands.

Then, he'd lost most of his guard; men he grew up with who protected him wherever he went. He'd watched innocent children taking up arms defending their town from the gilar and had ordered them into battle. He'd asked the fairy to leave safety and risk their lives in a battle of which they had no knowledge or investment.

Was he bitter and hardened? No, but he would risk much to end the war, perhaps more than his brothers. They had lived the war and its battlefields, but they saw little of the innocent and wonder left in the realm they protected.

"It's been a long year," he said.

Albertas took his eyes from scanning the lines assigned to him and the weight of his stare settled on Tyrus. "You did better than we could have ever hoped, little brother," he said with gravity often lacking from their conversations. "As father said last night…" He paused, squinting as he peered ahead. Tyrus looked as well, seeing a group of gilar leading a press and cutting down a large swath of defenders. His heart sank as he realized their father's position had been compromised.

"Father!" Albertas shouted and started to charge forward.

Lukas, larger and stronger than both his brothers, grabbed the eldest around the shoulders and spun him to a stop. Holding a struggling man, he met Tyrus' eye. "Go! I will hold him here."

The king and his heir were kept separate for a reason, and it was Lukas' job to keep Albertas alive. Tyrus gathered men around him and moved. They ran, shouting a war cry for

Ceru as they went. Gilar met them far too quickly, having penetrated further when the line broke.

Tyrus raised his shield, catching a gilar's strike against it and grunting under the blow. He stabbed forward, but his opponent shifted to the side, swinging in for another attacking drive. The blade *thunked* against his shield and *clanged* when he deflected with his own, shorter sword.

Block. Block. Parry. Strike.

He found the gilar's rhythm. Pressing into the next attack with his shield, he pushed the blade up and over his shoulder, using the gilar's momentum to help. With the diversion, he slipped forward and drove his sword up and into his opponent's chest. The gilar snarled as Tyrus twisted his blade as he withdrew, darting back to avoid a retaliatory strike.

The move was its last, as the gilar dropped to the ground, dead. Shaking sweat from his eyes, he left the body and continued forward. A slice across the back of an enemy soldier's legs gave one of his men the opening he needed to land a killing blow as Tyrus moved past. He spun, blocking another gilar's strike, and stabbed up into its armpit before kicking it away.

A slice slipped past his guard sometime after he lost his shield, opening a bloody line along his side. It tore him open at the joint in his armor, stinging when sweat dripped into the wound and movement tore his flesh further. Tyrus pushed the pain to the back of his mind and elbowed his attacker in the face. The gilar reared back from the blow, but not before its arm spines caught him and ripped another gash in his other side.

Despite the injuries, his backhand swing cut a line along the gilar's throat, ending the immediate threat. A gap cleared in the fighting around him, and Tyrus scanned the area, gauging where he stood compared to where his father had last been seen.

"Tyrus! Sir!" a voice called from a cluster of men defending their forward position. One waved him over from behind the others.

Before rushing over, Tyrus issued orders, shoring up the lines and repositioning the soldiers to hold against the continuing onslaught more effectively. Finally satisfied, he ran across and dropped at the kneeling man's side.

"Your Highness," he said. "The king."

The words were unnecessary. Garrett's face remained clear, despite the grievous wounds elsewhere. A deep gash across his chest showed bone, and his right hand was missing. Those two injuries might have killed him in time, but the death blow there was obvious. Two slices on either side of his neck told the story of a stab straight through. He would have died quickly, bleeding out in moments.

Tyrus stared at his father's dead eyes, looking blindly up at the bleached desert sky. He reached a hand up, surprised it was not shaking, and gently closed them, giving him a peace he did not feel himself. That moment deserved grief and farewell, but there was no time.

The men were holding off Kahnlair's forces, but they had lost ground and were too far forward, too spread out. Tyrus scooped up his father's helm and the ring he wore on a chain around his neck. He cleared his throat.

"Leave him," he ordered. "Fall back! Regroup!"

Along the path of their retreat, Tyrus found a new shield and used it well as he guided the men back into position. Only when the formation settled and had its new orders did he return to his position with the line of reinforcements.

Albertas appeared furious, shouting at Lukas as he paced. Their brother gave no response, stalwart in the defense of his charge, even in the face of such anger and vitriol. King Garrett had given him one order for the battle, that he see Albertas to the end.

Tyrus approached and saw something on his brother's face he never expected: terror. He stood frozen, watching with eyes blown wide until he started shaking his head.

"No," he said. "No."

Holding out the two items he had tucked away for the retreat, Tyrus said to him, "Your Majesty, you have the command."

CHAPTER FORTY

Var Istal – Kalachi Desert

After the horrendous exchange, Annalla returned to where Zara hovered, while Garrett and Argent were escorted to their respective positions along the front lines. Her blood burned with fire and anger, and her eyes held a pressure telling her she had tears left to shed. In her mind, she mashed everything into a tight little ball and stuffed it down deep, mentally using it to bolster her focus.

Zara jutted her chin. "The vampires rise."

She drew up the weapons and shields positioned for her and turned in time to see two catapults successfully fire. Zara gave her a wave that was half order and half farewell before they went separate ways. Annalla's path took her forward over the front lines of the enemy.

A physical gesture was not necessary, but she felt better reaching her hands forward and grasping the air as her power wrapped around the soaring boulders. She slammed her hands down, and both rocks ricocheted into Kahnlair's army below.

He had around twenty of the machines, and the rest started firing as the two armies engaged on the ground and the vampires closed in. Annalla bared her teeth in a grim smile as many of them crashed and broke. The expression turned to a grimace, though, when she could only stop two of the additional three fired successfully.

There was no time to dwell on the miss. Arrows shot at her from the ground, caught in her power, and the leading vampires attacked. Sword flashing, she ducked and darted around the slashing claws, dancing on air and dealing lethal cuts to her enemies. It was the kind of battle to make her blood sing: elegant and precise.

She moved a shield to the side, where a vampire ran headfirst into it and fell, to allow another one through her perimeter. With a twirl, she slashed out, cutting a long gash in the attacker's wing and sending it spiraling down. Flying blades bit into flesh, and she cut through the vampires back and forth across their center lines.

A mage strike hitting one of her shields drew her out of a battle-focused bliss. Annalla threw power into it to hold, and her defenses remained steady. She had increased the number of shields around her threefold since the battle in which she'd broken her leg.

Drawing her weapons into a defensive sequence, she hovered a moment and scanned for the mage's hiding place. According to Hephestar, magai shot either away from or toward themselves, so she could follow it back based on the angle of the strike. Unfortunately, with her and everything around her in constant movement, accuracy was limited.

With a rough estimate, she turned and dove, running in a line about thirty feet above the enemy soldiers. Another blast hit, but she was braced against it, ready. She lit up an area twenty feet in diameter. The fireball enclosed a barrier, holding her power back. Narrowing her focus, she burned hotter and let the temperatures pressure the mage's shields until they collapsed.

Rising, she tried to gauge how much more she could push and started the next hunt.

***

Five elven archers dodged out of the way as a vampire crashed to the ground among them. Larron had not expected his fear to spike as much as it was stationed 'safely' with the back lines of ranged attackers. Before the fairy, they had assigned soldiers to watch the skies for vampires descending to snatch unsuspecting fighters from above. They would dart in to swing at the vampire, trying to disrupt their attacks and potentially injure them while archers focused on distant targets instead.

Since gaining an air force of their own, the sky was as much of a mess as melee combat. Fairy and vampires darted in and out, sliding past each other in the air and circling back for more attacks. The erratic movements made it so origin and direction were not sufficient to determine friend from foe when seeking targets.

Archers paired up so one could target and fire while the other watched for dangers. Unlike the diving vampires, dead or injured aerial combatants had little to no control over their descent. If one of them fell, they fell fast and hard. Anyone on the ground risked serious injury or death if struck on impact.

Ignoring the nearby commotion, Larron sighted a vampire further ahead chasing an injured fairy. The moment of his release, Tydair pulled him by the collar and slammed him to the ground as he fell on top of him.

He barely noticed the thump of another impact as the air left his lungs and he struggled to draw another breath. Tydair scrambled up off Larron, and stabbed with his sword where the dust had yet to settle. Finally able to breathe, Larron wheezed in and regretted it instantly as the airborne sand clogged his lungs, making him cough.

"Larron!" Tydair called him over and whistled for a medic.

He crawled to where his partner worked and found two fairy on the ground with the dead vampire. Tydair already had pressure on the wounds of the first man, ignoring the seriously damaged raptor wings. The woman was wrapped in the vampire's wings, claws in her sides and fangs piercing her neck where it met her shoulder even though the creature was dead.

Carefully, he inspected the injuries and decided the stomach wounds were not likely puncturing major organs, so he worked the claws free and stuffed bandages beneath her clothing. The neck stab was riskier, and he did not want to free her too soon and make matters worse. He shifted to her broken bones and determined none were likely life-threatening.

A group of fairy landed behind them. "Larron."

He looked up at the voice to see the new fairy king directing the three others. "Darrin?" he said in surprise.

The young man gave a wry smirk as he knelt on the injured woman's other side. "Per the request of my colonels, I'm on medic runs today."

It made sense. Unlike the elven and human kings, Darrin had no heirs.

He gestured to the still-penetrating fangs. "I did not want to remove them until we could move her quickly, for fear she would bleed out."

Together, the six of them made quick work of the final field dressings, and two of the fairy took off with the patients in a matter of minutes.

Darrin gave one final look at Larron. "I'll be around, so call if you need me."

He nodded and wished him well as the group took off, then turned to find Tydair holding out his bow. Trading satisfied nods, they took up their positions once more.

***

A sparkle of fire shimmered, drawing Annalla's attention. The flame hovered over enemy troops and likely meant one of the magai assigned to the fairy had found one of their counterparts. She had already eliminated two magai, both with shields supplemented by Kahnlair. Based on the effort needed, she estimated she could only hit one, maybe two more before she had to change tactics to try to draw Kahnlair out.

As with the previous two times, Annalla blasted the area with a ball of fire, then narrowed in on the shielded location. Enemy arrows shot at her, and even a javelin or two were thrown. They did not make it anywhere near reaching her, as her barrier caught anything on target and reaching her active influence.

Despite the protections in place, she continued moving erratically around the general area of her fire. The arrows might not reach her, but there were plenty of magai remaining who were not within the fireball below.

The shield collapsed, and she turned to resume her patrol. As she collapsed the fire and drew the power back, a mage strike hit one of her shields hard enough to shatter it and rip it from her control. The larger center of the shield hit her, throwing her into a spin, and one of the shards bit into her cheek.

Righting herself, she swiveled her defenses to put more between her and her attacker before peering carefully along the line of attack. Despite the distance, she had little doubt as to the strike's origin. Two robed figures stood apart atop the defensive wall at the city's perimeter.

"Hehehe," she laughed a little hysterically, realizing the depth of power she was up against. "Oh, good. It worked." She hissed at the pain in her cheek when she spoke.

The robe on the left fluttered, and a second powerful

strike hit her forward shield. While it also shattered, Annalla took the brunt of the impact on the next layered shield. She pulled the large sliver from her flesh, tonguing the inside of her mouth where it penetrated through.

How can they target me from there? she wondered as she started moving again.

Another shield shattered, then another. She was running out of them too quickly to count. There was no chance of making a direct run for the wall.

"I need a diversion," she said and cursed herself for not grabbing a signal whistle.

Bobbing, weaving, and generally flying like a drunk bee, she scanned for the nearest fairy captain or leader. She found one and called him over to her, barely interjecting herself between him and the wall in time for yet another shield to shatter.

"Protector," the man said as he saluted, wide-eyed at the destruction.

"I need decoys," she told him. "A group of all papilio I can disappear into."

His eyes shifted from her, toward the wall, and back again. With a nod, he whistled up and motioned her to follow him. In quick order, a dozen fairy hovered around her. She drew in more weapons and shields to try to cover them all. When another blew apart into wooden shrapnel, she surged her power to grab the pieces and hold them in the curtain of objects.

Annalla scanned the gathered fairy. "I need to close in on the wall, but he is attacking too frequently."

They exchanged glances and nods. Two of the women undid their hair from sleek tails and started braiding.

"Can you get us all swords?" one of the women asked.

In response, Annalla drew up enough from the battlefield below.

The woman grabbed one and started issuing orders.

"Men, hover close to the women like you are reluctant to go in a different direction. Sunji, you're in line with the Protector, but peel off after we're away."

Splinters flew with another absorbed strike. "He will attack you," Annalla said, not wanting to pretend they would be safe on that assignment.

"That's the goal, Protector," she said. No hesitation. No regret. "End this. Drop your shields and weapons on go, and we all split."

They got into position, and she mentally counted down with the woman. *Three. Two. One. Go!*

Annalla shot up and left, wanting to come at the wall from that side. The shields and weapons she had held plummeted to the ground as she released them from her power. Mage strikes were silent until they hit, and it would be impossible to discern one scream from another with the battle raging. Regardless, she imagined she could make out her decoys crying out in pain as they were hit, though she did not slow to look.

No further attacks came her way, and she rose until the people on the wall were no more than specks to even her vision. She circled the city and dove, letting herself fall and pick up speed. Squinting into the air rushing past, she planned out the timing of her descent. Having done the maneuver carrying Larron and then Argent, Annalla did not doubt she could safely slow herself for a rapid attack.

The figures grew, facing away from her over the battlefield. One of the two pointed out at something and a group of vampires descended. Annalla closed in, approaching from behind. Her wings flared, creeping open and slowing her until she was safe to snap them open fully.

She reached out with her power to grip the massive shields of the gilar standing on the wall to the left of the figures where she wanted to land. Using them, she swept the mass of people off of and over the wall right before she pounded onto the walkway, rolling to absorb the impact. Still holding them, she brought two of the massive shields around to hover in front of her as the robed figures turned.

CHAPTER FORTY-ONE

Var Istal – Kalachi Desert

Annalla attacked as they turned in her direction. Fire engulfed them, only to encounter a barrier she could not feel beyond the void within her essential strike. Every time before, when she'd killed the magai, she'd felt pressure fighting back against the crush of her power. There, before her, hovered only an absence. The closest sensation she could think of was when she'd tried to use air on clothing people wore and sensed a void where the person existed that her air could not touch.

She pressed harder, hotter, and hoped to feel the gap falter or shrink. Instead, a blast shot out of the inferno, hitting her shield wall with a force massive enough to send one of the gilar shields flinging to the side. Dodging behind her remaining wall, she gripped it tighter with her power and dropped the fire.

The robed figures stood facing her in a circle of clear stone among the charred and blackened wall around them. Their stance was leisurely, not braced against an onslaught or primed to attack. Despite the massive power she threw at them, they appeared unfazed.

A chill ran through her and settled in her heart. The

closer person threw out a hand, and another mage strike impacted her shield. She held as the metal dented, but the effort sent a shock through her physically.

Water is closer here. Maybe I can blanket them, and they'll suffocate. The thought passed through her mind as she threw a smaller fireball at the pair, attempting to judge how large an area they protected. Based on the dispersion, it was at least a moderate arc in front of them.

Another gesture, another hit, and she considered closing in physically. If she could move faster than their shield adjustments, it would give her an advantage as her power waned.

Annalla poked her head up, gauging distance, and a blur sprung over the side of the wall and lunged at the closer figure. Sand-colored robes streamed, and daggers flashed in the sun beating down before sinking into the back of the closer figure. The person twisted around to face their attacker and hoods fell from their heads.

She recognized Patrice, clinging to the back of another woman trying to dislodge her. The enemy woman would be beautiful if not for the fury twisting her features. Her burnished bronze skin contrasted with Patrice's white fur as the irimoten dug her claws into the woman's cheek, scoring gashes along her face and ear.

They toppled back from the force of Patrice's leap, tumbling into the crenelations lining the back side of the wall. Patrice gave a final shove, pushing the woman over. She teetered a moment on the edge, a vicious snarl distorting her perfect features. The moment was all she needed to lash out before she disappeared over the side.

As she fell back, a blast hit Patrice dead center. Her smaller body folded in on itself as she shot backward and struck the opposite wall with a sickening crunch before crumbling to the ground.

Annalla stood, staring dumbfounded at her friend lying on the hot stone. A trickle of blood from the corner of her mouth marred her snow-white fur. The floaty robes she wore were not enough to hide the broken and twisted form beneath. Her chest did not rise with breath. Her eyelids remained closed.

They had both guessed the wrong target, and Patrice was dead because of it. Hot tears burned her eyes. Guilt churned in her gut, and she found it difficult to breathe. Had she done better and been able to expose them, Kahnlair would be dead and not his minion.

Kahnlair.

Her jaw clenched as she slowly swiveled her head toward the man responsible for all the pain and destruction. It seemed to her that his head tilted in curiosity beneath his hood as he stared down at Patrice's body.

The reaction, or lack thereof, was too much for her. Annalla screamed out her rage and struck. She threw everything at him, blazing the area white-hot while flinging anything loose her power could grasp at his position. The wall shuddered as she reached down, pulling forth the thorny desert plants to blanket the stones. She held her attack, the heat becoming intense enough to melt the shield lying forgotten on stones in front of her.

Her scream stuttered in her rough, dry throat. She fell to her knees, breathing hard as she allowed the fire to wane. It died away, revealing blackened branches, scorched stones, and drifting ash from the objects destroyed in the blaze. In the middle, Kahnlair stood casually in the center of a clear space, giving no indication he had even felt the heat from her fire.

He pulled back his hood and looked toward where his companion had fallen over the wall. "Well," he said, "she served her purpose."

Annalla wanted to cry, her heart breaking further. "Y-You're an elf?"

The man in the robe had light brown skin with slight blue-gray undertones, like weathered oak but smooth. His chestnut hair was pulled back into a braid in delicate, feathery loops. It was a hairstyle the elves wore to events and celebrations, or in times of peace.

Where the woman had been lusciously beautiful, Kahnlair was chiseled perfection. It had to be a lie, an illusion from his skill as an artist. The image was a feint to throw her off so he could attack while she was caught in disbelief.

Yet, no attack came. He stared at her with a sad smile on his face. It was the kind of smile you gave someone to commiserate when they learned a hard truth.

"I will show her," he said, speaking to the side, as though to someone standing at his shoulder, before he turned his face to peer out across the battle raging below. "Look at the destruction the humans have brought to our realm."

Her brow furrowed, unsure if he was speaking to her. "What?" she asked, then pointed in anger. "*You* did this! *You* brought this war!"

The look he gave her was one of disappointment, as though she was not being reasonable or rational. "No. I was once blind as you are. You do not yet understand how they are like a disease. I am working to cleanse Elaria."

"You are using gilar to kill your own people! How is that right?"

Kahnlair winced and muttered, "*Shh*, I know," but quickly smoothed his expression. "An unfortunate necessity. I am doing what I can to minimize the impact, but the gilar are easier to control than my people would have been to convince of the necessity of sacrifice." He turned to study her as though she were a tool presented for his inspection. "It will be easier now that you are here."

She shook her head, confused. "I am not going to help you," she said. "Stop the fighting. We can fix this if you surrender."

"*Shh!*" he snapped out to the side once more before looking at her again. "My course is set," he said with his face still tilted, making her wonder if he spoke to her or someone or something else. "You will not divert me from it. I am not as skilled with attacks as Tiria, but my shields are impenetrable."

Something clicked in her mind, the reason for the void and how he, and sometimes his magai, could defend against her power when Marto and others could not. "You are an essential."

His head tipped in acknowledgment as an aura grew around him. Despite the blinding sun pounding down on them, Kahnlair seemed to grow brighter to her senses. She did not think the effect was visual, but it presented to her as a bright light surrounding him and blanketing the area with a stuffy feeling and white noise.

"And you will make me stronger," he said, as part of the light lashed out at her like a striking snake.

If she imagined her essence within her like a sticky ball, the strike hit her, biting in and pulling until a chunk of it ripped off. Pain blasted through every nerve in her body. She could not even scream as her throat and lungs seized.

He manifests essence, came a distant thought as the incorporeal extension bit into her again. *I don't have essence yet.*

She would, someday, if she survived. People thought manifesting in itself was an essential power, but that was not true. Manifestations of essence were extremely rare and often less impactful in the physical world.

The latter was not the case for Kahnlair. Based on his mastery, Annalla guessed he had stolen the essence of many through the years, taking the very thing that connected them to life and bloating his own power to the point where he could make his magai nearly unstoppable.

Noise that wasn't noise blasted her ears as he continued

attacking. "Yes," he said in ecstasy on one breath before saying, "Forgive me," with his next.

Something has broken his mind, she thought at yet another indication he was not alone in his head. *It is no wonder he spoke with unfounded reasoning.*

He would win. He would gobble her down, take what remained of her power, destroy the army they'd brought to fight him, and sweep across Ceru. Would he stop there? She did not think so. Another slight would come to mind and he would seek to cleanse the next group, then the next. Not even the elves would be spared from the massacre in the end.

Annalla forced herself to stop writhing on the ground, even as another piece of her was consumed by his light. She pushed herself to her hands and knees and raised her dust and tear-streaked face to gaze upon him once more. He stood, palms forward on hands held wide in a gesture of welcome, an expression of bliss softening his features. The aura encompassed him, highlighting him as some elven deity.

In contrast, she kneeled on the ground. Her sweat-stained clothing clung to her body. Grime covered her skin and her face contorted as another stab of pain wracked her body. Her powers failed her. They were not enough.

She had only one option remaining. To complete his agenda, to see it through, he needed to survive their encounter. Her objective was simpler. She wanted to defeat him. There was no need for an 'after.' Her purpose in the world would be complete. She would protect her people.

Annalla looked to where Patrice's body had been before it had turned to ash in the firestorm of her anger. She breathed out a sigh of relief, and let go.

***

Jarin felt a weight settle on his chest as he struck with his sword, cleaving his opponent in half. A sensation felt only once before engulfed him as a ripple of power washed over him, inducing a moment of vertigo. "Morena," he whispered with longing and regret. He paused and scanned the field, seeking a head of blazing red hair.

"Jarin!" Geelomin shouted at him as he jumped forward, interjecting himself between one of his magai and the gilar rushing forward with Jarin distracted. "What happened?"

He did not know the answer, but a glow emanated from the city wall, drawing him in. It was not Morena. His friend had died at the river, never entering the unforgiving desert with them. Annalla was there, though, somewhere in the fight, searching for their enemy. He had nearly killed her once, an act for which he had yet to atone.

"Jarin!" Geelomin shouted again as a gilar's strike sent him tumbling to the side.

The gilar loomed over the elf lieutenant, raising its weapon to slide the blade home in his side. A human darted in, slamming his shield into the sword and away from Geelomin. He growled as he struck back, pressing forward and giving Geelomin time to rise to his feet.

With another glance at the flickering on the wall, Jarin shook himself and dove back into the fray. He thrust and swung, clearing the immediate area and pushing back those who had pressed into their line. The task of Geelomin and his unit was to shore up the area around him. He required space to work, and too often that left room for enemies to slip past his perimeter. The diverse unit Geelomin commanded had complementary skills they used to minimize that weakness around Jarin.

"Something is happening on the wall," he said in Jularian, hoping the enemy would not understand his words. "We need to get up there. Now."

Geelomin studied him, took stock of his people, and

nodded, then started giving new orders.

***

They were running out of arrows. Half the archer pairs had already been reassigned to melee support, reinforcing those lines as they dwindled from providing reinforcements for the front lines. In keeping with his promise to Annalla, Larron would be one of the last to advance. As the hours passed, though, that eventuality appeared more likely.

He drew and sighted carefully, determined to make every remaining shot count. The fairy were winning the sky, bit by bit, and the vampire numbers dwindled. His eye found one of those remaining and tracked as it harried an injured fairy retreating.

Before he could fire, a wave of dizziness washed over him. He released his draw and bent his head, blinking to try to clear the vertigo. While the feeling did not release, he seemed to be able to orient himself.

"Larron? Is something wrong?" Tydair asked.

The clarity of his partner's voice surprised him with the sense of pressure lingering in his ears. "I do not know," he said honestly and peered out over the battlefield.

Back and forth, his eyes roved the layers of fighting spread across the field of sand. The feeling reminded him of something—familiar in a way he could not place. A glimmer on the city's wall caught his eye.

"What is that?" he asked Tydair, pointing at the speck that might simply be a reflection of the sun rising toward noon. "Do you see it?"

Tydair squinted, his eyes flicking back and forth. He shook his head. "See what?"

"There." He stood behind him and pointed again. "It looks like a giant mirror, maybe?"

"I see nothing, my friend."

He pursed his lips in frustrated confusion at the reply. Concerned eyes flicked between him and the sky as Tydair guarded them while Larron tried to work through what was happening. His royal connection had taught him to never discount instinctual or innate feelings.

He rubbed his eyes and forehead. *When did this happen before?* He asked himself, because he *had* felt something like whatever was happening before that moment.

The memory hit him like a punch to the chest, feeling like something squeezed within him. "Morena," he whispered.

"What?"

Larron ignored the question and spun around, looking up at the sky. "Darrin!" he shouted. "Zara! I need a fairy now!" He did not have a signal whistle, but he put a couple of fingers to his lips and let out a piercing whistle his own way.

He kept shouting, over and over, despite the people around him being startled out of their shooting and looking around for whatever was terrifying him. Fear pushed him, and he had to force himself to slow his breathing when he began to feel dizzy.

"Larron, what's going on?"

He spun at the sound of Zara's voice behind him. Her landing had been swift enough to kick up some sand, and she looked at Larron a little warily when he gripped her shoulders.

"Finally!" he said as he shook the fairy leader. "I need you to fly me to the wall. We need to save her."

Zara glanced in the direction he pointed, then placed a hand on his shoulder. "Larron, we can't help her in this fight."

"I know, but she is killing herself," he said. "She is going to use her essence to kill them both. We must stop her." Larron tore his eyes from the wall to stare into Zara's. "Please."

Holding out her arms as though for a hug, Zara pursed her lips and tipped her head. "Come on, then."

Quickly checking to make certain his sword was secure, he latched onto the fairy and felt the woman's arms come around him as she took off. They weaved between combatants and dove from attacks, dodging them rather than engaging, as Zara made a rush straight for the wall. One dodge came a fraction too slow. Larron hissed as the vampire claws raked his arm, but he told Zara to keep going.

"Where?" Zara said into his ear so he could hear her over the rushing wind.

Hanging his head back, he looked ahead, trying to make sense of the world from his upside-down position and find what he sought. He felt it before he saw it. The power surge went from subtle to immense, and there was no longer any mistaking it for the same as just before Morena died. Larron's head swiveled to the source, seeing a blaze of light.

"There!" He pointed, wondering how anyone could miss the effects of the power being shed.

Light spun and danced over the wall. White and gold battled, shooting off prismatic colors at the edges and sending sparks drifting into the air. Beautiful and terrifying, Larron felt something in him calling to the swirling colors. They centered on someone, but his eyes could not focus on the person through the thrumming power.

Directing Zara behind the figure, he spun around when they landed and drew his sword. They found themselves amid a charred area, blackened by fire. The stones beneath their feet were cracked, either from the heat or the plants, whose remnants still lingered.

At the center of the destruction, an elf shrieked in pain, holding his head as he kneeled, hunched over. Annalla lay facedown a dozen paces away. Behind her, the top of the wall filled with gilar as he took stock of the situation. The closest rested the tip of his sword on Annalla's neck, looked over at Larron, and grinned.

CHAPTER FORTY-TWO

Var Istal – Kalachi Desert

"Stop!" Larron shouted at the gilar, taking a pose as threatening as he could, given their relative positions.

Behind him, he heard someone else drop from the sky. He trusted Zara to watch his back and warn him if the newcomers were unfriendly. In his peripheral vision, Geelomin stepped up beside him. He suspected Jarin had also been drawn by the power surge still swirling above the two downed figures, but the essential elf would have been needed to hold the line. The fairy remained on guard as he and Geelomin stared down the gilar.

The one holding the sword on Annalla's prone form snarled at them, fangs flashing, in what might be construed as a vicious grin. Its yellow eyes narrowed in focus, staring Larron down. Smooth scales shimmered in the noon sun as the gilar's bulging muscles rippled beneath. The light glinting off them revealed the sharpness of the spikes protruding from their arms and heads.

Gilar were intimidating at the best of times. Before Geelomin showed up, he had estimated his chances of survival against their numbers on the wall as a toss-up, thanks to the relatively narrow walkway limiting their numbers advantage. With reinforcements, they would likely win to escape, but Annalla would not.

"A trade," the gilar called over the elf's continued screaming, quieting as he grew hoarse.

Not daring to take his eyes off his opponent, Larron resisted looking around for something with which he *could* trade. "For what?"

Yellow eyes lowered slightly, and the grin shifted to a look of mingled disgust and anger. "Him."

Following his gaze, Larron studied the man for the first time. When they landed, he had been too concerned about finding Annalla and distracted by the dancing lights to pay much attention. An elf with chestnut hair and grayish-brown skin, his heritage could belong to any of the Woodlands. He wore robes the color of wet sand to protect him from the desert sun, and his face twisted in pain.

"Chesik?" he asked, more directing the question inwardly.

He thought he recognized the man as a traveler thought to have perished during one of his long expeditions almost a century ago. A sense of dread and nausea seeped into Larron as he wondered what circumstances brought the missing elf to be on the wall with Annalla in the middle of a war.

The gilar spat, then growled out, "Kahnlair."

"No," Geelomin said in denial. "Lies."

"He bound us," he said with a snarl, "enslaved us to his will. The elf made us his puppets until this one confronted him. We will have our retribution."

The elf in question whimpered, "Help me, Lady," then collapsed, crumpling forward as they spoke, and the spinning lights started to dim and compact. Streamers trailing off from the main glow became less frequent and drifted lazily instead of shooting off in different directions.

"You will give us the elf," the gilar said into the silence, pointing with his free hand so there was no mistaking whom he meant.

Larron shook his head slowly, forcing himself to avoid looking to where Annalla lay, dying. He couldn't trade for her. A life for a life was not an exchange an elf could make, no matter what the gilar said about Chesik. They had to know their chances of obtaining their goal by combat were limited with so many present.

"I cannot," he said.

"Give us the elf," it said with a sneer, "and I will order a retreat. The gilar will leave the field and concede this human city."

Something painful lodged in his chest and Larron looked out over the battlefield. The gilar were the core of the army. Their strength could only be matched by the agility of the elves, and the elves were outnumbered. Kahnlair's human soldiers were more numerous, but they were held in check by the gilar. Even when outnumbered, the humans feared the gilar more than they feared an overwhelming force on a battlefield.

At that moment, the allied army was losing. The fairy might win the sky, but many of their survivors would soon be down, ill from injuries from their fights with the vampires. They would not be able to help the forces on the ground, and they had been losing ground line by line as the hours dragged by.

If what the gilar said was true, the gilar would leave, the vampires would not be far behind, and the magai should no longer have Kahnlair's power supplementing their own. Larron's people could win. All it would take was the sacrifice of one of his kin.

"Larron, no," Geelomin said behind him. "You cannot be considering this. Volunteering yourself is one thing, but we do not sacrifice our people against their will!"

"He is the reason for this war," Zara stated bluntly. "Elf or no, it is nothing more than he deserves."

Geelomin's face was grim. "Chesik, if he is guilty as they claim, may deserve execution. But torture at the hands of the gilar is a cruelty we cannot condone."

Larron turned away from the battle raging below and finally looked at Annalla. The dim, glowing lights seemed to make her sun-streaked hair shimmer.

The elves would not send an elf unwillingly into the hands of their enemies, he thought. *No matter the cost, Chesik's life is worth protecting and defending as much as any of the lives fighting below. It is a truth the elves hold close. But those lives at stake are not only elves.*

Sanctuaries, family, friends, he recalled the oath he had taken in support of his fairy bonded. *The fairy might not sacrifice one person either, but she would. She would break her own heart to protect those under her wing.*

Larron looked back up at the gilar, and Geelomin stepped between them, reading something in his body language.

"I will not allow this, Larron," he said. Pain, frustration, and disappointment flashed in his eyes as he faced him down. "You do not have the authority."

A pained smile twisted his mouth. "Actually," Larron told him. "I do, if you will recall. As it relates to ending the war, I have been given the Voice of Kings. Step aside, Geelomin. That is an order."

Geelomin clenched his jaw, and his eyes widened in surprise. His knuckles whitened as he tightened his grip on his weapon. Disappointment morphed into the pain of betrayal, but he shifted away as instructed. His movement revealed the gilar, grinning wide at their obvious disagreement and discomfort.

He glared at the creature still holding a blade to Annalla's neck. The dancing lights around them were down to a vague fog, and he could not tell if she still breathed, neither of which boded well.

"Back away from the woman and sound your retreat," he told the gilar. "On my word, once the gilar are leaving, I will bring him to you and we will go our separate ways."

A quick, snarled conversation took place, lasting until the one in the front stabbed back with his elbow spines, impaling the eyes of a second. It slid, dead, to the ground as the leader nodded to the gilar on its other side.

"We have a bargain," he said to Larron as one of the others placed a horn to its lips and blew a series of guttural notes.

The gilar on the wall backed up, one slow step at a time, and after only moments, the movement below shifted. Partial retreats began, lines collapsed, and retreats turned into routs. Though their numbers were not massive, the gilar support provided a structure suddenly lacking.

Wanting to vomit, Larron moved to where Chesik lay still and quiet and bent down to pick him up. Carrying him like a child, he walked over to the gilar, unsure if he was more terrified they would attack him or keep their word.

He did not have to wait long to find out, as the lead gilar took the back of Chesik's clothing in a firm grip and lifted him like a doll. The unconscious man's head lolled as he was raised high. The gilar roared, echoed by a roar from the gilar down the line. They slapped each other's backs and started to retreat down the walkway, but Larron did not wait.

He couldn't breathe as he dropped to his knees at Annalla's side, pulling her into his arms and burying his head against her neck as he cried.

Come back and tell me it is okay, he thought to her, calling out with everything in him, the healer in him flaring to life with power as his heart broke. *Tell me I did what was necessary, even if it was not right.* "I am sorry, so sorry," he whispered into her hair, unsure of what he apologized for.

Annalla did not respond. She did not take a breath.

***

Her body faded away. She distantly felt herself fall, and her face struck the stone.

I wonder how long the body survives after separation, she idly thought. *The autonomous functions will likely continue...right? But there would be no sense of self.*

The answers didn't really matter, because once the essence was gone, things just...stopped. Done. The end. She thought the protections on the sanctuaries would last at least as long as her physical form remained 'alive.'

Another lash bit into her, tearing and swallowing the piece of her it took. She technically had no sight any longer. The world pulsed and glowed, but rather than actual light, it was more like the memory of light and space. She felt golden against the silvery entity opposite. The torn-off piece of her flickered like a star in the night sky.

Annalla thought it odd when she felt no pain at the attack. Her essence was literally being torn apart and consumed, and she only sensed it in a 'this is happening' way. Regardless, she knew it was not right and that the silver needed to be stopped.

Stretching forward a piece of herself, she latched onto the silver glow and tugged at it. Connecting with the opposing essence, she sensed it remained connected to the physical. *His power is concentrated in essence and thought.* The knowledge came to her, and she somehow knew it related to how her own ability in essence would manifest—would have manifested, eventually.

Grasping the piece of essence, she tore it off and held it in her incorporeal grasp. She understood the two paths she could take. One would save her, the other would not. As

Kahnlair was doing, she could also consume and absorb her opponent's essence. It would strengthen her as her own essence naturally faded as she worked, leaving enough power to potentially connect with her body again.

The alternative left her to fade.

She cradled the silver, considering it, then flung the thought off into the ether. It flew away at a surprising speed before dissipating. Imagining herself an excited child at present time, she ripped into the silver like wrapping paper and threw the pieces into the air. They shot off like fireworks, zipping into the night.

I thought it was day?

The idea drifted away with the next piece, and she continued her work. Some of the pieces remained golden, so she gobbled those up to give herself more time, since every piece he ate stole time from her. More and more, she dug until something snapped. A dark red, like blood. The horrid tether fluttered with her movements. She ignored it and carried on and on.

Her movements slowed. The golden glow faded and she could only pick at the silver like lint on a blanket. Some of it remained linked to the physical. Unlike Annalla, he had not separated, and she lacked the strength to pull it from him. Though, something in her knew he would never manifest again. The threat was ended.

Pick. Pick. Pick. *Soon now,* she thought lazily. Her senses fluttered, rippled out from a disturbance, and her last thoughts were of reaching for water.

CHAPTER FORTY-THREE

Var Istal – Kalachi Desert

Larron leaned against a window in the sitting room of the house he had been given. The people of Var Istal had their city back, but they were much fewer in number than before. Most had been sent to war or to feed the gilar over at least three decades. Despite their struggles, they had welcomed what remained of the allied army with open arms.

Guides took smaller groups back to the east gradually as people and supplies recovered, to not destroy the oases again since they had been restored from Kahnlair's destruction. The emergence—or discovery, rather, and wasn't that a wonder—of Larron's essential power, had been instrumental in saving countless wounded and accelerating the recovery of the locals from their malnutrition. As they waited for their turn to depart, recovered warriors were given accommodation in abandoned homes in exchange for helping to rebuild and restore. Already, much had been accomplished in the week since the battle.

The city was broken, but he could see the beauty beneath. Buildings rose without seams, as though carved from existing rock. Artistic carvings decorated the buildings, as well as gorgeous mosaics and hand-designed rugs. Many required cleaning or repair, but it was work that could be taken up by idle hands. Recovering their culture and lives would be as important as planting and harvesting.

"Come," he said in response to a knock at the door.

Zeris entered, looking grim. Regardless of their upcoming conversation, he was relieved his brother had survived. Argent had not. He and his bonded had fought valiantly until the end, neither leaving the other's side as they held an impossible line beyond all expectations.

"Larron," he said, standing straight and chewing his lip. It was the most awkward and uncomfortable Larron had ever seen his older brother.

He smiled wanly at him. "It is okay, Zeris. Say what you must. You will receive no objections from me."

Sighing, he closed his eyes as though in pain. When he opened them again, his stare held regret.

"Larron of the Derou," he said. "For your actions and abuse of authority, the Voice of Kings is revoked, and you are denied ever again receiving such honor and trust, forevermore. Additionally, for sacrificing an elf without opportunity for defense, you are hereby prohibited from returning to any Woodland for a period of no less than a century."

Zeris snorted in frustration at the conclusion of the proclamation. "Why did you do it, brother?"

"I did what was necessary."

"The ends *never* justify such means," he said, slashing a hand to emphasize his point. "You had only the word of the gilar! You do not know for certain Chesik was Kahnlair. We could have found another way! One that did not involve you sacrificing so much of yourself!"

Larron had no doubt Chesik was as the gilar claimed. Found in the center of Annalla's attacks and actively engaged in essential battle, there was little room for alternate explanations.

Perhaps more telling was the gilar holding to their promise. Escaping with Chesik in custody had been more important to them than a double-cross taking advantage of elven honor. Though, Geelomin had been of the opinion they simply preferred to see him sacrificing his morality.

Something horrible must have happened to Chesik. A traveler like Larron, he had not been around enough to have much interaction with other elves. Larron remembered him as a distractible but curious man. New places and new discoveries drove him to further reaches of the continent with each journey.

With Chesik, though, it had been more than the journeys. He loved learning and discovery, documenting his findings. So many of his trips took him away for extended periods that the elves did not count him among the missing until he had not been heard from in over a decade.

Most elves could not imagine one of their own changing so fundamentally they could do what Kahnlair did and become the cause of so much suffering. Their disbelief also led to his punishment. If his reasoning could not be true, then Larron was wrong.

"I will give your words due consideration," he finally said. "I sincerely regret I cannot offer you more."

Zeris shook his head as he stormed forward and wrapped Larron in a tight hug. He spoke into Larron's shoulder. "Jarin agrees with you. He was vehement in his support of your claims and actions. And you should know that you will *always* be my brother. Do not doubt that or my love for you, and do not lose yourself in the world while you are away. I expect your return when this period ends. And you *will* stay in contact."

Larron leaned back so he could look into his eyes. "Of course," he said. "I love you and our people. Believe that when I say: go home, Zeris. Erro deserves to see you alive and well."

Something in Zeris eased, and the remainder of his visit was less fraught with tension. They said their farewells. Elves were not limited to the Woodlands, so he had no concerns he would not see any friends during his banishment. After Zeris left, Darrin came out of the main bedroom.

"You'll be welcome in the sanctuaries," he told Larron. It would have been challenging for a fairy to tune out their conversation, but Annalla's friends were diligent in their vigil, and Zara had told her king of all that had transpired upon the city wall. "And the dwarves have offered to help us build settlements beyond the sanctuary bounds as well, at least near Essence."

Larron chuckled. "Thank you. You can be certain I will take you up on your offer. I might remain here first, though, and see if I can contribute to undoing some of the damage Kahnlair brought to these people."

"I'll leave you then," said the fairy king. "I believe she'll be stirring soon. Please pass on to her that Karl and Marto are expected to recover fully."

He saw his new friend out, then went into the room where Annalla slept. It had only been a week, so she retained most of her desert tan and the highlights in her hair. She had nearly died, and the toll the journey and battle had taken on her body still showed in her sunken eyes and hollow cheeks, but he had seen her in worse condition.

While he would not have made the trade with the gilar for her alone, her survival is what had made the trade worth it for him. Giving up Chesik had hurt him, hurt his heart. He did not know if he could live with himself and his decision if she had died.

Thanks to his power—a surprise to everyone—the injuries to her face and body had healed instantly when his essence had unfurled and reached out to her. Any healer mage could have done the same, but only he could have recalled her essence. He was an essential; a healer in his own way. There was speculation, but no one knew why his power had taken so long to manifest. Rather than trying to analyze it, he'd spent the first day and a half after the battle healing as many people as he could alongside the magai. Only later had he remembered Annalla's story about the fire essential whose power had also been delayed.

Sitting on the stool beside the bed, he took her hand in his and started talking. Not knowing what she heard and did not, he often gave her the same information over again.

"Friends first," he said. "I am told Marto will be fine. He and Karl were found late, so they were burned from sun exposure, but it seems the enemy thought them already dead and ignored their bodies. They were more worried about Karl's wings, but I was able to heal most of that damage. You will have to go easy on him if he challenges you to aerial combat, though.

"Geelomin lost half his team, but Thanon and Bealaras survived. I think Geelomin might be bonding with Fremya. You would like her. She is not intimidated by his stiff and assertive behavior. I think someday she might even convince him to forgive me.

"Tyrus and Nurtik are well, but they have given up their search for Patrice. We have officially counted her among the missing, likely killed in one of the mage blasts.

"As for the leaders, Albertas is king. Darrin is king. You do not know her, but Argent's daughter is king in the Auradian Woodland. Fwendilg died in the battle as well, and the Trazine Range clan will have an election to determine their next clanlord."

He sighed, thinking about all the damage done to the world and the rebuilding needed. The people of Elaria had been at war for two decades. As much as the land would need healing, the hearts of those living in it would as well. At least with the war ended, they could shift to struggling to live instead of simply struggling to survive. Eventually, there would be an end to the struggle.

And she would wake. He knew in his heart she would wake. Larron leaned forward to kiss her forehead. "We did it, Annalla," he whispered. "We saved the world."

Note to my readers

This is the end of the story of how the fairy people returned to save Elaria. Once left to fight on their own, long thought extinct, the lost race refused to abandon a world in need. For many generations, humans would cheer when a fairy flew above their villages. Many generations more would consider the fairy a good omen. Though they continued to dwell in the sanctuaries, they did not retreat from the world entirely.

If you were hoping for more of a love story for Annalla and Larron, you will have to wait. This is not the end for them. There is more for the pair to face and more to tell. I will not get to the rest of their story for a while yet, though. So, if you like a "happily ever after" ending, I recommend stopping here for now.

There is one more chapter. The epilogue follows, hinting at things to come for our heroes and for Elaria. Read at your own risk, though, as it will be years before this next story unfolds.

Thank you for visiting Elaria.

EPILOGUE

Var Istal – Kalachi Desert

Soon After the Battle's End

Annalla took a deep breath, her hand steady on the door handle, as she mentally prepared herself for the conversation to come. Dread settled into her gut, making her nauseous. Or maybe that was guilt rather than dread.

She had awoken a week ago, tired and as drained as she had been after fire and air had emerged so many months before. Friends visited daily, spreading out their time with her between her frequent naps to tell her everything going on in the desert city since Kahnlair's defeat. Every few days, another of the leaders would join a group leaving to return to their own lands.

Darrin would be one of the last to leave. He intended to coordinate two large groups again, each returning to where the two halves of the fairy army began. He needed to ensure the independent sanctuaries would remain balanced upon their return, which meant some individuals would be relocating to a new home. Though not unexpected, it highlighted the fairy's losses and put a damper on the victory.

Marto and Tyrus had cried when she'd told them about Patrice, and she joined them in their grief as a renewed wave of guilt surfaced. She was a hollow shell filled with self-recrimination. The only light in her life was Larron.

He took care of her in the house they had been given to share. The meals not brought as gifts were his creations. Every time he saw her, he smiled and helped her feel full, if only for a moment. He did it again then, when she opened the bedroom door and stepped into the open dining area.

"Annalla," he said, "dinner is almost ready."

At his gesture of invitation, she took a seat and watched him work. Bile churned in her throat, and she swallowed it down, forcing herself to relax. She watched his calm, sure movements, allowing them to distract her from her thoughts.

"So," he said as he placed a plate in front of each of them, taking the seat adjacent. "What has you looking grim?"

Annalla took a piece of bread and moved some of the food around. It probably tasted fantastic, but the thought of eating riled her stomach further. She pursed her lips, looking for a place to begin.

Larron sighed and set his fork down. "You want to leave," he said. They both knew he meant leaving more than Var Istal.

She nervously glanced up at him, trying to judge his temper. To her surprise, his soft smile held no anger, only sorrow and understanding. It made her want to cry again.

How to explain...

"Larron." She bit her lip. "I love you...but I do not love myself," she finally said. "We could be happy together. I could become who I need to be to make this life work. By all rights, I should stay and put in the effort."

She grimaced at how that last statement sounded, but Larron was laughing at her. Apparently, he elected to find her amusing rather than frustrating.

"That came out wrong," she grumbled. "Why are you smiling?"

He reached over and took her hand. "I have had centuries to live, travel, and understand who I am as an individual," he told her. "Your entire—and short, thus far—life has been about being and becoming what other people want and need. You molded yourself into the image your parents and people expected. The only time you had to simply *exist* was when you were suffering from memory loss and fighting for your life traveling with the Derou. Do you honestly believe I would want to continue that pattern for you?"

"I am the reason you were banished from your home!" she said. "How could you not be upset with me? I would be devastated if our roles were reversed and you were saying you needed to leave me."

"First," he said as he stopped smiling, "you are not the cause of my punishment. I will *not* be okay with you leaving me if you persist in believing otherwise. I specifically refused to trade for you, and you can ask Geelomin or Zara if you disbelieve me."

She shook her head. They could not lie to each other, not about something so important. "I believe you."

"Good," he said, his expression softening once more. "Second, you might be angry if I elected to walk away from you, but not if our circumstances were reversed. I will not believe you would refuse me something I truly needed. You are too noble for such behavior. I would go so far as to say you would believe the same if you knew and trusted yourself as you should…as you will."

Annalla squeezed his hand. "I do not deserve you."

"Hmm," he growled his disagreement and gave her a scolding look. "I need a promise from you, though, in exchange for being so understanding."

With a raised eyebrow, she asked, "What would that

be?"

His free hand rose as he leaned forward, cupping her nape and gently pulling her forward until their foreheads touched. "Don't die," he said, staring deep into her eyes.

***

Location Unknown

Later

The cave went down, deep beneath the surface where no light reached. She had fought to reach that place. Something in her felt it calling from so far away. It became impossible to ignore the draw any longer.

Down, into the darkness, with only a thin, winding path to guide her. Shortly after starting on the path, the flame lighting her way stuttered and went out, pitching her into inky blackness. Despite the dark, she continued, drawn on by something intangible.

She went on for what felt like hours. Down and down, it felt as though she floated in a void of nothingness, and she wondered if she still existed in the world. Eventually, the dark lifted. One point only, far below, a blue-black spark.

Eventually, the image resolved itself into a pillar standing at the center of a pool of water. Light reflected off the still surface; not a ripple marred the mirror sheen. Her heart pounded. Excitement? Fear? She wasn't sure, but she crossed the pool regardless.

Finally, before the pillar, she stared at an object carved with a rune. Her hand reached out, fingers trembling as they stretched forward. The tip of one brushed the artifact, and the cave lit up in her mind.

You want to be worthy, a voice said, speaking directly

into her mind. *I can help. Together, we can become great.*

Her hand closed around the piece, and she pulled it forward to rest against her heart.

THE END!

THANK YOU!

Thank you for traveling with me, Annalla, and Larron as they fought to save the world from Kahnlair's tyrannical crusade. .I hope you enjoyed the culmination of events, and that the twists and turns make you want to go back and read the series again to find the breadcrumbs I left along the way.

Characters are central to my writing, and I love all their unique personalities, even those who are no longer with us. I hope you have some favorites of your own.

Great reviews are critical for indie authors such as me. If you enjoy the book, please leave a rating or review, and recommend it to your friends! I appreciate all your support.

Looking for what is next? I do not have a preorder at this time. I am about 60% through writing a new young adult novel set in an alternate Earth that has been impacted by Annalla's departure.

If you want to stay in touch and hear about release information as it becomes available, look me up on social media or sign up for my quarterly newsletter or follow my blog at www.tiffanyshearn.com

Thank you for your support, and here's to many more books (and a sequel series) to come!

ACKNOWLEDGEMENTS

I am eternally grateful to the people in my life who support me and have contributed to my endeavors as an author. As always, any and all errors are mine alone.

To Samantha Millan, I promise I will get you the very rough draft of the next book series soon. I have a lot going on, so I appreciate your patience. Guy Parisi, your alpha edits remain invaluable, and your dedication to reading when you would rather an audiobook is appreciated.

Miguel Lobo, you have once again delivered an amazing rendition of the stick figure drawing and scene description I provided. You have brough Elaria to life. Maxine Meyer, I continue to appreciate your editorial advice and strive to continue to improve my craft.

To my beta readers Beba Andric and Éva Rona, thank you for your excellent reader feedback, I could not overcome those final hurdles without your keen observations.

The series would not be complete without all of you. Thank you!

ABOUT THE AUTHOR

Tiffany Shearn is a writer and author of the Hidden Series of Elaria, her first book *Hidden Memory* released in December of 2021 to great reviews. While working by day as an entrepreneur, a new role for her, Tiffany has spent more than two decades bringing her fantasy realm and characters to life. She is currently working on a new series in young adult fantasy.

Tiffany is a lifelong reader with a passion for the fantasy genre. She began writing in college when the stories in her head were vivid enough to distract her from lectures and now has four published works with more on the way. Tiffany lives just south of Seattle, Washington with her husband and their pets, Big Cat, and Little Cat. (www.tiffanyshearn.com)

Made in the USA
Columbia, SC
22 June 2024